PRAISE FOR *REDEEM THE LINES*

"As a middle-aged man born and living in Ireland. I can attest that the story line, with fascinating detail about Nate and Patrick, almost mirrors in reverse the journey of many Irishmen to the USA. Mike Murphy tells a gripping story of underworld situations as well as life in rural and urban Ireland in the 1990s.

Reading some of the sections took me back to bars and nightclubs I visited and historical family situations I experienced.

The story is descriptive and superbly crafted and provides honest backdrops for a changing and historical period in transatlantic travel and the situations people faced to try build a better life and livelihood."

—NIALL CULL, CEO, DLR Leisure, Dublin, Ireland

"*Redeem the Lines* is an eye opening and inspiring read. The friendship of Patrick and Nate occurs during a time of troubled cultural lines in 1990s Boston. Through Patrick and Nate's differences, their souls bond and show how human relationships can grow through conflict resolution and open minds."

—CHENOA MAXWELL, livelimitlessly.com

"Michael Murphy has expanded the saga of Patrick and Nate from the neighborhoods of Boston to the far reaches of Connemara, Ireland. Their exploits are at times bleak, often darkly humorous, and always compelling. Redemption comes in different ways, and Murphy weaves a complex tale of old loyalties challenged in a more modern world."

—CHRISTOPHER MURRAY, Boston Attorney

"*Redeem the Lines* is an engaging sequel to Neighborhood Lines, the story of Nate and Patrick, two young men coming of age in a city with strong racial and economic boundaries. As they transition into adulthood, the excitement doesn't slow down on this thrilling ride through the inner city of Boston."

—CORNELL MILLS, Roxbury, Boston, Massachusetts

"*Redeem the Lines* is a compelling story and a must-read. It tells the story of two young men from working class backgrounds whose lives intertwine over the years. The battle to overcome their inner demons is a war against themselves. Reading Murphy's book has left me reflecting about my own existence and about Dublin in the 80s."

—COLM PIERCE, colmpiercephotography.com, Dublin, Ireland

"Nate and Patrick, the lead characters in this story, have pushed me to think about what I truly stand for, as well as what I have come to tolerate in my world. Michael Patrick Murphy couldn't have written such an insightful tale had it not been for his own personal transformation.

Growing up Irish Catholic, I recall Father Sean Walsh as the only clergy member who didn't threaten me with damnation for my sins. He told me that redemption was a power to change for the better that I could find inside myself.

After reading Redeem the Lines, it dawned on me that the more things change, they do not have to stay the same. As such, I have befriended the characters in this story, and they inspire me to be the change that I truly want to see in the world.

The colorful people and riveting events make this book hard to put down. Pick it up—there may very well be something inside of this story that is meant for you."

—**JAMES MCPARTLAND,** founder, Access Performance International

"I am part of a family that participated in the METCO program, and I can attest that this is a riveting story that reveals that friendships can be forged despite being from different neighborhoods during the desegregated 1990s Boston. Murphy perfectly captures Patrick and Nate's challenges in their respective worlds as they both struggle to do what's right for their city, their families, and themselves."

—**FRED FORSGARD,** thespian, Boston, Massachusetts

REDEEM THE LINES

MICHAEL PATRICK MURPHY

RIVER GROVE
BOOKS

Published by River Grove Books
Austin, TX
www.rivergrovebooks.com

The following images are reproduced under license from Alamy, Inc. All rights reserved.
Page vi: Paul Revere monument at Paul Revere Mall in the North End of Boston. Massachusetts. Sean Pavone/Alamy Stock Photo.
Page 6: Funeral for victim of police beating. Jim West/Alamy Stock Photo.
Page 10: Jail cell at American Police Hall of Fame Titusville, Florida. Ilene MacDonald/Alamy Stock Photo.
Page 89: Roundstone, Co Galway, Ireland, the harbour with a regatta and a traditional pub. Design Pics Inc/Alamy Stock Photo.
Page 128: Quay Street, Galway, Ireland. Fabrizio Troiani/ Alamy Stock Photo.
Page 163: The Clarence Hotel in Dubling owned by U2 band members Bono and The Edge. Tim Cuff/Alamy Stock Photo.
Page 216: China Town in Boston. Enrico Della Pietra/Alamy Stock Photo.
Page 225: 1980s Combat zone adult entertainment area Washington Essex Boston Massachusetts USA. ClassicStock/Alamy Stock Photo.
Page 251: Boston skyline with outdoor basketball courts and baseball field in the foreground. Alan Myers/Alamy Stock Photo.
Page 309: Photograph taken during the aftermath of the London Docklands bombing. The London Docklands bombing (also known as the South Quay bombing or erroneously referred to as the Canary Wharf bombing) occurred on 9 February, 1996, when the Provisions Irish Republican Army (IRA) detonated a powerful truck bomb in South Quay (which is outside Canary Wharf). World History Archive/Alamy Stock Photo.

Page 183: This image is reproduced under license from Colm Pierce, www.colmpiercephotography.com

The following images are reproduced under license from Getty Images. All rights reserved.
Page 16: Democratic presidential candidate Bill Clinton. Tim Clary.
Page 18: The Eire Pub. Rick Friedman.
Page 30: Irish Boxers work out at the Petronelli Brothers gym in Brockton. Midea News Group/*Boston Herald* via Getty Images.
Page 33: First day of ceasefire in Northern Ireland. Mathieu Polak.
Page 52: Press conference displays cache of arms transported by Valhalla Boat. *Boston Globe*.
Page 99: Ireland starts easing level 5 COVID-19 restrictions. NurPhoto.
Page 105: Mountain sheep, Od Bog Road, Connemara, Ireland. Tim Graham.
Page 130: Boston police department anti-gang violence unit. *Boston Globe*.
Page 132: Jury studies Tiffany Moore Crime Scene. *Boston Globe*.
Page 133: Boston Mayor Menino tours neighborhoods impacted by gang violence. *Boston Globe*.
Page 183: James J. "whitey" Bulger named to FBI Ten Most Wanted fugitive list. *Boston Globe*.

Distributed by River Grove Books

Design and composition by Greenleaf Book Group and Kim Lance
Cover design by Greenleaf Book Group and Kim Lance

Publisher's Cataloging-in-Publication data is available.

Print ISBN: 978-1-63299-643-5

eBook ISBN: 978-1-63299-644-2

First Edition

CONTENTS

PROLOGUE

NATE SITS IN A DULL GRAY QUESTIONING ROOM INSIDE THE Boston PD headquarters on Tremont Street as a short, stalky Black cop he doesn't know and Sergeant Daly from the Irish neighborhood—a large, bald White cop—enter with suspicion plain on their faces. Daly drops two photos of a building going up in flames. A sign on the roof of the building that reads "Scrapyard" is engulfed by the inferno.

The Black cop sits down in front of Nate, stares him in the eyes, and says, "We know you were involved and you know something. But what I can't figure out is what your connection to Patrick is. And why?"

Nate leans back. "I have no idea what you're talking about," he says.

He glances at his interrogator and then at Daly and chuckles. "So, Daly, you haven't let him in on the history yet, huh?"

Daly paces back and forth with beads of sweat dripping off his skull. He pounds his fist on the table. "I knew you two were up to something," he says. "I told you two to keep your noses clean after all you been through lately."

"I haven't seen him since that night in the hospital with you, so let's stop wasting all of our time here. You wanna know what our connection is?" Nate asks, turning back to the Black cop.

"I met this White kid on the first day of school, the first day fifty Black freshmen entered a hundred-year-old White Irish school for the first time ever, back in '88. We shared most of our classes, and at the end of the first week, we had to do a project together. There we were, me a Black kid from Roxbury, and Patrick a White Irish kid from South Boston, walking the historic Freedom Trail and taking notes. Up downtown crossing, by the statehouse and Faneuil Hall, we had to follow a tourist map in our own city. By noon, we were just about done with the project, with only one more statue to visit. We were both uncomfortable being seen with the other on the streets. Standing at the edge of Faneuil Hall, we hesitated, looking down into the unchartered territory in the all-Italian neighborhood called the North End, where the Paul Revere statue stood tall—the last stop on the Freedom Trail.

The Paul Revere statue in Boston's North End
remains a symbol of the birth of America's freedom

"Beside that powerful horse statue was an empty basketball court with a set of dunk hoops. I pulled my ball out of my backpack to slam a few dunks. Patrick grabbed a rebound and took a few shots, so we played a little one-on-one.

"After a few minutes, we heard a few strange noises, like a faint blast of air had passed by our heads. Patrick scanned the area but didn't see anything, so he prepared to drive the lane. We heard the noise again, and I fell to the ground, an excruciating pain in my shoulder.

"Patrick dropped over me and started digging at the holes in my shoulder blade.

"I winced. 'What are you—?'

"'You've been shot,' Patrick said in a harsh whisper. 'I'm trying to get the pellets out.'

"He turned and yelled, 'What the fuck!' up to the window where the shot must have come from.

"Five Italian teenagers walked onto the court, swiftly approaching us.

"Patrick leaned into my ear and said, 'Follow my lead. Get ready.'

"He stood up and said, 'What the fuck? You could've took an eye out! We're leaving now, okay?'

"One of the biggest Italian kids said, 'What the fuck is wrong with you, bringing a n*gger in our neighborhood?'

"Patrick walked right up to him and blasted him right in the chin, knocking him out cold. Then he turned to me and said, 'Run, as fast you can. Let's go!'

"We ran all the way to South Station, never looking back. On the Red Line train home, I asked Patrick why he'd done that.

"'I'm sorry that happened,' he said. 'I should've known better. My father once said never to back down from injustice, and when you're outnumbered, to pick the meanest, biggest guy and take the best shot you can.'

"From that day on, I knew he was a different type of White boy, that's for sure. So, yeah, we got history—a lot of it. He has only been out of prison for a minute, but, from what I can see, if he had anything to do with this, he did the city a solid!"

Chapter 1

REBORN FREE

"YOU READY TO GO YET, KID?"

Inside the eight-foot-by-eight-foot cell, Patrick jumped to his feet.

Across the tiny space, Choppa, Patrick's cellmate, slowly stood up. He was a White man much older than Patrick, maybe in his fifties, although they had never talked about it. He was barrel chested, with intimidating, massive arms and a collection of Irish tattoos all over his skin, including a shamrock on his earlobe.

A guard let Patrick out of a holding cell where he had changed out of his jumpsuit and found that his old jeans still fit reasonably well, but his shirt and coat were way too tight. Four years of weightlifting had transformed his torso from a men's medium into an extra large. His shoes fit, although he knew already they would be dated when he put them on. So the first order of business was going to be getting some new clothes. For a few weeks now, Patrick had known he would be stepping into a changed world.

The guard opened up the cell.

"We're gonna let Choppa walk you out to the last gate."

Patrick stepped into the narrow corridor as the guard also waved Choppa out, closing the door behind them. As the clang of the door echoed, Patrick felt the emotion running deep between the two of them. They had become family.

"This gonna be an adjustment, kid?" Choppa started.

Yeah, the past four years has been an adjustment, Patrick thought. He put a smile on and said, "I'm just so pumped for a fresh start."

Patrick watched Choppa's face take on a glare of dead seriousness, and Patrick held his gaze on him for what he knew would be one of the last times.

"When you first walked in here, you were a boy three months out of high school. Now you're a man, and the world's a different place. Everyone in the neighborhood knows now you're a stand-up guy that can handle the worst life can throw at you. But no matter how tough it gets out there in the real world as an ex-con . . . don't ever come back here again!"

"I won't, but I got no regrets," Pat said. "At the end of the day, I'm not a rat." That was what had gotten him in here to begin with—not turning in his best friend. But even being in prison was better than being a rat. Everyone knew that.

The guard walked Patrick and Choppa through the grounds toward the front gate. He couldn't help turning the events of the past five years over and over in his mind, from the night of his graduation party through the almost four years of days and nights in prison for something he hadn't done.

———

IT HAD ALL STARTED WHEN THEY'D STEPPED OUT TO GET SOME fresh air. Pat had been walking the streets of South Boston late at night with his buddies Walsh and Sean, a good buzz going for all three of them. Sure, they saw the four Asian teens near the phone booth, but they didn't think anything of it. Sean instigated them as they passed, tapping one of the kids on the back. Sean was such an asshole. It was funny. At first, that seemed like the end of it.

But shit got out of control fast. The Asian kids came back in a car a few minutes later, intending to finish what Sean had started. They leapt out and started ripping antennas off cars parked nearby, whipping them around as weapons.

It was then that Patrick and the boys knew they were in deep shit. They raided the nearby dumpster to find weapons to counter. They only had a few seconds to grab anything that could hurt—an iron, a broken bottle, a shower curtain rod.

It was a total melee, everyone whaling on each other. By the time the cops showed up, one of the Asian kids was bleeding out on the sidewalk from his abdomen. Patrick and the other boys scattered, but he got caught.

The cops spelled it out for him back at the station, telling him in no uncertain terms that if that kid died, he'd be an accessory to murder—unless, of course, he spilled what had happened.

Patrick knew it was Walsh. He'd been defending himself with the broken bottle when the kid got injured. And Patrick knew that, if he told the cops, he'd get off easy. But Walsh was one of his best friends. And even if he weren't, no fucking way was he going to break the code of silence and rat someone out. He recalled the conversation he'd had with his mother, who knew the history of the neighborhood well.

"You think going to prison's bad?" Pat had told her. "Being a rat is like being excommunicated. I'll never get respect from anyone ever again. To cops, criminals, friends, and enemies, I'll be nothin'. Honestly, I'd rather be in prison."

"Hard as it is for me to hear," she'd replied, "I know that's your only choice."

"I'm sorry," he'd told her, and she had gone off into her bedroom, closing the door behind her.

In this case, someone had to hang because it involved a racial incident, a hate crime, or however the media molded it to appear. So, in the end, the judge made Patrick an example.

———

AS THE GUARD APPROACHED THE FRONT GATES, CHOPPA NOD-ded and extended his hand. Patrick shook it and gave him a hug. He saw his mother watching from the car. She was almost as excited as the day he was born; today, he was reborn free.

When Patrick had first arrived, Choppa had shaved the kid's head and had Pat grow out some scruff on his face to put some edges on his handsome young looks. But today, Pat was almost five years older, clean shaven, his hair high and tight—fresh for his ma and ready to face the world. The guard closed the gate behind him and yelled, "Yeah, stay far away from this place, skid."

Skid was slang for "prisoner," and Patrick grinned as he realized that, in just a few moments, as they drove away from the prison, the name would no longer apply.

The day was unseasonably warm, which meant about forty degrees, with no clouds. The conditions gave Pat a clear sight of his beloved mother, who had aged on the outside as much as Patrick had on the inside. There were fine lines around her eyes and mouth that had not been there before.

He stared out the window as his mother drove home and was startled by how different things felt to him. The Quiet Man was gone, replaced by a Starbucks, and another pub was now a Asian restaurant. They turned onto Telegraph Street, and Patrick was startled to see such a large group of Black teenagers laughing loudly all the way up to Southie High. He hadn't been gone that long, but the neighborhood lines had certainly shifted. They continued toward home, and Patrick noticed a large crowd gathering outside a funeral home.

"What happened?" Patrick asked, turning to face his mom.

"Mikey Smith hung himself," she replied sadly.

"How old was he?" Patrick asked. He remembered Mikey as a bright-eyed, exuberant youngster, always confident and full of positive energy. The idea that he could have been suicidal seemed unfathomable.

"Oh, sixteen or something. More than a dozen others have tried in the last six months—seven more from Southie ODed on heroin. The place is different, Paddy. These new pain pills are everywhere, and if you can't afford those, the heroin is like ten bucks a bag. Not sure this would be happening if Whitey was still here. These days, there's more color in the projects than a friggin' rainbow!"

Patrick stared in disbelief. He gazed out the window again and noticed how much more subdued the people were. Gone were the boisterous yells and the confident strides. They had been replaced by vacant expressions and listless shuffling.

As they drew closer to home, the sights became more familiar, and he was relieved to see some things were still the same. As he approached his house, he felt the excitement of connecting with his friends and family in the neighborhood. He was even going to reach out to his old friend Nate, who was from a Black neighborhood just a few miles away.

Chapter 2

A BOSTON CHURCH

AMID THE RESPECTFUL WHISPERING AND SOFT CRYING, NATE
entered the funeral in the Baptist church on Dorchester Avenue. About
six foot four and in his midtwenties, he walked slowly down the aisle to
the front of the church, to Jamal's mother.

She recognized him instantly, although some time had passed since
they had seen each other. But of course she would recognize him: Nate
and Jamal had grown up best friends, playing basketball together, eventually going to different colleges to become local college basketball stars.
She hugged Nate as he sat down, crying into his shoulder. Nate shut his
eyes tightly as he hugged her back, trying his best not to cry too.

The church was packed, with nearly the entire local Black community showing up to pay their respects. A large closed casket had been
placed in front of the altar. Nate felt sick, knowing he would never get
to see Jamal's face again. There had been no warning—no sickness or
long-term battle with cancer. Jamal had been slain—stabbed by a member of the Lenox Street Crew, one of over a dozen gangs plaguing the
Boston community.

Nate shook his head. Jamal wasn't even living here anymore; he'd
just been visiting home from Cleveland. Nate still didn't have the story
straight. *The Globe* had said that Jamal and the alleged murderer had
some kind of argument at a local nightclub called the Roxy. Later, in the
small hours of the morning, Jamal had arrived at his girlfriend's place,
where the alleged killer stabbed him. But who knew how the facts would
eventually shake out in the trial.

Jamal was well liked and had friends in every circle—even in the
gang community. But Nate had warned Jamal soon after graduating
that he couldn't be both a baller and a banger. "Keep your nose clean,"
Nate had warned. "Avoid the career criminals at all costs. Those guys
will drag you into trouble."

Nate knew this all too well. Gang violence had struck his own family.
His cousin Troy, a gang member, had been killed years ago, while his
other cousin, Tre, languished in Suffolk County Prison. Tre had founded
the Norfolk Kings with his younger brother, Slugs, and the new gang had
carved out a name for itself dealing coke and heroin in a highly contested
neighborhood. They'd invited Nate to join when he was in high school,

but he would have none of it. For him, it was always the straight and narrow. He wanted nothing to do with that way of life. Slugs claimed he was just an electrician now, but something about his expensive shoes and SUV seemed to indicate he was probably still banging.

He'd even seen street violence hit the seemingly untouchable White community. His friend Patrick had been a hockey star at Cathedral High. Nate had met him when the group he was a part of—a hundred underrepresented kids from all different ethnicities—was accepted as part of an interracial enrollment program organized by headmaster Father Lydon.

Pat had graduated high school and probably should have been destined for an athletic scholarship somewhere. But, as far as Nate knew, his friend was still doing time in Suffolk after a street brawl with an Asian gang. On the night of graduation, a Asian teenager was dead, and Patrick had been assigned blame for a crime he didn't commit because he wouldn't open his mouth.

Nate spotted Slugs somewhere in the middle of the room. They nodded to each other. Nate could tell he'd been crying.

Reverend Gibbs stood over the service in his black attire with the thick white collar. Nate knew him to be a well-liked man of God who had seen too many young Black men killed before their time. Nate had known him since he was little. Although he'd never really been religious, he'd always trusted Reverend Gibbs. Gibbs had come from the streets and had a way of connecting to people from all walks of life.

Gibbs approached Jamal's mother and put his hand on her shoulder as she tried to restrain her sobs.

"I not only sympathize for this mother of this wonderful young man, Jamal, who had a bright future in the NBA, but I empathize," Reverend Gibbs began, projecting his solid and comforting voice. "I have a son his same age, and every time he leaves this house, even though I am a man of God—saved, sanctified, and filled with his spirit—something pulls at me. I can't seem to sleep easily until my son comes home again. Anyone else in here feel like that?"

"Amen!" the congregation responded.

Amen, Nate thought. These young Black men were falling as if they were on the front lines.

Recognizing Nate, Gibbs put his hand on his shoulder next, in a gesture of solidarity and emotional support. The dam finally broke, and a tear ran down Nate's cheek.

"Now, I know my son's a good boy, but that doesn't matter these days," Gibbs explained. "The Bible tells us, 'Redeem the time, for the days are evil.' Our children aren't evil, but the days are. When they go out into these streets, no matter how good they are, evil is all around them."

The congregation exclaimed a chorus of disjointed amens.

"Now, I've tried to talk of the positive and about the love of God only. But I am reminded we are in the midst of war! Every positive has a negative; that's how the world exists. You cannot say there is good without acknowledging the evil!"

The words pierced Nate's soul. He locked eyes with Reverend Gibbs as if God were speaking directly to him. It was surreal, his best friend lying there dead in the casket, with his friends and his family all around him. Nate's heart was just so heavy. He had returned from Virginia last night as soon as he heard about the murder, and the gruesome reality of reentry to his old neighborhood was nearly too much to bear. Being a college student in another state was like a vacation from the reality he was born into on the Dorchester-Roxbury line in Boston.

All he could do was cry.

Chapter 3

NEW BEGINNING

Suffolk County 8x8 jail cell shared by
Patrick and Choppa for four and a half years

AT FIRST, PAT DIDN'T RECOGNIZE WHERE HE WAS WHEN HE woke up. After four years of being confined in Suffolk, everywhere else still felt alien. Waking up alone in a soft bed with walls and a window was a far cry from waking up on an ultra-thin mattress surrounded by bars, with a crusty cellmate still snoring just a few feet away.

The fog lifted after the first few seconds. He was back home, in his own room, in his own bed, in the house he'd grown up in. It was strange being back, to say the least. Pat had heard about this from some of the other prisoners; they said it was like reverse culture shock. People that go to live in different countries for months and years get acclimated and then have a hard time adjusting to their own culture when they return. It's not that their country changed; it's that they have.

Of course, Pat had never been to a foreign country. Hell, he'd hardly ever made it out of Boston. But he didn't have to. He'd been to Suffolk. It had its own rules, its own tribe, its own language and culture. That fuckin' place might as well have been a different planet.

Pat didn't miss it. *Fuck that place.*

He started his new morning routine, the one that he got to create for himself. That was the worst thing about prison, Pat thought: They take away all your choices, deciding for you when you get up, when and what you eat, when or if you go outside or shower. About the only thing you control is when you go to the bathroom, the "friends" you make on the inside, and what you read—and even these have strict parameters. You're never alone unless you're in solitary, which is the fucking worst place you can be. They take everything you have left while you sit in darkness, left to your own demons.

Pat had never considered what an epic experience it was to take a hot shower by himself until he was deprived of it. Now, he felt like royalty. There were no threats in this shower, nobody waiting for his guard to be down to try and take advantage of him. After that first day, when he proved himself as a fighter, he had simply assumed people wouldn't try to jump him in the shower. But some of those guys were just fucking crazy. He always fended them off if they tried it. Anyone who did would end up fucked up or unconscious or both. Nobody ever tried twice.

As he dressed, he caught a glance of his tattoo, small letters on his arm—the one he'd gotten on the afternoon of his graduation. It read *Vengeance Is Mine*—a reference to a Bible verse from Romans. He had gotten it because he thought he would get justice for his cousin PJ. Pat's eyes then rested on the photos of him and his high school buddies still on the wall near the mirror. There was Walsh, and Slick, and Sean the asshole. And there was his cousin PJ, gone way before his time. Rest in peace.

Fucking Sean.

Sean had got into some bad shit to make some money in the neighborhood, but that wasn't uncommon. It was practically expected. Everyone had a little side hustle, and most guys started when they were still in high school. PJ had started to help Sean with his operation, running little jobs here and there. At first, it was just weed, pills, whatever. But it quickly moved to coke. It was good money if you were willing to take the risk and you knew what you were doing.

Pat never got involved with that stuff, but not because he judged those who did. Even the local liquor store, the Packy, as locals called it, would deliver drugs if you knew the right way to ask. That was just one step up from getting liquor delivered if you were underage. The proprietors at the Packy didn't give a shit; let the fourteen-year-olds have it. The cops weren't going to stop them, and the kids were just going to get fucked up anyway. Why shouldn't they get a piece of the business?

But Sean was ambitious. He rose up through the ranks, starting as a barback at Triple O's and eventually making a name for himself working his own small group of wannabe hustlers. He dazzled PJ with stories of easy money. For a short while, PJ made more than he'd ever dreamed. But, one night, Sean sent him alone on a deal into the Black section of Dorchester, and he was shot and killed.

Pat winced a bit at the memory of his conversation with his mom the previous night. It still stung. His ma had spoken to Pat's friend Nate. Nate was the one who'd eventually figured out what had happened to PJ. Nate's cousin Tre had killed PJ, although he probably hadn't meant to. Tre had a side hustle too, dealing on his own turf as part of the Norfolk Kings. Tre had shot PJ in the leg, and he'd bled out at the hospital. Nate told Pat's ma that he never found out the exact details of that night. He had heard a few different stories: PJ was carrying way too much coke by himself or too much cash, or the guys he was buying from tried to rob him. They would never really know.

All Pat did know was that Sean shouldn't have sent PJ out alone that night with no support.

Besides Sean, Tre was definitely on Pat's shit list. Ma had told him that Nate believed if Pat found out Tre killed PJ while locked up in the same prison as Tre, Pat would have killed Tre, which would have meant Pat would never have been released from prison. Pat was pissed at first but as he thought about it, he realized Nate had done the right thing. He even decided to sit down and write Nate a letter about it, even though they hadn't seen each other in years. At this point, Nate had probably already graduated college.

Tre was still in Suffolk now. Pat couldn't quite let go what Tre had done, but it gave him some satisfaction to know that Tre would probably live out the rest of his years there.

Patrick drifted down the stairs to mail the letter. Ma had made eggs and toast, a little orange juice on the side. He could smell fresh coffee too, which he was still getting used to. Even the generic cheap stuff was way better than the stuff he drank in prison. She had gone out of her way to make him breakfast lately, maybe trying to appreciate that he was back and to treat him a little before he moved into a place on his own. She was giving him way more attention now as an ex-con than he ever got as a high school student. Maybe she felt a little guilty about that.

He grabbed the *Boston Globe* and flipped through it between bites. He always had to check in on the latest action of the Celtics and the Bruins. The Super Bowl was already over, not that he cared that much anyway; the Patriots never made the playoffs these days.

He went back to the front page. The headline leaped out at him: *DESPAIR TURNS TO SUICIDE*. The subhead underneath read, "17 Deaths by Suicide in South Boston in the Last Two Weeks." What the fuck? It was never this bad, not even in the Black neighborhoods of Roxbury and Dorchester—either that or it just never made the papers. Pat knew these deaths were all related to the cheap heroin that had flooded the streets since Whitey Bulger disappeared. He had gone on the lam right before Christmas, right as the Feds were ready to pounce on him.

No one knew where he went. Some people thought he ratted out to the FBI, but Pat didn't believe it for one second. Not Whitey. It would be a cold day in hell before that happened. He might run, but he'd never rat.

You could say a lot of things about Whitey, but when he was still in charge of the street, heroin was not an issue. Sure, you could get it, but it was expensive and rare. Whitey owned a piece of almost everything that was sold illegally in Boston, but cocaine was the most profitable. It was a party drug and could be destructive, but everyday people could still have a coke habit and remain functional. Sort of.

But now, Whitey's iron grip on the drug trade was gone. Now a thousand upstarts were vying to take his place, independent cowboys selling heroin cheaper than ever before. Black-market OxyContin—basically heroin in a pill—had just begun to circulate. Worse, anybody could get a bag of heroin for even cheaper—about ten bucks a bag. One dose and you were hooked. It wouldn't take long before people spent every penny they had and burned every bridge of friendship.

Fuck. This was getting to him. He had to get out of the house and get some air. He dumped his empty plate into the sink and grabbed the car keys.

"Ma, I'm out for a while."

———

DRIVING AROUND THE NEIGHBORHOOD DID LITTLE TO improve his mood. The whole vibe had changed, like a layer of desperation hovering in the air. A weight of defeat had replaced the pride and bravado that he remembered. Pat wanted to think that maybe he was just remembering things as rosier than they were, but he couldn't deny what he was seeing with his own eyes.

As he approached Andrew Square, a street zombie stopped in the middle of the road, blocking the way. They were the heroin junkies circling the drain, only a matter of time before they overdosed or killed themselves some other way. They all looked barely alive, gray skin with dark circles under their eyes, emaciated and walking around in a daze, desperate for their next fix. They were multiplying like rats. Somebody had to get this under control. Pat laid into his horn to wake up the poor bastard. The junkie seemed to come out of his trance and shuffled away from the road, going nowhere in particular. Pat drove off.

Enough of this shit. It was time to lighten up already. He hadn't really hung out with any of his friends since he got out of Suffolk, and he had a solid idea of where at least one of them might be hanging out on a Saturday afternoon—Adams Corner. It was time to reconnect. A cold beer sounded fucking fantastic. The Irish Village was an unofficial neighborhood a few miles or so south of Boston, with no projects around, and right now, Pat needed to take his mind off that whole mess. He drove toward Adams Street and Dorchester Avenue, home of one of his favorite places, the old Eire Pub.

AS HE CAME NEARER TO ADAMS CORNER, HE COULDN'T HELP but be curious as to how this historic Dorchester nook had changed over the last four years. He had a good feeling he would run into Slick, whom he hadn't seen since his graduation party and that whole fucked-up night. He'd been friends with Slick since he was eight, since PJ was their centerman and linemate on the ice. They were all pretty good at hockey back then.

As a young man in Dorchester, it wasn't like you called when you wanted to see your friends. You just showed up to places where you knew they would be. Back in high school, it would have been the street corner, the city park, the tracks, or the basketball courts. Maybe you might see people at Mass, but that wasn't really a hangout. Father Lydon would put on an event every now and then at Cathedral High to keep the kids out of trouble, but that wasn't always a regular thing. Most of the time, you just showed up at people's houses. Everyone knew everyone.

The Eire Pub was the afternoon spot to be. It was one of the places that was pure Boston, through and through. The place was fucking legendary—sports celebrities and famous politicians would make a point of visiting. Both Reagan and Clinton had famously stopped by and soaked in the fabled atmosphere. Clinton had actually dropped by just last week,

President Bill Clinton in Dorchester is helped
over a bar at the Eire Pub by Boston Mayor Ray Flynn

and the visit was commemorated by a photo of him getting on the bar and
hamming it up with the locals. It was a visit to honor Mayor Flynn, whom
Clinton had recently made the new ambassador to the Vatican in Ireland.

But it was really the locals that made the place special. Inside the Eire
was the real Boston, a place where no one really cared if you were rich
or poor, and you could just grab a beer and bullshit with the guys. This
wasn't a place to pick up girls but, rather, for men to relax and be men—
mostly regulars just hanging out.

As he approached the street corner, he spotted a tall, skinny guy
with bleach-blond hair smoking a butt. Son of a bitch. He knew he
would be here!

"Yo, Slick!" Pat belted out the car window.

Slick's head popped up, and he exhaled a cloud. Pat watched as the
recognition hit him.

"Holy fuck! Pat, is that you?" Slick asked. They shook hands. "You
are a fucking mountain now," Slick said, studying his new frame.

"And you look like a fucking degenerate," Pat replied. They shared a
laugh. Pat already felt better. But he wasn't lying. Slick had always been
the best dressed of his friends, but somehow the nice clothes just made
him look shadier.

"What the hell were they feeding you in prison?"

"Total fucking garbage," Pat answered, laughing. "And what the fuck you do to your hair?"

"You don't like the hair?" Slick asked. "Never mind. I don't fucking care if you do or don't." It was already on. Pat's best friends liked to demolish each other for sport.

"What you been up to, Slick?" Pat asked.

"Hey, man, no one's called me that for years. It's Treats now," he replied.

"Treats?" Pat asked. "What's that?"

"Let me buy you a Guinness," Treats said. "I'll explain inside."

Chapter 4

THE EIRE PUB

THE EIRE PUB HADN'T CHANGED A BIT, AND PAT GUESSED THE
bar had probably looked mostly the same since the doors opened back
in 1962, long before his time. Stepping into a familiar part of traditional Boston was refreshing. The old-fashioned bar was made of dark
wood, shiny from the constant cleaning. The walls were of a lighter
color, wood paneled and decorated with Bruins and Red Sox jerseys
and a few pictures of celebrities and politicians. Never completely spotless, it had a lived-in feel. Even the floor was a reddish-brown linoleum
that kind of had a permanent stain and wear to it no matter how much
the barbacks mopped.

The smell of cigarette smoke and suds permeated the air. As Pat suspected, the crowd was mild and of mixed ages. Treats took a seat toward the end of the long bar, and Pat pulled up one of the last stools.

He had only been inside the Eire a few times before prison, for lunch with Walsh's uncles. Most of the time, the crowd was generally members of the Boston Police or Fire Department, politicians, construction unions, or Boston Irish residents.

Pat had only spent four years in prison, but those years felt like they had aged him a whole decade. A simple place to chill out and drink for a minute with regular guys was much more appealing to him now than when he was eighteen.

Treats, with the exception of his new nickname, was pretty much the same. He was lanky and put-together, too preppy to be a tough guy. He appeared to be maybe a little wealthier than before, but Pat didn't want to ask him directly about it. People could get twitchy about that kind of thing. Maybe after they each had a little buzz going, he could get deeper into all that.

For now, they bullshitted about the lousy baseball season last year. Even in prison, Pat caught a few Red Sox games on TV or on the radio. The baseball strike cut their season short in August, but the team wasn't doing too good even if the season had continued. The Red Sox had fifty-four wins and sixty-one losses, which wasn't the worst, but the New York Yankees were leading them by seventeen games. The running score against their hated rivals was pretty much the only metric that most of the guys cared about. The curse was real.

After Treats was done bitching about how Clemens was the only starting pitcher on the team worth keeping, he started to wander off to other topics. Patrick struggled to interpret Treats's speech; he was years out of practice. Treats was from Dorchester, so he had a thick Boston accent, but that was not what made him hard to understand. His parents had immigrated from rural Ireland, and they had one of the thickest Irish brogues Pat had ever heard. So Treats had this weird mixture of intense Boston and country Irish. On top of that, he talked fast and kind of mumbled his words. When he was sober, his speech wasn't too bad, but after a few drinks, only his close friends and family could make sense of what he said.

"You been out for a few now, man. Where ya been?" Treats asked.

"Just taking it all in, you know?" Pat answered. "It's been kinda weird. Wasn't sure I was ready to socialize just yet."

Treats nodded, taking a long gulp from his Guinness. "Everyone knows you're a good kid and that the judge felt like making an example out of you. This city'll never get past the racial and mob history."

A dead silence filled the air.

Pat knew what Treats was probably thinking. Treats had never visited him in prison and probably felt a little embarrassed or guilty about it. But Pat didn't really hold it against him. It's a big thing to ask people to visit you in prison. It's the last place anybody wants to be, even for a fifteen-minute conversation.

"It is a little different around here these days, isn't it?" Treats said, kind of changing the subject. "There's no sheriff in town, and everyone's running wild."

"Yeah," Pat agreed. "I almost ran over a junkie on the way over here, around Andrew Square. It's a fucking shit show."

Treats shook his head. "Won't be long before you'll have to put bars on your windows and whack these guys with baseball bats to get 'em off your front stoop. Fuckin' junkies, man."

Treats sounded dispassionate about the whole thing. He took another long swig. "Still," he said with a knowing look in his eye, "the situation does open up some interesting opportunities."

Patrick leaned in. "You dealin'?" he asked. "I mean . . . more than usual?"

Treats just turned back and smirked. "It's no goddamn mystery. Everyone knows that if you want the good stuff, you talk to Treats."

"Treats," Pat whispered. "You're not . . . you're not dealing oxys, are you?"

"Fuck that shit," Treats shot back. He leaned in and lowered his voice. "No, man. No heroin, no angel dust, none of that wacko shit. Mainly just weed. Lots of weed. If anyone needs some party drugs, man—coke, ecstasy, shrooms, whatever, I can get my hands on that too. But I don't fuck around with needles or shit that makes you jump off a building."

"That's all you had to say, man," Pat said, relieved. Everyone had their hustle these days. But heroin and crack was where he drew the line. The blight on his neighborhood was growing fast, and it felt like it was going to get worse before it got better. If things didn't change, before long Boston would have a place of its own like skid row.

"What I meant," started Treats, "is that there's an upside to every situation. With so many pranksta running wild, it's easier to do business on the down low. There's so much going on, no one's going to bother with a small operation like me. I'm not trying to expand or anything. I mean, it's just weed. Easy money. I'd be a fool not to. The cops have bigger fish to fry."

Treats took out his pack of cigs and tapped them on the bar to pack the tobacco in. He lifted a cigarette to his mouth and lit it, waiting for Pat to react.

"Okay, you have me convinced." For a minute there, he thought Treats was trying to recruit him. But even if that was the case, Pat would have to say no. Dealing had never been his style.

"Listen," Treats said, exhaling a cloud of smoke, "I just got an interesting proposition for ya. Trust me; you're gonna love it."

"A proposition?" Pat asked, a little suspicious.

"It's not about the weed, you fuckin' Mary," laughed Treats.

Treats smiled and threw some cash on the bar to pick up the tab for both of them. It was a small thing, but Pat appreciated it.

"C'mon. Let's go," said Treats, already putting on his jacket.

———

TREATS'S NEW PLACE WASN'T TOO FAR FROM THE EIRE, IN THE heart of the Irish Village—a double decker he shared with his sister. He had the upper level, with an attic, a living room, and a kitchen. It was a pretty common layout for the whole neighborhood. For a family, it'd be pretty tight, but for Treats, it was more than enough space.

Treats led him to the attic hatch and unlocked a heavy padlock. He brought down the ladder, and they climbed up.

Pat laughed to himself when he saw the inside. It was like Treats had rebuilt his bedroom from high school. The attic looked less like a drug dealer's base of operations and more like a clubhouse. The walls were painted green and white, and he'd even brought some of his old posters to decorate—The Smiths, U2. He'd hung a new poster of Pamela

Anderson in a bikini. That girl was hot, but those boobs were definitely fake. Pat was more of a Paulina guy.

An open door led into the unfinished side of the attic with bins and lockboxes everywhere and six large, green trash bags along the side of the wall, one of them open. Pat guessed they were full of weed, probably divided into pounds and ounces. On the floor was a triple beam scale; you didn't have one of those unless you were measuring something precisely, like a lot of drugs. Weirdly, a few pairs of sneakers were lying around right next to a soldering gun. Pat didn't know what that was all about, since Treats hadn't mentioned any kind of smuggling operations—and weed, due to its sheer bulk, wasn't exactly something you soldered into a shoe. He had all kinds of stuff up here—some of his supply, a few stacks of cash in rubber bands, and construction tools. Nothing Pat hadn't seen before but maybe not all this much at once.

An old beat-up couch sat in the middle of the room, and a few stools were scattered about. Treats sat down, pulled a joint from his jacket, and lit up. He took a couple of hits and passed it to Pat.

"Fuck, why not?" Pat said, taking the joint.

He took in a few hits. He hadn't smoked weed since graduation night. And this shit was way better. The stuff they could get their hands on in high school was pretty much the dregs and shake that the dealers couldn't sell otherwise. A little stale and full of stems and seeds, that weed was what they used to call "dirt weed." But this shit was top of the line, he could tell. His old friend had developed some refined taste.

"I got a girlfriend now," said Treats, out of nowhere.

"Yeah? How's that goin'?" Pat asked.

"She's cool. Stacy. Hot brunette. Nursing student. She's from the Q, North Quincy. We're probably going to end up living together soon."

Treats was the kind of guy who could usually get almost any girl he wanted. It kind of surprised Pat that, at twenty-three, he was thinking about living with a girl instead of playing the field. Pat was about to respond when Treats continued.

"She's pregnant. She wants to keep it."

Treats's face fell a little when he said it. Pat wasn't going to ask if Treats wanted to keep it too.

"Hey, I almost joined the carriage race once," he said instead. "Kiley and I had a scare in high school. Scared the fuck out of me. Turned out to be a false alarm."

Poor Kiley. Pat's prison sentence had broken her heart. He hadn't worked up the nerve to see her since he got out. She was beautiful—and fun. No way was she still single, and he hadn't expected her to wait for him. But he hadn't thought about her in a while, and he wasn't going to let himself start now.

"Well, this one's real; trust me. She took like three pee tests and went to the doctor. This little guy's coming in six months," Treats said. He had a defeated expression.

"Sorry, man," said Pat. "Hey, you know, you might love it. Most guys come around to being a dad once the kid actually arrives. You were probably going to have a kid anyway. It's all just happening a little earlier than you planned."

"Well, that's why I had something interesting in mind. A little bachelor party. One last hurrah before I'm chained down. You know what I mean?" Treats asked.

"Like what? Head out to Atlantic City?" Pat hadn't gone on much vacation. With his ma being single and raising him and his two sisters, any spare money left over usually just went to his tuition at Cathedral.

"Way bigger than that, my friend," Treats said, smiling. "Wanna go to Ireland?"

Ireland? Pat could barely wrap his head around it. He'd never been out of the country before.

"What? You're kidding?"

"Ireland, bro! My cousin's getting married in this little village called Roundstone. She told me I could bring whoever I want. I figure you, me, Walsh. Stacy has exams, so she can't go. It's just the guys."

He started getting animated just talking about it, and he took another hit. "Listen, man . . . just think about it. You missed out on all the awesome parties just when life was getting interesting. This'll be like spring break, four years of college, and Woodstock all wrapped up into one trip. You'll fucking love it!"

Holy shit. Treats was actually making sense. Why the fuck not? Pat hadn't really blown off any steam since he got back. He'd missed all the milestones that all the other kids got to experience. Why not go on an adventure? He couldn't think of a reason not to go. Except maybe for his parole obligations and money!

"I don't have the money for this, man," he finally said. "What's it gonna be, like fifteen hundred just for the airline tickets?"

Treats smiled and pointed to some of the bags.

"No way. I'm not selling. Not even to get to Ireland," Pat said.

"No man, you got me all wrong. I'd never jeopardize your freedom. But if you know someone needing a connection or whatnot, just let me know about it. I'll give you a little commission. Something like that. I'll do the dealin'. I mean, only if you want, brother. No pressure."

Pat was skeptical, and Treats could tell, so he backed off a little.

"Tell you what, Pat. You just think about it. Maybe you can find some odd job or something before we go. The wedding's in a couple of months. Maybe I can help you get in with the union guys and work on a few sites in the meantime. But you do what you gotta do."

Pat nodded, thinking about it. He needed to get a job anyway. Maybe he could work a few temporary gigs.

"Either way"—Treats inhaled another monster hit from the joint and exhaled a cloud of sweet smoke—"you're coming with us."

It was hard to argue with the shit-eating grin on his face.

Chapter 5

JOB HUNT

"SORRY, KID, I'D LIKE TO GIVE YOU A CHANCE, BUT . . ."

Pat sat stoically in the chair across from the middle-aged and balding HR guy. He knew what he was about to hear, so he wasn't emotionally attached to the outcome. It was the seventh or eighth application he had filled out this week at construction sites all over the city.

Ordinarily, it would have been a pretty decent time to try and get a job at a site. In addition to all the regular construction all over the city, there was the Big Dig, a massive highway and tunnel project that had been going on for years. For an enterprising young man willing to work hard, there were tons of opportunities. Plus, it was still wicked cold this time of year, so fewer people were willing to work outside.

"Taking on an ex-con is too much of a risk. Nothing personal," the guy said. Pat had forgotten his name already. Herb? Frank? Who cared?

"Honestly," Pat countered, "I can bang nails and saw wood with the best of them. I don't have as much experience as the rest of these union guys, but I'm in great shape. I've probably got better stamina than some of your best men. And I learn fast."

"I'm sure you do," he said. "But that's not the issue. It's a liability concern. Why hire an ex-con when I can hire someone just as good who isn't?"

Pat had heard enough. This was another shut door. He half-heartedly thanked the guy and had already forgotten what his face looked like by the time he left the office. Maybe the work-union construction plan wasn't the best option. Maybe he had underestimated how hard it would be for most people to see beyond his past. He knew he could reach out to some people in the neighborhood for a favor, but he didn't want to start off owing somebody something. And painting a garage or helping some old guy in putting up a fence wasn't exactly something that would go anywhere.

He wandered into the street, trying to figure out his next move.

He could see the bind that guys like him were in. He had to make a living. He just wanted an ordinary life. But if no one would hire an ex-con, wouldn't that just force him into working under the table—dealing or doing something else that was probably illegal? It was a cliché but one that hit so close to home, now that he was on the outside. He'd vowed never to go back to prison, which meant trying to stay on the straight and narrow, but reality was making that prospect less and less likely. Forget getting to Ireland. At this rate, he'd be stuck living at home with his ma and sisters, working odd jobs just to have some pocket change. In his mind, Pat could already hear Treats giving him shit about not going on his party trip. But what the hell was he supposed to do?

Pat walked to where he had parked his mom's Ford Taurus and hopped in, warming up the engine in the late winter cold before he got the car moving.

Fuck all this. Maybe what he really needed to do was get his head clear with a good workout, maybe pound out some frustration on the heavy bag. His mind drifted to the past, to the place where he used to train every summer at the boxing gym. In prison, it was his skill at the sport that made all the difference in his survival.

O'Riley's Boxing Club, located in Quincy Center and less than ten minutes outside Boston, had an old-school reputation for training some of the toughest characters from all over the Boston area. It was all part of an informal network of boxing clubs that had such a profound influence on so many of the young men in the city. And out of all of them, O'Riley's was the best. It was the real deal and also happened to be the gym that the Police Athletic League boxing club used for its youth program.

Pat's cop friend, Sergeant Mike Daly, used to help run that program and trained there. Daly was one of those guys who knew both sides of the fence all too well. He'd spent his life in the boxing gyms while his brother did time in federal prison for dealing blow. Daly was the cop who had tried to save Pat from his prison sentence and had urged him to tell the truth and rat on Walsh. Pat had always liked Daly, and he appreciated his efforts. But no way would he ever rat, especially when his friends had all just been defending themselves that night. Pat saw himself as just as guilty—or as innocent—as any of them.

Pat had started training with his dad when he was six. He still kept a picture of his father and himself from that time on his nightstand. In the photo, his dad kneeled in the ring so Pat could reach him, with a boxing training pad on each hand. Pat was crouching in the photo and about to throw a monster right hook. After Pat's father disappeared, Daly would sometimes help Pat train.

Nowadays, Jimmy Fahy was the main trainer, and the owner was a local judge who funded the place. Jimmy had always taken a special interest in Pat. "You show a lot of talent," he'd once told Pat. "You're strong, fast, and there's your willingness to put in the work." Pat wasn't afraid of getting hit, even back then. Now, he was even more fearless. After the bare-knuckle trials by fire he'd faced in prison, nothing in the ring would scare him. And fuck, he needed the workout.

———

MORE PEOPLE WERE TRAINING THAN PAT WOULD HAVE expected for an early Thursday afternoon. It was good to be here. The place smelled bad, but that came with any good gym—a sign that people were working hard. A few guys were wailing on bags, others lifting on the sidelines. One guy was jumping rope; he was a few minutes into it, judging by his flop sweat. If this were the summer, he was sure he'd see some junior high and high school kids training too. The place itself wasn't much of a sight. With the dim lighting and two flights of stairs to walk down, it resembled a stale, dirty basement. But that was the kind of feel you wanted in a good boxing gym.

A couple of guys were sparring in the ring—hard to tell if they knew each other or not. People's personalities changed once they went into fight mode. If you got two best friends together in the ring and they were on the competitive side, they might look like they were trying to kill each other. Then afterward, they'd grab a beer. One of the greatest things about boxing was the way it tended to bond people. Friendship started with respect, and it was a lot easier to respect someone who had the guts to go toe to toe with you in the ring.

That was something Jimmy inherently understood. They didn't make them like Jimmy anymore. He must have been in his late forties at this point, and the dude was just a legend to everyone in the boxing community. He'd had a really good pro record back in his day and had fought all over. He'd even roomed with Tony Danza and spent time under Cus D'Amato—Mike Tyson's trainer in upstate New York. He was kind of a second father to young men all over the Boston area.

The gym was one of the only places Pat could think of that wasn't racially segregated across the bullshit neighborhood lines; there was none of that crap at O'Riley's. Black kids, White kids, Mexicans, Jewish, Asian—it didn't matter. Jimmy didn't care about any of that. It was all about the skill, the guts, the heart of the fighter. That was how you were judged. Did you give your all? Did you work hard? Did you never give up, even if you were hurting and losing? Did you respect your opponent by making him work for it? Did you respect yourself by playing to win?

Young men who would have torn each other apart because someone was in the wrong neighborhood were training together and making lifelong friends. The race jokes they made back home on their own turf weren't repeated in here. If you spent enough time at O'Riley's, you eventually stopped making those kinds of jokes entirely.

O'Riley's was probably the reason Pat made such good friends with Nate back in high school without thinking much about it. So many of his friends were hung up on the whole idea of Black kids "invading" Cathedral High School. In fact, Pat's ma had thrown a fit about it. Pat just saw it as the school reaching out to help out some underprivileged kids with a scholarship. He could still hear his mother complaining: "We had it just as bad as they did. And no one lifted a finger to help us."

Pat felt the same way then as he did now. What was the fuckin' big deal? It sure as hell didn't matter in here. Jimmy ran a tight ship and wouldn't put up with any casual racism in his gym. It didn't matter how much money you made, either. There were young college students working out next to construction guys, cops training with ex-cons, and so on. Boxing was the great equalizer.

As for Jimmy himself, he seemed to have his finger on the pulse of the city. Everybody knew and liked him—politicians, lawyers, cops, professional criminals, the mob, blue-collar guys, white-collar guys, two-bit criminals. Jimmy got respect. He was completely tapped in.

Part of that came from his rich life experience. He'd served some time for dealing coke out of a restaurant—or at least that was the story on the street. It wasn't the kind of thing you asked details about. Pat forgot how many years Jimmy had served in prison; that was way before his time. If Jimmy had any other secrets, he was successful in keeping them close to his chest. But because Jimmy had been on both sides of the law, he understood people and didn't judge where they came from or what they had done.

He looked around, eyes still adjusting to the dim light. *Holy shit.* There he was, a stocky silver-haired guy leaning up against the wall, watching the sparring guys, sort of talking to himself. Jimmy was always scouting for potential talent.

Pat picked up his stride and approached.

"Hey, Jimmy. It's been a while," he said.

It took Jimmy a moment, but the glimmer of recognition came into his eyes. "Patrick! Son of a bitch! I knew they wouldn't have you in there forever." Jimmy had known all about Pat's jail term. He had shown up at the sentencing, solely to offer support. He was that kind of guy. He shook Pat's hand firmly, with a wide and genuine smile.

Already, Pat's sour mood from his job search was turning around. "Good to see you, Jimmy. Looks like nothing much has changed around here," Pat said, returning the firm handshake.

"Boxing doesn't change. Come to think of it, people don't change that much either." He laughed. "I'm glad you stopped by."

"Honestly, I just want to work off some steam," Pat replied. "It's been a weird week."

"Well, be my guest. You know your way around. You need some gloves?" he asked. Patrick hadn't worn boxing gloves since before Suffolk. In that place they'd used socks over a pair of flip-flops as mitts. "I got some clean loaners in your size."

The notorious O'Riley's Boxing Club in Quincy Center,
where the toughest Boston fighters trained during the 90s

PAT PUT IN A MONSTER WORKOUT, WARMING UP WITH THE
speed bag and then committing some serious effort with the heavy bag,
throwing his substantially heavier and stronger twenty-three-year-old
frame into it. He beat it like it owed him money.

Before long, a whole hour went by, and Pat was exhausted and
dripping with sweat. Because he'd come to the gym spontaneously, he
didn't have his usual workout clothes. He happened to have an old pair
of sweats in the back seat, and he had a white undershirt on, so he had
just used those. It was kind of trashy, but whatever. The punching session
made him feel a hell of a lot better than he had before.

After he showered and toweled off, he stepped back out to catch up
with Jimmy and hand him his workout fee.

"No charge, Patrick. No way." Jimmy laughed. "Jesus Christ. But you
owe me for a new heavy bag now. You're a beast! You could knock out a
mule with that power! You can pay me later, when you have a job."

Pat hadn't mentioned he had yet to find work, but showing up in the
middle of the weekday was a good indication of his unemployment.

"At this rate, I'm not sure when that's gonna be, Jimmy," Pat argued. He tried to shove a ten-dollar bill in Jimmy's hand again, but Jimmy waved it away.

"Comin' up empty, huh?" Jimmy asked.

"Yeah, it's not going so well," Pat explained. "Turns out being an ex-con isn't exactly a selling point. You know how it is."

"Oh, believe me, I do. I do. But it's hypocritical, if you ask me. Good people wind up in the can too. And you don't gotta be a criminal to be a bad person."

"Yeah," Pat said. He liked Jimmy. He had a way of smoothing everything over, making everybody feel like they were on the same playing field.

"Listen," Jimmy started, "I'm actually looking for someone. You want to help out here for a while? I can't pay you much, but I can get you above minimum wage and I'll give you $20 a round to spar my pros. Just go easy on them! Help me set up and clean up, maybe hold the mitts for some of the guys. Maybe even coach a few of the kids on the weekends. And you can train all you want. What do you say?"

Now that was an interesting proposition. He hadn't even thought of that as an option, and it wasn't a bad idea. It wouldn't be nearly as much as he could make in construction, but that was kind of a pointless argument because none of those guys would hire him anyway. And he'd enjoy being in the boxing gym. He didn't mind if he had to mop the floors. If he worked five or six days a week from now until the wedding, maybe he'd have enough scraped up to go.

"Damn, Jimmy. That sounds pretty good," Patrick conceded. "Can I work five or six days a week? I'm trying to go to Ireland in a month, so I'd have to take a few weeks off around then. But I need the money for the trip."

Jimmy's eyes lit up. "The old country, huh? What's going on over there?"

"Just a much-needed vacation," answered Pat. "Prison doesn't offer much in the way of sightseeing."

"No, it sure the fuck doesn't. God, I hated it." Jimmy laughed. "Tell you what. Why don't you start on Monday?"

"I don't know. I gotta check in with my secretary," Pat joked. "Sure, man, I'll be here."

Ireland would maybe be a possibility after all.

———

A FEW MINUTES AFTER PAT LEFT, JIMMY SAT DOWN AT HIS OLD beat-up wooden desk in the corner of the gym to do some paperwork. The phone, which he always guessed must have been from the fifties, sat on the corner and rang abruptly. Its tone was nearly as loud as the boxing bell. Jimmy picked up.

"Yeah?"

"Jimmy. It's Choppa," said the gruff voice at the other end of the line.

"Choppa. What's up?" Jimmy asked.

"We need someone for that drop we talked about. Someone we can trust that won't ask too many questions."

"I get it. Someone you can trust," confirmed Jimmy. "You're never gonna believe this. I got just the guy. Guess who just told me he's going to Ireland?"

"Who?" Choppa asked, completely at a loss.

"Your old cellmate. Patrick."

Jimmy waited through a long pause.

"Hmmm. Yeah, that could work very nicely," Choppa said. "The timing is perfect, and we need the funding for the next effort. The cease-fire is about to be officially over."

Jimmy had suspected that this was about The Cause. He doubted from the start that the fragile peace between the IRA and the British government would hold—Choppa couldn't be the only one making moves for the IRA. It was a miracle the cease-fire had lasted all these months. For now, the broken peace was all but a foregone conclusion. But to make any move at all, The Cause needed money and resources.

"The English tried to demand a 'disarm' as a precondition for the peace talks." Choppa chuckled. "And it just so happens Whitey needs exile out of Piccadilly right fucking now. Safe harbor in exchange for a sizeable donation to the effort. That's the arrangement in the works."

Jimmy didn't say a word.

Back in the day, other than paying his vig, Jimmy always stayed clear

A young child sells newspapers on Londonderry Street
during the cease-fire in Northern Ireland

of the major Irish crews and somehow survived them despite hustling the
vig collectors with much lower than expected payoffs. He had known
Choppa throughout the seventies; they were tight. Part of that came
with respect. Jimmy hardly ever asked questions. Although he heard
rumors that Whitey had been spotted around Europe recently, nothing
had seemed solid until Choppa just confirmed it.

This was way more than Jimmy needed or wanted to know, that was
for sure. He was responding to the request that Choppa was searching
for a runner for some Ireland transaction drop, and that was it. That was
how the network worked—with trust.

"Look, Choppa," Jimmy said, finally breaking the silence, "I think the
kid is perfect. He's young, hungry, tough. Most importantly, he knows
how to keep his mouth shut."

"Make sure of it. And tell him only what he needs to know."

"You got it," Jimmy confirmed. He hung up the phone and sat back
in his creaky chair.

It was just a drop. He was sure the kid could handle it without too
much fuss.

Chapter 6

CATHEDRAL

IT WASN'T THE HAPPIEST OF HOMECOMINGS. JAMAL'S untimely death had hit Nate deep. He had always envisioned a joyous occasion coming back to the city he loved. Instead, his return felt bittersweet and complicated. Still, Nate was glad to be back home.

It had already been nine months since he graduated from the University of Virginia in Charlottesville, but he knew his return to Boston was inescapable. Nate had almost been afraid to come back; the city was in his blood, and he knew he wouldn't want to leave. He'd have to drag his girlfriend, Vanessa, back with him next time. He knew she would fall for the city. Or at least he knew he could persuade her to move there.

Nate gazed around, breathing in the familiar sights he loved so much. It was a strange feeling. He approached the block of the Cathedral Housing Project's playground, where so many memories he had with his best friend began to surface. He couldn't believe he would never see Jamal again.

It was midday when he stood at the 1400 block of Washington Street in the South End, in front of a pizza shop. Nate was just finishing his favorite for lunch—a giant slice of plain cheese with extra red pepper flakes from Harry O's Pizza. He stood there on the sidewalk, taking in the scene. Across the street towered the Cathedral of the Holy Cross, built in 1875, the mother church of Boston's archdiocese and built in the old-world cathedral style—the heavy stone grand and ornate, made to impress and last. It would not have been out of place in Dublin. His high school alma mater, Cathedral High School, was on one side of it. On the other was the Cathedral Housing Project.

Back in the day, a solid opportunity had arisen. Nate had been one of the first recipients of the Cathedral High outreach program. For the first time, Cathedral High had enrolled promising Black and other minority students from the surrounding areas at a significantly reduced cost. His mom had wept tears of joy the day he was accepted. She proclaimed it was truly a blessing and part of "God's will."

It was weird at first being in a mostly White school, but Nate learned to thrive. He just knew he had to be careful. People "like him" couldn't screw up even a little bit. As his mom kept telling him, he had to keep his nose clean and work twice as hard as White people. No one was going to give him any slack. Boston was still the kind of place where a police officer would pull you over just because you were Black and driving a decent car.

But Nate followed his mom's advice. He kept his head down and worked hard. He even befriended a White boy, Patrick, who became his friendly rival. It was such a shame what happened to Pat—finding himself in the wrong place at the wrong time like that on the night of graduation. He always felt like Pat had gotten a raw deal. It was the kind of thing that happened to young Black kids all the time. Pat probably never expected it to happen to him.

Nate glanced back at his alma mater's grounds and saw what he thought was a familiar face. *Was that . . . ?* Unsure, Nate crossed the street to the school, picking up his pace to see if it was indeed the man he recognized. Yes. Yes, it was.

It was his old Cathedral High headmaster, Father Lydon, the priest responsible for the outreach program at Cathedral High and like a surrogate parent to all those he had looked after. Father Lydon stood there, off the outside court in front of the school, shuffling students returning to class through the door.

"Yo! Father Lydon!" Nate shouted.

The old Irish priest snapped his head in Nate's direction. After a moment of recognition, his face beamed.

"Nathan!" Father Lydon called out. "Is that you?"

Nate jogged in to close the distance and shook Lydon's outstretched hands.

"It's me, Father. How you doin', man?" Nate said warmly.

"Oh fine, fine. It's such a surprise to see you. What brings you back? Weren't you in Charlottesville?" the headmaster asked.

"Well, it was some bad news, actually—"

"Oh my goodness, of course," said Father Lydon, his face dropping as he suddenly made the connection. "I'd forgotten you were so close with Jamal. I'm so sorry, Nate. Such an outstanding young man . . . You really tore up the courts together. My condolences, son."

Nate nodded. Lydon's voice calmed him. Many had offered Nate their condolences, but it felt different coming from Father Lydon.

"You still going to school?" he asked.

"Oh, I graduated!" said Nate, glad to change the subject. "I'm just here temporarily. But you can't keep me away from Boston. Since I'm here, I wanted to visit some friends and family, also my cousin Tre in Suffolk County Prison. I thought it'd be a great time to catch up with the city."

"It was a long sentence they handed Tre," Father Lydon said. "It's such a tragedy he couldn't steer clear of those gangs. I try to do everything I can to help all these young men stay on the straight and narrow, but sometimes . . . it's an uphill battle. Everyone thinks it won't be them that gets caught."

"Could have happened to any of us, Father. It could've happened to me! Between my cousin's bangin' and my aunt's drug history, at any moment I could've been shot dead or pinched. And that totally would've changed my life."

"You know, son, I think somehow you would have avoided all that, even if it had turned out differently. You've always had a good head on your shoulders."

"Well," Nate laughed, "you wouldn't believe it, but I got pinched the summer of our senior year in high school. Just for being at my aunt's house! They served a no-knock and took everyone. Let me go without charge, fortunately."

Father Lydon just shook his head. No-knock raids weren't unusual for the BPD, especially in the Black community. Neither of them needed to mention that the system was unfair.

"Anyway. I'm in a different world now. But I love this city so much. College was so great down south, but I keep getting that itch, Father. Like . . . like I needed to be here. I've been feeling like . . . if I want to pursue being a lawyer, I could study law right here in Boston."

Father Lydon grinned and patted Nate on the shoulder. He looked around the school grounds as if he were searching for something to say.

"What do you think?" Nate asked.

"It sounds like your mind's already made up. So, if you need a recommendation or a phone call on your behalf to your first-choice law school, I'm sure I can be of some influence, my friend."

Nate basked in Father Lydon's good intentions. He felt that Lydon meant what he was saying. That was just the kind of guy he was. He had even gone to visit Tre now and again in prison, just because Nate had asked him to check in on his cousin.

"Do you think this is right for me?" Nate asked.

"Well, if you want my opinion, then yes," Father Lydon said cautiously. "I think law school would fulfill the personal need you have to help others choose the right path and fight against the injustices in our city."

"I'm sensing a 'but,'" Nate said.

"But . . . as you know, the racism and corruption of this city, the political bureaucracy and shenanigans up at the statehouse—those will pose great challenges and frustration at every step along the way. It's bigger than just one man."

Nate nodded. He had no visions of being a one-man army or a knight in shining armor wiping the city clean of graft and corruption, and God knew what kind of criminal element was near the top. But he had his whole life ahead of him and felt a fire burning under his feet. What happened to Jamal had just added fuel to that fire; he felt he needed to do something—anything—to stop the steady flow of young Black men falling victim to gang violence. So many mothers burying their sons.

"As always, Father, you know I'm ready for a fight. Don't forget my first few days of school here, when this integration program started. I was in your office every day after squaring off against these Irish kids."

They both shared a laugh. Nate could chuckle about it now, but at the time, it had been pretty intense.

Father Lydon stared off into space for a moment, contemplating. "This isn't high school anymore, Nathan," he cautioned. "This is the real world out here."

"I know, Father, but—"

"It's bigger than even what is going on now," Lydon continued. "Years of history, a system that needs to be reimagined and reincarnated by a force of nature."

"Well, I intend to play a part in that reincarnation, Father. We're headed in the right direction, right? We have an Italian mayor now, the first non-Irish in sixty-five years. That's something, right?"

"Well, yes, by default," Father Lydon said with a laugh. "Because Clinton picked Mayor Flynn to be ambassador to the Vatican. But Mayor Menino is impressive, for sure! Let's take a walk, Nathan."

Father Lydon and Nate strolled in the direction of the Cathedral Housing Project. They stopped at the park bench overlooking the small playground. We do have a whole new set of problems out there now.

"Speaking of the Irish," Father Lydon began, changing the subject, "have you heard from your friend Patrick? He's been out for a little while now, you know."

Nate hesitated, not sure what to say—he wasn't confident his friendship with Pat was on solid footing.

"Yeah, I just heard he was out. Haven't seen him yet. He sent me a letter explaining that he finally understood why I didn't tell him my cousin Tre killed his cousin PJ. You get it, don't you, Father? If I told Pat, he would have killed Tre in there, and Pat would have spent life in prison. It seemed like the right call."

Father Lydon nodded in a way that he seemed like he understood.

"But I suspected you might have played a role in his understanding, Father. Did you help him see the light?"

The old priest just smiled, a knowing shine in his eye.

"Anyway," Nate continued, "you can read it for yourself."

Nate removed the folded and worn letter from his pocket. Father Lydon carefully unfolded it and began to read.

Dear Nate,

Just wanted to drop you a line to tell you I finally got out. I did learn to type a lot better in prison, so turns out I listened to that part of your advice. Are you on this email thing yet? Walsh, of all people, said he'd show me how. Can you believe it? They have it at the library, apparently. Father Lydon says no one's going to write regular letters like this anymore. We'll see, I guess.

Anyway, I'm sorry I didn't answer those letters you sent. I did appreciate them though. I've been doing a lot of thinking, and I didn't want to write you until I'd sorted through my thoughts, if that makes sense.

You were right about me thinking the world would just roll out the red carpet and give me what I wanted. Politics was probably never gonna happen anyway, but now I can at least focus on moving forward. I'm starting at Suffolk University in the fall.

Ma's helping me, but I'm going to pay her back bartending, since I'm finally old enough. I think I'm going to take business courses, and who knows? I might even buy a pub eventually. But one thing at a time.

Ma finally told me about Tre, or Mo. That's what we called him inside. I won't lie: I was pissed when I first heard. But I understand why you didn't say anything. You were thinking ahead, like you always do. I'm going to try to do that too.

Now I need to tell you something. Someone I've known my whole life (Sean—I don't think you ever met him) was the one who made PJ go to your neighborhood. Sean lost some dope for his bosses at the time, and he sent PJ to try to pick up some more. So the whole thing is as much Sean's fault as it was Tre's. And of course, PJ should've known better. But whatever. The world is screwed up. I don't have to tell you that.

I also wanted to say that you deserve every good thing that has happened to you. I spent a lot of time locked up in there, feeling like it wasn't fair. Like that college life was mine and, somehow, the universe screwed up and gave it to you. But you and your ma have worked hard for every damn bit of it. I watched you do it.

The bottom line is I was just feeling sorry for myself. I did some stupid shit. It wasn't as bad as what some of these people do and get away with, but that doesn't matter. I gotta take a page out of your book and focus on what I can control.

Are you coming back to Boston after college? I hope so. I don't think I could ever leave, although I'd like to move Ma to a nicer place. Danielle's dating some accountant or something, so hopefully that will work out for her, and Shannon is doing really well in high school. Kiley went away to college, but she's supposed to come home for the summer in a couple months, so we'll see if that goes anywhere for me.

If you come back this way, I hope you stop by. Maybe we can grab a drink, unless your ma's still smelling your breath every night, ha ha. I sent a letter to my parole officer requesting to leave the state. If I am granted, I may take a road trip down somewhere, maybe to Virginia—don't be surprised if you see me up in the stands watching you running game on the court!

Your friend,
Patrick

Father Lydon carefully folded the letter and handed it back to Nate. "The letter confirms the real connection between the two of you, as well as the pain," he told Nate. "Perhaps it also contains the beginnings of forgiveness."

"I was surprised. I expected Pat would never speak to me ever again, that he'd be so angry that I'd have to watch over my shoulder if I ever returned. We're on our own now, no one to mediate between us."

"What do you mean?" asked Lydon.

"Back in the day, you always had a way of helping us see each other's point of view. It's tough to see past your own world when you're still in high school."

"It's part of God's work," said Father Lydon.

"Yes, but, if it wasn't for you, Father, there would've been quite a few beefs that would have escalated to riot level. I remember that day right over there . . ." Nate pointed to the basketball court adjacent to the Cathedral High School front door. "Patrick and I almost went toe to toe as the helicopters flew overhead. It was crazy; the riots were going on at the same time at South Boston High. It's amazing how the crowd can swing our actions at the drop of a dime!"

"That's why cooler heads need to prevail," said Father Lydon. "You and Pat getting into a fight would have been pointless. And it's not who you two were."

Somehow, Nate thought, the priest seemed to know them better than they knew themselves.

Father Lydon sighed. "I'm just playing my part in keeping the peace and creating progress. I always recognized that you and Patrick had more in common than you could imagine. But it is God's plan for the journey for each of you to keep evolving along the way toward his light."

Nate stared out over the empty playground. These words were comforting. Father Lydon had a way of talking to him that made him feel understood and cared for. Not an easy thing to accomplish in this hood.

"You know," started Nate. "Patrick's a true friend and a real solid White boy. I never thought I would say that. But all things considered, even with everything that's happened, our friendship has taught me a lot. I hope the best for him."

"Me too, Nate," said Father Lydon. "He didn't deserve the punishment he received."

"Not sure how well he will fare out there in this world after his unnecessary stint, four years in lockup, and the ex-con label! But you know the saying, Father, 'Snitches dig ditches.' So I agree he did not have much of a choice."

"The few times I visited him," Father Lydon began, "he had a grimace in his eyes I had not seen before . . ." He was lost in the moment. "I know his soul well. He'll find his way. I'm sure you two will cross paths soon."

They sat in silence for a moment. Lydon stood up first. "Well, listen, Nate. I know you just got back into town, so let me know if I can help you out with anything at all."

Nate also stood and shook hands with the headmaster.

"Hey, I spoke to Reverend Gibbs a few months back," said Father Lydon. "If you want to start to get active locally, he has created a powerful forum for the Black community to come together to interact and intercept gang violence. They're trying to save lives. They're calling it the Ten Point Coalition."

This perked Nate's interest. Each minute he spent back on his own stomping grounds seemed to produce another reason to stay.

"Yes, I'll think about it. And I'll be in touch to cash in on that recommendation."

Nate briefly embraced Father Lydon. It was good to see him again.

Chapter 7

THE DIRTY DEED

IT WAS EARLY FRIDAY NIGHT, AND PAT WAS ALREADY TWO shots of whiskey and four beers in with Walsh. He knew they were just getting started. They were in the mood to blow the roof off Walsh's house. Walsh had just finished a hard week working on the Big Dig, and Pat was relieved he could help out at the boxing gym for a while. Walsh's fridge was packed with beer, and Pat knew that there was always an extra whiskey bottle stashed away somewhere. They were in no danger of running out of booze.

Walsh was one of the three people who had visited him in Suffolk. The other three were his ma, Nate—a few times when he was on break from college, and Father Lydon, who seemed to regard Pat as his spiritual responsibility. Walsh stopped visiting after a while but kept sending him encouraging notes; little things like that kept Pat going while he was counting the days to get out.

Pat and Walsh had been tight long before the stabbing incident with the Asian kids. They spent every year at school together, every summer break, and every neighborhood or school event. In everything, they were thick as thieves.

With the fight that sent Pat to prison, their bond became unbreakable. Pat had taken the heat for Walsh. If he hadn't served four years for him, Walsh would be serving twenty years or possibly life. As soon as they picked up those makeshift weapons from the dumpster, they knew it might get dicey, but they were guarding each other's lives. Had the situation been reversed, he knew Walsh would've done the same for him.

What Pat had done for Walsh was more than just a favor. It was like a covenant, sealed in sweat and blood. They were brothers for life now. And even though Walsh was spared from going to prison, it wasn't like it was smooth sailing for him.

Pat still found it weird, seeing Walsh's new disfigured face. Walsh told him the whole story when he returned from Suffolk. While Pat was serving his sentence, Sean had finally confessed that he'd sent PJ out alone on a drug deal the night he was killed by Tre and his people, and Walsh lost his shit. They had gotten into a drunken fight.

As soon as Walsh started wailing on him, Sean reached for the cask-strength whiskey bottle he had stolen from Triple O's and smashed it on Walsh's face, breaking his cheekbone and dousing him with whiskey. If that weren't bad enough, Sean's cigarette fell during the tussle and ignited the whiskey, lighting up Walsh's face like a torch. Then Sean bolted like a fucking little pansy-ass, leaving Walsh to douse his head in the sink and call for help by himself.

He'd been saying it like a refrain lately: *Fucking Sean.*

That cluster-fuck sent Walsh into the hospital for a month. But for Walsh's part, he didn't complain. He could still get work and didn't seem to have a problem attracting girls, despite—or because of—the intimidating scar on one side of his face. But Sean was pretty much persona non grata to both of them now.

Pat had heard that Sean fancied himself like Whitey now, amassing a crew and trying to get the lion's share of the neighborhood's hard drug trade. He wondered if Sean was dealing heroin. It was just further proof that Sean didn't give a shit about anybody. He was so greedy he would sell his own neighborhood up the river. He truly had evolved into a greasy little shitbag.

As Walsh always said, "What goes around comes around." It wasn't worth going after Sean if it meant maybe going back to jail. It was only a matter of time before a rival or the law would catch up with him. All you needed with that careless bastard was to let nature take care of itself.

Walsh certainly wasn't dwelling on it. He was never one to feel sorry for himself or obsess about the past. He was always just solid, taking college classes at the other Suffolk—the university—and working nights cleaning up at the statehouse. Even though his buddy Treats was getting deeper and deeper, Walsh didn't want any part of the drug-dealing life-style. But he didn't judge it either. And he really knew how to have a good time.

Walsh poured out another round of shots.

"To getting back on the horse, brother," said Walsh, lifting his glass. "Sláinte!"

"Sláinte!" Pat repeated the Irish toast right back to him, and they both downed their shots.

"So Treats tells me you're coming to Ireland with us?" Walsh asked.

"I think so. I mean, pretty sure. I'm not going to be making much at O'Riley's, but I can cobble enough together to pay for the trip. I'll be broke when I get back, though." Pat laughed.

"Well, I always got a couch if shit gets bad, man." Pat clinked his beer bottle with Walsh's on that comment; Walsh had his back. "They must be payin' you pretty good at the statehouse, huh?" He already knew the answer. It was a steady gig that you could make an easy weekly paycheck at, check-in at five p.m. after all the politicians left, and be out the door by nine p.m.

"Yeah. Not bad, not bad. Well, I've been working pretty hard the last few years. I don't spend much on things I don't need, so I've been saving a lot. Trying to work days on a few construction sites whenever I can too." Walsh always talked about joining the police department or the fire department—either one.

He seemed upbeat. A lot of guys would have turned into a total head case if they'd gone through what Walsh had, but out of all the people Pat grew up with, Walsh seemed to be one of the most well adjusted, despite the last few fucked-up years.

"I'm actually waiting to hear about going into the next Police Academy. There's a twenty-nine-week program," Walsh said.

"Walsh, that's awesome," Pat said. "Seriously? You're actually going to be a cop?"

"Just try to refrain from jokes." Walsh laughed. "I'll beat your ass if you call me a fucking pig."

"Well, you are a filthy animal," Pat jabbed.

"Oh, fuck off, mothafucka." Walsh laughed. He shifted around a bit, breaking off eye contact to stare at his drink. "Hey, Pat, I know you don't actually like talking about that night, but—"

Pat cut him off. "You would've done the same for me, man. We don't need to dwell on it." They'd already had this conversation, and it was already water under the bridge.

Walsh continued, "I know, I know. But I owe you my life. You saved me twice—once from getting killed in the street and once for saving me from a long sentence. We were outnumbered that night. I just wanted to get out of there alive. I'm sorry, man. I'm sorry you got the shit end of that deal."

Pat nodded and tried not to let the emotion crack his face. He didn't need to say all this; it was a given. Walsh dug into his back pocket and pulled out a thick envelope. He handed it to Pat.

"Here, man. It's about ten Gs in hundreds. Been saving fifty bucks a week for the last four years . . . for when you got out. This should pay for your Ireland trip and then some."

"I can't take this."

"You can. And we aren't discussing it, unless you're trying to piss me off."

Pat thumbed through the bills in disbelief. *This guy. This fucking guy.* If he lived a hundred years, he'd be lucky to make another friend even remotely as good as Walsh.

They hugged it out.

"Thanks, man. Seriously, thank you," Pat said. He didn't know what else to say. He knew it wasn't easy to save ten thousand dollars, even on union construction gigs. Walsh didn't need to make anything up to him. What a class act.

"Now you can keep all your O'Riley's money for yourself, brother," replied Walsh. "And when we get to Ireland, we can pull out all the stops."

Pat could just picture it, the three of them running amok in Ireland with no supervision and no brakes. Pat laughed to himself. It hardly seemed real. He tried not to question his current turn of luck and to just enjoy the ride.

He grabbed the whiskey bottle and poured Walsh and himself another round. Tonight, the spirits would flow.

Chapter 8

IRELAND MISSION

MIDWAY THROUGH THE FIRST WEEK OF WORKING AT THE boxing gym, Pat was already starting to feel better about the future. It felt good to be surrounded by other young men trying to better themselves and to have something to do that was productive. He wasn't getting rich, but at least it was an honest day's work, and it gave him a chance to figure out his next move.

And he wasn't a bum. He'd had enough idle time in prison, and he wasn't going to sit around complaining about his options. A job was a job. There was no way he was going to not work just because he had 10K in the bank; that wouldn't go very far if he had nothing else coming in. Walsh's contribution was generous, but Pat figured he'd probably blow through at least a third of that, maybe even half, on the Ireland trip alone—maybe even more if they really wanted to cause some damage. He chuckled to himself, unsure of what kind of international travel companions his friends would be. Walsh would be fine. Treats? Probably fine. Maybe. As for Ireland itself, he didn't really know what to expect.

He'd met plenty of Irish. So many of his friends and family would know someone who was moving to Boston, and everyone would always go out of their way to make the newcomers feel welcome. They'd show them around, take them to see a few sights, even get them fast-tracked into a job or one of the unions. Being from the old country offered you a little bit of celebrity, like it was your birthday or something. A whole network of people wanted to help set you up. It was certainly a better welcome than the original Irish got. Being Irish in the early 1900s often meant having trouble finding work or even getting service at a business or restaurant. It was hard for him to imagine—and amazing how much things had changed in less than a hundred years. The descendants of those first Irish immigrants must have adopted a "welcome wagon" approach to make sure that the brutal past wouldn't be repeated. And it was much more brutal than most people knew.

It was almost lunchtime, so Pat knew it was time to check out the locker room and give it another once-over. He dragged the cleaning cart over, collecting a few dirty towels along the way to be washed.

As he was wiping down the sinks, he spotted Jimmy in one of his signature white tanks leaning up against one of the lockers. Pat hadn't heard him come in.

"How's it going so far, kid?"

"Not bad at all," Pat replied. Something about working there felt like home. He'd spent most of the morning talking to Jimmy as he worked, catching him up on some of his lost years in prison. He wasn't the chatty type, but Jimmy had a way of making it easy to open up.

"That's great," Jimmy said. "But pace yourself. You don't need to get your life right back the first few months. Just take it day by day."

"Are you kiddin' me? I could do this all day." He wasn't lying. He could.

But there seemed something else behind Jimmy's smile, like he knew something.

"Listen, Pat. Why don't you step into my office? I've got some things to go over with you."

"What's up, Jimmy? Did I overstep my boundaries here?" asked Pat. He couldn't imagine he'd done something wrong.

Jimmy just laughed. "Far from it, kid. Let's have a talk."

Even though Jimmy's office was not that old, the way he had it decorated seemed like it had been preserved from the fifties. Everything had a sort of brown or sepia tone to it—brown desk, copper-colored floor, yellow walls. A few framed black-and-white photos of some of the guys he'd trained and even managed personally (he'd brought them some modest success as local champions) stood on the desk and on an adjacent shelf. There was a cool old-school picture of Marvin Hagler and Jimmy with long hair training side by side.

The chair Pat was sitting in was creaky and a little loose. Jimmy didn't splurge on little luxuries like comfortable furniture or modern desks. He was like a boxing monk, concerned only with the sport and bettering the skill of those willing to sacrifice. It seemed like all he wanted was to find his world champion.

Jimmy sat on the opposite side of the desk. He leaned back and put his arms behind his head.

"Patrick," began Jimmy, "how would you feel about a little outside opportunity? Something's come up recently, and I think it's a perfect fit."

Pat blinked. This was not what he'd been expecting. He felt honored that he was going to be considered for something important enough to be taken aside into Jimmy's office to discuss. He was also a touch surprised.

"What kind of opportunity? A fight in a smoker?" Pat asked.

Jimmy laughed. "No, that's too easy. I just gotta find someone who'll want to fight you. We have plenty of time for that—to jump you into a pro career fresh out of prison would be a disservice to you. Once your head is clear and settled in, we will start that dream and make it come true. But, before we get into that, I need you to understand what I'm about to say never leaves this room."

Pat's interest was piqued. Jimmy continued, "I need to know you're not going to share a word of what I'm about to tell you to anyone. You got that?"

What on earth was he talking about? Pat couldn't imagine what kind of secret a man like Jimmy needed to keep.

"You have my word," he said. "I won't tell anyone. What's this all about?"

"The people organizing this thing, they're operating at a high level. You understand? Trust me, you don't even want to know who they are. They just need a little help, and we're the ones that could do it."

Pat nodded, taking it in.

"The job'll take place in Ireland. We need you to pick up the contents of a safety deposit box in Dublin and deliver it to a location that will be disclosed later. I was asked by a few guys handling the logistics if I had the right person to pull it off low-key."

Holy fuck, Pat thought. *Was this really happening?* He wanted to say something, but nothing came out. His mind was full of questions. *Whoever these guys were, whether IRA, mob, or just someone high up keeping a low profile, they must be important.*

"I know you have questions," said Jimmy. "So go ahead."

"What's in the box?" asked Pat.

"Just a shitload of cash. They didn't tell me how much. What's important is who it's for."

This stopped Pat cold. *No way. Could he mean Whitey?*

Whitey was still on the run. No one knew where the fuck he'd gone. But he sure as hell couldn't use banks and credit cards, so he had to survive on cash alone. That meant he needed little stocks of it, supply lines to keep him flush all along the way. Pat knew Whitey was one of the most highly connected and intelligent career criminal bosses of the twentieth century. But even if he had stash boxes around the world, he couldn't be the one to go in and access them. Most likely he'd had that all planned out in advance.

Accepting this kind of gig was beyond dangerous. If caught, he might go back to prison. And no way was that happening. He was tempted to walk out right there, but . . . but what if he could pull it off? He couldn't lie to himself. There was something about this that excited him. It seemed important. And Boston had gone to shit since Whitey left. He wouldn't mind helping him out a little.

Was he really considering this?

It was hard not to like Whitey a little. He may have been a devil, but he was the devil that all the locals knew and were used to. Pat used to run into him every week at South Boston Liquor Mart, where Pat would buy scratchies and butts for his Nana. Whitey was often hanging around and would say hey. Whitey might have his known his dad—perhaps why he always got at least a friendly nod.

For all the rumored cold-blooded killing Whitey was supposed to have done, he seemed to be good to the kids in the neighborhood. At least, he was to Pat. Pat was somewhat friendly with some of Whitey's trusted underlings, and they were part of the community, the culture. When he was in high school, he'd sometimes go paintballing and shooting real guns at the ranges up at the New Hampshire state line with Whitey's top henchman, Kevin Welch.

Jimmy cleared his throat and leaned forward, balancing his elbows on his knees and placing his fingertips together. "Here's the deal, Pat. I know you're trying to stay on the straight and narrow. But you do this one job and you'll be set up—totally legitimate. Twenty-five thousand dollars, plus getting you hooked up with a bartending job or a long-term union construction gig. Hell, both, if you want. And after all that, if you want to focus on going pro"—he gestured toward some of his past champions on the wall—"we can get your head ready and focus on training."

Jesus Christ. Twenty-five thousand. Pat could bank that and immediately start working. He could save for a house, do everything on the up and up. With that kind of legitimacy, maybe he could even get Kiley to start taking him seriously again as a real prospect. With everybody on the inside getting him a job, he wouldn't have to worry about his ex-con past ever again. It would be a chance to start over from scratch, with a nice little nest egg in the bank.

It was tempting. Really tempting. But still a risk. But if he said "no," how would that be received? Bulger and his crew were not the types you said "no" to.

"How am I going to do this?" he asked. "I'm not even an Irish citizen. I can't just walk into a bank and take off with the contents of a safety deposit box. And I need to get a travel pass from my parole officer. I need proof of the family wedding connection."

"All right, listen to me, Pat. Daly and the judge have been asked to clear the parole obstacle, but they know nothing else, nothing about the drop. The planning has all been worked out. Choppa's arranged these kinds of drops for funding The Cause for almost a decade now, all from his prison cell."

"Wait," interrupted Pat. "Choppa? Choppa's in on this?"

As his cellmate, Pat had learned a lot about Choppa. He was born in Galway and emigrated to Southie in grade school. He ran a rival gang against Whitey way back in the day but eventually joined forces with him. Choppa had been out of Whitey's hair after the infamous debauched shipment of guns to the IRA. He had been on the run since '78. When he returned to Boston in '87, he was apprehended and went straight to prison on a thirty-year bid. Pat had seen firsthand how

Choppa communicated with his criminal networks through coded letters and private visits that no other prisoners got.

"Pat, you know his history. No one'll fuck with a veteran connected to the IRA and Whitey. That's why I asked Choppa to keep a close eye on

$1.2 million worth of weapons headed to the IRA from the Gloucester fishing trawler were seized by the Irish Naval Service after they were transferred to an Irish ship, the Marita Ann, off the coast of County Kerry, Ireland

you in prison. But now I owe him," Jimmy added, letting that extra piece of information settle.

Pat was struggling to keep up. "So you and Choppa were protecting me this whole time?"

Jimmy leaned back in his chair and sighed. "Listen, Patrick. After your first week away, your mother came to me, sick to her stomach. She wasn't sleeping and could barely eat. She asked how I could help protect you on the inside. She knew you were beat up and in solitary for fighting, and she asked me who I knew in there and what I could do. So I went to Choppa."

Patrick nodded his head in confirmation of the facts he had previously assumed.

"Why me, Jimmy? I'm not a criminal," Pat said. "I'm just a kid from Southie who's had a bit of bad luck."

"Right time, right place, Pat," Jimmy explained. "The job came up, and it has to be done now. You come along and tell me you're going to Ireland. It just happens to be a perfect alignment. A solid, tough, stand-up young man like yourself who's always done the right thing, knows how to keep his mouth shut, and has proven beyond doubt that he can handle himself like a professional law-abiding citizen—we couldn't ask for a better guy for the job. You're tight with Choppa. You're no rat, kid, and you never will be. They know they can trust you."

On that point, Pat knew in his heart that Jimmy was right. He would never be a fucking rat. He spent years proving that point. But still, this was a lot to consider. Pat nodded, soaking in the information.

"Plus," Jimmy went on, "if they sent an established guy, they'd be waiting for him. No one's gonna be looking for you. You're just a young guy from Boston on vacation." Jimmy studied Pat's face. "A young guy making up for lost time. I know you said Walsh has put aside some cash to help you, but it's nothing like what this can do for you."

Pat was already adding up the money in his head. Walsh's 10K, plus the 25K for the job, plus at least a year's income in construction or as a bartender. He would potentially be acccumulating, all combined, about 100K in comp. It would take him twenty years to save that kind of money on his own, working the kinds of shitty jobs they give ex-cons.

Jimmy took his silence as permission to keep going. "The box will be under your grandfather's name, with you as the beneficiary. You walk into the bank, sign some papers, and then you take it to the drop spot, and you're done. That's it. This is a first-round KO, kid. You got the highest level of FBI, IRA, Billy Bulger . . . hell, I wouldn't be surprised if President Bill Clinton has okayed this. There's no way anything is going to happen to you. They would all go down first, and that'll never happen. You know that!"

A thought dawned on him. Was this why Clinton had been in Boston, at the Eire Pub, shortly before Pat's assignment? He pondered on the possibility, also knowing that he would probably never truly know. The FBI had long been rumored to be in Whitey's pocket, and some even thought it was the Feds that had tipped him off ahead of the raid, enabling him to flee town before he got caught. Billy Bulger, Whitey's brother, was a state senator and president of the Massachusetts Senate. Some said he was practically Whitey's right-hand man in corruption on the state government end. Nana would always say, "One rules with a gavel, the other with a gun!"

Jimmy was essentially saying that the whole rotten apparatus of corrupt government was behind him and wouldn't let him get caught. He leaned back into his chair and added, "I mentioned your trip to Choppa last week because I had to get back to him on this, so I wanted to get his thoughts and see if this could be the break you need."

"What if I say no?" asked Pat.

Jimmy nodded in understanding. There wasn't an ounce of cruelty in his face. He replied, "Only if you want it, of course. I would never steer you into harm's way. I'm here for you, to help you in any way you want. You say 'yes' and do the job, you're set up. You say 'no,' then no harm, no foul; you keep working for me, and we move on. The rest's between you and Choppa; I'll leave that between you two cellies! Choice is yours, Pat."

It sounded like a game rigged in Pat's favor. If the Irish mob, the IRA, Billy Bulger, the FBI, and Whitey Bulger were behind him on this, then where was the real risk? All he had to do was basically be a courier for some cash. And then he'd be set for a good long while.

He thought of those failed job interviews—of all those other ex-cons who eventually ended up back in prison because they couldn't make a living doing anything aboveboard. He thought of his ma and his sisters, who'd hardly ever taken a vacation or splurged on themselves. He thought about having a shot with Kiley, maybe having a normal life with a house and a family. And he thought about all those poor saps who let poverty swallow them up, turning them into hopeless heroin zombies or worse.

This was a ticket to escape all of that. Little risk, big reward.

Pat stood up and outstretched his hand.

"I'm in," he said.

Jimmy shook Pat's hand and let out a warm and genuine laugh.

"Attaboy. I'll let Choppa know," Jimmy said. "Oh, yeah . . . He wanted me to pass along a message. He said, 'Tell Patrick his vengeance is now mine.' He said you'd understand."

Patrick was afraid of what that meant, precisely, but why? He left Jimmy's office with no small amount of butterflies in his stomach, and they weren't exactly the good kind.

Chapter 9

VISITING SUFFOLK PRISON

SUFFOLK COUNTY PRISON SUCKED. THERE WAS NO WAY around that fact. Nate hated the oppressive atmosphere of the place, the doom and gloom that felt like a growing cancer. The gloomy building sucked the air out of its surroundings, pregnant with the hate and rage and despair of the people entrapped within. Of course, Nate thought, the prison population was disproportionately Black.

The talking heads on TV liked saying that Black people commit more crime, but Nate scoffed at that. Sure, some of them deserved it. But there were plenty of White boys walking around free who had done plenty worse. Even a parole violation meant something different if you were White. Up and down the system, the dice were loaded against people like Tre, even if they were innocent. Which, unfortunately, wasn't the case.

The only thing that kept a lot of the prisoners from going out of their mind was visits from friends and relatives. It'd been far too long since Nate had gone to see Tre, and even though he was looking forward to seeing him, he felt forced to drown out the ugly atmosphere of the front gates with the music from his headphones and portable CD player.

He bobbed his head to the rhythm of "Gangsta's Paradise" by Coolio. It was everywhere right now—huge on the billboard charts. He mouthed the lyrics as they were spoken, knowing them by heart already.

Nate paused the CD to go through the metal detector at the security checkpoint. He knew the drill and robotically removed his headphones, keys, and loose change. After picking up his things on the other side, he approached the glass booth to get buzzed into the access lobby. It was usually a quick procedure to get the door open, but he could already tell something was off.

On the other side of the glass of the secured prison wall, two Black corrections officers talked quietly and continuously stole looks in his direction. Their hushed conversation seemed to go inappropriately long. Finally, the guards buzzed themselves through the security doors to greet him. He recognized the top guard and could see that something was wrong by the expression on his face.

"Yo, Nate. It's good to see you, man," said the top guard.

"Likewise, Enzo. What's goin' on?" asked Nate.

"Yo, um . . ." Enzo stammered. "Listen, man. I'm sorry, but we can't take you to see Tre."

"Why not?" Nate asked.

Enzo looked down. Whatever he wanted to say, he was dreading it. Enzo sighed, took a deep breath, and reengaged eye contact. "Tre was found dead two nights ago in his cell," he said. "I'm sorry to be the one to break it to you, kid."

Nate's stomach dropped out. All of a sudden, the guards seemed far away. Everything seemed to slip into black and white, and he collapsed into a heap on the floor, the guards failing to catch him on the way down. *Tre's dead? What the fuck? Why? How?*

Enzo and the second guard helped him back up to his feet.

"What the fuck happened?" asked Nate, his voice shaking as he fought back tears.

"We don't know. They tried to notify the next of kin, but they're also keeping it hush-hush until they find the cause of death."

Aunt Carol should have been on their list as next of kin. But Aunt Carol had been falling apart as of late. Sometimes it took her days to return calls. Maybe there was a message on her answering machine, still blinking red, waiting to be played.

"Man, something seems off, that's for sure," said Enzo, steadying Nate with a firm grip on his arm. "A few different gangs are claiming the kill."

His head was still swimming. He'd known this day would come eventually, but he couldn't believe it now that it was right in front of him.

Tre was like an older brother to him—an intimidating badass who was tough on Nate and had protected him on the streets his entire life. Nate was a tough kid who was strong with some scrap. But Tre was a beast. People knew if they fucked with Nate, Tre would gun them down in the blink of an eye, just for fun and the principle of it.

Nate gathered his thoughts. *Think. Think, goddammit.*

"Enzo, it doesn't add up. The streets have been quiet for a while. It's been over four weeks now with no beefs, and Tre knows everyone in here. He's been in here for at least two years . . . Has anyone new been moved in? Anyone transferred? With any affiliations at all?"

"No, nothing lately," the other guard replied. "But there's a story about a tampered witness that concealed one of Tre's murder charges. So he would've been staring at ten more years. But they're still investigating that."

"Let me talk with his cellmate for five minutes," Nate pleaded.

"No can do. He was the one found him dead, and he's lost his shit," Enzo explained. "No one but the cops get to talk to him."

A fog of disbelief descended over Nate. He always thought that Tre would be fine because he'd be in prison for the next fifteen years. Granted, it was not the place you wanted to be, but it was at least safe from the violence of the streets. After he got out, he'd be stronger and wiser. Sure, Tre would most likely restart an operation running weight up and down the East Coast. But at least he'd be smarter about it, maybe covering his tracks and leaving the hits to the young men he would recruit along the way.

There'd been no doubt about Tre's ability to build a small drug empire out of virtually nothing. Nate was fourteen when Tre started the Norfolk Kings. Tre was just twenty. But he had built it up fast, carving out his territory with an itchy trigger finger and a small group of loyalists, including his brother, Slugs.

Over a decade later, it had evolved into a tight organization. Nate was aware that Tre had maintained a level of control from prison, but the Norfolk Kings ran into new territory. Dozens of other would-be drug kingpins were flooding into the power vacuum, including the Norfolk Kings' longtime rival, the Vamp Hill Kings. For ambitious gangs, that put a target on the Norfolk Kings. Tre would have been right in the crosshairs. Was that what had happened?

Nate excused himself to sit in a chair. He held his head in his hands, trying to resist the uncomfortable, light-headed feeling. *Breathe, damn it*, Nate thought. *Just breathe, and try to think.*

He peered around and caught a glimpse of an older White guy with a tiny shamrock tattoo on his earlobe leaving the visiting area and returning to the inside. The man reminded him of Patrick and that Boston Irish life. Nearby was another young, stocky White guy walking away from the visitor's area's glass panels and phones. He only caught a quick glimpse, but it seemed like that guy definitely resembled someone from Patrick's group of friends. Maybe it was that punk Sean that he'd mentioned in the letter?

Nate always remembered the faces of Pat's friends. Walsh and Treats were clean-cut Catholic schoolboys, but Sean and PJ seemed more like trouble. That Irish old-timer on the inside—he just appeared like a seasoned career criminal or a politician.

He couldn't help but think Pat and some of the Irish convict crews were in there together at the same time. Could this finally be the avenged murder of PJ, Pat's best friend and cousin, whom Tre had coldheartedly killed during their sophomore year in high school? Nate didn't want to believe it. After all, Patrick had been out for at least a few months now. Why risk everything after he was free?

Nonetheless, despite the Irish crowd being different from his own, he knew for sure they wouldn't think twice to kill.

His thoughts were running crazy, and he had to get out of there. Already, he was mentally forming the list of facts he needed to gather and people he needed to call. His mother, Aunt Carol, Slugs, and Reverend Gibbs were all on the short list.

He didn't know where to start for the facts. But something inside him wouldn't rest until he had answers.

Chapter 10

SEND-OFF PARTY

THE NEXT FEW WEEKS FLEW BY. PAT KEPT HIMSELF BUSY AT the gym working regular hours and working out afterward. He'd be out the door of his house at seven every morning and wouldn't return until around eight at night. Ma kept leftovers set out for him, so all he had to do was nuke a plate in the microwave or heat up something quickly on the stove. She was never the greatest cook, but anything she made was a ton better than what Pat had gotten in prison. Plus, now that he was earning a little money, he could help her out with groceries.

She wasn't quite sure how to take the Ireland trip. "You just got home a few months ago; now you're going on vacation? What about the job hunt or parole? How're you going to pay for it? Do these people at the wedding know you guys are coming?"

Pat answered all the questions, attempting to soothe his ma's rough nerves. He changed little details; he'd gotten the money for his trip from his job, for instance. He didn't say a word about Walsh's donation. And of course, there was no way he'd mention anything Jimmy had talked about.

She was paranoid about him getting in some kind of trouble again. Maybe she had a sense he wasn't telling her everything.

On the other hand, she seemed to be living vicariously through him. Like most people of Irish heritage living in Boston, she dreamed of visiting Ireland. It was on her bucket list, and Pat could detect a touch of jealousy.

Maybe she was a little proud of him too. He could have easily just taken the first few months at home off, not searching for work, sitting around the bar and getting drunk every night. But he didn't do any of those things. Sure, he'd party a little on the weekend, but no different from any other working twenty-three-year-old would do.

As the day to leave for Ireland got closer, he could feel his ma loosening up a little about the whole idea. On the Sunday before his trip, she insisted on a proper send-off after Mass.

The afternoon party was pretty mellow. Ma made herself an old-fashioned with some of the better whiskey she kept in the liquor cabinet; that was something she made on special occasions. Treats and Walsh arrived together. Treats had two brand-new boxes of Adidas Gazelle sneakers, which he handed to his two friends as a generous departing gift. He looked high but not enough to make Pat's ma notice. Pat's sisters invited some of their school friends over, so there were some young kids in the mix, cranking up the stereo.

Pat was trying out his new sneakers and joking around with Treats and Walsh in the living room when he spotted Father Lydon approaching the front stoop from the sidewalk. It was good to see him. Loyalty went a long way with Pat, especially these days. He would never forget that Father Lydon was one of the few who had regularly visited him in prison. Back then, it was Father Lydon who had asked Pat the question that started to get him to think clearly. "What would have happened if you had found out and then acted on that information, exacting revenge on Tre in jail?"

Well, Pat would have killed Tre, of course. And then Pat would have never left prison. So Nate had done the right thing. But it took the conversation with Father Lydon for him to finally realize that.

Pat went to shake Lydon's hand. "Good to see you, Father," he said.

"And you, son. You seem to be in a better place than the last time I saw you."

"Just needed some time to cool down. Believe me, I'm glad to be home," Pat replied.

"Mind if we step outside for a moment?" Father Lydon asked.

Pat gulped. He couldn't help the constant low-level paranoia he'd felt ever since accepting the clandestine job from Jimmy. It was a weird feeling, almost like when he used to occasionally smoke weed between classes at Cathedral and felt like everybody could tell he was stoned.

Once they were far enough away from the front stoop, Father Lydon said, "I thought you should know. Nate's family reached out to me and informed me that Tre was killed in a prison cell not too far from the one you were in."

Of course Lydon would know, thought Pat. *Everyone tells him everything.* He felt a chill run up his spine, immediately recalling Choppa's recent message.

"What happened?"

"They couldn't get a clear read on the security cameras. No one really knows yet," said Father Lydon.

Good old Choppa. Covering his bases as usual, Pat thought.

"I know you have complicated feelings about Tre, son. But I just thought you should know. Maybe you might want to reach out to Nate and offer your prayers."

Pat glanced down and nodded. He didn't really want Father Lydon to see the expression on his face. Although he did feel bad for Nate, he wasn't the least bit sorry that Tre was gone. But he couldn't help but wonder how it all had gone down; there was something sketchy about this prison hit that didn't make sense.

"You're right, Father. I should talk to him. We haven't really spoken since I got out. I wrote him a letter trying to make things right between us, but I haven't heard from him since," said Pat, focusing on the ground. "I'll reach out. But I probably won't see him in person until I get back."

Father Lydon nodded in approval. "You're a good kid, Pat. Don't let all the darkness around you change who you are or where you're heading. And don't forget where you came from and who your friends are."

Pat wasn't sure exactly what he meant by "the darkness"—probably just the state of affairs and the neighborhood or maybe his depressive and angry mood when he first got out of Suffolk. The few months already felt like a year. It didn't matter. Father Lydon was on his side and was probably just doing his best to give him a pep talk.

"Thanks, Father. Now, if I'm not mistaken, you seem to be missing a drink. Let's get warmed up inside and get that taken care of," said Pat.

Father Lydon nodded. They began their walk back to the front stoop.

On the way, he heard a car door slam from across the street. As Father Lydon rejoined the party, Pat turned around to see who was coming.

It was Kiley. Really her. Climbing out of the passenger side. A rush of blood went to Pat's face. Was she coming here? Kiley caught his eye and froze for a second. Out of the driver's side came a tall guy, someone he didn't recognize. Probably her new boyfriend.

Kiley caught his eye and waved. Pat just waved back. She smiled, then turned back toward her house. Pat wasn't sure if he was relieved or disappointed she wasn't coming over. Memories flooded his system. He had been her first. It was nearly five years ago they were together, but seeing her again . . .

He shrugged the thought off and made himself turn and go back inside, trying to get a handle on himself. As he reentered the house from the freezing cold, he felt warm all over, and he had not even had any shots yet.

Chapter 11

O'RILEY'S

IT HAD BEEN SEVERAL DAYS SINCE NATE HAD RECEIVED THE news about Tre during his visit to Suffolk County Prison. He stumbled from the spare bedroom at Aunt Carol's house, bleary-eyed and rubbing his face. Ordinarily, he was a heavy sleeper and able to drift off in seconds. Even though he had graduated, he was still used to the grueling college schedule of studying and basketball, a routine that had made it easy to fall asleep instantaneously. But last night, he hadn't been so lucky. He had tossed and turned all night. Somewhere around five a.m., he'd finally fallen into an exhausted sleep, but his body woke him a mere three hours later. He silently cursed.

Before he could even make his coffee, the haunting of his mind began again in earnest. Tre had been murdered. Someone in Suffolk County had killed him, but Nate couldn't discover any of the details, including how he was killed. The streets were ringing with rumors from rival gangs, but they had no suspects. It still sounded like bullshit to him.

No further information was available, and no detective had taken up the case. Why would they? Who the fuck would care about a Black drug dealer killed in prison? They probably asked the rudimentary questions they were trained to ask for the report, bypassed an investigation entirely, and shipped it off to the cold-case files. There, it would gather dust and cobwebs, forgotten. Another Black body in Boston was buried unceremoniously.

Tre's mom, Aunt Carol, should have been the one to receive the call. Ever since Tre had been sentenced, she'd taken a turn for the worse. She no longer helped plan any church events with Reverend Gibbs, and she avoided the church entirely. Mom suspected Aunt Carol had turned to the bottle. Nate didn't know either way, but that would explain why she wasn't spending much time at home; he hadn't really seen her since he had returned to Boston.

He had dreaded telling Aunt Carol. She'd already lost her eldest, Troy, to gang violence, and now Tre. This was the kind of news that could put her in the hospital. She could barely get out of bed the last few days.

He still wasn't sure why Tre's brother, Slugs, hadn't been notified by the prison to begin with. Tre had mentioned there was a bit of bad blood between them after the trial. Slugs had been running with the Norfolk Kings gang, same as Tre, but it was Tre who ended up getting caught. There was substantial resentment there.

Not that Slugs got off easy. After being shot in a little turf battle, he had been confined to a wheelchair for almost a year. He'd had to relearn how to walk in rehab. He got by pretty well these days with a cane and had just earned his electrician's license. Slugs would never be going back to the gangbanging life. He'd already paid too much in blood and tears.

Slugs put on a brave face, but he could tell that it hit him harder than he was letting on. Nate imagined it was survivor's guilt; he'd never really had a chance to patch things up with Tre before this happened, and now he never would.

Tre was murdered.

The phrase stuck in his head, cycling over and over.

Tre was murdered.

Nate rubbed his temples, begging his mind for these intrusive thoughts to stop. Still, the last fucking thing he needed was a head shrinker. Talking with a complete stranger about his near murderous grief seemed like a horrible idea. He'd grown up Black in Boston; he was used to surviving, even thriving, without help. He didn't bat an eye at heavy responsibility and had long since proven himself. College on an athletic scholarship had been an advanced boot camp in discipline. He never slept in, never skipped classes. He put every single thing he had into it. All he did was study, get tutoring, go to class, go to basketball practice, and study some more. He knew he would have to work twice as hard as any regular White kid just to be taken seriously. It wasn't fair, but he'd long since given up any expectation of the world being fair.

He tried once to explain that to his buddy Patrick from high school, who'd had a lot going for him until he found himself in the wrong place at the wrong time. They'd been pretty close for a while. Nate had visited Pat a few times in prison, but their relationship soured when Nate called him out for having a bullshit chip on his shoulder. Pat was under the impression that opportunities were just handed to him because Nate was Black, opportunities that he didn't earn.

Nate was even-tempered, but he let his friend have it for that. He still remembered the glare on Pat's face when he told him, "Well, that's not how life works for kids like me. We have to fight and push and pray and fight some more, or we wind up dead. Sometimes we do everything right and we end up dead anyway."

At the time, Pat had doubled down on his anger. All Pat wanted was for Nate to find out who had killed his cousin, PJ. Nate knew it was Tre but wouldn't tell. That damn fool would have killed Tre and then spent his remaining days behind bars. The last thing he'd told Pat was to behave himself. "Maybe I'll catch you on the outside," were his last words to Pat.

As fate would have it, Tre was dead anyway, and he finally understood Pat's anger. It was starting to build, and Nate needed a place to put it. There was an order to things, and no way was he letting this go. There was nothing the BPD could do if he decided to investigate on his own time, as a private citizen. Not that they would give a shit if he did.

Besides, Nate was connected to a world that the White cops couldn't easily enter, had they even wanted to. Having spent all that time with Tre and Slugs in his youth gave him the street cred he needed to pass through certain doors without arousing suspicion. Not many people could claim that their cousins were part of the Norfolk Kings. He kind of knew how the other side worked. He could probably find out more from the Black community in a few days than the cops could in an entire month. Somebody had seen something or knew something. Almost everyone in the hood knew someone in prison; he just had to find those people.

Nate methodically prepared his coffee, busying his hands while his mind worked things through.

So what rocks could he flip over? Where was a place where connected people congregated? Where could he get a pulse on what was happening behind the scenes? Where would the different neighborhoods converge and he could blend in?

Nate's head snapped up. The Unity Sports and Cultural Club, down on Dunbar Street, in Dorchester, and—oh, of *course*—O'Riley's Boxing Club. He was sure he could get pointed in the right direction. A place with some cops, some criminals, and some fighters was a good place to start.

He flipped the coffee maker to "ON" and sat at the kitchen table, staring out the picture window. The voice in his head was still going, but its tune had shifted.

Tre was murdered. And I'm going to find out who did it and why.

———

IT WAS NATE'S FIRST TIME AT O'RILEY'S SINCE HIS HIGH school days. He missed the era of working out all day during the summers, either on the court or in the gym. His training trips here to Quincy would be with a beating heart of the Black community named Papa Ray. Papa Ray knew everything going on in the streets.

Taking a quick scan around, he felt like the gym still had the soul of an old-school boxing club, like in the movie *Rocky*. The sounds were the same—the rhythmic *bap bap* sounds of the speed bags, the low thuds of the punching bags, the *whip-tap* sounds of jumping rope. It smelled like padding and sweat, with a fine layer of cleaning supplies on top of that. It looked lived in and dimmed around the edges, well used and practical.

Nate was more of a baller than a boxer, but he knew the basics. It was a great workout, and he could efficiently work it into his cross-training regimen for staying fit. Many athletes supplemented their physical fitness with boxing. It was always practical to have a few slick moves up your sleeve in case of any trouble. And everyone knew of Jimmy's history. *Maybe he would be willing to talk to me too*, Nate thought.

He scanned the place, searching for any familiar faces. No one at first glance, but then he did see someone he recognized. An older, bald Black man, probably in his late fifties, coaching a young Black fighter who seemed to be about fourteen, sparring with a White kid around the same age. The man was standing at the edge of the ring, leaning back, his arms intertwined in the ropes. Peering across the ring, Nate spotted Jimmy in the same pose. Seeing them together confirmed it for him. Sure enough, it was Papa Ray.

Papa Ray orbited in a similar realm as Jimmy. He was an older trainer from Roxbury who'd been bringing Black fighters to O'Riley's for decades. He'd travel to different gyms around the city and bring half a dozen Black guys to train and spar. He was well known and loved in the boxing world and was tight with Jimmy. Nate had known him since he was a kid and had always liked him. He was kind of everybody's uncle.

As Nate recalled, typically Papa Ray would come over every few weeks, and he and Jimmy would size up their fighters for sparring. From what he heard, it was always a respectful training session. Jimmy was direct and crystal clear, never tolerating any racial bullshit in his gym. He had fighters of all ethnicities coming in and out from all parts of this city and New England.

In a city with as much racial strife as Boston—largely due to the forced busing of the seventies—it was rare to find a community where race didn't seem to matter. Many White folks would pay lip service to "equality" while still behaving oppositely. It wasn't like that here, where a level of mutual respect always organically existed.

Nate made a slow circle of the perimeter of the room, examining his surroundings. He saw a Black fighter around his age, someone who looked like he went here a lot.

"Yo. You know if a guy named Patrick's been coming around here?" Nate asked the fighter.

The fighter wordlessly pointed his glove in Jimmy and Papa Ray's direction and got back to his punching bag. Nate nodded and walked over to the legendary trainers.

He greeted Papa Ray first, who tried to place him at first, then lit up when he recognized his face. They shook hands firmly.

"What's up, Papa Ray?" Nate said.

"Nathan. So good to see you! What brings you back in town?" Papa Ray said with a smile.

"I thought I was just here for a week for Jamal's funeral. But then I went to visit Tre, and . . ." Nate trailed off. Papa Ray seemed to already know the news. "Anyway, while I'm here, I thought I'd catch up with Pat," he said.

Just then, Nate saw Jimmy approaching with a squinty face, like he was trying to remember how he knew Nate. It had been years since they'd seen each other.

Jimmy shook hands, exchanged polite greetings with Nate briefly, and then returned to training the fighters.

Papa Ray put his hand on Nate's shoulder. "I'm so sorry about Jamal and Tre, Nathan," he said, lowering his voice. "The word got out quick. Such a terrible thing."

Nate nodded. It was still hard to talk about it.

"I'm glad you've taken the rights steps in life," Papa Ray told him. "You know Tre could never keep himself out of trouble. Always had these big ideas."

"Thanks," he replied, finally finding the words. "We all take our own paths."

"Well, your mother was never going to let you follow your cousin's. She'd beat your ass right back home when she caught you out on the corner! That's for sure!"

"Yeah." He smiled. "She always kept me busy as hell, eyes on the prize. No way was I going to get stuck here, man, and be a corner boy."

"So I guess you're not ballin' anymore? I thought I'd never see you after you went down to Virginia. Your mom still down there? What's the game plan now, big player?"

"She's still down in Charlottesville," Nate replied. "She likes it. I'm not sure what's next. Maybe law school, just not sure where yet, man. Most likely I'll stay down south, but you know . . . it's always hard to stay away from Beantown, man. I love this place."

Papa Ray nodded with a smile.

"I know exactly what you mean," he said.

"Maybe I'll come back after law school," said Nate, grabbing the top rope of the ring. "Maybe I can make a difference. Hey, think about how many people you helped, doing what you do!"

"That's a helluva kind thing to say, Nate," he said. "Mainly, I just help people help themselves. They just need a little push is all. But I like the sound of it. Keep in touch. Maybe I can put in a good word for you someday on your way up!"

Nate laughed politely. He wasn't sure what Papa Ray could do for his legal career, but he appreciated the sentiment. It wasn't out of the question that he could call in some kind of favor if Nate ended up going to law school in Boston. He was well connected, a lot like Jimmy, with friends in many places.

After all, he was standing in O'Riley's Boxing Gym, owned and funded by a judge and Jimmy, a former criminal who also owned a shady bar in Roxbury called Pug's Pub near Dudley and Blue Hill Avenue, a real run-down area. It had been there for a few decades. Back in high school, Nate would always say to Patrick that it just didn't make sense, an Irish guy owning a bar in Roxbury.

"Speaking of the word," Nate said, changing the subject, "I was just trying to figure out what word on the street is, man. If you hear anything about what happened to Tre, can you please let me know? Seems weird, you know, them having no dirt up at the prison."

Papa Ray nodded grimly. "I'm sure the details will roll out soon," he replied. "Someone'll claim it, even if they didn't do it."

"Oh, and hey—have you seen my old friend Pat around here?" Nate asked. "I thought maybe he might know something."

Papa Ray shook his head no. "This is the first time I've been here in a while."

"All right, lemme know if you hear anything. I'll be seeing you soon."

Nate turned to leave the gym and spotted Jimmy along the way out, talking with one of the fourteen-year-old fighters by the speed bags. When he saw Nate was headed out, he approached him.

"Hey, Nate. Yeah, sorry it took me a while to recognize you back there. I do remember you . . . from way back," Jimmy said. "Patrick said he could never get you off the court to get you in here."

"Well, I always was the better ball player," Nate said, half joking. "Have you seen him around?"

"He's out of town for a few weeks now," Jimmy replied. "Just left, in fact."

"Any idea where?" Nate asked.

Jimmy shrugged his shoulders. "Didn't tell me. Just said he'd be back in a couple of weeks."

Hmm. Why would Pat not mention where he was going, if they were having a conversation about him going somewhere? And the timing was odd—but not necessarily incriminating. It could be a coincidence that Pat just happened to leave in the wake of Tre's death.

Nate reached into his pocket, pulled out a card, and offered it to Jimmy. "Tell you what," he said. "That's my number. If you see him, can you have him call me?"

"Sure thing, kid. And when I talk with him, I'll tell him you stopped by."

They shook hands, and Nate went for the door. Something about that interchange with Jimmy rubbed him the wrong way. But he couldn't put his finger on what exactly felt off. As Nate ran up the stairs and exited onto the sidewalk, he kept his head down to avoid making eye contact with the regular cast of shady characters standing in front of Dunkin's all day. As he looked up for one brief moment, there was Patrick himself, standing right in front of him, about to head down into the gym.

They both froze, staring at one another like time had turned into slow motion, and rightfully so. Nate estimated it had been about five years now since they'd shared free air with no glass or guards between them. They immediately embraced with a hug.

"I came by to catch up with you, man, but Jimmy just said you were out of town," Nate said.

"So sorry, Nate. I'm heading to the airport right now, and I'm late as hell. Plane takes off in less than two hours. I just came by to grab my gloves and backpack," Patrick responded.

"Damn, man. We have so much to talk through."

"I know we do, Nate. I know what's on your mind—I spoke to Father Lydon—but don't worry. I won't keep anything from you. Only you do that shit!" Patrick said.

"Oh, man, you couldn't leave me hanging without a low blow, huh?" Nate said.

They shook hands, and Patrick ran off down the stairs.

Nate leaned on a storefront grate and kicked it, causing a loud rattle. He was overcome with an unresolved feeling of frustration. But there hadn't been enough time to bring up Tre; the conversation would only have escalated in the wrong direction.

Chapter 12

DUMB LUCK

PAT WAS A LITTLE MORE NERVOUS THAN HE EXPECTED HE would be on the day he was flying out of Boston. It wasn't any of the logistics. Jimmy had helped him get his passport expedited and given him a few important details about where he'd be going after the wedding. Treats advised him on the kinds of things to pack, since he was familiar with the climate they'd be flying to. Walsh was cool as a cucumber. He was good with details and sort of took charge of the day's planning. He even offered to drive and put his car in long-term parking, because, as he put it, "I don't trust the fucking cabbies who always try to rip you off at Logan."

Pat had woken up feeling unnerved. He'd never been on a plane before, never been out of the country, didn't know if he would get airsick or not. He didn't think he was claustrophobic, but who knew how he would feel once he got on the plane.

And then there was the mission. There were still some pretty big fucking blanks on who he was supposed to meet and where he was supposed to stay after the wedding was finished. Jimmy insisted that he'd get word to him when the time was right and that it was important that he only get information when he absolutely needed it. Pat could see how that would make sense. If anything went sideways, he could deny he knew anything, because he actually wouldn't.

But he was still going to have to explain to Walsh and Treats later why he would be gone for a while or had to miss the return flight. He wasn't sure what story he would go with yet, and, either way, keeping anything from them did not sit well with him. Maybe he would make up that they overbooked and he decided to stay a couple of days. Overbooking was still a thing, wasn't it?

But he couldn't get ahead of himself. He tried to put the mission in a separate box because it was pretty fucking exciting to finally have a little vacation. As they crossed the Massachusetts Turnpike into the brand-new Ted Williams Tunnel, Pat gawked at the docks of the Seaport District. All the landscape was new.

It was a cold, dreary day, but that wouldn't change once they were over the ocean. It wasn't like they were flying to the tropics. Roundstone would probably be cold and gray too. But it would be a different wide-open country, and right now, different seemed good.

After Walsh dropped off the car in long-term parking, they shuttled into the main terminal without a hitch. It wasn't exactly peak travel season, so traffic at the airport was pretty smooth. At least, that's what Treats was telling him. He couldn't imagine being one of these suits who traveled four or five days a week. What a life.

The whole security line experience was a bit surreal. All the security guys with badges, cops with two-way radios, metal detectors, and X-ray machines for luggage reminded him of being checked into prison. Pat surveyed the area. No one else seemed to be troubled. All the suited guys and fancy ladies in business attire appeared practically bored by the experience.

He relaxed a little after clearing the metal detectors and picking his bags up on the other side of the conveyer belt. Why had he been nervous? He had nothing to hide in his luggage. Any secrets he had were in his head, where they couldn't be reached.

They were way early, so they headed to one of the bars near their gate for drinks. Treats was already in party mode and bought them a round of Jameson shots before they settled in with a few pints of Guinness. Despite Walsh's earlier contribution, neither of them would let Pat drop a dime on the bar.

As a light buzz kicked in, Pat felt his anxiety start to fade. Already, his mind was on how much fun he was about to have, instead of all the things he needed to do. Treats was already speed mumbling something about how many honeys he was gonna hook up with in Ireland and how Irish girls were the best in bed. Were they? Pat had no idea.

Midway through the next round, Treats suddenly clammed up and stared out beyond the bar. Something had his attention.

"What is it?" Pat asked. It wasn't like Treats to get instantly serious. What the hell? Was it a psycho ex or something?

"It's fine. It'll be fine. Don't worry about it," replied Treats.

"Every time you say something's fine, something's about to get fucked," said Walsh, scanning in the direction that Treats was facing. Pat also glanced around, trying to figure out what had Treats so spooked.

"For fuck's sake," whispered Treats, "don't everyone turn at once."

Walsh turned back around, but Pat stole a few glances. Then he thought he saw what Treats might have been upset about. Two police officers were patrolling with dogs, German shepherds.

"We'll be fine," Treats said again, even less convincing than before.

"Treats. What are you worried about?" Pat asked. "We're not carrying anything."

Treats just closed his eyes and smiled.

Walsh set his drink down and leaned back.

"Are we?" asked Pat.

"Yeah, a little," admitted Treats.

Walsh turned beat red. He swore through gritted teeth, "Mothafucka."

Pat, his throat suddenly tight, whispered, "What is it?"

Treats took a deep breath and mumbled matter-of-factly, "About fifty tabs of E in my shoes, a half ounce of weed in my carry-on, and a bag of coke taped between my ass cheeks."

Patrick's stomach dropped out. In his mind's eye, he could already see that twenty-five thousand from the job vaporizing into thin air, his fingers getting broken one at a time by one of Bulger's guys, and another ten to fifteen years in Suffolk. No, no, no. Not today.

"You fuckin' jackass. What the fuck were you thinking?" asked Pat.

His mind flashed back to him smoking joints with Treats in his attic and the sneakers next to the soldering gun. Crafty bastard had soldered the drugs inside the soles of his shoes. Jesus, how often had he done this?

Couldn't Treats cool it for one day while they traveled through two international airports that were lousy with cops? And to risk everything just to make sure they had drugs to party with when they got to Ireland? This fucking guy!

A vein was already popping out of Walsh's forehead. He put his arm around Treats to whisper in his ear. It wasn't exactly a friendly gesture.

"You can't do this to me, Treats," Walsh said. "I'm going to the academy. I've got to have a spotless record. You get caught, I had nothing to do with you. You got it? You're not gonna fuck things up for me."

Walsh looked at Patrick, then down at his sneakers that had been gifted from Treats, and asked, "Do we have drugs in our fucking sneakers right now too?"

Treats responded with a calm smirk as if he were trying to convince himself. "Come on, guys, there are tricks," Treats explained. "My shoes are airtight; the tabs are soldered inside the rubber. Besides, those dogs don't know shit for E. They're not trained for it. Other shit's wrapped in that industrial turkey bag plastic. It's what the fuckin' cartels use to ship drugs across international waters in shipping containers—airtight; no smells can escape. We'll be fine. Your sneakers are empty. They're decoys. Our best bet is to play it cool."

Walsh and Patrick separated from one another, standing up one at a time to take a seat at opposite ends of the bar. The three of them made eye contact with each other to determine the next move.

For the moment, the officers didn't seem to be focused in their direction. They were in the international terminal, and a flight from Israel had just arrived. As the passengers disembarked and entered the airport, the police officers and the dogs worked the crowd, the dog sniffing in a disciplined pattern to cover as much territory as possible.

Pat wasn't sure what the play was here. Did they simply leave to avoid detection, giving up their expensive airline tickets? Even if they did lose hundreds of dollars, it would be worth avoiding getting caught. Or should they double down and stay? *Maybe I should go to the boarding area*, he thought.

Treats waved the waitress over to his high-top table and ordered another round of shots.

Their few seconds of separated peace abruptly ended when they heard one of the German shepherds barking. Pat whipped his head around to see what was happening. The K-9 cops had huddled around a Middle Eastern businessman in a sharp suit and gestured toward his briefcase. The dog sniffed the briefcase and barked again. They couldn't hear the conversation, but it appeared like some back and forth was happening with the cops and the suit.

The situation got heated fast. The suited guy was animated, gesturing wildly with his arms. The cops confiscated his briefcase. One cop opened it up and took a peek. He then slammed the briefcase shut.

Like someone had flipped a switch, the mood changed. The cop without the briefcase manhandled the traveler's arm behind his back and grabbed his shoulder. The suit panicked, broke free, and made a dash toward the exit. Both cops released their dogs and pursued him on foot, apprehending him in seconds.

Patrick and Walsh rejoined Treats to watch the arrest play out. They appeared to be free and clear.

"How sure are you those turkey bags will avoid detection?" Walsh asked.

"If it works for the cartels, it works for me," said Treats.

Pat wasn't sure if Treats was bullshitting or not. Treats was a small-time dealer. How the fuck would he know what the cartels were up to? "Act normal," said Treats as he lifted his shot glass for a toast. "Sláinte."

"Sláinte," answered Pat and Walsh at the same time. What choice did they have? They downed the shots, and Pat tried to remain calm. Walsh was still muttering to himself, fuming with doubt.

Then again, they couldn't argue with his logic. If they made an exit strategy now, it could pique the interest of the officers. And even if the officers didn't notice, the German shepherds would.

The two officers were making another sweep and heading toward the bar. Pat froze, eyeing what was happening.

One of the dogs came close to the bar and did a sniffing sweep of everyone sitting at the stools. When they came to where Treats was sitting, the dog stopped. Pat could feel his heart beating in his ears and a rush of adrenaline as he gripped his Guinness, expecting the worst.

Instead, the dog just lay down, yawned, and started licking his balls. Treats and Walsh busted out laughing. Pat exhaled.

"That's okay, boy. Let's go get you something to eat. It's time for your break," said the officer, leading the dog away from the bar. The officer nodded at the boys as if to say, "Sorry you had to see that." The other dog, some distance away, was headed toward another gate. For now, they apparently had averted disaster.

"Luck of the Irish, boys," said Treats through a smile.

"Don't you fucking even," replied Pat.

"We're still thousands of miles away from Roundstone, you fuckin' pinhead," said Walsh. "I almost needed to change my goddamn underwear!"

They were still laughing. What could have been a brutal arrest instead ended with just a dog licking his junk.

Soon afterward, they overheard the announcement from their gate that their plane was boarding. Pat downed what remained of his Guinness and shot his friend one more dirty look before they got on the plane. "Do me a favor, Treats. No more surprises, okay?" he pleaded.

Treats nodded and made an expression like *Who, me?* as he chuckled to himself.

Pat could still feel his heart racing as he boarded the plane.

———

THE THREE OF THEM WERE SEATED RIGHT NEXT TO EACH other. Walsh and Treats offered Pat the window seat since he'd never been on a plane before. Treats also said that if, by any chance, he got airsick, looking out the window would help. Walsh got the middle, and Treats insisted on the aisle so his long legs would be less cramped; he was the tallest of the three. They could have sprung for first class, but why spend all that money on a good seat when they could spend it on alcohol and parties?

Pat found himself enjoying the rush and velocity as the plane took off. His eyes stayed glued to the landscape as they climbed higher and higher. It was weird seeing Boston all at once, from thousands of feet away, the way the birds see it. He couldn't exactly see where his house was, but he could pin down the neighborhood. The city appeared a lot cleaner from this far away. As the plane rose in elevation, it was kind of cool seeing clouds from the opposite perspective, far below the plane.

After they got settled in, the first order of business was getting more drinks. They all ordered whiskey and sodas—the beer was absolute crap—and asked to keep them coming. Pat thought the flight attendant was cute, so he flirted with her a little. She had a lilting Irish accent, with blonde curly hair, and was all smiles to the boys.

They were all four drinks in by the time they boarded the plane, so they were feeling pretty good. Treats and Walsh were already joking about how the ball-licker dog had all saved their asses. Pat was still a little angry, but now that they were out of danger, he recognized what a funny story it was.

Walsh blurted out, "There was no luck about it. That dog would rather clock out than smell your nasty ass!" Even Treats cracked up at that one.

The in-flight movie was *Speed*, with Keanu Reeves. They'd all seen it already at Walsh's house, but it was still a pretty good one.

The whiskeys kept coming. Where were they now? Six? Eight? The little nip bottles were already piling up in the seat pockets. Walsh was already down for the count, but Treats looked restless. Somewhere around the scene where Keanu hunts down Dennis Hopper in the subway, Treats got up to use the lavatory. Pat closed his eyes for a minute, just listening to the movie on the headphones.

He must have dozed off, because when he opened his eyes again, they were in the end credits. Walsh was snoring beside him, but Treats's seat was still empty. Where the fuck was he?

The cute flight attendant walked over and leaned down with a concerned expression on her face. "You might want to come back here and deal with your friend," she said.

Oh, fuck. What the fuck did he do now? Pat was already bracing for the worst.

Pat unbuckled his seat belt and carefully climbed over Walsh so as not to wake him. He walked down the long aisle toward the lavatory at the back of the plane and could see Treats in mid-argument with another stewardess. She was older, and she sounded pissed. As Pat got closer, he could make out what was being said.

"Honestly, I told you," Treats explained. "I'm deathly afraid of flying. My cousins died in a plane crash when I was young. I was just smoking a cigarette to relax."

Treats had a knack for saying whatever the fuck popped into his head. He'd always been like that, an epic bullshitter. He'd never had cousins who died in a plane crash. This bastard was grasping at straws, and he was fucking lit. This wasn't going to go well.

"And I told you, sir, we don't care," she shot back. She held a ziplock bag in front of Treats's face. "Disabling a smoke detector with a plastic bag is a federal offense. And so is smoking on an airplane."

"Please, sweetie . . ." Treats tried bravely.

"Don't 'sweetie' me. The Garda will be waiting on the ground when we land. You can try to negotiate with them. Now get back to your seat."

This was bad. The Garda was the Irish national police force. They wouldn't fuck around with these kinds of charges. Why would they go easy on a bunch of American douchebags who totally disregarded their laws? Treats could be in serious trouble, and the last fucking thing Pat needed was the attention of the Irish law pointed in his direction or any kind of story that leaked to the media. Twice on the first day, he felt the entire mission had been jeopardized. Over what? Party drugs?

His fucking buddy was turning into a liability. He couldn't believe they had all narrowly escaped Boston law enforcement only to be faced with the Garda—which had to be far worse. He was going to have to find a way to turn this around.

The flight attendants formed a sort of phalanx and herded both of the men back to their seats. The mean one stood right next to them until their seat belts were buckled.

"If there's any more trouble, the captain has authorized us to restrain you," she said. "Don't make us do that."

Treats nodded and smiled. Walsh must have woken up while the commotion was happening. His face said he'd already guessed trouble. Walsh stared at Treats. Pat thought he smelled funny.

"Were you smoking weed?" Walsh asked.

"No, but I wish it was a blunt," Treats said through a laughing whisper. "It was a cigarette. I'd already flushed it when they forced the door open."

All Pat could do was stare at Treats, and Walsh did the same, his mouth gaping open. All for a fucking butt.

Pat unbuckled and slipped past the boys and into the aisle. He crouched down and whispered to Treats. He had to tell it to him straight. Pat gritted his teeth. It took everything he had not to clock him right then.

"Listen, Treats. I told you I am never going back to prison. You have two choices. You shut the fuck up and sit still 'til we land, or I knock you the fuck out right now and you can sleep out the rest of the flight. What you brought with us is enough to put us away for years. You cannot fuck around with this shit. You got it? I'm serious. I'll knock you the fuck out right now. You know I will."

Treats nodded in silence.

"So what's it gonna be?" He wasn't moving until he got an answer.

"I think I'll take a little nap. I'm all talked out anyway," Treats said through a smirk. This motherfucker.

Well, that was one problem down. Now he had to go deal with the flight attendants and try to clean up Treats's trail of disregard. Maybe he could work on the young blonde one and see if he could charm her into changing her mind. The older one—forget it.

He walked back and spotted her in the galley.

"Hi, it's Brenda, right?" he started. He'd gotten her name when they were ordering drinks earlier. Brenda looked up and smiled at him, an errant blonde curl escaping her little hat.

"Well, if it isn't one of the little hell-raisers," she said. "I wouldn't waste your breath trying to save your friend. That's a pretty serious offense. The captain didn't like it at all."

"Hey, I'm really sorry about my friend. He's . . . psychologically damaged. You know, traumatized. This is the first time he's been on a plane since . . . the incident with his cousins. Honestly, I'm worried sick about him," Pat said, laying it on thick.

"It sounds like a terrible thing he went through," she said, softening a little. She was giving him that ogle, the one where Pat knew a girl was looking at him in a sexual way. She was already touching his arm, expressing her concern.

"All I'm saying is you don't have to worry about him. I just gave him a sedative, and he won't be giving you any more trouble," he spun. It was half true, in that if there were any more trouble, the sedative would be his fists.

"Please, there's no need to call the Garda," he continued. "We're actually on our way to his cousin's wedding in Roundstone—the only cousin he has left. It would just crush him if anything got in the way of that reunion. He's really at the end of his rope."

Brenda stared into his eyes, and he could see she was struggling to discern if he was telling the truth. He held his gaze. She sighed. "Do I have your word?" she asked. "No more problems?"

"I swear to God, Brenda. I swear to God," Pat affirmed.

"All right. I'll talk to my supervisor and the captain. We haven't actually notified the Garda yet. But if there's one more incident, if he so much as raises his voice, we won't hesitate to call it in. Okay?"

"It's a deal, Brenda. Thank you. Seriously, thank you. You have no idea how much this will mean to him." Brenda squeezed his arm, and Pat flashed her his most heartfelt smile. He turned around and headed back to his seat.

When he was all buckled back in, he told Walsh how he had smoothed over the situation. Treats was already fast asleep. Walsh shook his head.

"You're a snake charmer, Pat," he said, laughing. "Thank fucking God."

He thought a few more drinks would do wonders to calm himself down. It had only been half a day, and he'd already almost had two heart attacks. When the next round of drinks came, it was Brenda who delivered them. She smiled at them and winked at Pat as she handed him his cocktail napkin.

When she left, Pat flipped the cocktail napkin over. There, on the back side in blue ink, she'd left him her phone number.

Chapter 13

IRELAND

THE LOUD IN-FLIGHT CHIME INDICATING THAT THEY WOULD be landing soon woke Pat from his sleep. The good news was he still had a bit of a buzz, so he wouldn't be dealing with a hangover just yet.

As his bleary eyes adjusted, he noticed their little in-flight party's aftermath. Small whiskey bottles overflowed out of their seat pockets, and Walsh and Treats were both covered in crumbs. Their cocktail napkins were all over the floor. Walsh was already awake and making a half-hearted attempt to clean up. They all reeked of booze. Treats had his sunglasses and earphones on and was still fast asleep, drool oozing from the corner of his mouth. He was a class act, this guy.

Pat peered out the window to catch a glimpse of the scenery. They were approaching the airport of Shannon, a much smaller airport than Pat had expected for an international hub—maybe room for about twelve planes parked at once. The airport was nestled on one side right up near an estuary that flowed in from the Atlantic Ocean. On the other side, the place was surrounded by an emerald grassy countryside, geometric patches of farmland bordered by trees, all in various shades of green. It was about what he pictured Ireland would be like.

The city itself seemed tiny—maybe the size of Stockbridge or one of those other backwater towns in rural Massachusetts. It was gray and raining, just like back home this time of year.

The landing was a little more unsettling than Pat would have liked. He'd never felt the sudden jolt of landing gear colliding with landing strip pavement; it felt a lot more out of control than he would think landing would feel like. He was ready to get the hell off this plane and get another drink.

The three men stood and shuffled single file off the plane, all still groggy and trying to get it together. Pat flashed another smile at Brenda on the way out, who smiled right back. Treats and Walsh kept quiet. For now, it looked like they'd managed to dodge a bullet. If that was indeed the case, it was no less a miracle that Pat had talked his way out of trouble. Had they dealt with the Garda, the rest of Treats's stash would have been on the table.

Pat suddenly had the realization that they were being herded into customs. Oh Christ, they still had to deal with customs. Treats's stash had escaped undetected on the way out of Boston, but Pat had no idea what to expect here.

Treats didn't appear to be worried, but that wasn't saying much. If anyone could benefit from an enhanced sense of what was risky and what wasn't, it'd be Treats. But Treats had made this trip before, and chances were he'd probably brought an epic fuck-ton of drugs that time too. Maybe he did know what he was doing?

The line was a breeze. Pat began to relax when he saw that Treats had gotten the kid-gloves treatment by immigration. They asked him a few questions, and he answered in his natural accent. That probably helped. Officials stamped his passport and sent him on through.

Walsh's experience was just as smooth, as was Pat's. Pat couldn't believe how easy it was to smuggle drugs into Ireland. Maybe that's why Treats had thought it was not a big deal from the beginning.

Inside, the main terminal was a far cry from the bustling Logan airport. This place had kind of a sleepy feel. Plus, they were arriving during the off-season. Hardly anybody was in line at the car rental parks. They got a good deal on a small gray sedan.

"All right, boys. I'm driving since I know my way around," said Treats.

"Dude, you're still fucked up from the flight. I'm not getting in the car with you," Walsh shot back.

"Relax," answered Treats. "That was hours ago. I've had time to sober up."

If it were any other person, that claim would be doubtful. But Pat knew Treats. Treats had such a high tolerance that it would take a tranquilizer shot from an elephant gun to bring that fucker down.

"Where to first?" asked Pat. The wedding wasn't for a few days, and Pat was a little fuzzy on what the itinerary would be. He was sort of handing the reins off for this part of the trip.

"The Twelve Bens Bar. My uncle Manus lives about five doors down. It's along the way, in Galway. Then we'll stop at my uncle John's farmhouse in Roundstone."

Walsh pointed to an airport bar placard advertising a special on Irish coffees. "That sign says the Irish coffee was invented in Shannon. Is that true?" Walsh asked.

"Yeah, I think so," said Treats.

"Well then, we're grabbing some Irish coffees for the road," he said, already making a beeline for the bar.

"Fine, ya fuckin' tourist," sighed Treats.

———

ONCE THEY WERE ON THE ROAD, PAT WAS GLAD TREATS WAS driving and not him. For one thing, everyone drove on the left side, and the steering wheel was on the right. That was a total mind fuck. Plus, the rain was coming down in sheets, and they were spending most of the journey on a small two-lane highway.

On the other hand, Treats was driving like a maniac, taking curves at high speeds and coming within inches of oncoming cars going the opposite way. He'd already hydroplaned a few times. Of course, Pat knew that Treats drove like this when he was stone-cold sober. It really wouldn't have made any difference.

Woosh! Treats made a sudden adjustment on a curve that momentarily sent them to the shoulder of the road and back. A large shipping truck had gone over the line, and Treats had to evade. *Jesus Christ.*

Pat was already a touch jittery from the Irish coffee—a strong brew with a healthy dose of whiskey, maybe even a double. But if the coffee hadn't roused him up, Treats's driving had sure as hell done the trick. After only ten minutes into the journey, Pat was white-knuckling it.

To distract himself from fixating on the high-speed obstacle course, Pat gazed outside to take in the countryside. What he could see through the rain was pure beauty. Expansive rolling hills of grassland flew by, dotted by trees and occasionally livestock. Stone fences overgrown with moss protected both the edge of the road and divided some of the properties they had passed. In the distance was a mountain range. The setting was as far from the urban environment that Pat was familiar with as he could get, and was a welcome change of scenery.

After about an hour of the high-speed tour of the Irish countryside, they arrived at the edge of Galway. The rain was still coming down pretty hard, so it was difficult to see. Treats slowed down coming into town. Some of the farmhouses on the outskirts were similar to each other—white-stone exteriors with thatched roofs. Some of them could have easily been a few hundred years old. As they came closer to town, the houses started looking a little more modern.

"Here we go," Treats said, turning down the street that must have been familiar to him. He pulled up to a white cottage with a hanging sign that read *The Twelve Bens Bar*. The place was ancient, maybe as old as the farmhouses or older.

Happy to get out of the car, they stretched their legs and quickly got inside. The rain wasn't letting up.

Inside felt like a preserved museum dedicated to drinking. Signs that had been up decades or longer adorned the walls. The whole place was mostly one room, with an old stone fireplace on one end, complete with a roaring fire. The place was downright cozy, like a scene from an old painting. An old bartender wearing a cap and a brown apron greeted them. A few old-timers and younger regulars sat at the bar, a few couples at the tables. The place smelled like pipe smoke and beer.

Treats approached the bartender with his usual swagger. "Three pints of Guinness, please."

Because it was so thick and foamy, the Guinness was slow to pour. As the bartender was tending to the head on the drinks, Treats struck up a conversation with him.

"I'm searchin' for a guy named Manus. My mother told me he was my father, and I'm a love child," he announced loudly.

Pat winced. Any chance to be inconspicuous was blown. They'd already looked out of place as it was, and now half the bar was peeking up from their drinks and clocking them all as foreigners disturbing the peace. You could hear a pin drop.

And what the hell was he talking about? Wasn't this "Manus" his uncle? Walsh and Pat traded bewildered glances. Treats turned back at Pat and Walsh and winked at them. *Oh, boy, here we go.* Walsh started cracking up.

"Yeah, I've come from Boston to reconnect," Treats added.

Still not a peep out of the bartender, who went back to putting the finishing touches on the pints of Guinness, leaving a sizable head on each glass. It was a refreshing ceremonial moment for their first Guinness in the homeland.

"The fresh coat of paint really livens up the place," Treats observed. The bartender brought over the three pints and put both hands on the bar.

"You opening a tab, boyo?" he asked dryly.

Treats opened his wallet and fished out a twenty. As he laid it down on the bar, he finally broke it to him.

"I'm just kidding, man. Manus is my uncle. We're from Boston on our way to Roundstone for a wedding. You know there's another Twelve Bens Bar on Adams Street in Dorchester? The same family owners."

A flash of recognition ignited in the old bartender's eyes, and a smile finally cracked. Then a burst of deep laughter started from his gut as he set the pints of Guinness in front of Treats.

"You shifty little bastard, acting the maggot. Of course we know Manus; he practically lives here. Should have known you were related by the bullshit you're spoutin' off," he said through a chuckle.

That broke the tension. A few locals joined the bartender in his laughter, and then Walsh and Pat joined in. The mood changed from hostile to welcoming, like someone had flipped a switch. The boys made themselves comfortable saddling up at the bar and talking with the locals.

Pat learned that the Twelve Bens in Dorchester was one of those bars that the hardcore Irish, first-generation immigrants who had been born in Ireland had adopted as one of their watering holes back in Boston and thereby re-created there; he'd never known this about the

Twelve Bens back home. Most of the locals called these guys "turkeys," which was either a term of endearment or a slur, depending on how people would say it. The turkeys tended to hang out in different places than second- or third-generation Irish. The Twelve Bens welcomed turkeys with open arms, so naturally it might be known to a few people here in the home country.

The bartender insisted on pouring them a complimentary round of whiskey to welcome them to Ireland, which Pat accepted with enthusiasm. The way Pat saw it was, "Why stop now?" This was the roaring good time that Treats had promised them. And they were barely getting started.

———

TWO DRINKS LATER, THE RAIN HAD FINALLY LET UP A BIT. THE boys said their goodbyes and piled up in the car for the short ride to Murvey, a little village inside Roundstone harbor.

Treats lit up a blunt and passed it around. Pat felt nice and smooth after, sober enough to still function in front of Treats's family but relaxed enough not to get nervous. With one glance at Walsh, Pat guessed he felt the same way too.

As for Treats, he always seemed like a fool living on a knife's edge, never concerned about any danger. But what did he have to worry about at this point? The challenging part, smuggling the drugs into Ireland, was behind them. All they had to do now was look forward to enjoying their contraband supply.

They'd pretty much hotboxed the car, so Treats told them to roll down the windows as they pulled into Murvey. As the clouds of smoke billowed out of the cabin, Pat caught a first glimpse of the town they'd be staying in for a few days.

The scenery was breathtaking. All the stories that Pat had heard about the old country's beauty were true. They saw more of the rolling hills up close, and far away, Pat could see horses grazing in a vast pasture. As they drove closer to the village, the hills were lined by blooming trees on each side. They passed a small harbor on their left, with a couple of fishing boats docked in the slips. The narrow two-lane road was lined with a

The Roundstone Harbour in Roundstone, Co. Galway, Ireland

short stone wall protecting the street from the edge of the harbor's waters. Treats told them that the wall was a gathering place to take in the fantastic view or share a drink with locals. There were no open container laws here, or at least no one took them seriously.

The other side of the road was lined with a solid flank of stone houses nestled right beside each other, with an occasional alley between them. The village emerged like it was lost in time. As far as Pat knew, there wasn't any city in America that looked like this.

Treats made a few turns. The houses had thinned out. Treats said only a couple hundred people lived in town, and it wasn't one of those resort communities. Tourists hadn't discovered it yet. This was a local, sleepy farm and fishing village, a great place to relax and disappear for a while, but not necessarily a great place to blend in. They'd stick out here even more than they did in Galway.

It was late in the afternoon when they pulled up the road to a farmhouse surrounded by fields and trees. It was a home straight out of the 1800s, practically the size of a barn. Its construction resembled the old country houses they'd seen on the way over: white-stone walls, gray thatched roofs.

An Irish red setter rushed out the front door to excitedly greet the newcomers. Its barks announced their arrival to Treats's relatives inside. The motley crew of cousins and aunts and uncles poured out the front door.

Pat mentally cleaned up before the proper family greeting. They'd washed up a bit back at the bar, taking a "Spanish shower"—what Treats explained was just a washing of the face and hands and underarms and applying fresh deodorant. All three of them combed their hair in the car. Now it was just a matter of getting their heads screwed on straight and trying to make it through the family welcome without coming off as a bunch of drunk vagrants. And they weren't falling down yet, so they stood a chance.

The family took turns giving them all hugs and shaking their hands. Pat heard so many names that there was no chance he was going to remember them all. All he could remember was Uncle John, a stocky mountain of a man with silver hair and deep laugh lines on his weathered face. Shaking his hand was like shaking a rough bear's paw. This was a man who worked with his hands for a living.

After all their greetings were exchanged without incident, Treats's relatives ushered them into the family room near the giant fireplace to have a cup of tea. The room was perfectly suited for a large gathering of friends and family. Old and comfy furniture and an oversized coffee table full of teatime treats awaited them.

"Tea's a big deal here," Treats explained. "You'd never invite someone into your home without offering it. And you have it at least four times a day, so get used to it!" Pat and Walsh nodded. Tea was certainly nothing to complain about, and after a damp spring day, it was downright comforting. Also, after smoking that blunt in the car, Pat was getting hunger pangs. Those little sweet rolls and other baked treats offered up with the tea smelled like they would hit the spot. He could certainly get used to this.

"So, how was the flight?" asked Uncle John, taking a roll from a tray.

Pat fought to retain his composure and not break up laughing right there. He was half tempted to say, "The flying was a fucking nightmare, a complete shit show, and I was ready to murder Treats on the spot. And we almost had an international incident." Perhaps they'd be amused? Probably not.

"It was good, sir," offered Walsh, saving Pat from thinking of something. "Mostly, we just slept."

"Yeah, pretty uneventful. When I was awake, I was just filling out crosswords the whole time," said Treats, a whopper of a lie that Pat was sure his family saw through, judging by the smirk on Uncle John's face.

"So you came all the way out here just to go to Thomas's cousin's wedding? That's a journey, friends," said Uncle John.

"Yes, sir," said Pat, surprised at hearing Treats's real given name. "Well, I'd never been to the old country. I'm third-generation Irish American; my grandparents were fresh off the boat in Boston. I've always wanted to visit."

"And what do you think so far, lads?" asked one of the male cousins who seemed close to their age. Jaffe—that was his name, Pat suddenly remembered.

"Well, we've only seen Ireland on the drive from Shannon, but I've never seen a place so green," answered Pat honestly. He'd been cooped up so long in prison and then in Boston that he'd had no idea how much he needed to just be in nature and see wide-open country. He felt safe here. This place was comfortable, like it had been waiting here for him this whole time. Most of all, he felt free. No one had any preconceived notion of who Pat was out here, besides that he was an American. The constant reminders of the decay in his neighborhood were gone. Even though he knew he'd only be staying a few weeks, it felt like a fresh start. He could breathe here, something that he'd missed while he was in prison.

They eventually moved on from tea to dinner, a hearty plate of roast beef, mashed potatoes, roasted carrots, corn, and freshly baked bread with home-churned butter. Pat was ravenous at this point. All they'd had for lunch was whiskey and Guinness—not exactly a meal. The food was much better than anything his ma had ever made him. All three of them had seconds.

After some post-dinner whiskey with the family, Pat was ready to turn in. Uncle John showed them to a small guesthouse about three hundred yards away from the main home. The short walk over smelled like clean air and fresh grass. Pat spotted a few wild rabbits jumping away from their path.

Once inside, John showed them the amenities. Three twin beds were set up in what appeared to be a converted nursery. The three men had their own little kitchen and bathroom that they would share. The rooms were all on one floor, with a view overlooking the back part of the property. They said their good nights and got ready to crash. At least, Pat tried to. Treats insisted they all have a couple more drinks and smoke another blunt. He'd already brought some cans of beer from the fridge in the main house. Walsh seemed game, but Pat was ready to pass out. After his first beer, he gave in. If he tried to sleep, the other two would keep him up anyway, so why fight it?

They got to telling stories from high school, and before they knew it, it was three a.m. Pat drank from a reclined position, half sitting up in bed. He listened to Treats as long as he could before he faded out, a half-empty beer can in his hand, his last thought that he couldn't remember the last time he had felt this relaxed.

Chapter 14

UPSIDE DOWN

PAT HAD NEVER EATEN SUCH A COLOSSAL BREAKFAST IN HIS life. It was a massive assault of fresh breakfast food, the likes of which beggared belief. He almost couldn't comprehend the spread laid out on the table, like a banquet for a small army.

"This is a traditional Irish breakfast, maybe just a little more elaborate than usual because of all the family guests," Treats explained. "Most everything here comes from the farm or is made fresh, except maybe for that marmalade."

The mountainous plate of bacon is what caught Pat's eye first—massive thick cuts fried to a crispy and dark finish. Fresh eggs from the farm hens, sunny-side up, were already served on the plate. A mashed potato hash with vegetables was another star attraction. And the food kept coming—giant sausages, mushrooms, roasted tomatoes, homemade bread with freshly churned butter. And copious amounts of tea flowed into their cups. The flavor combination of everything together felt like a natural high. This spread was practically mythical.

Auntie Kay waited until midway through breakfast before she started interrogating Treats. "Heard you howlin' at the moon last night from up in the guesthouse," she said, giving Treats a bit of side-eye.

"Not quite howlin', Auntie. Just takin' it all in," answered Treats.

"Wasn't aware there was a concert happening in our back pasture," Auntie Kay replied.

"Well, there is now," said Treats, laughing. He then stifled his laugh when he saw Auntie Kay was still burning.

"You boys better watch yourselves. If you follow this young man's lead, you'll end up over a cliff, like complete eejits," she said, a stony expression on her face.

"I'll make sure they don't get in any trouble, Kay," offered Treats. Walsh snorted and almost choked on what he was eating. And Pat had to agree; putting Treats in charge was letting the mental patient run the asylum.

"Well, based on what I've seen so far, you'll make right bags of that too," retorted Auntie Kay. This time, a hint of a smile crept onto her face. That was enough information to confirm for Pat what he long suspected: that his family was used to his shenanigans. Treats was an instigator. He didn't know how to be any different.

In response, Treats just smiled and shut his trap. With all this incredible foodstuff, it was pretty easy to stop talking. Walsh hadn't said a thing since he sat down.

By the time Pat had finished breakfast, he wasn't sure how he was going to drag himself off the chair. He hadn't thought he was that hungry before sitting down, but once he'd gotten started, it was hard to stop. There was something intangibly delicious about all that fresh food. It hadn't sat on shelves anywhere. It had no preservatives, no packaging, no weird hidden crap. They were eating as close to the source as you could get.

"It's important to eat pure, bro," whispered Treats through a smirk. "That way, you can get the maximum impact of the drugs later."

"Yeah, I remember you selling me that about alcohol too the first time you got me drunk," Patrick said, his tone a little sharper than he had intended it to be. Was Treats beginning to irritate him, or was that just the jet lag?

NIGHTTIME FELL, AND PAT SAT ON THE COUCH, HEAVILY anchored by the unstoppable onslaught of calorie intake. Breakfast was followed by eleven o'clock tea, a giant lunch, afternoon tea, and another incredible dinner. Pat tried to fight off the drowsiness and natural malaise that came from engorging himself all day. Walsh, slumped in a comfy chair, was struggling with the same.

Treats, for his part, still seemed full of energy. He chain-smoked and paced, herding some of the older cousins together for a trip to the local village bar. By now, Pat was ready to get out too. If he sat any longer, he would just doze off, trying to digest the massive bricks in his stomach.

"Treats, we gotta get the fuck outta here," begged Pat. "I can't take it anymore. We gotta do something, move around, anything. I'm gonna slip into a coma over here."

"I can't eat any more potato pancakes," said Walsh. "Seriously. I'm gonna burst."

"All right. Then we're out!" Treats barked.

After a quick round of Jamesons, they piled into the little rental. A few of the cousins were going in their own cars, except for Jaffe, who was taking his motorcycle. On the drive over, Treats informed them there was only one bar in town, although there were several more a short drive away in neighboring towns. The local watering hole was simply called King's Bar, a modest one-room establishment. Pat didn't care where they were going, as long as they could stand up, walk around, and have a few drinks.

They pulled up to King's Bar, slightly down the street. With full bellies and a smooth high going, they drifted into the bar. Like most of the Roundstone businesses, the bar was tucked into the bottom floor of a converted house-like structure, with apartment homes above the bar. The establishment's face was tiny, barely wider than fifteen feet or so, marked by bright purple paint, which defined it as separate from the rest of the building. A picnic bench and table sat outside near the door. There was no bouncer.

Treats opened the front door and ushered them inside. The place was long and narrow, shaped like a shoebox, with the bar at the very back wall. Barstools and tables lined one wall, and bench-style booths the other. The wooden bar itself maybe only had room for about four people. Little Irish flags hung by a string of lights lining the ceiling molding. Prints of Irish paintings and Guinness advertising adorned the walls. The place felt warm, with soft lighting giving everything a sort of sepia color.

The bar was about half full with mostly men over fifty having a pint.

Almost everyone was wearing a sweater or a fleece jacket to stave off the spring chill. A few younger locals were milling about. Everyone seemed to know each other. Many turned around, trying to see what they could make of the newcomers. But Pat thought he could see a glimmer of recognition on their faces. Maybe they'd heard they were coming?

Treats ordered a round of shots for them and also ponied up for the first round of pints. Pat settled in at the only space left at the wooden bar, and an old man with giant bushy eyebrows struck up a conversation with him.

"You must be one of the boys from Boston," said the man, his tone friendly.

"It's that obvious, huh?" chuckled Pat.

"Well, your reputation precedes you, lad. Everyone knows 'bout the upcoming wedding. Plus, practically the whole village could smell your car comin' in yesterday. People talk around here."

Pat winced a little. The air was pretty pure around here, and so were the people. Any kind of smell like that must have lingered to noses used to clean air.

"We probably need an oil change," improvised Pat.

"Smelled more like a prairie fire to me," said the old man with a laugh. "I'm sure it's out by now."

If the old man knew about them, then probably everybody in the bar had already heard. Pat knew these stories would get out of hand.

Jaffe and some of the other cousins and aunts starting filing in, and before they knew it, the bar was packed with both family and local villagers. The vibe had picked up, and suddenly, the place was lively with chatter. Some of Treats's extended family hadn't seen each other in years, and others were making some first-time introductions. Walsh appeared to be having a great time, mingling with the villagers.

Pat spotted a familiar face he wasn't expecting—Lanie, Treats's twenty-three-year-old cousin from Dorchester. The admittedly cute girl had walked in with a man who must have been her boyfriend. Pat had met Lanie a few times at Treats's parties when he was growing up but hadn't seen her in at least four years, since before he was sentenced. He reintroduced himself and shook hands with her boyfriend, Matt, and made some small talk about Dorchester and how they were all enjoying their first trip to Ireland.

On his way to get his third round, Pat ran into Jaffe, the somewhat serious-faced cousin he had met back at the farmhouse. Pat guessed Jaffe was close to thirty. He hadn't really had a chance to talk with him. While he was ordering his Guinness, Pat spotted an IRA tattoo on his forearm that he recognized. *Tiocfaidh ár lá*, it read, meaning "Our day will come." Choppa had the same one across his back.

"Committed to The Cause, are ya?" asked Patrick, immediately regretting the question. Must have been the Guinness and weed. Why would he start a conversation on a topic he was trying to avoid?

"Anyone true to our country should be," answered Jaffe. "We've all had enough of the queen treating us like dogs."

Well, that certainly changed the mood. It was probably bad form to bring up the IRA at a bar. It would be like talking politics back home at the Eire. All it did was foment a lot of bad feelings and sometimes stir up trouble. But part of Pat was dying to share that he had always supported a United Ireland. He remembered the endless nights in the cell with Choppa, talking about the deep history of the Republic and Choppa's efforts in Boston, shipping guns to his contacts on the island. That was a full education in itself—and now he was part of an important mission with some of those same contacts. His task was orchestrated at the highest levels.

He changed the subject by buying Jaffe a shot. Jaffe retaliated by buying him one too. Now, Pat was already four rounds in, and his Guinness had just arrived. It was going to be an interesting night.

Right on cue, Pat heard some shouting from the middle of the bar, over by the tables. It was Lanie, having a complete fit, shouting something at Treats. Confused, Pat left Jaffe at the barstool and approached Treats and Lanie to see what their deal was.

Holy shit. Treats had lit up a joint in the back corner of the bar!

He was still smoking it as Lanie was giving him the third degree. Pat scanned the room and met Walsh's eyes; he had also just recognized what was happening. Pat tensed up, thinking they might have to get Treats out of trouble yet again.

"What the fuck's wrong with you?" Lanie shouted. "You're smoking a fucking joint inside the bar? So fucking disrespectful!"

If the weed smoke hadn't caught everyone's attention, Lanie's shouting certainly did. Now everyone was staring at the altercation.

"Look, Lanie—" Treats started in a casual tone that seemed sure to only enrage her further.

"Don't 'look Lanie' me. Your aunts and uncles are here. This isn't Lucky's in Boston, you fucking idiot!"

Treats responded by blowing smoke in her face. Then she slapped him. Pat didn't see the rage come out in Treats very often, but it was coming out now. Pat and Walsh maneuvered closer, and so did Lanie's boyfriend, Matt.

"Shut the fuck up, you bitch," Treats growled through gritted teeth. "Don't tell me what to do in front of my fucking family."

At this, Matt inserted himself between Lanie and Treats, trying to stare him down. Walsh seized Treats's joint and put it out, pocketing what was left, then grabbed one of Treats's arms. Pat grabbed Treats's other arm.

"This is a family issue, Matt. It's none of your fucking business," said Treats.

"It's not my business until you threaten my girl, Slick," Matt retorted. Pat realized that they must've gone way back, although he couldn't recall ever seeing him before.

A few of the bigger men from the village stood ready, moving on one side or the other of Treats and Matt. They were poised to help pull them away from each other too, in case Treats squirmed free of Pat and Walsh.

A quick accounting of the situation led Pat to believe that Matt wasn't going to do anything. Already, Matt was breaking eye contact with Treats and going back to Lanie, attempting to soothe her. She stormed outside; Matt was close behind.

Meanwhile, the mixed crowd of relatives and villagers all stared with their mouths gaping open. Even the bartender was craning his neck to see if the situation would disintegrate. If this were a bar back in Boston, he would have already reached for a bat. As for the rest of the crowd, they emitted a small chorus of gasps and whispers.

A loud motorcycle revved up right outside the bar, interrupting the drama of all the hushed gossip. Pat and Walsh dragged Treats outside to cool off, like bouncers taking out a drunk, and there they spotted Jaffe, already on his bike.

"C'mon you fuckin' Yanks," Jaffe told them. "Follow me to Clifden. The mood'll be right! You've stirred the shit out of this one!"

Treats had fucked this up completely, as usual, and they needed to head to a place that had a better vibe. If they stayed, Pat and Walsh would be guilty by association. It was time to get the fuck out of there before things got worse. The last thing Pat wanted to do was get into a brawl in front of Treats's extended family.

Half the brawls Pat had ever been involved in had to do with defending someone in his own group who had done something stupid or attacking someone who had wronged them. That's just what you did: you defended your crew, right or wrong. As far as Pat was concerned, Treats may have been an idiot, but he was *their* idiot. Anyone who laid hands on him would be met with force in kind. That's why it was best to stop the fight before it started. Once it got going, Pat and Walsh would be honor bound to fight in solidarity.

Clifden was about eleven miles northwest but an easy drive on roads with hardly any traffic. Pat wasn't going to let Treats drive and took over the wheel. Maybe it was just the drinks chilling him out, but driving on the left side didn't seem that intimidating anymore. How hard could it be? Walsh was already relighting the extinguished joint and passing it to Treats.

Pat fumbled around with the controls and started the car. Jaffe revved his engine again. Pat honked his horn a few times, signaling he was ready. Jaffe responded by taking off like a gunshot, forcing Pat to lay on the gas to keep up. With that, the rental car rolled off into the moonlight.

———

BY THE TIME THEY'D ARRIVED IN CLIFDEN, TREATS WAS noticeably more relaxed. This cooldown could have been a combination of things. For one, Treats's attention span was shorter than a squirrel's. He lived in the now, so although his temper may have flared, it was all over, and he was ready to get back to having a good time. Before entering the bar, they'd shared another joint with Jaffe, by the side of the road. In any event, it would have been hard for Treats to stay angry when he had a solid foundation of marijuana in his system. Treats insisted the pre-bar joint was required "for safety." After they finished, they were all clear to drink with impunity. Jaffe showed them inside.

They found themselves at Lowry's Music and Whiskey Bar, a lively joint with more upbeat energy and a younger crowd. The bar was old fashioned, precisely what an American would expect a well-trafficked Irish pub to present like. The walls and floors were of dark wood, and the wooden bar was lined with dark red barstools. The place smelled fantastic; they had a homestyle kitchen in the back. Young people were milling around.

Jaffe was becoming a fast friend to them. He had a bit of a wily vibe, someone who thrived on big risks. Jaffe knew where all the local watering holes were within a twenty-five-mile radius and was already proving to Pat that he could drink with the best of them.

Walsh and Treats had gone outside for a quick smoke, and while Pat was waiting on their next round of pints, Pat spotted Jaffe riffling through something on a stool. Jaffe made eye contact, but he just smiled and carried on with what he was doing. On closer inspection, Pat could see he was going through a lady's purse, lifting some cash and a pack of smokes.

Patrick waved him over. "What the fuck are you doing, man?"

"Found money. If she's thick enough to leave her handbag lying about, it's fair play." He then put the purse back right where he found it.

Pat had buddies who used to go tailgating back in high school, which meant something different in Boston. While a delivery truck was bringing in goods to a shop or store, kids would rush the truck and steal what was inside. It was pretty easy. If you only stole a little bit, the driver was often none the wiser. But purse snatching was kind of low, not something Pat would have ever considered. It made him think twice about Jaffe. Illegal drugs were one thing. What they did to their own bodies was hurting no one. But stealing from innocent women was sketchy.

Given their drunken state, Pat thought it would probably be best to leave it alone, but at least he could stop Jaffe from doing it again. When Walsh returned, Pat told him to keep an eye out to see if Jaffe was doing anything shifty. "The best way to do that is to keep him close and by keeping his cup full," Pat told Walsh.

True to form, that wasn't the last round they would be drinking. A couple of hours in, Pat had lost track of how many they'd had. Ten? Twelve? Hard to keep the math straight. Treats had escalated to drinking whiskey and returned to fuming about Lanie and Matt.

"That mothafucka. Gimme the keys," demanded Treats.

"Whoa, whoa, calm down," said Pat. "They're probably all gone now anyway."

"Easy, man. We're havin' a great time over here," chimed in Walsh.

"I'm gonna pound that asshole's face. Slap him hard upside the head. Are you comin' or not?" slurred Treats. Man, was he fucked up, Pat thought. He didn't even know why he was mad. Sure, Lanie had pissed him off, but somehow all his rage had shifted to her boyfriend. It didn't have to make sense; it was the whiskey talking.

Jaffe, on the other hand, was all about it. If they were going to fly back to the bar all half-cocked and sniffing for a fight, he wanted in on it too. "Time to go, boys," he said, dropping some cash on the bar for the last round. Then, they followed him out the door. Pat didn't have a map, so he would just have to follow Jaffe's motorcycle. He guessed they were all in on Treats's stupid crusade.

Once again, Jaffe went off like a rocket, even faster than last time. Pat was struggling to keep up. The dirt roads were all winding, and there weren't any streetlights once they got out of Clifden. It was mostly farm country, dark and overgrown. Plus, Pat was starting to see double. It wasn't the drunkest he'd ever driven, but his state wasn't conducive to high-speed racing. Pat did his best to follow the dust cloud Jaffe was leaving in his wake. As they sped in pursuit, the car was catching air on little bumps.

These roads were a fucking nightmare. There was no fucking signage, hairpin turns popped up by complete surprise, and animals were everywhere. Pat had already dodged a couple of sheep and a cow. Did these fucking animals just wander the roads at night?

"Fuck! How the fuck you see the road in light like this?" grunted Pat, entirely focused on keeping up.

"It's easy! Just follow the moon, brother!" Treats shouted.

Treats was right. The moon was full, and the sky was clear, so at least they had some of that light to go on. But more importantly, little streams and canals by the side of the road reflected the moonlight. The roads were built next to the waterways, so the water appeared like a narrow glowing border that marked where the edge of the road was. Roughly. If Pat focused on that, he got a clearer picture of where he was going.

"I'm gonna wail on that piece of shit Matt!" shouted Treats. He was working himself into a froth. Walsh tried to offer him a joint, but he wasn't having it.

"Calm down," started Pat. "We're in the middle of fucking Farmville in Ireland flying down the road in the pitch dark, and you want to beat the shit out of a guy from Dorchester? I don't even know where the fuck you're gonna find him at one in the morning."

"Fuck that piece of shit!" Treats yelled.

"Chill out, Treats. Chill the fuck out, man," Pat said in a calm voice. He wasn't going to get in a screaming match with a whiskeyed-up Treats.

"Oh, sure. If you had a beef with the guy, there'd be no say in the matter for us. You'd just expect us to—"

Walsh screamed, interrupting Treats. The car was off the road in a patch of high grass, still at high speed.

"OH FUCK!" screamed Pat. He fought to get back on the road. He managed to slow the car down to a crawl, but it was tipped sideways at about a forty-five-degree angle near a sidehill's crest. The wheels were stuck in tall grass, weeds, and mud. Pat tried to steer out of it and hit the gas, but the maneuver didn't work. The car reached a tipping point and began to roll. The bottom dropped out of his stomach, and time seemed to freeze as everything went topsy-turvy. The vehicle rolled four or five times down the soft slope, throwing them around like rag dolls. They landed upside down with a thud, wheels facing the sky.

It was dead silence for a few seconds. None of them were wearing seat belts, so they were all awkwardly lying on their heads, shoulders, and backs. They were covered in beer cans, fast food trash, and ashes from the ashtray. Some of the glass had shattered and dusted their hair.

"You guys all right? You okay?" asked Pat.

Following another moment of silence, Treats piped up. "Fuuuuuuck. You fuckin' *idiot*. What the fuck we gonna do now?"

"I'm okay, man. I think I have glass in my hair," said Walsh. "Did you really just flip the car going five miles per hour?"

"Shut the fuck up, Walsh," answered Pat.

They crawled out of the car, careful not to snag or cut themselves on any glass. Then they stood up and checked themselves out. Pat brushed some of the shattered safety glass out of their hair and clothes. He'd be pretty bruised tomorrow, but he wasn't feeling any pain at the moment.

Once they established they were all okay, Treats laid back into Pat. "Jesus Christ. Why the fuck did I let you drive? You haven't driven in four fuckin' years! And you're drivin' in Ireland? Drunk?"

Treats stared them down until Walsh broke a grin. Then Treats cracked up.

It wasn't like it would have been any different if Walsh or Treats had been driving. As far as Pat knew, this could have been the best possible outcome in the doomed mission to go back and beat the shit out of Matt in the middle of the night. Treats probably would have launched them into a cow or off a cliff.

Pat examined the rental car. One of the axles seemed to be bent. All the windows were broken. Even if they could get it running again, it would be a magnet for law enforcement to stop them. This thing was probably totaled.

"I think maybe it's best we sort this all out in the a.m.," said Pat.

"It's already the a.m.," laughed Walsh.

"The house is about a mile or two from here. I think we can just follow the road we were already on," said Treats.

They started down the road, walking at a leisurely pace. Treats offered them some bumps of coke for the journey, but Pat was still too adrenalized. Walsh also declined. They settled instead for the beautiful walk back home in the moonlight.

———

THE SWEET RELIEF OF SLEEP WAS SHORT-LIVED. PAT DIDN'T remember much past walking home in the dead of night on the country road. He couldn't even remember coming in through the front door. All he knew was his deep peace was being shattered by furious knocking, a sound that seemed both loud and miles away, much farther than the rental they had left upturned in a smoking heap. Maybe, if he ignored the sound, it would go away.

The thunderous knocks only got louder and more heated. Finally, he could hear the front door beyond their bedroom explode open with fury. And then their own bedroom door flew open, with enough force to nearly shatter the hinges.

He opened his eyes a crack, revealing an enraged Auntie Kay, huffing and puffing with laser beams practically coming out of her eyes. Pat pulled the blanket back over his head in a futile gesture to evade her wrath. Maybe Treats would take the brunt of this one. Again.

She stomped over to Treats's bed, bumping the night table. Beer cans rattled to the floor, making a piercing sound that made Pat wince.

"You think this is fucking Jamaica?" she began. "You think this is spring break, you miserable half-cocked Yanks? You can just act like a melter and light up a joint wherever the fuck you are, and everyone else has to just fuck off?"

Pat peeked from the covers and could see by Walsh's face and Treats's wide eyes that they were equally terrified. She was shouting at all of them and at no one in particular at the same time, as if she wasn't sure which one of them she wanted to kill first.

"Your mom'll be beside herself. Half of Ireland will hear about your shenanigans before the wedding even happens!"

Treats put his hands up, gesturing to take it easy. "Auntie Kay, it wasn't even me!" he implored.

"Oh, everyone's going to get plenty!" she barked. She hadn't even gotten to the bit about the car yet. Did she know about the car?

"And then you Yanks decide to fly the car upside down, leaving it all banjaxed in the ditch?"

Shit, thought Pat. *How the fuck did she know? It must have been Jaffe. That bastard! Left us in the dust to walk home and ratted us out after!* Pat covered his head again. But Auntie Kay grabbed the blanket and sheets and flung it off his head. She stared at him, shaking her head. "For fuck's sake, lad! I thought you were going to keep your nose clean!"

"Oh, Auntie," Pat tried. "Treats was all messed up, so I had to take responsibility to drive. And these roads, Auntie—I'm not used to the roads. I'm drivin' on the left side, and the roads are all dirt, there are no lights, and sheep everywhere—"

"If the roads aren't pleasin' to ya, then maybe you should drive slowly until you get your wits about ya," she said. "It's exactly the wrong time to be takin' a bet to race with the devil!"

Pat wasn't sure if the devil she referred to was Jaffe or more of a weird metaphorical devil, like courting trouble or something. He opened his mouth to respond, but nothing much was coming out. Auntie Kay took that as her cue.

"Well, you better straighten out and not embarrass us here. This is a respectable community, not some drug-fueled beach orgy in Ibiza," she said, her finger in Pat's face. "Three days. Three days you goddamn derelicts have been here."

She marched out and slammed the door. All of them sat in silence. Walsh made an "ooh boy" kind of whistle.

Treats piped up first. "Well, I think that went far better than it could have," he announced, smiling.

———

THEY MANAGED TO COLLECT THEMSELVES AND WANDER OUT of the guesthouse, and they congregated around the kitchen table. It was close to ten a.m. They had long since missed breakfast, and no one dared ask Auntie Kay to fix them up something. There were plenty of leftovers in the fridge, so the boys made a meal of sausages and potatoes and toast with jam. After last night's bender, the food hit the spot. A pot of coffee pumped some life into them.

None of them said anything for a while. Treats was content to smoke his cigarette and stare off into the distance. Pat and Walsh nursed their coffees. Pat's wheels were turning as he tried to figure out what they should do about the car. He felt guilty. They were in this mess because of his driving. They needed that car, for the wedding, for the country tour, and for Pat's mission. He sure as hell wasn't going to phone Jimmy to explain that he needed another car because he flew the other one off the road after sixteen or more drinks. Not exactly the kind of message to inspire confidence.

He thought back to Jaffe and some of the conversations they'd had last night at Lowry's. Jaffe had connections over here like Pat had in Boston. If they needed to get something done, they could use the local network of friends and family. And he'd already seen that Jaffe wasn't concerned about ethics or petty crime. That would make it a little easier. Pat considered involving Treats but then thought against it. Treats was family here, but he wasn't really connected outside his immediate circle

106

like Jaffe was. And Treats had lured them into enough trouble already. He didn't want him to somehow pooch the task to recover the car.

That meant they needed Jaffe's help. And Pat should go alone. Walsh could try to keep Treats on planet Earth and out of trouble for at least a few hours. Even if they just went back to doing drugs in the guesthouse, it would be better than Treats being at large in the community.

Pat stood up and zipped up his coat.

"I got an idea, guys. We still have to get back to the wedding in Galway and then up to Dublin. And I have something to do in Northern Ireland after that. We need a car. Why don't you guys cool off here, try to lay low for a bit."

"What about Auntie Kay?" asked Walsh. He was serious.

"Stay out of her way until she cools off," said Pat.

Walsh glanced at Treats, who just smiled and nodded and shoved some more toast dripping with jam into his mouth.

———

IT WASN'T HARD TO FIND JAFFE IN ROUNDSTONE. THE PREVI-ous night, he'd mentioned that he usually hung out by the harbor. It would make sense; that seemed to be where all the locals convened. King's Bar was within view, and if anyone wanted the local gossip, they could hang out there or at the stone wall overlooking the harbor.

Pat spotted Jaffe smoking outside of King's Bar. Jaffe just laughed when he saw them.

"It's a car, not a plane!" Jaffe said, slapping his hand upside Pat's back. Pat couldn't help but laugh a little too. They'd walked away from the accident, hadn't they?

Jaffe finished his cigarette and invited Pat inside the bar. It was practically empty, so they had their choice of seats right up at the bar.

"A little hair of the dog?" asked Jaffe, already ordering him a Guinness.

"Sure," responded Pat. Anything to help kill his throbbing headache.

"Sorry I left you back there, man. I figured you'd find your way home eventually," Jaffe explained.

"Oh, we made it home all right. By foot!" Pat responded.

"It's a pretty walk in the moonlight, isn't it?"

Pat wanted to be mad, but he just wasn't. "Pretty" was an understatement. The countryside around these parts was indescribably beautiful. At night, all bathed in moonlight, it was downright . . . mystical. Despite the fear of imminent death moments earlier, that walk had made it almost worth crashing the car.

"Yeah. It's something else," replied Pat.

"You know, I was blind drunk. Had I backtracked, I probably would have ended up in the ditch too," offered Jaffe.

Pat started to say something but thought against it. He needed Jaffe's help, so he wasn't going to get pissy about last night. Instead, he just raised his glass to clink Jaffe's.

"Sláinte," toasted Pat.

"Sláinte," Jaffe said with a wink.

"Listen, Jaffe, I'm curious about something. How the fuck did Auntie Kay know about the car?" asked Pat.

Jaffe cocked his head back and let out a bellow of laughter.

"How the fuck did she know? Pat. The whole damn town knows. It's the farmers, man. This is their turf, and they all wake up early. By five a.m., I'm bettin' most of Roundstone County knew!"

"Bullshit," said Pat, not believing him.

"Oh yeah? Watch this," retorted Jaffe.

Jaffe waved down the bartender and gestured toward Pat. "Hey, Miles," he said, "do you know who this is?"

"Yeah," answered the bartender without missing a beat. "That's one of the Yanks that flew upside down."

Pat groaned and put his face in his hands. This was just fucking embarrassing.

"So, how you going to get the car out?" Jaffe asked.

"About that. I need your help," responded Pat.

———

AT ABOUT FOUR IN THE AFTERNOON, PAT WAS RIDING SHOT-gun in a flatbed truck with a new car perched on the back. The driver had a hat with the rental company's logo on it. Treats and Walsh stepped outside as the heavy vehicle rolled up the gravelly road.

Pat gestured to the driver to unload the car right there.

"Where's the other car?" asked the driver.

"You can just drop that one right here. These guys are desperate to get to Galway. They're late for a wedding," Pat said.

The driver squinted to see Pat and Walsh about thirty feet away. They still were a little worse for wear from the night before and had donned jeans and T-shirts. Then he spoke to Pat.

"I'm not supposed to drop the car off until I see the other car," said the driver, humorlessly.

Pat leaned in. "Listen, mate. Help out a few Boston fellas. We got a lot of shit we got to do. See those guys?" Pat pointed and waved at Treats and Walsh near the front door. They awkwardly waved back. "Just drop that new rental so they can follow us to the car right behind you. Stay right here."

Pat jumped out of the cab of the truck and walked toward Treats and Walsh.

"What the fuck's going on?" asked Walsh.

"Just follow my lead. I'll explain later. Treats, can you take the new rental and follow us to where we left the old rental on the side of the road?"

Treats just nodded and smiled, a glimmer of recognition in his eyes. With that, the truck driver unloaded the car, and Pat climbed back into the truck. Treats and Walsh jumped in the rental and led the truck to the old one's location.

The road wound all over the place, with treacherous obstacles nearly every step of the way. Sometimes it was a deep ditch with no guardrail, sometimes a downhill stretch that could take you off-road and tumbling down a little ravine. Nothing was paved. How fast had he been driving last night? Way too fucking fast for this road.

After a short stretch, Pat told the driver to slow down to a crawl. He gestured at an empty spot on a flat area off the side of the road. It was not, of course, where he had left the car. "What the fuck?" he exclaimed, doing the best acting of his life. "It was right here when we left it, broken down on the side of the road!"

"What did you say was wrong with it?" he asked.

"Engine just cut out. We had to walk home. Oh God, I hope it wasn't stolen," Pat said, running with the story.

"Wait. I see something down there," said the driver. He pulled up another ten feet or so. There, resting at the bottom of the ditch upside down was the rental car. However, all of the wheels were gone. The radio and license plates were gone too. As for the rest of it, it appeared that someone had taken mallets to the car and taken turns smashing it.

"Oh my God!" said Pat, peeking over at the driver to see how he was reacting. The driver's mouth gaped open in shock.

"The car's been stripped," the driver said flatly. "I guess they took everything."

It took everything Pat had not to bust up laughing at his little ruse. "You Irish sure are crazy around here!" he exclaimed. "I guess that's why they invented insurance!"

"Of course you guys are covered. I'll just need your signature so you can be on your way, then I'll have to make some calls to figure out what they want me to do."

After Treats signed the new rental agreement, the driver told them not to worry about the wreck in the ditch. They were calling in another tow truck to help him load it up.

Treats started the new rental car and lowered his window, giving the peace sign to the driver. Pat nodded and tipped his baseball cap.

"Thanks for the help, man. Good luck!" he said. The driver tipped his hat back.

They drove away slowly and tried their best to be out of sight before they burst out laughing.

"What the fuck did you do, Pat?" asked Walsh.

"Jaffe's connected to a little crew that does some car work. He just called his local mates and had them strip the car," Pat told them.

"So now we have a new rental car, and Jaffe's got some extra pocket change. I'd call that a win-win, huh boys?" said Treats, through a grin. "One thing, though."

"What's that, man?" Walsh inquired.

"From now on, I'm driving," answered Treats.

Chapter 15

THE REVEREND

NATE PACED ON THE STREET IN FRONT OF THE ELLA BAKER Community House, his headphones on, his heart racing. He still felt the constant anxiety of Tre's death; it infected him like a sickness. Moving helped to dissipate the nervous energy and confusion. If he held still for too long, the pain would catch up with him all at once.

He knew the neighborhood well. The center was right beside his old church and just a few blocks away from the tiny apartment he had grown up in on Washington Street. And inside the old church was his beloved old Reverend Gibbs.

Gibbs had been his family's religious leader for as long as he could remember, and Nate's mom was one of his staunchest fans. In her eyes, Gibbs could walk on water.

No doubt, he was a different kind of reverend than most here in Boston. He'd grown up in Philly and had been a gang member before changing the course of his life through faith. Nate couldn't deny the power of a belief system that could turn someone around so profoundly as it had Gibbs.

Aunt Carol was a big fan too, wherever she was now. Perhaps Tre's death was just too much for her and she'd left town for a few days, he thought. Even though that didn't seem like her at all.

Nate checked his watch. He was a little early for his scheduled walk with the reverend. He'd called him a few days after he came up empty at the gym. As a community leader, Gibbs might be privy to information that could help Nate start on a trail. Anything was worth a shot at this point. The police weren't doing a damn thing.

Reverend Gibbs exited the old church and spotted Nate right away. He flashed a big smile, one that seemed genuine. Nate felt comforted seeing that smile again and couldn't help but grin himself. He stopped his CD player and removed his headphones.

Gibbs closed the distance and hugged him. "I'm glad you reached out," he said, sizing up Nate. "You all grow up so fast. It seems like yesterday you were still in junior high. And look at you! I'm sure you've done your momma proud."

"Hey, Rev. I know it's been . . . a long time. I came back to attend Jamal's funeral, and your sermon hasn't left my mind."

"Those were God's words," Gibbs said, staring him directly in the eyes. "I'm just a messenger. This is a war of good versus evil."

"I know, Rev. I wanted to see Tre while I was here, but when I visited Suffolk a few days ago . . ." He felt his voice shaking and took a deep breath.

"Let's walk, Nate. Take your time. It'll come."

They strolled down the street. The movement calmed him, that feeling of being in more control by being in constant motion.

"Anyway, as I'm sure you know, he's gone. I can't find out anything other than they found him dead in his cell. No one's telling me anything."

Reverend Gibbs listened, his expression changing to concern.

"I'm aware, Nate. And so sorry for your loss. I'm afraid of what it means for this community. It's bigger than just Tre."

"What do you mean?" Nate asked.

"I'm afraid this is going to spark a lot of gunfire in the streets. A cycle of retaliation. Your cousin Alvin is already proclaiming a bounty for vengeance."

Nate almost laughed. He hadn't heard Slugs called by his real name since high school. The name didn't seem to match his physical appearance; he was a heavyset man who towered over the rest of the family. The combination of his height, weight, and limp made him appear much older than he was.

It disturbed him that Slugs was thinking about returning to a life of violence, an act that could rip him out of his barely stable electrician's existence and thrust him back onto the wrong side of the law. He'd worked so hard to escape that life!

"They're both not doing too good, Reverend," said Nate. "Aunt Carol has been MIA since Tre died, and Slugs is just stewing. I don't know what he's up to. It's too bad I didn't know about the bounty until now. I'm sure his strategy's already in motion." Nate paused. "Will it ever stop, Reverend? This is exactly why I left. And I was considering coming back for good. Before I left, I thought I'd confirm a few things about potentially starting law school around here. What the fuck was I thinking?"

"You can't run from your home, Nate. You can't run away from your people or the evil you are suffering. You have to face it head-on, support your family . . . make an impact. I believe that's why you returned. I believe it's God's plan."

"I had a conversation with Father Lydon when I first got back," Nate said. "I thought I'd come back to become a lawyer and fight corruption right here in Boston. But now . . . I can't see past Jamal's and Tre's deaths. All I see is bloodshed."

Reverend Gibbs nodded knowingly. "You're being guided. You've got to pay attention to the signs. Use your hurt. Let it motivate you. Keep your ears open—keep trying to get through to Slugs and your aunt, Carol. See what they think. Who do they think did it and why?"

Nate let that sink in, nodding. They walked in silence for a few moments as he turned things over.

"You know, Nate, me and a few of the other men of the church have started something we believe will make a significant positive impact on the city. We're stepping up and taking matters into our own hands."

"You've got my attention," Nate said.

"It's called the Ten Point Coalition. I'll explain more later. But tonight, we'll be out there, walking the streets together between ten p.m. and two a.m."

"Walking the streets?" Nate asked. "Like a patrol?"

"Something like that. We'll be interacting, solving problems, promoting antiviolence. It works. We've managed to negotiate a cease-fire that's lasted for weeks."

"But with Tre's death . . ." Nate began.

"That will certainly end the peace," answered Reverend Gibbs. "Which is why we have to double our efforts."

"Wow. Well, I'm impressed with what you've been able to accomplish so far. You guys getting the BPD involved?" Nate asked.

Gibbs paused, and Nate could see he was likely searching for the diplomatic words to say. "We'll have to see about that, Nate. I'm not sure what the trust level is there yet. Still a lot of bad blood, with what happened to Reverend Williams."

Nate winced. He knew precisely what Gibbs was talking about, even though he'd been in Virginia at the time. Last year, a no-knock raid on the wrong house had resulted in the SWAT team busting down the door of Reverend Williams's apartment. The poor old man had dropped dead of a heart attack, taking his last breaths as a police officer pinned him to the floor. It was all over the *Boston Herald*. For the police to kill a man of the faith, even by accident . . . well, Nate could understand why both the Black and religious communities still had trouble trusting the cops. Too many "accidents" seemed to hurt the Black people specifically, over and over again.

"We have a ways to go with the cops, but I don't believe anything is impossible," explained Gibbs. "But in the meantime, be careful, Nate . . . of who you are asking questions and why. There's a way to go about these things. You have to protect yourself."

He knew Reverend Gibbs was right. He had probably been a little careless already.

"Stop by tomorrow, Nate," Gibbs told him. "I'd like you to meet some people at the Community House. I think it'll be worth your while."

"Sounds good," Nate confirmed. Shaking his hand, he parted with Reverend Gibbs and slowly walked back to his car. One thing for sure, he thought, was that Gibbs had a knack for making people feel better. For the first time since Tre died, he didn't feel alone.

Chapter 16

GALWAY

WHEN AUNTIE KAY SAW THE NEW RENTAL CAR IN THE GRAVEL driveway, she just sighed and shook her head.

"Thomas," she said, "you could fall into a cow patty and end up smelling like a rose. But sometimes it ain't good for you. Or us, either."

She could barely make eye contact with the rest of them and seemed to be fuming through much of dinner. Uncle John was quiet too, but he didn't seem angry. In this case, he seemed to defer to his wife. Any show of compassion for the boys might break solidarity and cause trouble on the home front. But Pat thought he detected a hint of wistful jealousy in Uncle John's face. Uncle John had probably been a hellion in his youth too.

As for the rest of the cousins, chatter went on over the table as usual. Even though a large part of the family was staying at the farmhouse, the wedding would take place in Galway, about an hour away by car. Already, there was excitement in the air about everyone getting together; lively Galway was a far cry from the sleepy farm community of Roundstone.

Pat was beginning to wonder how much longer Treats's family would put up with this nonsense. The Americans may have already overstayed their welcome, but if they had, Treats wasn't going to be the one to tell his friends.

It was Walsh that jumped in and proposed a change of venue. They had retreated to the guesthouse for the routine after-dinner joint, all of them uncharacteristically quiet. Midway through the joint, he spoke up.

"Maybe we should let things cool off over here. Stay somewhere else for a while?"

Pat nodded. It was a relief to hear someone say it. They had to get out of there before they attracted even more attention. Each hour they stayed in Roundstone, Pat was worried that something would happen to pooch the whole Jimmy job.

"You might have something there, Walsh," answered Treats in a rare moment of wisdom. "Why don't we head up to Galway for a while. Time to crash in on Uncle Manus; he did offer us a place to stay if we needed it. We can let the dust settle here. With us out of Auntie Kay and Uncle John's hair, they might be a little more in the forgiving mood when they see us in a few days."

"Why didn't we stay there in the first place?" asked Walsh.

"You wouldn't have wanted to miss Roundstone, mate. Would you want to go home knowing you missed seeing country like this?" Treats inquired.

He was right. Who would want to miss such incredible vistas, home-cooked food, and local village culture that they couldn't get anywhere else? There wasn't anything like this back in the States, not as far as Pat knew or had seen.

Treats was already pitching them on the next batch of trouble. "Let's get a little taste of the city life. That's one thing you can't get here. And you can meet my cousin Wally. He's around our age and a little more accustomed to the city pace than the people around here." The way he said "city pace" was obviously loaded. Pat knew that Treats took the party aspect of this trip very seriously. Anything to keep the reality of the baby coming at bay.

"Sounds good to me, man," offered Pat.

"It's settled then," said Treats, smiling. "First thing tomorrow, we drive to Galway. I'll phone Aunt Maggie and Uncle Manus and let them know we're coming. Then we can head out and meet some of the honeys."

That sounded better than good to Pat. It had been over four years since he had touched a woman.

———

"FIRST THING IN THE MORNING" WAS A RELATIVE TERM. They'd spent a good portion of the night going through a case of beer and getting high out of their skulls. Treats grabbed Walsh's Gazelle sneakers and ripped out the sole, magically pulling out a small compact bag. Addressing Walsh, he said, "Sorry, I must have got confused; yours weren't the decoys!"

Walsh lowered and shook his head, covering it with his hands. What could he do?

By the time they had themselves sorted and packed, it was close to noon. Aunt Kay seemed both relieved and sorry to see them go. She made them take a few biscuits and other treats for the road, and she and Uncle John good-naturedly joined them in a single shot of whiskey before they said their goodbyes.

"Try not to turn up dead before the wedding," she said, probably only half kidding.

"And if you do, don't get found 'til after the wedding!" Uncle John added with a deep laugh. Pat thought that was a pretty good one.

They both waved off the boys as Treats rolled the car out of the driveway and kept waving until they couldn't see them.

Treats, with the mild exception of the shot of whiskey, was remarkably sober and clearheaded and took to the wheel with enthusiasm. Walsh volunteered to drive, but Treats was in too much of a gung-ho mood to step down. He needed something to do at all times, and navigating the Irish countryside gave him plenty of stimulation.

Pat never got tired of the landscape—the rolling hills and wide-open fields, the scenic mountains on the distant horizon, and what seemed like millions of shades of green. For once, Treats was not driving like a fucking maniac, so Pat felt like he could let his guard down and relax. He was in the back, and after about fifteen minutes, he lay down to take a little rest.

When he awoke, they were just pulling into the outskirts of Galway.

"Ahh, the beautiful Barna Road Moycullen area," Treats explained. "Kind of like American suburbia." Homes were grouped in subdivisions, and the city center was just a short drive away. Treats rolled to a stop in front of a modest white-stone house and laid on the horn.

A woman came bounding out and down the front stoop. She may have been in her mid- to late forties, with a mess of brown curly hair, and she was wearing jeans and a bulky sweater. She was grinning from ear to ear. Right behind her was a fresh-faced college-aged kid. Treats had barely stepped out of the car before Aunt Maggie hugged him and nearly knocked him off his feet, and Cousin Wally followed suit. Maggie welcomed them and ushered them inside. Before long, they were having sandwiches and tea, and she set in on asking about their trip. By merely a peek from Treats, Pat could tell they were about to conspire on a cleaned-up version. Somehow they would have to omit the joint in the bar, the high-speed chase through the countryside, and the flipped car. He could tell it was a struggle for Treats because even though it painted them in a bad light, it was already an epic story. Taking all the good stuff out was just painful.

"So how was Roundstone? Was there anything for you young lads to do out there?" asked Aunt Maggie.

"Oh, sure. We all had a pint down at the bar. But it was a sleepy place, not really made for making trouble," Treats said in pathetically sanitized misdirection.

"Really? I didn't even know Roundstone had a bar. I thought it was nothing but fishing boats, sheep, and pasture," mused Maggie.

"Yeah, lots of wide-open country, Auntie," replied Treats. "It was beautiful. We actually went out for a midnight drive."

Pat swallowed any kind of expression that might have been on his face. He was watching Wally's reaction and could make out that he suspected they weren't telling the whole story.

Aunt Maggie explained that Uncle Manus would be coming home late from work and that he would have to catch up later, at dinner.

"Wally, why don't you show the boys around town later tonight?" suggested Aunt Maggie. "I'm sure you know a few spots where you can stretch your legs and grab a drink."

DINNER WAS UNEVENTFUL, OUTSIDE OF THE FANTASTIC BEEF stew that was the main course. Uncle Manus was tired and happy to see the end of Friday. He made small talk with the boys and drank a beer with them before retiring to the TV room to smoke and turn his mind off for a while.

"Hope you don't mind, boys, but it's been a long week. I'm probably gonna watch the news and turn in early," he said. "But I'm sure Wally's game to show you the ins and outs of a Friday night in Galway."

"We're set, Da. Don't wait up for us," said Wally. Uncle Manus waved him off with a smile, already engrossed in the TV listings.

"What's the plan, guys?" asked Walsh once they were out of earshot.

"I figure we get dressed and hit the club. We can drop some E on the way over. That way, we'll start rolling shortly after we get there," said Wally.

"What's it like?" asked Pat.

"E? Oh, you're in for a treat, mate. Your first time is always the best. Brain chemistry or something," said Wally, seeming to delight in showing Pat the ropes. "It's like, you're happy all the time. It's easy to talk to people, and music is super intense. In a good way." That sounded outstanding to Pat. He was feeling pretty goddamn good already.

———

PAT HAD SHOWERED AND CHANGED AND WAS READY TO GO. AS he was giving one last review of himself in the mirror, he heard the phone ring. Moments later, Wally came into the guest room.

"It's for you, Pat. Says he's your uncle," said Wally.

Fuck. Was that Jimmy? How had Jimmy found him here?

"I'll take it in here, thanks," answered Pat. He picked up the phone and heard Jimmy's trademark, high-pitched raspy voice.

"How ya doin', kid? Any trouble so far? You got helicopters circling yet?" Jimmy joked.

"Nah, Jimmy. Just goin' out for the night. We just came in from Roundstone." Patrick spoke in a low voice so that no one would hear. Treats was downstairs, but Walsh could come out of the shower at any second.

"That's not what I heard," Jimmy replied.

Was Jimmy keeping close tabs on him? He breathed in and tried not to sound nervous. "Heard from who?" he asked.

"Relax. Treats's sister gave me some phone numbers to call for places you'd be staying. This was second on the list."

He kept forgetting that Jimmy knew everyone and probably wanted to know a little about where they were just in case they needed help. Hopefully, nobody had told him everything they had done so far.

"Everything's good. I got this. Just laying low, having a few drinks tonight. Nothing crazy." Which was the truth, mostly.

"That's good to hear, Patrick. Stay loose, and roll with it. You know what I'm sayin'?"

"Everything's going smooth. I'll call you as soon as I get to Dublin," said Pat.

"One more thing," Jimmy said. "Nate stopped by O'Riley's. He was talking with Papa Ray for a bit and was asking for you. I told him you were on vacation. I don't know if it means anything, but I thought you should know."

Pat didn't know what Nate needed to discuss with him, but imagined maybe he wanted to pump him for information concerning Tre.

"Thanks, Jimmy," responded Pat. "I did run into him on his way out of the gym, but I was in a hurry with the flight and all. I'll connect with him when I get back."

"All right, kid. Keep your head on straight."

"You got it. Take care, man."

As Pat hung up the phone, Walsh came in from the bathroom, freshly showered. They were just about ready to roll. There was a certain freedom in not knowing what would happen next and still being all right with that, a feeling he had not felt since high school.

Wally offered to drive. While they were still parked, he opened up his pack and gave them each a little yellow tablet prepackaged in a tiny ziplock bag.

"These are Mitsubishi. Excellent high, mate. I've had them before," said Wally. "Just be sure to drink water, though, okay?"

Pat nodded and studied the pill. Sure enough, it had a little engraving of an M on the face of it. This must have been how the ecstasy dealers put their individual brand on things. He popped the pill and washed it down with his can of beer.

As Wally drove them into the city, Pat noticed how so many of the streets had the same kind of design. All the buildings were right next to each other and began at the edge of the sidewalk. There were hardly any alleys, and the streets were narrow. It gave the city a sort of walled feeling, so it wasn't easy to see around corners and could get tight. Some of the streets were paved with modern asphalt, and others were the original brick. They were in a district loaded with restaurants and bars, and little strings of lights and small colorful flags were hung between the buildings, above and across the street. This gave everything a lively, festival-like feel.

"This area has the best club, the Dragonfly," said Wally as he slowed down to search for parking. Once he found a spot on a little side street, they parked and shared a joint.

As Pat walked to the club, the air was electric. Live music from different bars echoed through the streets, creating an uplifting backdrop of sound.

They turned the corner and saw a line of people waiting to get into the club. An entire row of dolled-up ladies exploded into Pat's field of vision. Holy shit. Practically all of them were tens. One had a top that looked like a purple butterfly, barely covering her, with a tight skirt that left little to the imagination. She seemed shiny, somehow. Pat felt a rush, like going up on a roller coaster but at high speed. He felt like his stomach had dropped out, yet pleasurably. A wave of happiness washed over him, and an overwhelming sense of well-being flowed through him. He was invulnerable, and the world was a candy store. Was this even real? His vision seemed to pulse a bit with the *thump* of the electronic drums coming from behind the club's closed doors.

"Wally," said Pat, "I think something is happening."

"Yeah, I feel it too. You're going up. You might get a bit dizzy at first. Just breathe with it and you'll feel fine," Wally said through a smile.

"Rub your hands through your hair," Treats said.

Pat ran his fingers through the hair on the side of his head. Whoa. It felt like a million little pinpricks of pleasure popping on his scalp. The sensation was incredible.

"Dude, stop playing with your hair. Everyone's gonna know you're high," whispered Walsh.

Pat nodded and put his hands down. He couldn't stop staring at the different girls as he walked by. Was it just the ecstasy, or were Irish lassies just this beautiful?

Wally led them to the bouncer in front, who was manning a little velvet rope. The bouncer greeted him with a smile and a handshake; obviously, these two knew each other. After some quick back and forth, the bouncer unchained the velvet rope and ushered them right in.

The club itself could have been any dance club in Boston. The layout was essentially the same—a large bar at one end, a vast dance floor, and a few booths and tables for bottle service. A VIP area upstairs glowed with soft light. Lights and lasers adorned the ceiling, emitting pink and red beams, and a DJ on a raised platform was spinning techno hits. The beats were jumping, and Pat loved the feeling of the bass vibration in his body. All of his senses felt dialed to eleven. A few people bopped on the dance floor, but the place wasn't at full throttle yet.

Treats muscled his way through the crowd to get to the bar, where the young male bartenders were slammed with orders and serving all the pretty women first. Pat didn't mind waiting; he could spend all night just staring at the ladies ordering drinks. Treats tried to hasten the ordering process by waving some bills around, a gesture that Pat knew most bartenders hated. It was the visual equivalent of snapping fingers. But it worked this time.

Treats finally got the bartender's attention and gave him a couple of twenties.

"Listen, mate, the cash is for you, but when we want a drink, don't make us wait," he yelled over the music. The bartender held his gaze for a moment, then nodded, clearly annoyed.

Pat tasted his beer, but it seemed more bitter than usual. He put it down and let himself feel the rhythm.

"Something wrong with the beer?" Treats asked.

"It just doesn't taste good to me on this stuff," answered Pat. It was hard to focus in here—so many attractive women.

"I know what you need. I'll get you a screwdriver. Trust me—OJ is amazing when you're rolling." Treats winked.

Treats approached the bar, and Pat watched him wave his hand, but the bartenders collectively ignored him. It was worse than the first time. "Jump Around" by House of Pain started to play loudly and crank up the entire crowd. After a few minutes, Treats seemingly gave up and lit a cigarette. He took a few dramatic drags of the cig and then flicked it straight at the bartender he had tipped.

Pat watched the half-smoked cigarette arc through the air and hit the bartender square in the face, crashing into his nose in a flurry of sparks and ash. The bartender batted at his face and searched for where the projectile had come from. Then, he locked eyes with a smiling Treats, toasting the bartender in the air with his pint of beer.

"I told you not to make us wait, mothafucka!" shouted Treats over the music.

Pat braced for impact; they had hardly been there forty-five minutes and they were all about to get kicked out.

The bartender's face moved from incredulous to filled with rage. He rang an old tip bell at the bar and pointed at Treats. Three bouncers came from nowhere and surrounded him. Then they forced him back out the front door and into the streets.

The three of them regrouped out front. Even though it was not happening to him, Pat was watching someone else's movie, and the production was highly entertaining. He took a deep breath of the night air. It was much better for them to be outside. They were in a courtyard-like area with tons of young people enjoying the spring evening. Plenty of opportunities to meet some girls. But he would have to let Treats go on his own for a while if he was going to have any chance. A euphoria started building again inside, and all he wanted to do was connect with someone.

"C'mon, let's go to another bar," implored Treats, lighting up another cigarette. He still acted pissed off; the E had clearly done nothing to temper his rage.

"You guys go ahead. I think I want to wander around outside for a while," Pat answered, fixated on a group of girls in their early twenties smoking on the corner.

"I think I'll keep an eye on Pat," said Wally. "First time . . . he might need some backup." Wally's eyes were transfixed on the same group of three girls that Pat was staring at.

"I'll go with Treats," said Walsh. "We'll just be around the corner. Find us at one of those bars."

Pat and Wally nodded and set their attention on chatting up the girls. They were from a town outside Galway, staying at a local hostel and questing for adventure.

It had only been a short while before Pat heard a tremendous racket from around the corner. First, he heard the unmistakable sound of glass shattering. Then a loud crash, followed by four or five more crashes, as if something big had knocked a bunch of things down.

Pat paused but didn't want to stop telling his story. He'd told the girls about the plane ride to Ireland and was working his way through the whole "Yanks that flew upside down" tale. He was just getting to the point where he flipped the car. It was super easy to talk and flirt while on E. Words just poured out.

Wally craned his neck to see if he could tell where the commotion was coming from. "I think it's coming from around the corner," he surmised.

Pat heard some shouting but shrugged it off and picked up where he left off, telling the wild tales to the girls. Then he saw Walsh appear from around the corner, running at full speed toward Pat. Oh no. What fresh shit had Treats stepped in now?

"It's Treats. He's in a fight!" Walsh yelled. "They're gonna rip him apart!"

Pat's gears shifted instantaneously, his body tensing for a split second and the muscle memory preparing him for a serious fight. Then he bolted around the corner, with Walsh and Wally close behind.

When he came around the corner, it didn't take a master detective to determine what'd happened. A bar's glass storefront had been shattered. A basketball-sized hole punctured the bottom, the cracks spiderwebbing out from there. Farther down the street, five motorcycles in a row were lying sideways and slightly on top of one another. In his mind's eye, Pat re-created the crime scene. Treats had sent something through the bar's storefront, kept walking, then kicked over one of the motorcycles, which hit the next, and they'd all fallen like dominoes. Those bikes were, at the very least, pretty scratched up.

Not far from the bikes was Treats in a fighting stance, dancing around and trying to avoid a five-on-one beating from a bunch of angry bikers. Pat wouldn't be surprised if they pulled a weapon.

Pat surmised this whole scene in only a split second. This was the kind of situation he'd been born for. Since age five, he'd been training, and the last four years in prison had enhanced his skills exponentially. Jimmy had molded him, and Choppa had sharpened him into a weapon. Pat had taken on guys nearly twice his size in the prison yard; a few bikers weren't going to scare him, although he would certainly have preferred to talk this out. Pat rushed into the group encircling Treats, putting his hands up in peace to stop the potential melee. Immediately, he felt a punch off the back of his head that almost dropped him to his knees. He turned, instinctively blasting one with a straight left and incapacitating the man who had popped him. These guys were pissed beyond the point of no return. He knew right away this fight was not ending peacefully. Wally and Walsh went in after him and laid a few punches into the guy who was already down. That guy wasn't going to get up for at least a few minutes. Neither Wally nor Walsh was nearly as good a fighter as Pat, but what they did have was solidarity.

Now it was four on four, although, really, it was more like Pat and Treats versus all the bikers. The ecstasy did nothing to slow Pat down. It only seemed to heighten his senses. With that and the adrenaline, he was an efficient machine. One guy swung wild. Pat effortlessly blocked and gave him such a formidable body blow that he hunched over and left the circle. Treats knocked the crap out of him as he was bent over, and that guy was on the floor. Now it was three.

Two of the guys rushed Pat, but Pat was fast. He'd had hardly anything to drink, and these guys were fighting four or five drinks deep. He danced around the punches, evading and only blocking when he had to. While one was swinging, he ducked and hit the guy behind him. As that guy's nose exploded into a broken mess, Walsh and Wally went in and took him down.

The other guy had his eyes set on Treats. To his credit, Treats got a couple of good punches in before taking a right hook to the face. Pat stepped in with a right hook and knocked the guy flat on his back.

That left the bikers' biggest and slowest, a bearded, tough-looking brute who was now outnumbered four to one.

"Let's even up these odds," said Pat, gesturing for the boys to step back. Treats made a "not bad" face and lifted his hands in the air, gesturing that he would stay out of it. Walsh and Wally did the same.

The big guy swung first and was miles away from touching Pat. Pat hit hard to his body with a right-left-right combo, then danced back. The big guy rushed to get closer. Since he had a longer reach, he thought he could get the advantage.

But the guy was untrained and slow. Even if he had eighty pounds on Pat, he would be no match for him. Pat distracted him with his left, faking like he would punch with that hand, and then unloaded with his right uppercut.

The big guy fell straight back, like a tree in the forest. Timber.

A crowd had gathered, and he could hear sirens coming around the corner. *Fuck*, thought Pat. The Garda was coming.

He melted back into the crowd. Wally gestured to come closer to him, and Pat happily obliged; best to pretend they didn't know Treats. Once the coast was clear of the Garda, they could all regroup. A few officers were already out of their cars and searching the crowd.

Treats and Walsh were slowly making their way toward them through the thick crowd in the street, but they were intercepted by the Garda and forced toward a paddy wagon. The back of the wagon was wide open. Pat could see Treats standing just outside and Walsh sitting inside.

He moved a little closer to see if he could tell what was going on. The Garda had started asking Treats questions. As he was answering, a pint glass flew from the crowd and hit him in the head, shattering on his temple—one of the angry bikers, no doubt. He yelped and started bleeding from the fresh cut and swore a blue streak. The cop ignored the incident and didn't even turn in the direction the glass had come from.

"*Fuck*. You didn't see that? What the fuck, man?" Treats asked, wiping the blood off the side of his head and rubbing his hands on his jeans.

The young Garda officer laughed as he was writing things in his report. "Hey, you probably deserved it," he said dryly.

Walsh was hot and losing his temper. Maybe the combination of the drugs and adrenaline was getting to him, but he started blurting out in anger.

"Unbelievable! We roll out the red carpet in Boston for you turkeys when you show up, and this is what you got for us?"

The young Garda officer glared at Walsh, locked eyes, and put his report and pen back in his pocket. Then he looked over at Treats.

"All right. Sorry, pal. Let's go. His mouth just got himself some company tonight," said the Garda, cuffing Treats and ushering him into the paddy wagon.

"Wait!" Treats begged.

But it was too late. The Garda shut the doors, walked back around front, and drove off. Pat just stood there, blinking. What the hell was he supposed to do? If he'd done anything, he might have ended up in the paddy wagon too. And the longer he stayed, the more chances that witnesses would recognize him. Then he would start to get questioned by the other Garda present. He turned to Wally, who was no longer next to him. He'd disappeared.

"Your mates are toast 'til morning," said a familiar voice.

Pat spun around. It was Rebecca, one of the two coeds he had been talking to before the whole situation went to shit. Jennifer stood beside her, not quite as tall but just as cute. And they still wanted to talk to him, even though he had blood all over his knuckles.

"I guess it's gonna be a cold sleep in the drunk tank tonight for them, huh?" Jennifer asked.

Pat nodded. The adrenaline and ecstasy had him feeling a particular kind of rush. He suddenly forgot about the bar and his friends' antics. All he could see was the two girls in front of him. Everything else was far away and dreamlike.

"Well, it feels like I'm in good hands, girls," Pat smiled, offering them each an arm.

"Oh, we better watch this one. He could charm the knickers off a nun!" Rebecca laughed.

A late night in beautiful Galway City

"C'mon, Boston boy. We'll get you cleaned up back at the hostel," Jennifer said, leading him down a side street. The mere sensation of their soft hands on his arms sent waves of pleasure through him. If just taking his arms felt this good, he couldn't imagine what would happen when more clothes started coming off.

Chapter 17

COMMUNITY

NATE ALREADY HAD SECOND THOUGHTS ABOUT REVEREND Gibbs's invitation to stop by at the Ella Baker Community House. The more he thought about the Ten Point Coalition, the less sure he was about it. He appreciated Gibbs trying to help, but Nate wasn't sure getting involved with some church organization was the right move—if that was what they were asking him to do.

Then again, he wasn't sure what the Coalition would have to say. The least he could do was hear them out. Gibbs had a way of moving people to action. Maybe, at the very least, he might see some possibilities that he hadn't seen before.

When he neared the bottom of the Community House stairs—the ones leading into the basement, where everyone was convening—he heard voices. A conversation was already in progress. He stopped to listen, trying to get an angle on what he was walking into. Only Papa Ray and Gibbs were supposed to be there, but you never knew.

"No way in hell I trust any of them, Papa—there is no breaking down this BPD code," declared Reverend Gibbs. "I need to gain this trust with my own two eyes before I let this blow up in our faces."

Nate was getting the gist. They wanted him to gather information of some kind. They were arguing about who they could confide in. That doubt meant things were on shaky ground and that risk was involved. Armed with that knowledge, Nate could better evaluate what he was walking into. It didn't exactly sound safe.

He entered the room, and the discussion stopped. Nate said nothing, only nodding toward Reverend Gibbs and Papa Ray. *Okay, I'm here,* thought Nate. *No need to be conspiratorial. Just lay it out.*

Gibbs stood up and offered Nate a chair at a round wooden table. The room itself was spacious and perfectly ordinary, the kind of basement you could set up ping-pong games or cafeteria tables for a pancake breakfast. Columns of stacked chairs lined the walls. It was both a rec center and a meeting hall, with not much effort to make it permanently one thing or the other.

Nate jumped right in.

"All right, Rev, I'm listening," said Nate after he sat down. "For starters, I don't need anyone watching after me out there. I can handle myself. No disrespect, Papa, but this stays between the three of us only, no way BPD can know. I like Sergeant Daly, but no way."

Both Papa Ray and Gibbs raised their eyebrows at Nate's announcement. Papa shook his head, not saying a word yet.

Gibbs took the lead. "Let me give you a little context before you make any decisions, Nate. See, Menino owes me for his Black community support and votes. And it doesn't stop there. He needs our community to help him end these terrible times that plague this city."

"We've had enough," added Papa Ray. "And by 'we,' I mean Blacks at large, who always seem to be on the losing end of decisions made by

Boston Police Department anti-gang violence unit searches
a car and pats down youth suspects in a Boston neighborhood

White community leaders. Menino knows how fed up we all are with his department. The corruption, Nate . . . These police officers routinely shake down the kids selling drugs, then rob them. The mishandling, the lies, the incompetence. My God, Nate. This list goes on and on. I don't have to tell you. Remember all the misjudgments and bad assumptions in the Charles Stuart case?"

Nate nodded in agreement. No one could forget the Charles Stuart case. He was that guy who had called the police and claimed a Black man had shot his pregnant wife. Stuart gave the police a physical description, and then all hell broke loose. The cops tore apart the neighborhoods, searching for anyone who loosely fit the bill. It was nothing less than a whole-scale invasion, terrorizing entire Black communities. They'd even busted into Tre and Slugs's place.

It turned out the whole story was a sham. Stuart had made it up. He'd shot his own wife and taken some of the life insurance money. His brother outed him, and rather than face judgment, Stuart jumped off the Tobin Bridge straight into the Mystic. But not before dozens of Black men were arrested and falsely accused. The police were too quick to believe the violent Black criminal story. They wanted it to be true. They exposed their racist predispositions, naked for everyone to see.

"Now we're dealing with this Mulligan case—that detective who was shot execution style," continued Gibbs. "They're trying to pin it on a Black boy out buying diapers."

"Never mind how they have handled the Tiffany Moore case," chimed in Papa Ray. "Remember? That young girl killed in the crossfire, sitting on the mailbox a few years back? Or how they're handling the killing of Jermaine Goffigan—the nine-year-old shot in the chest while counting his Halloween candy? They convicted an innocent Black man who served three years before they realized they made a mistake."

Reverend Gibbs punctuated everything Papa Ray said with a constant commentary of *mm-hmm*s and *yes, brother*s.

"They don't have a clue," concluded Gibbs. "They're just playing pin the murder on the Black man, any Black man, guilty or not!"

Reverend Gibbs folded his arms, satisfied he had convincingly made his point.

The Jury examines the crime scene where Darlene Tiffany Moore was killed as she sat atop the mailbox on Humbolt Avenue in Boston's Roxbury

Everything they'd said had struck a chord. He knew about all these cases; every Black man and woman in Boston did. Just as one outrage ended, another injustice began. The Goffigan situation was particularly painful. That kid could have been any of his younger cousins. A life snuffed out because of a senseless random bullet. And to make matters even worse, another young man's life was destroyed after he was falsely accused.

Nate took a pause and swallowed painfully. "I know the Goffigan family well, Reverend," he began, his words measured. "It's been very sad and frustrating to see."

Reverend Gibbs leaned in, zeroing in on him. "Nate, I have my contacts in the department. We've all confirmed it's not safe to collaborate."

Papa Ray shook his head and looked down. Nate could tell there was still some disagreement between the two men. Papa still seemed to want to partner with the police, but not Gibbs.

"I have a better plan," Gibbs proposed. "As I said last week, the mayor and I discussed the Ten Point Coalition and how we could possibly work with the BPD and how they can help in the cease-fire plan. I shut it down for now but left one door open for the future."

Boston Mayor Thomas M. Menino talks with residents on Magnolia Street
in the Roxbury neighborhood of Boston while touring areas of the
city recently impacted by gang violence

"What door would that be?" Nate asked.

"We discussed this rare opportunity regarding your involvement, as well as all the details around your family's gang history with the Norfolk Kings, that you've been gone for five years, but everyone knows you since you were a kid. And that now you're back. And that Tre has been killed . . . You're the perfect confidential source that can help us understand the beefs and the players. And how to reduce the bloodshed."

"What exactly do you want me to do?" asked Nate.

"Menino agreed to a plan where we run this through an FBI task force—Operation Eagle Eye. You'd be a CI working within that operation, which makes you documented on a safer and more highly secure level."

"What would I be focusing on?" Nate inquired.

"For now, their main focus is on getting information on the heroin and crack. Where it's coming from, where it's going, et cetera."

Nate leaned back, contemplating. What they were asking him to do was dangerous. He wasn't willing to do anything that might get his cousin or any of his family in trouble, but if the people who killed Tre were connected to the larger takeover of the drug supply in this city, he'd be willing to follow where the trail led.

"Well," Nate began, "it's better than the BPD. I'm not sure I trust the FBI around here either. But regardless, I'm going to do it. I have to. I'm meeting Slugs tonight."

Regardless, Nate thought, *Slugs knows I'm standing with the Kings on this!*

Papa Ray and Reverend Gibbs shook Nate's hand to make it official. They would go over details and how Nate would report to them later.

For now, Papa Ray seemed to be relieved by the official sanction of Menino and the FBI running the operation, and having the FBI involved was a good compromise over the BPD. Still, those FBI bastards were probably corrupt too. One needed only to check recent headlines to see how they'd been in cahoots with Whitey Bulger for years.

But that was then, and this is now, conceded Nate. He could only hope that whomever he'd be dealing with in the FBI would have his heart in the right place.

Reverend Gibbs grabbed his coat and put his arm around Nate.

"Now that we figured that out," Gibbs said, "I would feel much better if we can keep this between us. Underground. We just need to keep you alive, son."

Nate stood up, a new determination settling in. He felt all the awfulness—the death, the corruption, the gangs—was focusing him like never before. He was on a mission.

"You're a different man now," said Papa Ray. "A man that's reached a point where he'll do anything it takes to save his community, no matter how the chips are stacked against him. You have no choice now; you're doing God's will."

Nate took in all the reverend was saying, silently agreeing.

"All right, guys. I'll see you next week," he said and headed up the staircase.

Chapter 18

THE HOSTEL

THE SULTRY PLEASURES OF THE NIGHT STRETCHED INTO THE morning. One of the girls had wasted no time stripping him down to nothing, and Patrick felt the energy and love in the air. Maybe it was the fact that he was a charming Irish boy from Boston just visiting that had Rebecca feeling so eccentric. The drug made it impossible to either sleep or climax, but it didn't matter. The skin-on-skin delight of two women writhing on him was feast enough for the senses. He didn't know when or how he would have this opportunity again; he'd never felt so free in his entire life!

By eleven a.m., the drug's effects started to wear off, and with the oncoming headache, the reality of the situation was beginning to dawn on him. He had to get his things, figure out where he was, and try to figure out how to get Treats and Walsh out of the clink or the drunk tank or wherever the hell the Garda was holding them. The headache was intensifying, his mouth had a cottony taste, and he was a little sore all over.

Rebecca and Jennifer were naked and sound asleep, exhausted by the acrobatics of the evening. Pat began the treasure hunt of finding where his clothes had landed. His underwear? On the lampshade. Jeans? In the bathroom. Shirt? Under two sets of thong panties on the floor, underneath the bed.

After collecting his things, Pat took one last look at the girls. Somehow, all three of them had shared the bottom bunk of a stacked pair of twin beds. There was another bunk bed on the opposite wall. Had anyone else been there last night? Pat couldn't recall. No one else was here right now, but he saw a duffel bag at the end of the bed.

Pat stumbled out of the hostel into the brightness of the streets of Galway, pausing to observe his surroundings. Where was the bar from here? He tried to get his bearings, but nothing looked at all familiar.

After orienting himself, Pat was able to find his way back to the car by retracing his steps with Rebecca and Jennifer all the way back to the corner where Treats had unleashed himself on the motorcycles. He was sure of the spot, partly because he could still see bits of broken glass and metal on the cobblestone street. More telling, he could see a fresh sheet of plywood over the storefront window.

From there, all he had to do was remember the path to where they had parked near The Dragonfly. Pat felt annoyed by the chore, with negative emotions rising along with his headache. The hangover was far more piercing than what he generally experienced with whiskey.

Eventually, he found the car unmolested, parked where they had left it. Wally, knowing nothing of his car flipping escapade, had given him the rental car keys last night, just in case they got separated from Treats.

Pat tried his hand at driving on the left side again, this time unburdened by drunkenness and windy country roads. He couldn't remember the exact route back, but he had a pretty good sense of direction once he started seeing familiar landmarks. Eventually, he found his way back to Aunt Maggie and Uncle Manus's place.

Expecting to see a worried and frazzled Aunt Maggie, she instead greeted him warmly at the door, seemingly feeling fine and unperturbed.

"Morning, Maggie!" Pat said cheerfully. "You haven't seen Wally or Thomas or Walsh, have you?"

Maggie tossed back her head and laughed.

"Poor dear, you must be worried sick. Manus and Wally went to negotiate with the Garda. Left about an hour ago, will probably be home soon," she explained. "Manus is good friends with some of the boys at the station. He'll likely get them out with a warning."

Pat's shoulders relaxed. Once again, they had evaded the law—sort of.

"But how'd Wally get home? I had the car keys," Pat asked.

"He ran all the way home! Must have been at least seven miles. But he didn't run through the roads; he cut across the fields!" Aunt Maggie giggled. "Poor lad was exhausted!"

Pat chuckled at this. What a maniac! He wondered why Wally had disappeared on him; that still didn't make sense. Maybe he was afraid the Garda would pick him up too?

Maggie turned on the burner for the kettle. "Can I get you a cuppa, lad?" she asked, and he nodded in the affirmative. Water, in any form, sounded great right now.

"You lads sure know how to flatten the walls when you travel." Aunt Maggie snickered.

Chapter 19

BLUE HILL AVENUE DINER

NATE WATCHED FROM HIS CAR, PARKED ACROSS THE STREET from the old diner on Blue Hill Avenue. Papa Ray and Reverend Gibbs sat at the booth in the corner. Nate imagined the coffee rings adorning the laminate surface between them and the scattered remnants of sugar packets and single-serving creamers. In their company, two cops hunched over the table, deep in conversation for at least the last forty-five minutes.

Nate knew this entire conversation was about him. Papa Ray had let him know that this was the decisive moment to keep Nate's CI operation from the BPD. He watched Gibbs act as the mediator of the group. Gibbs was relaxed, addressing everyone as a group, gesturing in the way Nate had come to know politicians did. Papa Ray had deep furrows on his forehead, nodding vigorously at parts of the conversation and clearly holding back during other parts. He sat back with folded arms, and Nate could see he was trying to stay neutral, despite his strong opinions.

The cops didn't seem to be on the same page. Both were young and tall, but the similarities ended there. Sergeant Daly was White and Irish, clean-shaven, with a clenched jaw and tense lips. The high and tight crew cut screamed military precision and old Boston heritage. The other cop, Officer Miller, was Black and a little thicker, with a body like a linebacker. He nodded occasionally and mostly listened.

Abruptly, Daly pounded the table and threw up his hands in dramatic fashion as if to announce he was done. Stuck toward the window, Officer Miller had to awkwardly shuffle out of his seat to let him out. This action was all too much; Nate jumped out of his car with his hat down low and walked into the café, then right up to the register. He sat down at the counter and grabbed a coffee. His back facing them, he was now within earshot of this conversation—just another patron sipping his coffee.

"You don't understand police work!" barked Daly, grabbing his hat on the way out. "None of you do. You wanna play pretend and get yourselves killed. You're not going to do it with my permission."

"They're just trying to help, Daly," responded Miller with his palms up. "Calm down and hear them out. I think they may be onto something."

"I've heard enough," proclaimed Daly. He turned his back and started walking out, his hat under his arm. Then he stopped and turned around. He opened his mouth as if he had something to say, then appeared to shift gears.

"Thanks for the coffee," he said flatly. Then he turned back around and exited the diner.

Miller gazed apologetically at Gibbs and Papa Ray.

"Listen. It's a tough proposition. I appreciate where you guys are coming from, but it's going to take some doing. A lot of these guys are protective of their territory. You know what I'm saying, Rev?"

"It might take some time. It's not easy for any of us," Gibbs conceded.

Miller reached his hand out and shook Reverend Gibbs's and Papa Ray's hands. Then he turned to leave.

As soon as he was sure Miller was gone, Gibbs let out a deep sigh.

"Well, hell. That could have gone better," Papa Ray said, his arms still folded.

"I don't trust them," said Gibbs, dropping the diplomatic pretense. "I mean, I definitely don't trust Daly. Why should I trust the head of the gang unit? It seems like every other week I'm consoling a new Black family whose kid is harassed by a White cop. Or worse—shot."

"I've known him for a decade, Rev," countered Papa Ray. "He's been in the gang unit forever, and he was a fighter. I helped train him, for goodness sake."

Gibbs leaned over the table intently. "Papa, I told you, only one person can know who our CI is." It was a dangerous job, especially if the CI got caught in the wrong place at the wrong time by either cop or criminal. Confidential informants had to skate two worlds on a razor's edge. Most of them weren't even doing it voluntarily; the cops usually had something on them, and informing was a way to stay out of trouble. Nate knew that some of the police force trained at O'Riley's and that over time, Papa Ray had heard just about everything. Nate had heard he had even been approached to be a CI himself, back in the day, but had emphatically refused. He would have been fantastic given his connections, but he had no clear motivation to do so. As he told so many young fighters—including Nate—back in the day, "Just because you could doesn't mean you should."

"This is now an FBI task force CI," continued Gibbs. "It deepens our security. Now the BPD will know there's a CI out there, but he'll remain concealed."

"Why do they trust you?" asked Papa Ray. "This is unusual, even for you. From gang member to reverend to FBI liaison? How in the hell is this even working?"

"The FBI and Menino have bought into this CI operation on my terms because of my history with Menino. He knows that it only works if his identity remains concealed indefinitely. I threatened that the Ten Point would only begin a collaboration with the city if this one goes smoothly."

Papa Ray was putting all the pieces together. Mayor Menino was a skilled politician and now also the official ambassador to the Holy See. In a staunch Roman Catholic town, this gave him a lot of credit among the white Irish, even though Menino was Italian by heritage.

Reverend Gibbs boasted, "My close ties with Menino and being one of the rapidly rising Ten Point Coalition figures has given me a lot of leverage with the city."

"But to bring in Nate as a CI," protested Papa Ray.

"Look, the FBI's already got an operation underway on the heroin and crack distribution," answered Gibbs. "Nate's perfectly positioned, and Lord help me, he's the right man for this work. It's as if it's God's plan."

"What do you mean?"

"Think about it. The timeliness of Nate's return to the city, his very close known affiliations with his cousins and aunt to the Norfolk Kings, and then to top it off, Tre, his cousin, was one of the top dogs of the Kings. And he gets taken out in prison over control of distribution! It's too real not to take advantage of and save lives out here. The truth of the matter is that Nate will be poking his nose around town with or without us."

"I understand, Rev. I do. I do," replied Papa Ray. "But we can't risk a young brother like Nate without having a few people looking out for him. He can get popped any second in the blink of an eye. He has blurred vision, man. His best friend and cousin were just killed. He's not ready for this . . . has his whole life in front of him, law school. Oh, Rev, you need drop that ego, brother!"

Gibbs reached out his hands and grabbed Papa Ray's in solidarity and compassion. Nate had seen this expression at too many funerals, the faces of parents fearing for their Black children all over the city. And even though Papa Ray was no blood relation, he was pleading on Nate's behalf as if he were his own. It made Nate feel even more determined to get involved.

"Okay, Papa," answered Gibbs firmly. "I'll let you know when I decide who the contact will be. You've got to trust Nate's instincts. He's been tearin' up these streets since he was a little boy. He knows his hood inside and out . . . and always found a way to keep himself out of trouble and alive! I'm not about to compromise his life and all the information he can provide because I told the untrustworthy BPD—no way."

"All right, Rev," conceded Papa Ray. "Remember now, Nate agreed on the condition that I am involved. You heard him. He didn't trust some of the group of clergy involved in the Ten Point Coalition. He trusts you, but he thinks this is a money grab by the churches and some of the crooked men that run them. Don't prove him right." Papa Ray leaned back and released Gibbs's hands. "I need to know as soon as we have someone from BDP checking in on Nate's survival. Those two guys I trust."

"You have my word, Papa," promised Gibbs. "All right. Let's go. We have to reach out to Nate. We can meet at the Community House basement and let him in on the details."

Papa Ray nodded and laid a cash tip on the table. With Nate's life in the balance, it would be a hell of a thing to be wrong, and Nate could see the worry on Ray's face. Papa and Gibbs walked right behind Nate, without a clue. This is exactly what Nate wanted, to be in control of his fate, knowing all sides of this deal going down.

Chapter 20

RECEPTION

THEY PULLED UP SLOWLY INTO THE ROUNDABOUT IN FRONT of the reception hall. Despite Treats having forbidden Pat from driving ever again while on this trip, he was the only logical choice. Pat had consumed only a few shots and had only taken a couple of hits off the weed and hash joints, which, in this group, made him the only responsible option. Walsh and Treats had ingested complex layers of coke and ecstasy and multiple shots of alcohol on top of that. Once they stepped out of the car, Pat wasn't even sure whether Treats and Walsh would stay tethered to the ground or shoot off into orbit.

They had fully intended to go to the actual ceremony. Pat, Treats, and Walsh stayed behind at the house while Manus, Aunt Maggie, and Wally shuttled other relatives to the church. The Boston boys showered and dressed and were ready far sooner than expected—which meant they had plenty of time to dive back into the bag of drugs.

"We can't show up this fucked up. We can't have the Darkness walk into the church," Treats had said, back at the house, straight-faced, rolling on ecstasy.

Pat had snickered. "The Darkness. Like we're all going to burst into flames."

"I wouldn't wish me showing up at my own wedding ceremony, never mind someone else's," Treats had joked.

"That gives me an idea," Pat had said. "Maybe if we show up late to the reception, everyone'll be too fucked up to notice."

It was a good compromise, and they'd gone with it.

Now, just as he'd suspected, he'd have to herd these cats into their supposed assigned seats at the tables in the reception hall. How well this was going to go would depend on Treats not being there at all, so Pat was just going to settle for completing their reception visit with no violence. Public embarrassment and dirty looks were a foregone conclusion at this point.

They'd already missed the formal dinner, but there were still plenty of small-plate snacks at the buffet table. The band had started up, and many of the guests were dancing already, although they hadn't quite reached full tilt. The bride and groom were visiting different tables.

Pat scanned for their assigned table, continually checking behind him to make sure Walsh and Treats were close by. They struggled with all the stimuli, wide-eyed, with giant pupils and permanent grins stretched across their sweating faces. Both were sweating profusely. One look at these guys and anyone would know they were high out of their gourds.

Once Pat found the table, he showed Walsh and Treats their chairs. They were seated at a table with part of the groom's family. The seated middle-aged couple looked like they were good people having a wholesome time. Pat already felt sorry for what he knew the boys were about to inflict upon them.

"Hi!" Treats announced while getting into his chair. "I'm the Prince of Dorchester."

The couple wore a mild look of surprise on their faces, like they were waiting for more information.

"Oh, don't worry about a thing. Nothing to worry about at all," Treats continued. "But as prince, I must warn you in advance: I have gonorrhea of the mouth."

Walsh sized up Treats with a stupid stare and started giggling. Pat wasn't even sure they had heard him correctly. It was hard to understand Treats under normal circumstances, and right now, under the influence, his mouth sounded like it was full of marbles. The old couple had their jaws frozen open, their surprise hanging in the air for a moment before they burst into laughter.

"What did you say, lad?" asked the husband with a bemused smile on his face.

"I'm sorry. You don't have to listen to him. I'm Pat, this is Walsh, and our friend with the mouth problem is our shy friend Thomas," said Pat, using his friend's given name and trying to put a fresh coat of politeness over the weird start of the conversation. "He just means that he blurts things out sometimes. We're kind of used to it."

"Yeah, maybe you guys can help me come out of my shell," said Treats, peering in the wife's direction and giving her a wink. Luckily, the lady had a sense of humor and giggled.

"Where can we get booze around here? You guys want any booze?" Treats asked the couple. They pointed to their half-full wine glasses and shook their heads. "No? How about some party favors?" he asked.

Pat was already hunting for a place that he could dig a hole and die in. The couple giggled again uncomfortably and shook their heads again. Treats shot up from his chair and bounded across the dance floor to the bar.

"I'll get the shots!" Treats shouted over his shoulder, loud enough that half the dance floor could hear him. Pat could hear a few of the older guests gasping. Walsh laughed helplessly.

And so the conversation went for quite some time. After Treats returned with a round of shots for everybody—that he insisted the couple drink— he personally demonstrated what "gonorrhea of the mouth" sounded like. He would have everyone laughing for the first three sentences, and then the fourth and the fifth would be downright jaw dropping. It became a cycle—shock, laughs, then awe. Every time the couple tried to participate, Treats interrupted with a conversational grenade.

The husband finally dared to disrupt Treats's stream-of-consciousness rant to introduce themselves. "We've all heard about the Yanks that flew upside down in Roundstone," he said, smirking.

"Hey!" Walsh shouted. "We're famous!"

"We even know some of your friends from back home. I'm Mickey, and this is Lara. We're family of the Concannons from Hyde Park," said Mickey.

Hyde Park was a neighborhood in Boston, just a touch southwest from Dorchester. The Concannons were friends with Treats's family. When Treats would have a party, inevitably, some of the Concannon boys would show up. Both Pat and Walsh had hung out with them on and off over the years, and they'd all been nearly as wild as Treats. Maybe that's why the couple hadn't run away screaming yet. They were familiar with this particular brand of crazy.

Pat leaned over to Walsh and whispered, "This Irish world is getting smaller by the minute, but if they know the Concannons, I feel better already!"

After a few minutes, Mickey and Lara excused themselves to socialize with some of the other wedding guests. Walsh was so high he was content just staring off into the dance floor. Treats and Patrick scanned the crowd to see which girls were single and old enough to fraternize with.

Events became more of a blur as the night went on. Pat remembered dancing with a few of the girls and ordering a few more drinks. He didn't ordinarily drink champagne, but it was actually pretty good. Treats disappeared on and off, no doubt sneaking off to recruit and corrupt some of the guests so he wouldn't have to do drugs alone. Walsh had wandered off somewhere, but Pat was too busy talking up a cute redhead at the bar to be worried about it.

At one point, Pat ran into Aunt Kay, who'd had just enough champagne to be happy to see him. She did, however, deliver a warning, albeit in a lighthearted tone.

"All the folks from Roundstone have made it clear you boys are supposed to behave yourselves and not embarrass the family," she lectured with a severe face. She held her expression still, locking eyes with Pat. Then she softened and laughed. "So I was relieved you chose not to show up to the ceremony!"

She slapped Pat's back, and they both shared a laugh. If only Aunt Kay knew what they had been up to since then, and that they still had the whole city of Dublin to tear up tomorrow.

Still, he was worried about Jimmy and Choppa. If Jimmy knew how to contact them at Aunt Maggie's, chances were he might know more of what they'd been up to. Pat was set to check in with him again tomorrow morning, so he was hoping for the best.

Which reminded him: poor Maggie must have been caught up with their now legendary stay in Roundstone. But so far, she'd said nothing.

After a few more glasses of champagne, Pat found a couch in a lounge area to relax. He was just going to sit down, but all the champagne was enough to make him drowsy. He leaned his head back and let his eyes close for a few minutes.

He wasn't sure how long he was out before he was awakened by someone shaking him. Opening his eyes revealed it was Treats.

"Have you seen Walshy?" Treats slurred. "I've been looking for about fifteen minutes."

Pat was surprised Treats could still speak English. "I'll help you find him," he said.

They patrolled the place, checking the bathrooms first to see if he'd just passed out. He wasn't in the stalls. Maybe one of the girls had taken him home? It was possible he wouldn't have thought to say goodbye.

"Maybe he's just having a smoke outside," suggested Treats.

They exited the reception hall's front door into the roundabout lined with parked cars. It was dark outside, which meant he must have been asleep for at least an hour. A few lawn chairs were scattered haphazardly, and someone was staggering right in the middle of clutter. Well, it *was* a wedding, after all. They weren't the only ones getting fucked up.

Walking closer, they could see it was Walsh, ranting to himself in complete gibberish. *Well, that explains the chairs*, thought Pat. Walsh picked up another garden chair and hurled it toward the cars in the roundabout. It turned end over end before colliding with a parked car. Then, a light on top of the car flashed on.

"That's the Garda," Pat said dryly, rubbing his forehead with his fingers. They'd been doing great, no big trouble so far. Why did Walsh have to throw a chair at the only police car parked in the roundabout?

Treats giggled and seemed delighted someone else was getting in trouble instead of him. Nonetheless, Pat thought, they were going to have to try and save him.

They watched the Garda officer step out of the car and slowly approach Walsh.

"You make sure Walsh is okay. I'll talk to the Garda," said Treats.

Great, thought Pat. *Treats has verbally horrified every innocent human that he has come in contact with all night and feels he is the one to diffuse this situation.*

They both walked toward the officer with their hands open and up, showing they weren't armed and not aggressive. So far, Pat's impression of the Garda was they were not as quick to violence as American cops. Still, he didn't want to experience anything that would change that impression.

"Evenin', Officer. So sorry about your car. We've been celebrating for the wedding, and this little guy got away from us. Looks like a little too much champagne, eh?"

To his credit, this seemed to disarm the Garda, and his face softened. He shined a light on Walsh's face. "He okay?" he asked.

"Sorry, Officer," said Walsh, weaving and staggering just trying to stand still.

"I'm sure he meant to keep the chair throwing confined to the grass," explained Treats.

Pat stepped forward to give Walsh a hand and a shoulder and helped him sit down on one of the few remaining garden chairs. "Calm down," he whispered. "We'll handle this. You don't want to spend another night in the tank, do ya?"

Walsh shook his head. "Fuck no," he said, followed by completely garbled words. Pat was sure that if he just left him in the chair for five minutes, he'd forget whatever the hell he was angry about and fall fast asleep.

Pat turned his attention back to Treats, midway through his conversation with the Garda.

"Yeah, we came in from Boston last week. I've got family here from Boston, Roundstone, Galway, and Clifden. I regretfully brought my angry friend here along with me. I mean, he's a Yank. What are you gonna do?"

Treats casting Walsh as the chief troublemaker was hysterical. But his approach seemed to be working. After a few minutes, the officer bid them good night and headed back to his car. He pulled out of the roundabout and drove off.

Treats flashed his trademark grin. "No way in hell was I spending another night in an Irish jail," he said, outstretching his hand to help

Walsh up. Pat and Treats got on either side of him and helped him walk back to the reception. The bar was already closed, and now was as good a time as any to say their goodbyes, before they got in any more trouble and while Walsh could still walk. Tomorrow they would start for Dublin, where the real mission could begin.

Chapter 21

REUNION

IT WAS A FEW HOURS PAST DUSK IN BOSTON, THAT TIME OF night where the casual happy hour crowd was about to head home, while the serious drinkers were just getting started.

Nate walked briskly through the streets he knew so well, a habit he'd had since a kid. It was hard to get in any trouble if you always kept moving. In his hood especially, that was tragically true.

He crossed the street over to a little bar called King Tut's, tucked near Washington Street and Blue Hill Avenue. Walking into the dark cave of an establishment, Nate pushed through a few clouds of smoke and grabbed a creaky wooden stool at the old bar. There weren't many familiar faces. It'd been at least four years since he'd come here last. A few regulars hunched over their drinks, barely registering that Nate had come in.

The bartender, at least, looked familiar. Nate couldn't remember his name, but he recognized him from back in the day. He was an old-timer, a hardened Black man well into his middle age. In high school, Nate suspected that the bartender knew his ID was fake but looked the other way. He had never been much of a drinker anyway. Most of the time, he was meeting up with his cousins, who inevitably got into way more trouble than he ever did.

The bartender turned in his direction, his one scraggly eyebrow going up as if to ask, *You ordering something or what?*

"How about a Johnny Walker, straight up?" Nate asked.

The bartender reached for the bottle. "One of them days, hey?"

Nate nodded. He couldn't help but like the guy.

"Haven't I seen you around here?" the bartender asked.

A few regulars glanced in Nate's direction to see if they could place him but looked away. If they had known Nate from back in the day, they had since forgotten him.

"Oh, it's been a minute," Nate began. "But yeah, I've been around here my whole life. I'm just waiting for my cousin to join me."

"Yeah, you look kinda familiar. But I mind my own business, all right."

The bartender set Nate's drink in front of him and moved to the next customer. Nate appreciated that he didn't pry. He wasn't really in the mood to explain himself to strangers.

Nate could hear the massive front door swing open. He turned toward it and smiled in recognition. A heavyset and bald Black man in his late twenties or early thirties approached, supporting himself with a cane and sporting a Sacramento Kings hat. Nate would have recognized him anywhere; this was his beast of a cousin, Alvin, known everywhere else simply as Slugs. He took his time, scanning the bar and looking everyone in the eye. It was an intimidating gaze, one that could easily be perceived as a threat. When he stared in Nate's direction, he stopped. Then his expression softened and his eyes lit up.

"Yo, yo!" he shouted in Nate's direction. A few regulars appeared to brace themselves for impact, perhaps preparing for a quick exit.

Nate rose from his chair to meet Slugs, taking a good look at him as he approached. They immediately embraced in a powerful bear hug, patting each other's backs and gripping tight. They had been running around in these streets since they could walk.

The bar crowd visibly relaxed. "Yo, Sonny!" Slugs shouted at the bartender. "Get a round of drinks for everyone! I need to toast with my boy Nate over here!"

Like a ritual he'd performed countless times, the bartender wordlessly lined up a row of shot glasses and poured twelve shots of whiskey. Slugs grabbed two of the glasses and gave one to Nate. As he raised his glass, about five more young Black men crowded the bar, all wearing Kings jerseys and hats.

"If you don't know," announced Slugs to the bar, "now you know. One of the OG of the Kings, my brother Tre, was taken out a few nights ago up at Suffolk. Of course they called it a suicide, but that's just the typical bullshit up there, y'all. Tre, rest in peace, my brother. We got you down here!"

Slugs looked around, making eye contact with everyone, and then downed his shot in one gulp. Nate followed his lead, and Slugs reached over and grabbed him by the head, putting him in a playful headlock.

"I lost my older brother, and now my younger brother shows up out of nowhere," Slugs said when he'd released him. "Much love, cuz. Much love. Now let's get down over here. Let's get into it." Slugs showed Nate to a small table and sat down to start the drinks flowing. Their conversation overlapped for the first few rounds as they talked over each other, laughing and crying while reminiscing about the years past.

After they'd broken the ice and conversation slowed down, Nate lowered his voice and leaned closer in, not wanting what he said next to be overheard by those around him.

"So . . ." Nate began. "So what the fuck are you hearing out there? I was up at the prison and couldn't get a straight story of how this shit went down."

Slugs shook his head. "No way he killed himself, man," he asserted. "Tre was never going out like that—no matter how many years they had on him."

"There's so much shit going on out here in this city, man," Nate replied. "I thought it couldn't get any worse, and bam! And you—I thought you were laying low and out of this shit."

Slugs folded his arms on the table. "Listen, Nate. Norfolk Kings lay pretty low, but there are a few allies and a few rivals that need to be dealt with. When there's money to be made, I occasionally get involved in making connections or whatever. Tre and I had a way of communicating out here, which certainly helped me supplement. That's all it was! But right now, we don't know who'd have had the balls to execute this. But it makes sense, Nate. Because it puts a major dent in the Kings' supply source, now that Tre's gone."

"So now what?" he asked, unsure of where this was leading.

"We'll find out something soon enough," Slugs answered. "In the meantime, I need to help reestablish Tre's connection—he was coordinating the shipments coming in from Miami. Without a source, these guys will fall apart real fast, and that's bad for everybody. And about Tre," Slugs added, "everyone knows to keep their ear out on anything so we can put two and two together and figure who took him out. Then it's my turn. For real."

He could tell that Slugs wasn't kidding on that front. If he ever did find out who'd done it, Nate suspected not even the devil himself would be able to stop him from enacting his revenge.

Slugs didn't scare easily. He had been given his nickname by Tre when they were teenagers, even though Tre was always the real triggerman on most of the shootings. But it was Slugs who was still perceived as the real heavy. He was always around the deal, intimidating the whole room with his size. The joke went that it would take multiple rounds of slugs to stop him. The name had stuck.

Nate thought that Slugs had gone completely straight after he'd been shot five years ago, over on Dot Avenue in a drug deal gone wrong. Some fool was always trying to prove something. Slugs should have died for all the blood he lost—and for a while, he was in a wheelchair. But he was a fighter, and with enough rehab, he worked up the strength to walk again, with just a limp as a permanent reminder. But not even that experience would sever Slugs's connection with the Kings. Once a Norfolk King, always a King.

Slugs returned to the bar to get another round, leaving Nate to ponder his thoughts. He couldn't believe he'd only been back in Boston a short time and was already profoundly involved. It felt surreal yet not surprising, and overwhelming all at the same time. One thing for sure: he felt he had a huge opportunity to stop some bloodshed—maybe even protect the Kings down the line. Of course, there was no way he could tell Slugs he was a CI. The best he could do was protect him if shit went down.

After a few more drinks, Slugs accompanied Nate out the front door. A few guys followed them, a sort of informal entourage of some of the Kings who looked after Slugs. The cold air bit them hard on the way out, and everybody covered their mouths with their hands. They all gathered on the corner to say their goodbyes. After they parted ways, Slugs opened up his black Ford Explorer parked on the street and gestured for Nate to get in.

Slugs started the car to warm up the engine and get the heat going. After a few moments, he pulled away from the curb to drive Nate home. As he did so, he reached under his seat.

"What you got there?" Nate asked, curious.

Slugs opened his hand to reveal a shiny chrome .38 revolver. He placed it on Nate's thigh. Nate stared at it, unsure, not wanting to touch it just yet. He'd seen his cousins packing all types of guns growing up. Slugs maintained eye contact and nodded as if to say, *It's yours. Take it.*

Nate couldn't say he hadn't known this was coming. He was in pretty deep now, at multiple levels. He needed to protect himself out here. It would be suicide if he didn't. He wondered what the FBI would say or the reverend . . . or Papa Ray. They'd never clearly covered this question, but they expected him to stay alive by any means necessary. How could he not be armed? They were asking him to swim in a sea full of sharks.

"Listen," said Slugs calmly. "This is clean, fresh out of the box. Tre always kept a stash of guns for moments like this. Keep it close to you. You never know, and can't be caught empty-handed if you're around here, cuz. You're blood, and I just can't have you taken out too, all right?"

Nate nodded. Slugs was right. This was his way of protecting him.

"You feel me," Slugs continued. "I know this ain't your thing, but even if you have to fire a warning shot in the air just to back some mothafuckas off, it's better than burying you too. But like Tre always says, no shells with the revolver."

Nate listened intently, turning the gun over in his hands to examine it.

"Look, I could have any one of those corner boys riding with me, but I know you're as fired up as me on this. Besides, you're one of the smartest niggas I know. We need each other to keep each other alive, bro. I love you like a brother, and you're the only one left I got."

Nate took the gun and slipped it in his pocket, just like he'd seen Tre and Slugs do back in the day. He had seen his cousins packing heat since he was ten years old. Even though Nate was never officially a Norfolk King, he was family, a permanent honorary member by default. Even so, he never imagined he'd be riding along with the Kings as an adult.

"Slugs," Nate said, breaking his silence, "we got this. I'll let you know if we need more than eight rounds."

Nate knew that most of the people on the street would be talking. They'd be saying that Slugs is out there poking around with his cousin who's back in town. His original plans were to lie low—but this was one appearance that would get real traction on his mission. He could track where the massive amounts of heroin were coming in, start to uncover who had killed Tre, and protect the interests of Slugs and the Kings all at the same time.

Lots of sides to keep track of, thought Nate. *This is a step up that requires caution at every moment.*

Chapter 22

EAST DUBLIN

AS USUAL, NONE OF THEM WERE READY BRIGHT AND EARLY for the road trip to Dublin. Eight hours wasn't quite enough to sleep off the previous day's bender. Getting up around nine in the morning had seemed reasonable at the time but felt less so when the first alarm came blaring at Pat. By the time they were ready to go, it was already eleven.

At breakfast, Pat made an excuse that he wanted to straighten up the guest room before he left. This would buy him enough time to make another secret check-in call to Jimmy back in Boston.

After he dialed, Jimmy picked up right away, even though it was five in the morning back home.

"Patrick, how are ya? It's nice to hear your voice, kid," Jimmy said. He sounded wide awake.

"I'm pretty good, Jimmy. We're packing up the car and about to drive to Dublin," Pat replied, not wanting to elaborate too much.

"That's good. That's good. Listen. You sure everything is under control? You got this?"

"No problems, man. We had a great time at the wedding and no major incidents," Pat replied. Relatively speaking, the statement "no major incidents" was correct. No one was injured or in jail. Yet.

"I stopped in at Eire Pub yesterday and heard some stories about a few guys tearing up Ireland," Jimmy said.

Pat winced, wondering if he had underestimated the power of rumors getting around. He knew the power of a good big-fish story.

"You know how people talk, Jimmy. They embellish a little to make a better story," Pat offered. But he knew this was flimsy. You couldn't fool a guy like Jimmy, someone who had seen pretty much everything. His bullshit detector was finely honed at this point.

"This is the opposite of what we discussed," said Jimmy. "We said fly under the radar and don't fuck this up. If anyone else hears these shit stories, it may cause a problem."

"Jimmy—"

"I'm not kidding. If I hear one more thing slightly out of order, it's mission aborted: no payment, no job—nothin'. Way too much planning has gone into this. Don't be stupid now. I'm trying to give you a fresh start here! Understand?"

"Yes. I understand," Pat offered. "Listen. We were just having a good time and didn't mean to get out of hand. We'll blend in much more in Dublin. I don't want to do anything to jeopardize what you set up here."

"Good. I'll hold you to that. You excited to meet the boys at the gym?"

Pat knew he had to drop off the money at one of the boxing gyms in Dublin. It was full of guys who knew Jimmy and had underworld connections to one thing or another—IRA, organized crime, underground fights, the works.

"Yeah, Jimmy. I'm excited to get in and meet those guys, maybe spar with a few of those fighters we talked about. Listen, I'll call you when I get done spending some time at the gym. Seriously, no worries. I got it all under control," assured Pat.

"All right, kid. I'll look forward to that call. Have a good drive, and keep your head about you."

"You got it, Jimmy."

Patrick hung up the phone and let out a deep sigh. He would have to slip out of party mode and get serious for the rest of this trip—at least the best he could, notwithstanding his best friends being the devils on his shoulders.

As he was herding everyone into the car, Wally stopped them discreetly in the hall to give them a small paper lunch sack. Inside was a little hash, wrapped in plastic for their journey. Pat appreciated the token but was a little wary of anything that might contribute to future issues at this point.

"Helluva two days, mates. Come back any time," Wally said, shaking their hands.

They said their goodbyes and packed into the car. Uncle Manus had already gone to work at the site, so it was just Aunt Maggie and Wally waving them off. With Treats in the driver's seat, they pulled out of the small driveway and started the Dublin journey. Pat could already feel the dramatic shift in his mind. He had a job to do, and he was going to do it.

They stopped at a convenience store on the way out of the city so Pat and Walsh could pick up some coffee and snacks for the road. When they got back to the car, Treats was ripping a fat line of cocaine off the armrest in the driver's seat.

"Dude," said Walsh, shaking his head and laughing, "you're fucking crazy."

"You want me to stay awake, don't ya? It's just like having a couple cups of coffee," Treats said, shrugging it off.

Pat kept quiet. Yes, on one hand, Treats's alertness would likely be enhanced, at least for a short period. And Pat couldn't really say anything; he was the one who had flipped the car after God knows how many drinks. On the other hand, all that coke would likely exacerbate Treats's propensity for risk and danger. But Pat wasn't his babysitter, either.

"All right, man. If you get a little jittery, Walsh can drive," said Pat, in a sort of compromise.

"You mean like this?" Treats mimed freaking out and having a seizure, shaking exaggeratedly. "Don't worry, mates. Unlike Pat here, I know how to fly a plane."

Jesus, thought Pat. *He is never going to let that go.*

———

ABOUT MIDWAY TO DUBLIN, THEY DROVE THROUGH A ROUND-about to connect with another road. As he was circling, Treats broke the silence.

"All right. What's your flavor? A few more rippas? We got about one and a half hours left until Dublin."

Pat was torn. Would it be better to accept and go along to get along? Or refuse and have to explain himself? If he started acting suspicious, Treats would sense something was up. A few lines in the middle of the day wasn't going to kill him. And the drive had so far been kind of boring; the novelty of the wide-open country had long since worn off, and this route wasn't nearly as scenic as the one between Galway and Roundstone had been. A little coke might liven things up. But he also had responsibilities.

"What's the matter with you, brother? You all right?" Treats asked.

"I'm good, man," Pat said, pulling from his inner debate.

Treats held his gaze on Pat, waiting for the catch.

"I think we need to tone it down a bit," Pat admitted. "We only have a few days left. At the rate we're going, it's amazing we're still alive and you've only been arrested once."

"We still got time, mate," said Treats, grinning. "The last hurrah isn't over yet. Dublin's a real city! It's finally gonna get crazy!"

This wasn't what Pat wanted to hear. Instead of pulling the ripcord on the parachute to slow down, Treats seemed intent on swan diving into the ground at full speed. He pulled over and started lining up the rails of blow. Like any cocaine enthusiast, he had a small mirror for this very purpose.

"First thing we need to do is hit this club tonight called The Kitchen." Treats announced this excitedly, interrupting himself to rip one of the three lines. "U2 owns it, and when we get there, we need to re-up on the disco biscuits to carry us through!"

Patrick was brewing inside now. He wasn't a fucking saint, and he was willing to push the envelope a little. But hadn't they done that already? Wasn't the last week nothing but a nonstop party, the bacchanal that Treats was so eager to experience? Weren't they doubling down on a hand they had barely been winning? Pat had a sinking feeling that their luck would eventually run out.

He held his silence, still turning the dilemma over in his head. Was it better to put a hard stop on Treats, knowing that he might rebel even harder? Or to give him a little leeway so he didn't go completely crazy?

"All right. But I'm driving the rest of the way, and we need to tone it down," Pat said. He meant business.

Treats passed the mirror to Walsh so he could snort the second line.

"All right, Patrick, you're up. Don't get all calm on me now," Treats implored. "Let's meet some girls and have some fun. That's all."

Walsh passed the mirror with the remaining line, but Pat handed it back to Treats.

"Remember," Treats said, bending over the mirror to snort the last line, "I'm going home to deal with the reality of a pregnant girlfriend who wants to keep it."

Pat nodded. He knew that Treats was just trying to hold reality at bay for a few days longer. Pat's jaw clenched, but he said nothing. He felt he was endangering the mission either way. If he mentioned the mission, it was compromised. If he didn't bring up the mission, it would lead to his companions making stupid risks because they had no idea the stakes that Pat was playing with.

Walsh was starting to look pissed too. His expression said this was the first time he had heard about the pregnant girlfriend. Suddenly, Treats's risk-prone behavior started to make a lot more sense. Pat could see Walsh's jaw grinding as he worked things over in his head.

"Patrick, you need to calm down," Treats said, matching his gaze.

"No, man, I think you need to," answered Pat. "This could be the best time in your life someday if you don't keep fucking everything up, man. Let's keep our shit together and make it back to Boston alive. You've been on a death wish ever since we walked through Logan like a pack of Puerto Rican drug mules."

An uncomfortable silence settled into the vehicle. After all he had gone through in prison, his fuse felt much more frightening and real.

They held the stare awhile before Treats broke it. Treats put the cocaine away and opened the car door so he could switch places with Pat. It wasn't any promise to stop partying but merely a silent acknowledgment that he would let Pat drive, and for the immediate moment, he would stop doing drugs. Probably until they got to the hotel room in Dublin.

Pat settled into the driver's seat and started the car. His anger passed, like an ominous cloud that had blown over. But he knew Treats would be a problem, and he and Walsh would eventually have to deal with it.

———

VIEWING THE DUBLIN SKYLINE FROM THEIR LUXURY HOTEL
room lifted Pat's spirits. The sun was setting, and Pat could see practically
the whole city from their wraparound balcony. The view was excellent,
even from the inside. True to his last-days-on-earth form, Treats had
booked a penthouse with all the modern amenities. The room took up
a top corner of the hotel, so they had almost a 360-degree view of the
city. The golden light of dusk flooded the balcony and the room's inte-
rior, giving the air a sort of magical and joyful quality. The animosity
of the car ride was already forgotten and in the past, like a Boston bar
fight between friends. After the punches were done, you could still have
a drink together.

Pat and Walsh leaned on the balcony railing, drinking bottles of beer
from the minibar. They all held their silence for a while, simply letting
the view speak for itself. Pat then clinked his bottle with Walsh in an
impromptu "cheers." He was suddenly feeling . . . poetic.

"To embracing this reunification on this once-in-a-lifetime crazy
journey that's been unpredictable at every turn," he said.

Treats lifted his beer as well.

"We did it, fellas," Pat continued. "Returning to the old country is on
every Boston Irish bucket list."

Walsh clinked his bottle to Pat's again.

"Well said, brother. Well said. That's a fucking proper toast." Walsh
laughed.

"Look at Hemingway over here," said Treats, bending over to snort
another line. "Did a lot of reading in prison, yeah?"

"Fucker! I did a lot of reading *before* prison," Pat shot back, playing.
Walsh and Treats both laughed, while Treats held up his hands in the air
in a "don't shoot me" gesture. Pat felt a moment of serene appreciation
for his new life on the outside and his loyal friends. They were batshit
lunatics, and they were his brothers. Nothing could break that. He took
in the whole atmosphere, glancing both at his friends and the skyline.
Treats turned the hotel radio up, which was playing the U2 song "I Still
Haven't Found What I'm Looking For."

"Sure is great to be here, fellas," he told them, "no matter how fucking crazy we are."

———

FULLY LOADED ON RECREATIONAL DRUGS AND BOOZE, THEY strolled up to The Kitchen like they owned the place. Pat felt there was something unmistakably "American" about their vibe, further distinguished by their Boston heritage, and he teetered on the edge of embracing this with pride rather than feeling like an outsider. At the door, Treats slipped a hundred euros to the bouncer, who reacted to them with a mild sort of shock. Were they celebrities? Gangsters? Both? An air of dangerous fun surrounded them, the kind of energy that instantly drew people in. Was it Pat's imagination, or did a few people stare at them, maybe thinking they were somebody as they easily passed by the line snaking around the block?

The Kitchen was unlike any club Pat had ever experienced. There was certainly nothing quite like it in Boston. Once through the front door, they climbed a short staircase that opened into a cavernous room. It was huge—easily space for at least five hundred people. The place had a minimalist, trippy vibe about it. Most of the walls and hallways were curved, except for the two bars, which, unlike the rest of the club, felt more traditional, lined with beechwood and tended by barkeeps of the supermodel variety. Booths and dining areas were arranged near the bar for those who chose to dine or drink as a group. The dance area was just beyond the seating and was dimly lit, with state-of-the-art lights and booming sound. This contrasted with an old-fashioned disco ball, which reflected the other visual effects, like roaming spotlights and lasers. An atmospheric pool, shallow and underlit, surrounded the dance floor like a moat and enhanced the bass speakers' sound.

Treats told him that the band U2 had carefully scouted the place before they bought the Clarence Hotel. They then turned the former basement kitchen into The Kitchen Nightclub, which had barely been open a year. Treats insisted that it was the trendiest place to be.

Patrick and Walsh made their way to the bar first. Pat was determined to buy the first round of drinks this time, a sort of low-key competition

The Clarence Hotel in Dublin, owned by U2 band members Bono and The Edge

to beat Treats to the punch. Treats was already preoccupied with scoring some more ecstasy. In this place, Pat thought, that should be relatively easy. The funny thing was, Treats kind of threw off the vibe of someone who was already on ecstasy. Pat wouldn't be surprised if people tried to get some from him.

Walsh and Pat flirted with the girls around them—all friendly, beautiful women with the whole night ahead of them. It was hard to know where to focus his attention. He was trying to get a drink when something caught his eye to his right.

Whoa.

She was a vision, whoever she was—long, jet-black hair and an angelic face, with big, oval, green spotlights for eyes. Her skin had the appearance of creamy porcelain. She was wearing a well-fitted blue dress with an unzipped black leather jacket, which allowed a view of her plunging neckline.

He didn't mean to stare. But he hadn't felt an instant attraction to a woman like this since Kiley. It was electric.

Snap out of it, thought Pat. *You'll miss your opportunity.* The bar was mobbed with drinkers, and she was having trouble getting the bartender to notice her. All the stools were taken.

"Let me order for you," said Pat. "Place is packed."

She smiled, sizing him up in an instant and seemingly liking what she saw.

"Well, that's kind of ya," she said in a thick brogue.

"What will you have?" Pat asked.

"A French 76," she said.

Pat had no idea what a French 76 was, but he ordered it for her anyway, instantly getting the bartender's attention since he had already tipped in advance.

"What's your name, dear?" asked Pat.

"It's Siobhan," she said with a smile. Siobhan. Of course, her name was beautiful too, thought Pat.

"I'm Pat."

"Pat, the Yank. Not too many Yanks in this club," she said.

"Don't hold it against me. My family's Irish," replied Pat. "Here, why don't you sit down on my stool."

She gladly accepted and hopped up on the stool, grabbing one of Pat's shoulders for support—and maybe getting a preview of how strong he was. She purposely brushed close to him with her body as she adjusted herself in her seat.

"Well, we'll just have to find something else to hold against you tonight then," she said with a smirk. "Won't we?"

The French 76 arrived in a coupe glass. Siobhan raised it to her lips and took a sip, never breaking her stare at Pat. She moved her stool over a touch, creating a small opening at the bar. She patted the bar, gesturing for Pat to sidle up next to her.

Pat forgot about Walsh, about Treats, about the mission, about everything. The whole world slipped away, and it was just Siobhan, only Siobhan.

———

BACK AT THE HOTEL, SIOBHAN AND PAT SAT ON THE COUCH just inside the room. Walsh had his back to them looking out over the railing. They were all intoxicated past the buzz point, where everything feels fun, comfortable, weightless, and without consequence. Pat knew Walsh couldn't hear what they were whispering to each other, but he could see everything over his shoulder.

It happened suddenly. Pat went in for a kiss, and Siobhan kissed back passionately. Then it was as if a dam broke. They attacked each other, ripping off each other's clothes in urgent desire, aggressively grappling with each other. It felt like a beautiful moment Pat hadn't experienced since before prison. Sure, Pat had hooked up with those hostel girls, but he had been so wasted on ecstasy he hardly remembered anything. This was different, the kind of girl Pat would go steady with back home.

He knew Walsh didn't get his kicks from being a voyeur, but he did notice Walsh lit another cigarette and continued to occasionally observe from outside. Pat killed the lights. He noticed Walsh's vague silhouette with the ember of his cigarette burning in the darkness.

Siobhan tumbled with Pat and grappled to get on top of him. She reveled in his struggle and pushed down on his chest. She writhed on him and started to grind hard. They tussled and pulsed, finding a slow and strong rhythm. Her moans were getting louder, no doubt loud enough to cause a noise complaint.

As her singing pleasure started to rise to an approaching climax, the door flew open and the lights came on. In blew Hurricane Treats.

"Goddammit, Treats," whispered Patrick, shaking his head. His timing was atrocious.

Treats barreled into the room, somewhat disoriented by the coupling happening right before his eyes. Siobhan yelped and immediately covered up with pillows from the couch, dismounting Pat simultaneously, while Pat swore a blue streak in slurred speech.

"Treats. You mothafucka," was the only intelligible thing that came out of Pat's mouth.

Looking up, Treats clocked Walsh still sitting on the chair on the balcony.

"Wow. What the fuck is going on here?" Treats asked.

Pat shot back. "I'm right in the middle of something, Treats. For fuck sake."

"Joke's on me, I guess," started Treats. "Walsh? What the fuck are you doing out there? Where're the other girls?"

Walsh flicked his cigarette off the balcony and leapt into action. He came in from the balcony and grabbed Treats by the arm.

"C'mon, Treats. Let's go. Let 'em be," Walsh entreated.

Treats seemed agitated and wild-eyed. "I got hustled down there by this clown. Some turkey sold me fuckin' Tylenol and told me it was ecstasy. He obviously doesn't know what the *fuck* he just did to himself."

Patrick did his best to cover up Siobhan further, grabbing a throw blanket from the couch and covering her whole body. He was steaming. He couldn't give a flying fuck about the counterfeit ecstasy story.

Treats opened his mouth, but Walsh body-checked him hard and grabbed him, forcing him back through the door. Walsh made sure to slam it from the outside, shutting them both out of the room.

Pat and Siobhan sat awkwardly with the lights on for a few breaths, hearing Walsh through the door. "Time to go find the dude that ripped you off, Treats," Walsh asserted. "We're not gonna do anything without Patrick, anyway. Let's just head back down there, okay?"

Treats seemed to get the message, and they could hear stomping down the hall toward the elevator.

Siobhan sighed.

"Oh fuck it, you crazy Yanks," she blurted out.

Siobhan pushed Pat back down and resumed her position, ready to finish what they'd started and maybe begin all over again. They were now completely alone, the universe shrinking to just the two of them. These were primal, passionate forces that could not be extinguished, and the momentary interruption was quickly forgotten.

Chapter 23

OLD FLAME

IT WAS NEARING EVENING IN NATE'S OLD NEIGHBORHOOD, and he knew he had to call down to Virginia to notify his mother and Vanessa that he wouldn't be coming back for a while. Nate was already setting up interviews and searching for an apartment. He could only stay at Aunt Carol's house for so long.

"It's going to be at least a few weeks until I make it back, and I'm definitely planning to attend law school up here in Boston in the fall," Nate told Vanessa.

He could hear the disappointment in her voice. "Nate, you told your mother and me this wouldn't happen, and you know I'm not leaving here, or my family!"

The phone went silent, then the disconnection beeps began. The fact that he'd be starting law school in eight months, combined with the recurring tones certainly felt like a breakup hung in the air. Nate didn't know what would happen next, but if Vanessa wanted to join him eventually, she'd need to move to Boston. But did he want that? The reality was, she wouldn't leave her life behind, and he wouldn't ask that of her. It was over.

He knew he wanted to talk to someone. He felt alone more than ever right now in this life. Nate threw on a jacket and checked himself in the mirror before leaving the house. But there was only one person who could calm him down and relate to his emotions.

He wondered if he should feel guilty; he had already made up his mind to visit his old high school girlfriend, Betina, who still lived in the same hood. She was Jamal's cousin. They had split up after his senior year ended, right before he went down to Virginia for college ball. But they'd been friends forever, ever since they were kids. He felt it inevitable that they would eventually reconnect. It was a small world. After Jamal's and Tre's deaths, everyone knew that Nate was back in town. And that included Betina, who had called him about an hour earlier.

"Stop by tonight around seven. My roommates are going out," she said. "It'll be good to see you, Nate!"

He walked briskly in the twilight, breathing in the fresh spring air—at least as fresh as it got in this part of Boston. He knew the route to Betina's place by heart. She lived in the college apartments on Lenox, right behind Northeastern University.

He was still knocking on the door when Betina threw it open. She squealed and threw her arms around him, planting a big kiss on his face. She took his hand and led him back to her bedroom to "talk." She closed the door and locked it, and then they lay down on the bed as if no time had passed at all, wordlessly undressing each other.

As Betina grabbed Nate's waist, she felt the .38 revolver tucked into his waistband. She froze, then sat up and back, still half undressed.

"What the fuck is this, Nate?" Betina asked.

"It's nothing. Don't worry about it," Nate said.

"I felt it out there when I hugged you," Betina scolded. "I don't get it. You said you were coming back for law school and you was gonna be all high-and-mighty nigga! What's going on?"

Nate placed his hands on hers. "Listen, Betina. You need to stop trippin'. Slugs's been on a mission ever since Tre was killed. I'm with him on this."

"So?" Betina asked, with one eyebrow arching up.

"So, there was no way in hell I was going to stroll over with nothing. You know what street this apartment is on?"

Betina stared at him knowingly. Every Black person in the city knew how dangerous and violent this part of town had been.

"Fuck no," Nate continued. "You want me to be another statistic? I still can't believe this shit. There's been over six hundred murders in the last five years."

"I know, I know," Betina said, looking down. "And the Goffigans."

"And you know, it was that Lenox Street dude just stabbed Jamal in the fuckin' chest, killed him. Snatched his fuckin' life. Gone. Mothafucka wore a shirt that said *I love Jamal* in court."

Betina grabbed Nate's face and stared him in the eyes.

"Well, make sure you don't get caught with that, Nate, or you'll be dead by the cops. Never mind the Lenox Street Crew!"

Nate returned the intense gaze and went in to kiss her again.

"Don't worry," she said, pulling him close. "I got you, babe."

They both lay back down on the bed.

"So tell me what," Betina said playfully. "You missed me as soon as you came back to town, huh?"

He smiled and stroked her face. "You know I always have a place for you in my heart, boo," he said softly, holding soft eye contact. "I feel you, Betina. You're doing your thang, and I'm happy for you. I just want you to know that I might need you at some point. So be there, all right?"

Betina shook her head. "You buggin'," she said. "This isn't you, Nate. Your cousins reaped what they sowed. What you getting involved for?"

"Wow." Nate grimaced. "You used to say the same shit in high school. They're my family, my blood. I look at it differently. They played the hand they were dealt. That ain't all on them, now. Don't get me wrong, girl."

She looked at him longingly again, seemingly willing to overlook any petty difference in opinion about what he needed to do with his cousins.

"We done this before, Nate," Betina said. "Oh, I already got you going, and you're gonna forget that girl down south real fast."

Nate took the chrome .38 out of his waistband and laid it on the bedside table. The rest of their clothes fell on the carpet beside the bed. Nate welcomed the warm touch of his first love, her familiar form greeting him, picking up right where they'd left off.

Nate whispered, "I'm sorry I just popped out up here out of nowhere, but you were the only one that would understand what was going on in my mind right now."

At those words, she held him tighter.

Chapter 24

DROP MISSION

"TELL ME AGAIN, SLOWLY," SAID PAT.

Walsh led Pat to the outside balcony. Walsh's hand shook as he fumbled with his cigarette. He had a panic-stricken look in his eye. He relayed the story to Pat once more: "He had the balls to go after a con artist in a crowded club with no follow-up plan. He walked into the bathroom, accused the guy of selling Tylenol instead of X, then bottled him over the head. He stopped to get a shot before booking it down the street to the food stand where I was at," Walsh said, all in one breath. "Then he walks over to an alley barely a block away, and within spitting distance of the scene he was trying to get away from, he fools around with a hooker. After a while, I went over to the alley and found the prostitute crying and getting herself together. She told me a truck came out of nowhere, and some goons snatched him up like luggage."

Pat didn't find any of it unbelievable. All this shit was completely within the realm of Treats's behavior. Sooner or later, living this far out on the edge, his luck was bound to run out.

But the timing. Fuck.

It was already one a.m. Jimmy had just told him he had to be at the bank no later than nine. There was a package waiting for him at the hotel lobby with all his fake credentials to retrieve the safety deposit box. He went over the cover story in his head again. He was his grandfather's chief beneficiary, and grandpa had just recently passed. He just had to go over the paperwork to memorize all the obvious details they might ask him.

And what if something else went wrong? If he got caught fraudulently trying to get a safety deposit box, he knew he was going back to prison. He wouldn't be able to call Jimmy to bail him out. They would disavow him altogether. The whole mission would be scuttled, and he'd be left high and dry.

"What the fuck are we going to do, man?" Walsh asked. Pat grabbed one of Walsh's cigs from the pack on the table and lit up. He had to think. His eyes darted over the Dublin skyline, looking at everything and nothing all at the same time. His thoughts raced.

Should they spend the night looking for Treats? What if something happened to them? What if he couldn't get to the bank on time? Jimmy might be forgiving, but the Whitey Bulger connections involved here wouldn't be. And he was sure they would all be benefiting in some way, shape, or form—even Jimmy. Nothing was done in this world for free! A few broken bones might be the least he would face. He could wake up dead at the bottom of a river or be dumped in some back alley.

Pat began to pace. Even if they could look for Treats, where would they start? They couldn't go to the Garda. He couldn't use Jimmy's network without jeopardizing the mission. What the fuck were they supposed to do? Wander out blindly into the night shouting Treats's name? No plan whatsoever? The guy could be anywhere by now, anyway. That truck may have been headed to another city for all they knew.

Walsh had no idea about Pat's mission. What was he supposed to tell him about this important thing he had to do in the morning? How was that supposed to be more important than saving Treats?

Wait a minute. That's what he could tell Walsh. Jimmy's network.

"Listen, Walsh," Pat said, finally breaking the silence. "I've been in contact with Jimmy this whole time. He wants me to meet some of his friends at a boxing club somewhere in Dublin. It's just like back home. These guys are all connected. Maybe they can give us an idea about what to do."

"Good old Jimmy. He's got connections everywhere," Walsh replied.

"He just wanted to check in with me, that's all. He's making sure we're still alive, wanted to make sure I was having a good time. Thought I might like to see what the boxing world is like here in Ireland," bluffed Pat.

"So, what are you saying?" Walsh asked.

"We stay here tonight. There's nothing we can do for Treats right now.

What the fuck are we supposed to do? Go screaming into the night, all fucked up on booze and drugs? We'll probably get jumped as easy targets by anyone out this late."

Walsh nodded, listening.

"Listen. Those guys who grabbed Treats are criminals. They might hurt him, rough him up a bit. But they know someone'll be looking for him. So they'll either throw him in a ditch or think he's worth some money. Maybe they'll find out how they can extort something out of him."

Walsh thought about it, seemingly turning the plan over in his mind.

"It just doesn't seem right not doing anything about it," Walsh said, shaking his head.

"We're more of a liability to him in this state of mind. We gotta calm down and do this methodically. Get more options tomorrow," said Pat, a plan starting to form in his head.

"I'm going to go down to the gym alone tomorrow," continued Pat.

"But—" started Walsh.

"They're not expecting you, bro. They'll help out where they can, as a favor to Jimmy. But I think they'll clam up if I bring along a stranger."

Pat had no clue if the guys at the boxing gym would help him at all, if they were in a position to help, or if it was even proper to ask. The most important thing was delivering the cash. After that was done, he would have more leeway to devise a plan to recover Treats.

Walsh smoked his cigarette to the nub and tossed it off the balcony. "Okay. What do you want me to do?" he asked.

"The first thing we should do is change rooms. We'll make up some bullshit reason, get something cheaper. Treats still has his key. They could possibly come back here for us too," Pat said.

Walsh nodded, relieved that there was something he could do to pour his physical energy into. He began to pack, starting with the drugs.

BY SIX IN THE MORNING, PAT WAS DRESSED AND READY. HE spent the extra time going through the paperwork from the package left for him from the front desk—a notarized document affirming him as the beneficiary. But there were no written instructions. All he had was the address of the bank that Jimmy had given him on the phone hours earlier.

His mind wandered back to Siobhan. He had asked for privacy during his call with Jimmy. She'd said she wanted to sleep in her own bed anyway but left her number on the nightstand and kissed him on her way out. She'd want to see him again—if he found a way out of this mess. That was a pretty big fucking *if.*

Pat reminded himself this was no big deal. He would walk into the bank, sign a few papers, walk out with the package. Then he'd take the rental car over to the boxing gym and deliver it. Once this mission was out of the way, he could focus on his missing friend.

Walsh was out cold, passed out on one of the queen beds. They'd switched rooms in the middle of the night, opting for a cheaper room on the floor below. They still had a balcony, but the view wasn't nearly as good. It didn't matter. They'd probably not be staying long.

Pat had that nervous feeling again, the same one he'd had his second day in prison, as if forces were conspiring against him. He tried to shake it off, but the anxiety was building. At this rate, he'd be a complete basket case by the time he got to the bank.

He needed to take a walk to calm the fuck down, so he left the room, closing the door quietly behind him. He took a large backpack, knowing he'd need something to transport the cash. He'd pace outside on the streets for a while, burn off the excess energy, and then put his game face on.

———

ONCE HE ARRIVED AT THE BANK, HIS FEAR GOT WORSE. NO one was threatening him or questioning his identity. He just had massive paranoia in the back of his mind that the security gates would come down without warning, trapping him in the bank with armed private security. No one had briefed him on an escape or backup plan. He either was going to be successful or not.

The bank itself looked much like any other bank you might find in the States. Certainly, the building was older and made of old red brick, but the inside had all the familiar things you might find anywhere—rows of tellers behind bulletproof glass, shiny floors, management offices in the back.

Pat informed the teller that he was there to retrieve a safety deposit box. She nodded and called over her supervisor. A middle-aged man in a navy suit walked over and shook Pat's hand.

"Hello, sir. I'm Mr. Donovan. Come with me, and I'll take you to the vaults."

"Thank you," Pat replied.

"Ah, you're from the States, are ya? What brings you here?" Mr. Donovan asked, leading him across the floor to a door.

"My grandfather passed, so I'm here to settle up some affairs," said Pat. He didn't really want the small talk but figured it'd be worse if he were too quiet.

"Terribly sorry to hear it, sir. This way."

Mr. Donovan opened the door with a security card. It clicked open, revealing a stairway to the basement.

"We keep our vaults down here, behind several layers of protection," said Mr. Donovan, leading Pat downstairs. He heard the door close behind him. A claustrophobic feeling crept over him, and he tried to shake it off.

The stairs led to another door at the bottom, which opened with a key from Mr. Donovan's pocket. It opened into an anteroom with a small plexiglass window for a teller. Once more, Pat heard the door to this room close behind him. Keep calm, he kept telling himself. For all he knew, Mr. Donovan was in on this as well.

"You can register and check in with Mrs. Kelley here. She'll assist you with your deposit box," Mr. Donovan said. "When you're finished, I'll lead you back upstairs."

Pat nodded and approached the teller. The vault door was to his left, guarded by two of the bank's armed security.

"All right, sir. I just need three forms of ID and the beneficiary document."

Pat went into his jacket pocket and pulled out the passport, ID, birth certificate, and beneficiary document that would transfer the sum. How Jimmy's contacts got the money put in his actual grandfather's name, he'd never know. As he took them out, a few documents fell to the floor. He mentally winced and bent down to pick them up, his hands still trembling from nerves.

"Sorry—a little jet lagged."

Mrs. Kelley was all smiles as Pat handed over the documents. If she was suspicious, she didn't show it. Jesus, he was horrible at this. If someone went back to view the footage, his behavior might seem suspicious. Or maybe they would just think he had butterfingers. Pat focused and tried to recover his momentum.

"Okay, sir, just sign here," said Mrs. Kelley. She handed him a small key, marked #948.

He signed slowly, careful not to misspell his name from nerves.

"Come with me, please," chirped Mrs. Kelley. She left her station, and the vault door unlocked. Once the door swung open, she was waiting on the other side. This would be door number three, Pat noted mentally.

Mrs. Kelley led him into a room with shiny rows of small metallic lockers. They were stacked right on top of each other in rows, together forming the wall. Each box had two keyholes for access. Pat assumed that both the box holder's key and the bank's key were required to open each box. She inserted her key, and Pat followed suit. The panel swung open to the right, and inside was a long box with a handle.

"The privacy room is right through that door if you want to examine the contents. Just let me know when you're finished."

Pat nodded and transported the box to a brightly lit room with an island in the middle. He hoisted the box on the island and lifted the top panel.

"Holy shit," Pat whispered.

He'd never seen so much cash in his life. Stacks of hundreds were packed so tightly into the box that there wasn't room for a single bill more. He was guessing each bundle held about ten thousand dollars. There must have been at least a half million in there.

He transplanted the cash from the box to his backpack, careful not to disturb the bills' pristine condition. As Mrs. Kelley led him back into the main registration area, Pat felt the uneasy burden of carrying this obscene amount of money. He couldn't wait to get to the boxing gym to unload it.

"Get everything you need, sir?" asked Mr. Donovan.

Pat nodded. Mr. Donovan led him up the stairs and back into the central area of the bank. Pat nodded in appreciation and shook Mr. Donovan's hand. Then he walked out the front door, into the glorious sun of a bright Dublin morning.

Chapter 25

THE OG

NATE GAZED OUT THE FORD EXPLORER'S PASSENGER WINDOW, watching all the familiar sights of Blue Hill Avenue pass by as Slugs drove in the early afternoon sun. They'd just passed King Tut's, an establishment that looked completely different in the light of day. Nate saw a few pedestrians hanging around, some looking dazed and strung out. *The market is still ripe*, Nate thought, *if the Norfolk Kings can hold on to it.*

The thought of getting more and more involved was jacking up the constant hum of Nate's background anxiety. Nate tapped his finger and shook his leg absentmindedly, his nervous energy needing an outlet for escape. Slugs was too busy bobbing in time to the bass of the stereo and spitting the lyrics to Luniz's "I Got 5 on It" to notice.

"These guys can't be running out of product every two weeks," he said, opening the business conversation. "That was the motive, Nate. You cut off the supply and watch the crew fight among themselves and deteriorate."

Nate nodded in agreement. It certainly felt like someone was trying to break up the Norfolk Kings and take their business for themselves.

"Whoever did this to Tre cut us off at the head," Slugs said. "They knew what they were doing. We need to reestablish the pipeline and then watch. Once the mothafuckas see it didn't work, the next move will be telling! That's when I'll get my fuckin' revenge."

"All right, man. Sounds like a plan," Nate said, somehow doubting it would be that easy. "So who's this connect that we're meeting here? You sure we okay? We good?"

"Yeah. Yeah. We're fine. Don't be trippin'. You remember Ricky?" Slugs asked.

Nate looked back at Slugs blankly, trying to remember anyone by that name.

"Well, maybe you don't," said Slugs. "He got put away eight years in '87—was teaching Tre and me how to pump product when we was kids. He's an OG in this game, and he just got out. He'll definitely know something about Tre's connect, help get things back on track—maybe even know who might have wanted to take Tre out."

Slugs slowed to park on the Norfolk Street corner off of Woodrow, stopping in front of a run-down triple-decker. They were in a primarily residential neighborhood with a lot of rented units. By day, this neighborhood was sketchy at best, recalled Nate. By night, you wouldn't want to walk around here unless you were packing.

"I'll do the talking," Slugs said, wriggling his massive frame out of the Explorer. Nate nodded, swallowing hard. They made their way up the stairs.

———

"SHIT. I *KNOW* YOU AIN'T TRYIN' TO GET ME INVOLVED AFTER I only been out a week, yo," Ricky said.

Ricky sat across from them on his ratty sofa in his bare-bones living room. He was a big man, like Slugs, but even taller—about six foot four. He had a distant, almost sideways look, as if he were skeptical about everything he was seeing or hearing. Nate had no doubt this man had spent the last eight years in prison. Before Slugs could reply, Ricky went on. "Get the fuck outta here, Slugs. You young soft-ass niggas got no business in this game, and I'm stuck here with this fuckin' ball and chain on my ankle now," he said, looking directly at Nate while pointing to his ankle bracelet. Nate caught a glimpse of what looked like a few bullet scars just above Ricky's ankle.

Nate fought his instincts to say anything at all. He knew he could easily pass as belonging to a tough-looking crew. After all, he'd grown up around his cousins and the Norfolk Kings, and he knew these streets like the back of his hand. But he'd never truly lived the gang life, and someone prison hardened like Ricky could sniff him out as "soft" from a mile away.

Slugs jumped in. "Ricky, you started this for all of us around here back in the eighties. Nate's been here with us his whole life. He remembers when that first Kings tag went up on your corner, just up the street."

Slugs's attempt to defend Nate wasn't wrong. Nate had never been a banger, but he'd always be family with the Kings because of Slugs and Tre and his history in the neighborhood. He was familiar with their whole world, although often through hearing about it secondhand. But nothing about the Norfolk Kings would shock him. Just because he wasn't a banger didn't mean he was naive.

"Now we coming to you for just a little information," Slugs explained. "Not trying to get you wrapped up in nothin'. I remember when you and Tre started the flow of product coming through Miami. And I know you and Tre had patched up those shipments coming through Jersey now."

Nate studied Ricky's face, which was stone cold, guarded.

"Thing is," Slugs continued, "there's nothing. No source right now that we can supply this crew with. And that's real bad for business. I don't have to tell you that; you know. And for the Kings in general, everything is in limbo right now. So we just tryin' to set up a flow for them, that's all. We tryin' to get it set back up, you know, man?"

Ricky sighed and leaned back, taking it in. He wasn't ready to spill anything yet. He took another sip of his Schlitz and waited.

Slugs was first to break the silence. "You ain't heard nothin' on what happened in there with Tre?"

Ricky's face softened, as if remembering who all this was for. He rubbed the bridge of his nose, took another swig, and punctuated it by putting the bottle down forcefully on the side table made from milk crates.

Slugs leaned in and tried again.

"All right, all right, all right. Yo, me and Tre built this from nothin', and at times we butt heads a lot, but we handled our business in all ways. That's why niggas knew we were not to be fucked with. Tre was always ready to pop off, and he did anytime someone was stepping to us."

Nate thought back to when Tre first started his rival gang right in the heart of other gangs' territory. It was Castle Gate on one side of the neighborhood and the Vamp Hill Kings on the other. Nate thought Tre must've had a death wish to even dream of starting a new operation there. He'd begged Tre to reconsider, saying, "All of them will shoot down a couple Black kids tryin' to run up in their territory without blinking. How can you not understand that?"

He'd never forgotten Tre's reaction, "Maybe we shoot them first."

That was the first time Nate realized Tre was packing and totally serious about the violence. Dude was committed. He knew then he would have no problem pulling the trigger, and Ricky seemed to confirm that.

Ricky finally broke his silence.

"Now, I don't know what happened to Tre, but if I hear anything, I'll let you know. You watch out for them Vamp Hill niggas; they always coming for us. The beef Tre and I had with them goes back to the beginning of time. They got a few stash houses and drug dens out there. One of them on the corner of Columbus and Mass Aves, the community calls it Hell House."

Slugs subtly nodded, taking it all in.

"In the meantime," Ricky went on, "I'll put you in touch with the right person to try and reestablish the flow from Miami." He paused to take another swig of his Schlitz, then lifted his index finger to make a point. "But that's it. I'm just setting up the intro. You stay the fuck away from this house until I call for you. I don't wanna see no BPD coming this way."

Slugs nodded in agreement.

"And keep my name out of them bangers' mouths," Ricky added. "I'm outta this game. It's done changed."

Slugs and Nate rose to take their leave.

"One more thing," Ricky warned, with a steady eye locked on Nate. "Make sure you punks don't get yourselves popped off out there!"

It had only been a few days, but already, the gun in Nate's waistband felt like a lifeline in a sea of danger. He was still hoping he never had to use it.

———

AFTER SLUGS HAD DROPPED HIM OFF, NATE MADE HIS WAY back to the Ella Baker Community House and slinked down the back staircase, making sure no one was watching him or following him along the way. There, in the basement, Papa Ray and Reverend Gibbs sat awaiting his arrival.

"Hey," said Gibbs. "How's it going out there?"

Nate settled into a chair and folded his hands in front of him on the table.

"So far, here's what I know," Nate reported. "Slugs is paranoid. He's angry, but he's patient when it comes to finding out what happened to Tre."

Papa Ray nodded while Reverend Gibbs took notes on a legal pad.

"In the meantime, he's just trying to reestablish the pipeline Tre had in place. The Kings out there are getting itchy, think they need to reclaim their presence, their identity, you know. They're running out of product every other week, getting played by a few other crews, so I feel something will ignite soon. Vamp Hill is just about to wipe them out for good. Today, we met someone to help reestablish the connect—"

Gibbs jumped on Nate's words. "Who was it?" he demanded. "What's his name?"

Nate hesitated, then raised his hands in protest. "Rev, I can't give it to you now. He isn't in the game—just got out. Slugs was just prying him for info and trying to get an introduction to their supply."

Gibbs shared a look with Papa Ray. Papa stayed silent, folding his arms, seemingly content to listen for now. "Nate," Gibbs pleaded, "any information is helpful here."

"Rev, this is damn good info. You have got to trust me. I know what I'm doing, and I'm not risking anything that can be tied back to me. Nothing."

"But Nate—" protested Gibbs, not giving up the point.

"I told you," responded Nate, "all I'm trying to do is feed you information on bloodshed that we can stop in real time, not the drug business or ratting on some OG that doesn't even want to be back in."

Gibbs looked down at his notes and sighed. He put his pen down.

"Nate," he began, "you're missing the bigger opportunity here. And at some point, I'd like to communicate with the mayor and the FBI and provide some valuable intel."

Papa Ray leaned forward. "Now listen," he said patiently, directing his speech to both of them. "One week at a time. One month at a time. One piece of information at a time. We have to be patient, fellas, so the real major impact that we can make is felt on these streets."

Leave it to Papa Ray to be the voice of reason, Nate thought.

"Rev, I'm gonna get there. I'm just getting started—getting to know what's going on out there. Give me another few weeks and I can provide some valuable info on the crack and heroin. But for now, I'm focused on stopping the bloodshed. These guys are ready to pop off on anyone just to prove something; I can feel it. But word is Vamp Hill is going to make a move as well and take out a few more key players, and I don't know if one of them could be Slugs."

"That's great info, Nate. It makes a lot of sense. We approached them the other night on the street, had an interesting conversation. We're focused on the Vamp Hill Kings, and their potential to execute more killings is real." Gibbs shook his head as he mentioned Vamp Hill. His sense of exasperation was palpable.

It's one thing to say I want to stop the bloodshed, thought Nate. But how hard would it be to keep his priorities straight once the BPD and the FBI got more involved? For now, he'd still have to ride along the knife's edge and hope he could keep his clarity as he plunged deeper into the Kings' world. He took a deep breath before saying anything further.

Chapter 26

STREET BOXING CLUB

EVEN THOUGH THE BACKPACK FULL OF HUNDRED-DOLLAR bills hung heavy on his shoulder, Pat felt weightless and free walking into the sunshine. A tremendous burden was about to be lifted off his back.

That feeling lasted only a few moments as the gravity of what he was carrying reemerged in his mind. He wasn't there yet. It was far too early to celebrate. He still had to make it to the gym with the money intact. Waves of anxiety washed back over him as he refocused on the next steps.

To everyone else on the packed Dublin streets, it was another typical day, and Pat was just a nameless face lost in the crowd, seemingly on his way to work like everyone else. Dubliners who saw him were clueless to

The FBI's relationship with Whitey Bulger exposed
the decades of corruption within the Bureau

the half million dollars he was carrying and to the fact that he was a cash mule acting for a notorious criminal, one of the FBI's Most Wanted.

Whitey Bulger was the FBI's white whale. He had humiliated the agency, slipping out of their fingers at the moment the city was going to sweep him up on unbeatable charges going back decades. But he had been tipped off, and he vanished into thin air. Their case would have been airtight. But too many on the inside were secretly working with Whitey to help take down rival gangs, and now the whole agency was paying the price. They'd stop at nothing to get him to save face by enacting vengeance. Of course they would call it "justice."

Pat laughed to himself. *Good luck finding him, guys.* Not even the people working to help him knew where he was. Whitey was of three worlds; he'd been a prisoner, a king of the Boston streets, and now a fugitive. Whitey was always thinking on multiple levels at every angle. If anyone could disappear without a trace, it was Whitey.

It gave Pat some comfort to think of Whitey's high-level connections that would, by association, likely protect him from getting caught. Everyone back home knew that Whitey's brother Billy was president of the Massachusetts Senate. Not only that, but the top fed, John Connolly, was rumored to have been the one who tipped Whitey off.

And those were just the connections that everyone knew about! God knows how many others Whitey held in his vice grip. Pat had his own suspicions that Clinton himself had signed off on his disappearance. He always felt the president was sketchy as hell. But if that were the case, that meant there was an even higher level of protection surrounding Whitey—which was good news for Pat.

Then again, anything could happen at any given time to anybody. Once you started walking around feeling like you were untouchable, that's when you got fucked. Questions popped into Pat's head. Was there a leak somewhere in the chain of communication that could put him in harm's way—someone in the IRA, or a rogue enemy from Boston, or Scotland Yard, or Interpol?

Back in high school and later, while reading voraciously in prison, Pat's favorite topic was history. It taught him that evil is everywhere at the highest level. Money is the root of it all.

He found his way to the rental car, parked on a side street to avoid scrutiny. Perhaps it was best they'd had a practice car to destroy before getting a new replacement for the Dublin mission. Having a car that was too beaten up was just as bad as having something too flashy. The name of the game was to blend in.

Pat opened the trunk and put the backpack inside, covering it with a blanket. Getting into the driver's seat, he breathed heavily, starting the car and gripping the steering wheel tight. Even though he knew the money was in the trunk, it felt weird having it out of his sight, even if only for a short drive. He pulled out into the street and glanced down at the map in his lap. He knew the upcoming ride would be the most nerve-racking twenty minutes of his life.

If something went wrong, Jimmy and the higher-ups could simply write off any casualty of the mission. That's what he had signed up for, whether he liked it or not. Jimmy liked him, for sure. But he wasn't going to hang for him.

"Get your shit together," Pat whispered, driving slowly and sticking to his preplanned route. It was bad enough he had to continually focus just to drive on the left side of the road. He had to operate flawlessly and try not to get detoured by any wrong turns. An accident or a stop by the Garda could be a disaster. Maybe he had seen too many movies, but he couldn't stop himself from constantly checking the rearview mirror to see if anyone was following him.

Once he reached the gym and locked the bag of money in the pre-arranged locker, he'd be done and free. Other than trying to get Treats, of course. He could still see traces of cocaine powder that Treats had left on the dash from their ride to Dublin. Taking another deep breath, he vowed that, somehow, he would find his buddy.

He reviewed the next steps in his head. Once at the gym, he was to shake hands with Coley. The gesture would let Coley know that his guys should get to the locker as soon as Pat was done making the drop. Jimmy came up with one extra measure to call the gym line back home and let it ring once; that would let him know the drop was complete and Pat was safe.

As he drove, Patrick scanned every car from every angle. He checked ahead, consulted his rearview, scanned the side mirrors, and even studied the pedestrians on the side of the street. The last thing he needed was to get jacked.

Patrick parked his car near this Sheriff Street alley in Dublin Ireland
Photo by Colm Pierce

Pat felt he was crossing invisible neighborhood lines as he headed into a different part of town, with a different feel. The area was called Sheriff Street; it was rundown and permeated a palpable danger, almost like home. IRA murals decorated the sides of decaying, ancient buildings. He'd seen a few of these before, back in Southie, but never to this extent. He was in the thick of it.

He found a parking spot not too far away from the gym. If he had to bolt out of there, he didn't want to be too far. He turned the engine off and sat still for a few moments, watching the cars drive by and the people walk about.

Prison had prepared him to live on the edge of heightened awareness and distrust. To get into that state of mind, you had to pay fucking attention. He scanned the area, taking note of the people entering and leaving the gym. A simple sign out front read "Street Boxing Club."

After surveying the area to his satisfaction, Pat took a few centering breaths. He could feel his heart slowing down as he focused on the matter at hand.

His last leg was here, a hundred-yard walk across a shady Dublin street. The stillness of the air and the silence of the streets made everything seem like it was moving in slow motion. All he had to do was open the trunk and walk through those doors, and he was practically home free.

This was his chance to undo what had been done. It would be a solid mission to not only get back on track but to give him a head start. He could gain back the five years lost in prison. He knew he would never commit a crime or get involved in anything corrupt again. Not after this, anyway. He just wanted life to be normal and to be able to have the cash to start fresh.

Pat slowly opened the car door. He circled to the trunk and lifted it open, checking the bag and feeling for the cash inside. Of course it was right where he had just put it. He swung the bag onto his shoulder and walked toward the gym.

The instant he opened the doors to the gym, he felt a familiar sense of comfort. It was a feeling of home, something so familiar and close to his childhood. He felt his shoulders relax as he listened to the layered sounds of boxing. He took in the slower and deeper sounds of fists hitting the heavy bag contrasted with the speed bags' faster and higher-pitched sounds, all punctuated with the bell. Many eyes noticed the stranger coming in but didn't seem to pay him any mind. They were putting in a mid-round workout.

An old-timer, probably in his late fifties and dressed in street clothes, walked up to meet Pat from somewhere near the ring. He came forward with his hand outstretched.

"Paddy! It's Coley. You made it like fuckin' clockwork, mate," he said, all smiles.

"Coley. It's great to meet you, sir," Pat replied, shaking his hand.

"Grab a locker, get wrapped up, and come see me. Jimmy told me you couldn't wait to hit those mitts. I got a few guys to put some work in with you," Coley said.

"I've been partying like a rock star for eight days," groaned Pat. "This could be messy!"

They shared a laugh. Coley slapped his shoulder in a gesture Pat took to mean, "I've been there, brother." On the front burner of his mind, Pat knew Coley was making a bit of a show for anyone watching. Coley had to sell the purpose of Pat's visit. He was just here to box. He wasn't here to drop off half a million dollars for an internationally wanted criminal. Nope, definitely not that. Pat played along with Coley, each acting their part perfectly.

Pat made his way to the locker room. It smelled like sweat and leather and bleach, just like O'Riley's. He searched for the locker Jimmy had told him, number seventy-four, and paused for a moment, enjoying the weight of all the cash. He would probably never know what it felt like to hold half a million dollars ever again. Pat removed a small bag from the backpack that contained his workout clothes. Then he zipped up the backpack, put it in the locker, and closed it shut. He secured the locker with a combination lock that Jimmy had given him.

That was it. The drop was done. Pat exhaled, feeling some of the stress leave his body.

He reached into his workout bag for his fighting clothes and put them on. Then he retrieved his boxing wraps and began the ritual of wrapping his hands. Just putting the wraps on his left hand started to sharpen his mind.

Dressed for the ring, Pat made his way to the front desk, saying hello to a few fighters along the way. A young kid was handling the front desk, probably working in exchange for membership.

"Can I use the phone?" Pat asked.

The kid nodded toward the corner of the desk, where Coley had placed an old phone in the corner. He picked up and dialed Jimmy, let the phone ring once, then hung up. Everyone along the chain from Jimmy to Choppa to Whitey or whoever else had orchestrated this plan would know that the drop was done.

Now, he was ready to fucking box.

———

GETTING BACK INTO THE RING WAS A BREATH OF FRESH AIR, regardless of how much weed, hash, and ecstasy was still running through his system. Before his trip, he had been working out every day with Jimmy. It'd been nearly a week now since he'd had a proper workout, not counting the fight with the five bikers.

About twenty minutes into his sparring workout, he felt himself shaking off the past week. His body felt renewed, as if the sleep deprivation from last night and the hangover didn't even exist. He felt invigorated. He could forget about all of it and just do what always took his mind off everything else: dancing in the ring with his fast, powerful hands.

In between short sparring rounds with others putting in their workouts, Pat sat on the edge of the ring with Coley, talking. Other fighters, probably regulars, observed the two guys' interaction with curiosity. Coley gestured for Pat to get into the ring. Coley followed right after, his hand pads on and ready to test Pat's skill. The mitt session with Coley got the attention of almost everyone. Coley was evidently the patron saint of boxing in this gym. He was an old-timer, but like Jimmy, he probably knew the art of boxing better than almost anyone.

The session started slowly. Pat could tell Coley was feeling him out, trying to get a sense of what kind of fighter he was—and Coley picked up immediately that he was a dominant left-handed puncher, a southpaw. Being a southpaw added to Pat's already rising reputation: good southpaws were rare and difficult to counter. After a few minutes, during which Coley tested Pat's straight left and hook on the mitt for power, he challenged Pat to pick up speed. Pat's blood and juices began to flow with the added challenge, and so did the punches connecting with Coley's mitts. The other boxers surrounded the ring, watching the newcomer intently.

His evaluation of Pat's skill seemingly complete, Coley tapped out and stepped out of the ring. He waved over another fighter to jump in. This guy was younger than Pat, a bit leaner, about the same height. The kid skipped the introductions and came in blazing, already warmed up from the heavy bag. Patrick felt him out, pulling his punches slightly. He didn't want to hurt the kid. But even going light on him, he obviously had the upper hand.

The kid lost patience with Pat's expert defense and got wild, sacrificing accuracy and strategy for power and speed. Big mistake. Pat used his split-second judgment and muscle memory to find an opening between the kid's punches and laid in with a Mickey Ward body shot that dropped him on one knee.

He stayed down, gasping, folding his arms to grip his side.

"You all right, kid?" Pat asked.

The kid nodded. He reached out his glove to tap Pat's out of respect. Pat tapped back, and then Coley helped the kid out of the ring.

"All right, man, that's enough for me for one day," said Pat. "I got nothing left."

"One more, pal," requested Coley. "This guy could use some practice going up against a southpaw. He has a fight next week."

Pat liked Coley, and he didn't want to be rude. He had to keep this relationship on the up and up as much as possible. "Whatever you say, Coley," he said, humoring him. "But one or two rounds is all I got."

Coley nodded and gestured for someone behind him to step forward. The guy who stepped into the ring was the most prominent fighter in the gym, maybe outweighing Pat by ten to twenty pounds. This Irishman was no joke. He was tatted up from head to toe, bouncing and dancing to psych himself up.

This guy was a showboat. Pat was sure he could take him, but it wouldn't be as easy as the last guy. He wasn't going to be pulling his punches this time.

They began with a little friendly pitter-patter. It was almost playful—feeling each other out, looking for any potential chinks in the armor. That lasted maybe a minute or two before both fighters intensified.

The crowd grew. Everyone, it seemed, wanted to see this Yank get knocked around by what Pat guessed was probably the best fighter among them. The Irishman had the home advantage and was lauded with cheers every time one of his punches connected. Pat was a curiosity and the villain of the moment. This Yank was messing with their hero.

Patrick knew this world all too well. Nothing here intimidated him; he'd seen it all.

Coley was coaching both corners, saying, "Take it easy" once in a while to keep passions cooled. His words went a long way in keeping a curious crowd from becoming an angry mob. Coley ran this place. The spectators would follow his lead.

He rang the bell, indicating the end of the first round.

Pat retreated to his corner. To their credit, one of the young kids offered him a water bottle. That was a nice touch of class, whoever that was. The rest of the crowd mobbed to the Irishman's side, patting him on the shoulder and shouting encouragement and cheers. From Pat's perspective, the guy looked enraged. Perhaps he was surprised that Pat was putting up a tougher fight than he'd expected.

The second round escalated as soon as the bell rang. The Irishman's temper exploded, going for headshots with powerful punches. Pat returned the attack, each of them getting a few good hits in. Still, he could see this guy's overconfidence was his weakness.

Acting on a hunch, Pat played possum, as if he were exhausted and couldn't match the pace or power of the Irishman. He retreated to the corner to make a show of catching his breath. But really, he was just luring his opponent in, looking for an opening to lay into him.

But this guy was coming to show his skill to his peers and Coley. He wanted to win decisively and dramatically, cementing his reputation as the local hero. He charged Pat, thinking the fight was practically already over. But Patrick had no more patience for the badass Irishman and decided to turn the tables on him. He had no more restraint or time. He had no business being in there anyway with all he had been through. Before the Irishman could get to him in the corner, Pat leaped forward and closed the distance, catching the Irishman by surprise. They grappled, stuck in a lock for a moment. Then Pat danced back and unleashed his straight left bomb. It hit the Irishman like a cannonball.

The Irishman dropped to a knee. The crowd reacted at first with a gasp, then a silent shock. Then grumblings began.

The Irishman stood up, but his head was swimming. Pat had rung his bell hard. One more attack and Pat could knock him out cold. He staggered forward for another shot at Pat.

But Pat waved it off, already starting to take off his gloves. "Sorry, I'm done, guys. Thanks for having me," he said. The grumblings and jeers intensified, followed by a few scattered claps. Despite the fact that Pat was a Yank and an outsider, at least a few of these guys had some sportsmanship, and even the Irishman gave a respectful nod. That was one of the great things about boxing: you could get the tar beaten out of you but still earn at least some respect. It was well earned.

As Pat came out of the ring, Coley patted him on the back. "Thank you, lad—a helluva challenge for my boy. Good fighting," he said. Pat could see why Jimmy liked him.

Now that the fight was over, the agenda of the moment rolled back into his mind. For a while, he'd completely forgotten about Treats. Pat figured he probably would have returned to the hotel by now. He always managed to find his way out of shit somehow. That asshole could sell hams in a synagogue. Hopefully, Pat could roll back, find Treats in the room, and they could all just jump on the plane and fly home.

Back in the locker room, he showered up, dried off, and grabbed his empty backpack. On the way out, he shook hands with a few fighters before Coley greeted him at the front door.

"Hey, what you did here today will never be forgotten. You're on the right side of history, my friend," Coley whispered. At first, Patrick thought he was referring to his boxing skills, but he quickly realized it was something much deeper and had to do with the drop.

Outside, a few of the guys were grouped together, talking. Pat recognized one of the guys as the one he had knocked down in the first round. He offered to shake his hand, and the kid half-heartedly complied. The others made some small talk. A Yank had never come into their boxing club and showed everybody up before. This was a rare event.

One of them asked, "How long you here?"

"One more night in this great city in this beautiful country, and then I'm headed back to Boston," Pat replied, in all sincerity.

Another of the men, taller and tougher looking, asked, "What's up for the evening, lad? You want us to take you out on the town?"

Patrick laughed to himself. That was the last fucking thing he needed. "No thanks, mate. We had just about all we can take. Last night, we really tied one on at The Kitchen and are still trying to recover," he answered. Taking a second glance at the guy who'd invited him out on the town, he felt a glimmer of recognition. Where'd he seen this guy before? He couldn't put his finger on it.

The man shook his hand again and said, "Well, go and rest up if it's your last night. I'm sure you'll get a second wind, though! Where you staying? We'll get you a proper Dublin *biodh turas deas agat*!"

Pat took that to mean *bon voyage* or something similar. Everyday Irish speech was full of these little Gaelic expressions. Most of the time, he just had to guess by context.

"We're at the Westbury. You might catch us at the bar," Pat responded. He doubted any of these guys were serious about taking him out.

The man nodded and smiled. Pat shook a few more hands and walked back across the street to his car. He walked briskly, already thinking about rejoining with Walsh to find their errant friend. With any luck, they'd both be waiting for him with a shot glass in hand at the hotel bar.

Chapter 27

SEARCH AND RESCUE

PAT BURST INTO THE HOTEL ROOM IN ANTICIPATION, HOPING to see Treats smoking a butt or ripping a fat line. But Treats was conspicuously absent. The minibar had gone unmolested. The bag of drugs was untouched. Uncharacteristic silence hung in the air.

Walsh sat out on the balcony by himself, staring out into the city. By the looks of the ashtray, he'd been chain-smoking. He glanced back, wide-eyed, perhaps hoping it was Treats who had just come in. His face fell when he saw Pat.

"Hey, man, nothing? No word?" Pat asked.

Walsh shook his head. Pat could see the lost look of disbelief and despair on Walsh's face. He rarely ever looked like this; it just wasn't him.

"No, man. I'm worried this time," Walsh said, lighting up another cigarette. "He would never do this. No call, no contact for this long. No way. Never."

Pat nodded in agreement. Something was definitely wrong. If this were back home, they'd already be looking for him at the bottom of the harbor.

"I even went by the local precinct to see if they had any dude from Boston locked up. Nothing." Walsh took a long drag off the cigarette, as if trying to extract wisdom and comfort from it. He met Pat's eyes, clearly thinking. "What happened at the gym, man? You were gone for so long . . . I've been freaking out."

He had to reveal part of the truth, at least. He owed that much to Walsh.

"Shit," Pat began. "Believe it or not, Walshy, I was doing something crazy for Jimmy. It was planned out for a while."

Walsh glared at him, his face reddening. Walsh opened his mouth to say something, but Pat jumped in first. "I'll tell you when I can. Don't ask me right now. We got to deal with this," he said, dancing around the truth. "The boxing club was in the shady Sheriff Street area, and I got a workout in with a great trainer named Coley Finnegan. I sparred a few rounds with two of his guys."

Walsh chucked his cigarette, already smoked down to the nub, off the balcony. "What the fuck—you sparred? You know I would've killed to have been there! I could have met you. I've always been in your corner, bro; you know that."

Pat could see the hurt and confusion all over Walsh's face. How could he have kept this from his best friend? They'd been through so much. Patrick's stint in prison had tested the relationship at the ultimate level, yet it had come out stronger for it. Walsh owed Pat his life—or at least twenty years of it. Even with that, Pat could see that this was a difficult moment for Walsh to surrender to the unknown.

"Trust me," Pat said sincerely. "I'll let you in on it. Seriously. But I can't just yet."

Walsh nodded. The trust was still there. But Pat could tell he still needed something to do other than smoke through two more packs of Marlboros.

"Okay, man," Walsh relented. "But what the fuck do we do now?"

Pat joined Walsh at his perch, leaning on the balcony railing beside him, looking out over the skyline. "I don't know where to begin, man," he confessed, desperate for a plan. "That hooker gave us nothing other than a mob or crime group that had her scared as shit."

"Can't we call Jimmy or go back down to that gym to ask around?" Walsh asked. "Somebody's gotta know who runs shit around here. And if anyone learns anything later on, they'll reach out for us."

It wasn't a bad plan, given the limited scope of Walsh's knowledge, thought Pat. But the added X factor of the mission and all the shadowy players that came with it gave him pause. Too risky. "Not sure I can do that right now," he told Walsh. "We need to keep this on the down-low and wait on calling in Jimmy and this guy Coley."

Walsh nodded.

"But . . . there were a bunch of guys down there, some sketchy too," Pat recounted, thinking aloud. "One of them asked if we wanted to hang out . . . said something in Gaelic—something like giving us a *bon voyage* Dublin style. I got a read on one of them when I said we were at the club last night."

"You think he knows something?" Walsh asked.

"It seemed off, but now that I think about it . . . I'm not sure. I said maybe and said we were staying in the hotel next door so they could find us in the bar. Then maybe we could hit the pavement."

"It's a long shot, man," Walsh admitted. "But it might be the only lead we have."

Pat nodded. "We'll get him back, Walshy. He's a goddamned swindler that could talk a dog off a meat wagon. He's gotta be okay. I just know it."

———

THE AFTERNOON SUN WAS STILL BRIGHT, AND PAT ENTERED the hotel bar with high hopes. Walsh trailed behind him.

He knew they might be in it for the long haul tonight. If some of these guys from the gym actually did show up, they'd probably want to toss back more than a few. As professional drinkers, Pat and Walsh knew to eat a big dinner to get the body prepped for savage intoxication. When they were through, several empty plates of entrées and appetizers littered the table. And they were already on their third round of Guinness.

"I'm going to call the concierge over and chat him up," said Walsh. "You wanna go see about the bartender?"

Pat nodded. He made his way back to the bar to get a jump on the next round and maybe see if he could coax any usable intelligence out of the barman. If anyone knew anything, it would be the bartender. He was at the center of all the drunken conversations in one of the best hotels in town.

After a few minutes, Pat returned to the table with a couple of shots to compare notes with Walsh.

"Sláinte," said Pat, clinking his shot glass with Walsh.

"Sláinte!" Walsh replied, downing his shot. After the familiar sharp "thud" of empty shot glasses on the table, they got down to business.

"So what did you find out?" asked Walsh.

"I got a few leads. I was telling him I boxed at the club earlier. He knew the place and some of the people there, so he opened up nicely. There is definitely a serious organization overseeing everything here. That's about as far as I got. What did the concierge say?"

"I got him to open up too after I told him I was going to be a Boston cop," said Walsh. "He mentioned some crew called GTL. They're kind of like how Whitey's crew ran Boston. They control everything. The whole fucking thing, from the churches to boxing promotion to drugs."

Pat's ears perked up. He leaned in, thinking.

"Hmm. Now . . . how do we get to them at the right level? I'd rather not request contact through one of these guys. Let's just find out what specific bar they roll in and see what happens," suggested Pat. "Time is fuckin' ticking, man. We been here fishing for two hours. Let's finish this pint and hustle over to a spot that they're known to hang at. Hopefully, they'll get the idea and help lead us to where the fuck he is."

"Not if they fuckin' killed him, Patrick," said Walsh.

"Listen, he disappeared at two a.m. last night," answered Pat. "It's only been twelve hours. He might be in bad shape, but I just know in my gut he's still alive. He's a fresh prick, but he's fucking harmless! He can't be killed for bottling someone in the bathroom and grabbing his cash."

"Really?" Walsh asked with a raised eyebrow. "Why not? If this happened back home at Triple O's, I wouldn't be surprised if they were digging a hole for him right now."

"You've got a point," Pat admitted. "But Treats didn't know who they were. It wasn't blatant disrespect."

"Let's settle up and get on the road," Walsh said.

Pat agreed. They couldn't accomplish much more here other than adding another layer of intoxication. Pat walked over to settle with the bartender, his back momentarily to Walsh. When he had paid and turned around, he saw Walsh was already stirring up some trouble with two guys at the table next to theirs. One of the men laughed heartily, and although it didn't sound foreboding, Pat hustled back anyway and joined Walsh at the table, sitting right next to him. He gave the laughing stranger a quick glance. It was him; he recognized the guy he'd seen outside the gym. The stranger, in turn, sized up Pat too. They shook hands, relieving some of the unspoken tension that had apparently put Walsh on the defensive.

"The name's Martin. Pretty impressive morning with you, southpaw. First guy was pretty easy. Second guy was one of the best around. Well done," said Martin.

Pat, caught a little off guard, searched for something to say. But at least they wouldn't have to look for these guys anymore.

"What you say, me and my fellas with your crew tonight? Sounds like some *craic* for the history books," Martin continued. "As long as we don't kill anyone or each other!"

Martin tipped his glass, and once again, he bellowed a laugh loud enough for the street to hear. This time his friends joined in.

Pat and Walsh looked at each other, searching for how to handle the cocksure Martin and his cronies. This guy was coming off as a man who was confident and connected to a certain degree.

Walsh was clearly holding his silence and waiting for Pat to make the first move.

"We would love that, Martin," Pat responded. "Sounds like a plan, but we may need help with something . . . so as long as we can keep this between us and not Coley Finnegan."

"Coley Finnegan?" Martin responded. "We keep everything from that man but the boxing gloves. He's old school and focused on fighting a different war!"

Martin's entourage raised their glasses. Pat was still uncertain of what to make of them, opting for silence. At least at the moment. It was hard not to crack a smile.

When the laughter died down, Martin leaned back in his chair and folded his hands.

"So what can we help with, Patrick?" Martin asked.

"I got a fuckin' problem, mate," Pat admitted. "We went to The Kitchen last night. Then . . . something happened, and our friend has been missing ever since. All we have to go on is this hooker that he was with who said someone pulled up in a truck and snatched him. We got nothin' after that."

Martin nodded knowingly. He leaned in slowly, placing his hands neatly on the table and folding them. Everything was deliberate. "So . . . when you say something 'happened,' you don't mean that your mate comes into our bar, ambushes our man in the bathroom, bottles him in the stall, stomps on him, then takes his cash and a bag of pills, do you?" Martin asked.

Pat felt the blood drain from his face. It was a fucking checkmate move.

"And then," Martin continued, "he stops at the bar on the way out to have a shot with your man here, then walks around the corner to bang a hooker in the alley like he's out for a stroll in the park? Yeah, fucking bollocks eh."

Pat's chin was practically on the floor and, by the look on Walsh's face, he wasn't faring any better. They were busted and at the mercy of whoever the fuck these guys were. Patrick took a breath and collected himself.

"I knew there was something more to you, Martin," Pat said in a calm and steady voice. "Where the fuck is he? Can you tell me right now he's okay?"

"Easy, lad." Martin laughed. "You're not in Boston anymore. It all depends on what you consider 'okay.'" He took a pause for dramatic effect, taking a sip from his drink before he continued. "I can tell you he's alive," he said finally.

"All right, let's cut the bullshit," answered Pat, finding his confidence. "What the fuck's going on and what do we gotta do? No disrespect. We had no idea what he was up to or who we were dealing with."

Martin nodded. He sat upright and unfolded his hands. "You see, Patrick, it's not good having my dealer walk out of the bathroom with his head all bloody. You're a reasonable guy. What type of message is that?"

Pat considered in silence. Martin wasn't wrong. If this were back home, this could have been a fatal mistake when dealing with whoever ruled the streets. Walsh was right.

"Better yet," Martin added, "what type of punishment fits that? You fuckin' Yanks have been touring the country like a rabid rock band—like you own the place. And *your* fucked-up friend is telling the story that *my* dealers are selling counterfeit drugs." Martin took another sip from his drink and went back into it. "Do you know what that does to an organi-zation? No? It breaks it down at the core, and someone ends up proper fucked!"

Pat wasn't sure how this was going to end. Already he was visualizing getting tied to a chair and kneecapped or far fucking worse.

"By the way, it's not my drugs that are counterfeit. That was pharmaceutical-grade ecstasy. It's you fucking Yanks. You've pushed your damn brains past the limits, and now they're fried! After days of doing ecstasy, your man won't feel jack shit. On top of that, the dealer he hit over the head is a son of a much, much more powerful man."

This wasn't good. Pat felt the facts pile on like cement shoes.

"Listen, Martin," Walsh proposed. "We're resourceful guys. What do we gotta do?"

"What's this guy worth to you?" Martin asked.

"If you mean money, it's the end of the trip and we don't have much in hand right now," Patrick said. "Our flight leaves tomorrow night."

"I figured that as well," Martin said, nodding. "When I saw you at the gym, and you said you were from Boston and were at The Kitchen last night, I put it all together and immediately got an idea. An idea that'll make me a lot of money. A lot. And I'll be glad to turn your crazy ass friend over to you if you play along. So, like I said, we're going to have one hell of a Dublin *bíodh turas deas agat.*"

Pat didn't like the sound of it, and from Walsh's clenched jaw, he could tell Walsh didn't either. But what could he do? He had to at least hear the proposal.

"All right, Martin. I'm listening," offered Pat.

"Well, my friend, all you have to do is show up here tonight at ten. You might wanna rest up a bit, 'cause you'll be squaring off under the moonlight," said Martin, slipping Pat a small piece of paper with an address on it.

Squaring off? What the fuck was this guy talking about? Pat unfolded the piece of paper. It was an address. He wasn't exactly sure where it was. He handed the paper to Walsh.

"What? A fight? With who? After today, I got nothing left, man. You mean a street fight?" Pat asked.

"Call it what you will," smirked Martin. "But we call it an old-fashioned straightener. And yes, no gloves! You lucked out, lads!"

Pat and Walsh exchanged a look. This was their shot. If they wanted Treats back, they'd have to do what Martin asked. If they ran away, they might never see Treats again. Pat tried to find a different angle, but there were none.

"Don't get any ideas," warned Martin. "You want your friend to come home with you in one piece, don't you?"

Pat and Walsh both nodded.

"You should thank me," Martin said through a smile. "I created a solution to the problem. The higher-ups went for it, so don't fuck it up! All you have to do is show up at the address I gave you. Thirty miles west of Dublin, Yanks!"

"So what—I fight, and, win or lose, he just leaves with us?" Pat asked.

"Yup. But don't fuckin' lose 'cause I am putting extra cash on you," Martin said. "I got the inside scout tip! No one else'll bet on you, that's for sure!" Martin let fly another chilling laugh. The rest of his crew snickered along with him.

"Martin," Pat said, "I gotta see Treats now or at least before tonight. I gotta know if—"

"He's already out at the farm. He don't look so good. But he's breathin'," Martin reassured through his toothy grin. "We'll call your room in a few hours." He rose from his chair and tipped his hat. He tossed a few bills onto the table for the drinks. In perfect sync, his right-hand man and the rest of his entourage also rose. They turned and filed out of the bar into the street.

Pat and Walsh sat in silence for a few moments, staring out the door Martin and his goons had just exited.

"Pat, I know this sounds bad, but in the big picture, Treats has another horseshoe up his ass once again," said Walsh. "He could be dead or in a much worse situation."

Patrick let out an exasperated chuckle and shook his head. "Easy for you to say!" he exclaimed. "I gotta fight some turkey psychopath in the most exhausted shape of my life."

"Well, you've seen much tougher situations in your life. Just think of it as us driving over to Garvey Park to square off with an Adam's corner kid."

Pat knew the reference well. Adam's corner was nearby Garvey Park in Boston, a heavy White-Irish area. Guys with beefs from opposing neighborhoods would often square off and throw down there. There were a few other parks like that—Dot Park, Hemenway Park, Faxon Park, to name a few. Pat couldn't count how many times he'd fought in one random skirmish or another.

But this was different. In the parks, Pat almost always had the upper hand. These Irish guys were trained fighters in a place known for producing some of the world's best boxers. And with no gloves! He'd be walking into the lion's den. Pat was already exhausted from this morning, but he didn't see much choice in the matter. He had to do what he had to do.

"You know, I just wanted to have one night to close out our trip," sighed Pat, shaking his head. "I would have grabbed dinner, maybe seen Siobhan one more time, and headed home, Walshy."

"That would've been too easy." Walsh laughed. "Let's go crash in the room for a few hours. After tonight, it'll all be over."

———

THE TRANSITION FROM A MODERN COSMOPOLITAN CITY TO the rural countryside in the middle of nowhere happened fast. They had the benefit of a three-quarters-full moon to guide them on the dirt country road devoid of any lights. It reminded Pat of Roundstone all over again, with the moon casting a pale light and long shadows all over the countryside.

Walsh had insisted on driving so Pat could focus on the upcoming fight. In the back of his mind, Pat thought Walsh might have still been afraid he'd flip the car again. But without Treats around, that joke went unsaid.

He'd actually gotten some decent sleep in the afternoon. His body was wiped out, and the beer had helped put him down. Most of all, the knowledge that Treats was possibly alive and within spitting distance gave him hope. But with just wrapped and taped-up hands, and no gloves, the possibility of injury was much higher. These guys wouldn't be fucking around.

Pat squinted and saw a small road to the left branching off from the dirt road. It led up a modest hill, where they could see lights and maybe a few campfires.

"I think this is it," said Walsh. He turned left and headed up the hill.

When they got to the hill's down-sloping side, they saw open fields and a farmhouse just ahead. A short distance from the farmhouse was a huge barn. The adjacent fields served as an impromptu parking lot for dozens of cars. They could see the light of more cars coming in the distance.

"What the fuck? Is all of Ireland here?" Pat asked. He hadn't been expecting the fight to be a massive event.

"These people love this shit," Walsh said. "It's the old country. They got nothing else to do."

They parked on the edge of a field and made their way to the barn, where all the ruckus was coming from. The crowd noise felt like that of any run-of-the-mill, wholesome event, like a music festival or a bonfire party. Except, instead, it was going to be guys beating the shit out of each other. The closer they got to the barn, the more enormous Pat realized it was, easily double the size of any of the barns he'd seen before.

The giant doors were wide open. When they entered, Patrick could see an open area the size of a hockey rink. He guessed this was where they most likely put on horse shows or maybe auctioned livestock. It was now filled with Irishmen, boozed up and ready to see the action. Clouds of smoke hung in the air from all the cigarettes and pipes.

A few scattered faces noticed Pat and Walsh, and then the recognition grew. In seconds, nearly everyone was sizing up Pat and commenting to each other. He was most likely the main event. The sudden appearance of a contender boosted the crowd's energy. They were getting rowdier by the moment.

Pat knew that he and Walsh fit the bill perfectly. The scarring on Walsh's face gave him a mean, scary look. Pat was lean and ripped; he'd been told many a time before that he had a look in his eye like he would rip your throat out and not think twice. Pat was fully aware of the importance of making an impression on their entrance. And it was authentic. They didn't have to front; they'd grown up in the toughest part of Boston.

From seemingly nowhere, Martin materialized from the crowd. He shook their hands, as if this wasn't extortion, and led them to a stable in the back where they could get ready.

"Where the fuck is Treats, Martin?" Pat demanded. "I am not doing this until I see him."

"Listen, I'll grab him," said Martin. "You get ready and get to the center. You're up next. Look up to the left-hand side. He'll be up there looking down, watching you."

Pat studied Martin's face. He seemed to be telling the truth, but Pat had long since learned not to trust anybody, especially if they already have your balls in a vice.

"After this, he'll be at your car ready to go," Martin explained. "I suggest you get the hell out of here fast! I anticipate there will be a lot of angry losers around here."

Pat shot him a look. "Why's that?"

"Don't get me wrong. This is one helluva fighter you're up against, lad. But Treats gave me the history on you, so I'm betting Boston." Martin shook his hand, grasping Pat's forearm with his other hand, then slapped him on the shoulder before turning to leave.

A few paces away, Martin turned his head back and shouted over the noise of the crowd. "That Treats is one funny bastard!" he yelled, letting loose his trademark laugh as he walked away.

Pat spent the next few minutes putting the wraps on his hands. Unceremoniously, he and Walsh started to tear their way through the rowdy crowd to get to the center, a dirt square marked by four trash barrels.

"Treats is going to owe you his life," said Walsh.

Pat just nodded. It was time to spring the devil from hell and race away to escape the flames.

Chapter 28

BARN BRAWL

AS THE CROWD GREW LOUDER, PAT INCREASED HIS PREFIGHT focus. He warmed up by drilling with some footwork and jabs into the air, which helped get his mind and body synced up to the present where everything was happening right now, so he could let instinct take over.

He looked around and soaked up the atmosphere, focusing on where exactly he was and what was happening. It was a little prefight intelligence. Who were these people exactly, and what was at stake here? What environment was he fighting in, and how would the crowd react? All important questions, should the shit hit the fan any worse than it already had.

Pat could take a few educated guesses based on things he already knew. He'd heard bare-knuckle fights here in Ireland were usually like street fight grudge matches between two people from different communities to resolve some kind of grievance. Fighting was both a universal language and an agreed-upon solution. Typically, a public fight would end the matter one way or the other, and the resolution was often clean and definitive.

The fights were stand-up, bare-knuckle bouts. The fighters just had wraps to secure the hands. Someone well respected would be the mutually agreed-upon ref. Things could always get out of control fast. Jimmy had told Pat about a boxing event he attended in Ireland with the Boston Police Athletic League, a semiannual charity event where some of the best of Boston-Irish boxers from the PAL would fight the best of some of the local fighters in Ireland from small communities all over the country. The fights were an all-day deal, and then the Boston group would stay in these cottages.

One night, after the fights, all the Irish and the Boston group got together for a cookout-type gathering. A couple of kids who had fought each other during the day were trying to play nice by drinking together. One thing led to another, and they ended up squaring off. Then the situation escalated quickly and became a battle of the Boston Irish versus the Ireland Irish. The argument got ugly, with the Irish kids in caravans of cars circling the cottages, throwing bottles and rocks and breaking windows. It was such a dramatic incident that the prime minister of Ireland made a public apology to the BPD members that were involved.

Why was fighting so deeply embedded in the Irish DNA? Being among the lowest ranks of the White race for centuries and surviving the Irish genocide—the Great Hunger, the Potato Famine—was generational pain Pat had heard about over and over again since the day he was born. In Ireland, fights could be held anywhere—on a farm, in the street, in someone's backyard, or in the middle of the woods. Entire communities would come to watch the fighters go at each other. It was a family affair, just part of the culture.

But this was different. This fight was clearly a money opportunity engineered by a Dublin organized crime group that none would dare cross.

Pat was at a disadvantage, knowing nothing about this mystery fighter's history, character, or fighting tendencies. Would he be facing the tattooed fighter he'd fought earlier today? Or would it be some other demented underground bare-knuckle Irish boxer?

With Walsh at his side, Pat ventured closer to the crowd to identify where the fighter could be. He scanned the motley crew of characters of the large group. Through a circle of scally caps, Pat spotted the broad back of a man having his hands wrapped. The man had a shaved head with a tattoo covering the whole back of his skull. The tattoo was of a large Celtic cross with St. Patrick in front of it—a religious symbol but also a symbol of national pride.

"Go size him up, and get a good look at those wraps," Pat whispered.

After a quick nod, Walsh dashed off to take a look. Pat had to be extra careful. If not for the organized crime group aspect, he wouldn't have distrusted squaring off with a fellow Irishman, but when it came to making money, anything could happen. The opponent could be using a loaded wrap—with hidden foreign objects that would make the fist hit harder or heavier or even tear flesh. It was harder to hide in just a wrap than in a glove, but a skilled operator could still do it.

Walsh was back at his side. "Seems like the man's got some skill. He's about your size. Crowd seems to like him. Wraps look legit, though. Nothing funny."

Pat was ready. He stuck out his hands for Walsh to help with the tape over the wraps. Walsh had done this before at several of Pat's tournaments back in Jimmy's gym.

As Walsh finished up, Pat glanced up at the large picture window on the second level. He noticed some people milling around up there, probably some of the higher-ups of the organization using it as sort of a skybox for the underground brawls.

"Let's get it done, brother," said Walsh. "The sooner it's over, the sooner we go home."

"What did you think of the other guy?" Pat asked.

"He's a bald, former redhead stepchild fucking beast, but you got this!" exclaimed Walsh.

Pat nodded and smiled, reassured by the vote of confidence. He took another glance around and spotted what he assumed were Martin's guys. They were taking last-minute cash bets from the crowd. The hodge-podge group of fans was sizing up this unknown opponent from Boston. They were here to catch a unique scrap, one they wouldn't typically get.

He looked up and let his eyes wander back to the picture window. *Wait. Is that... ?* He squinted to try and get a better look. *Yes. It is Treats, that little fucker.* He was sitting down, surrounded by a bunch of older guys in suits. Treats looked pretty banged up, with a couple of black eyes and split lip.

Suddenly, Pat's opponent was right in front of him, seeming to materialize from fucking nowhere. To Pat, he looked like one of the original Celtic Viking warriors. On the left side of the redheaded warrior's chest, he had a tattoo of a fist with bloody knuckles that read *The Tip Terror*.

"You ready, Yank?" said the warrior.

Pat nodded, stone-faced.

Another man stepped forward. From his demeanor and dress, Pat instantly surmised this was the ref. No doubt he was in Martin's pocket, but at least they had a ref. "All right, lads. No clinching; we'll break you up," he said in a practiced pitch. "If a KO, I'll give you a standing ten-count before you reengage. No three-KO rule. I'll call it as I see it. Go to it, lads."

The fighters both nodded in agreement. Then the Tip Terror tapped fists with Pat. "You're going down, Boston," he said, locking eyes with Pat. They walked back to their respective corners. With the roar of the crowd, they prepared for the first round.

The ref looked up at the picture window, then nodded to someone in the booth. Then he brought his fingers to his mouth and blew an ear-piercing whistle.

It was on. Patrick entered the center of the four-barrel circle.

The two men squared off, feeling each other out. The Tip Terror had an orthodox stance, a right-handed boxer. Pat faced him with a southpaw stance, leading with his right hand and right foot forward so he could jab with his right and pack a wallop with his left.

There was a small murmur from the crowd when they recognized his left-handed stance. Pat was uncertain whether the word had gotten out from his little demo fight this morning that he was a southpaw. It could have been privileged info that Martin and his men kept to themselves for the betting advantage.

It was still the opening moments. The fighters traded quick jabs, with occasional straights to feel out each other's power. Pat could tell he was facing—at the very least—an equal. He couldn't get cocky here.

They both tried a few combinations on each other, a few connecting quickly, but nothing dramatic. They seemed to counter each other's every move. The match was feeling too even, too equal. At some point, some-one had to break out of the pattern.

As if reading his mind, the Tip Terror began to amp up the pressure. Pat dodged and countered at a quickened pace. They were almost at the end of the first round. He continued to jab and dance, dodging the dead-liest of the Terror's punches. Then the Tip Terror broke his rhythm and unloaded a monster overhand right, straight to Patrick's forehead. It hit him like a bus.

The crowd went nuts.

Pat staggered back, shaken. The ref whistled, signifying the end of round one. Pat turned to his corner to find Walsh and collapsed on the stool. He craned his neck as Walsh spouted water into his mouth from a plastic bottle. He only had sixty seconds to recover and strategize.

"What the fuck, dude?" groaned Pat. "Dude hits like a freight train, man. He's throwing it like a grenade."

"Yeah, yeah, yeah," said Walsh, talking fast. "Listen. It's okay. That's probably all he's got. One-trick pony. Make him miss big with his overhand, then hit him with uppercuts and then come back with your left. Bink, bink, boom—all right?"

Pat nodded. He wasn't going to fall for it again. When Tip's punch came up this time, Pat's face wouldn't be at the end of it. He'd know the signs and the timing.

The ref whistled, and Pat erupted out of his seat with fierce motivation. They squared off again. As before, they traded jabs, but the pace was faster and more explosive. Pat tried various combinations, and a few punches landed but nothing devastating. The Tip Terror tried his own combinations, but nothing significantly connected. They were both getting pissed off and went more aggressive, which forced them to clinch.

The ref broke them up as soon as he saw it. They were serious about their rules; this was definitely a legit bare-knuckle street fight with some integrity. The two fighters separated and immediately went back into the fray.

TT was loose now and punching with energy and fury. Pat could already feel himself slipping behind. If he kept up this intense pace, the Tip Terror could just wear him out, catch him off guard, and unload his trick punch. That might be the end of it.

The onslaught kept coming. The Terror unleashed another combination. Pat blocked a few punches, but a couple connected. He was clearly on the defensive, which had to change real quick. He stepped back to get some room, still reeling from the hits, but his timing was terrible. The Terror threw his overhand right bomb and made a direct hit on Pat's forehead again. Pat lost balance, dropped to a knee, and then staggered back into his corner, where Walsh was waiting. Just as Pat started to fall down, the ref whistled and ended the second round. Walsh grabbed Pat and helped him balance, saving him the embarrassment of just plopping down on his ass.

"Patrick, listen. Look up there," said Walsh, pointing up at the picture window.

Patrick, in a temporary daze, looked up into the booth. "Yeah, I know. I saw him too," he groaned. Treats was standing among a few old-timers, with a cigarette, a fucking lowball whiskey glass in hand, and that motherfuckin' shit-eating grin.

"That dickhead's watching you fight right now," Walsh said. "Now end this fucking right now so we can grab that fuckin' idiot and beat the fuck out of him and go home!"

Glaring, Pat spit blood like it was venom. He could feel the rage building up in him like a volcano. Walsh knew precisely what to say to piss him off. And he'd been spot on. Seeing Treats comfortable with a drink in hand was enough to make him blow his stack and go nuclear on this guy.

Pat was standing steady now, his eyes focused, his mind clear, his heart full of fire and fury. The ref whistled to start the round, and he launched a few jabs and got into a stance that he knew would bait the Tip Terror's right overhand. There was no way this Celtic warrior could resist ringing Pat's bell a third time.

Sure enough, the Terror threw his monster right, but Pat dash-stepped to the left, throwing two power uppercuts to the warrior's face before he even knew what hit him. The Tip Terror dropped to one knee.

The crowd gasped, then roared with disbelief.

But the Tip Terror wasn't giving up just yet. He slowly rose and shook it off, getting back into his orthodox stance and ready to charge. But just as he started advancing, a gush of blood began to pour from a nasty-looking slice right above his eyebrow that went up about an inch and a half toward the center of his forehead. Someone from the Terror's entourage jumped into the ring and dabbed it with a shirt.

Holy fuck. This gash was flopping in the wind, a giant flap of flesh hanging off the man's face. This bastard was going to need at least eighteen stitches to fix that gaping wound. And he'd have a nasty scar to keep as a Boston souvenir.

The fight was over. No way could he fight in that condition. The ref nodded and blew the whistle while the crowd erupted in deafening shouts and boos.

The ref slid next to Pat and lifted Pat's arm in victory—appropriately, his left arm. By the reaction of the crowd, Pat surmised most of them had betted against him. *Well, fuck them*, he thought.

Uppercuts were Pat's favorite, the kind of uppercuts that Mike Tyson used to throw. Pat had Jimmy to partially thank for his uppercut technique. Jimmy had spent time in the Catskills with Cus D'Amato, the infamous manager of boxers like Tyson and Patterson and Torres. He'd trained some of the old-school greats too. No one knew the uppercut like Cus D'Amato. Jimmy took everything he learned from Cus and drilled it into his fighters over and over. Pat had learned from the best.

Pat was slowly returning to sanity, but he knew he still had plenty of leftover rage to take on Treats. All in good time. He looked up at the booth and saw Treats already coming down the stairs. Behind him was Martin, smiling. "We better get the fuck outta here quick, Pat," Walsh said. "The natives are getting restless."

Of course they fucking are, thought Pat. *They always get a little rowdy and pissed when the loser still wants to fight.* "All right, let's get outta here now," he said. "Treats can catch up. Looks like Martin is keeping his word."

Treats was probably a good thirty feet behind them at least, but he'd just have to book it; they sure as hell weren't sticking around.

A rush of cold air hit them as they left the barn. They were in the first wave of the dispersing crowd and wasted no time getting to the car. Walsh started the engine right away as Treats caught up and jumped in the back. Before he could even slam the door, Walsh took off like a bullet, speeding down the dirt road and leaving a billowing cloud of dust.

Patrick turned around and glared at Treats for just a few seconds. Then he threw a quick shot at him with his power left. It connected in a satisfying hit, and Treats howled in response. Patrick turned back around in silence.

"What the fuck was that for?" Treats asked, still rubbing his jaw.

"I can't wait to hear all of your bullshit," Pat yelled back. "We thought you were fuckin' dead, you idiot. You've been on a death wish this whole trip, the opposite of what I signed on for, fuckhead." He turned back around and gave Treats his death stare.

Treats, for his part, seemed wise enough to keep his mouth shut for the moment.

"You look fine," said Pat, disgusted. "Two black eyes and some cuts, and then you're drinking and smoking with the same fuckin' characters that snatched you?"

Walsh held his tongue, checking the rearview mirror for anyone who may have been following them.

"I almost *did* die!" Treats protested. "Those guys are no joke! But then, I just tried to make the best of the situation, Patrick! Do you think I wasn't gonna get involved in a wager, my friend, especially when you're the underdog?"

There he goes, thought Patrick. The fountain of bullshit just kept coming.

"Fuck that!" Treats continued, on a rant. "When it came down to it, I speak the same language as them. And to top it off, I made us a fair cut on that bout too! Just for your troubles, Patrick."

Pat turned back around to face the front, exasperated. He didn't know whether to laugh or fucking punch him again. "For fuck's sake, of course you did," he said. He stuck his hand back, palm open, without even looking at Treats.

Treats slapped his open hand with a thick stack of cash. Pat yanked his hand back and flipped through it. Hundred-euro notes. Pat was guessing around five grand. He smiled and shook his head. Treats wasn't off the hook yet, but this sure fucking helped. "Keep it," Treats said, putting his arms behind his head and leaning back. "You've earned it."

Pat did the math. Ten Gs from Walsh, five Gs from Treats, and twenty-five Gs for the job. That was forty grand. Not a bad haul for one trip. All he had to do was get home safely without further incident, which he could definitely do—provided he could keep himself from murdering Treats in his sleep.

"What happened?" Walsh asked, finally piping up.

"I'll tell you how it all went down back at the hotel bar," Treats said, cracking his big smile. It took Pat everything he had not to smash that shit-eating grin into orbit.

Chapter 29

LAST NIGHT

THERE'S NOTHING QUITE LIKE A HOT SHOWER RIGHT AFTER A serious fight, Pat thought, relishing the high-pressure water power-blasting his arms and shoulders. Worries melted off him as the water rinsed off the grime and blood and sweat. The stress of losing Treats and the fear surrounding the drop-off was gone, like so many droplets down the drain. No goons from Martin or the IRA or anyone associated with Jimmy would be coming to make him disappear. All he had to do was make it back to Boston, and he was home free.

He wouldn't be done with the pain for a while; he knew from experience that this was the intermediary period, where the body was still adrenalized for hours after the fight. He felt a little sore, sure. But it would be tomorrow when things would really start to hurt. It'd probably take two weeks before his body recovered. But none of that mattered. He'd accomplished the mission. Treats was safe. And Siobhan was coming over.

It was still before midnight. The first thing Pat did the moment the boys got back to the hotel room was to call Siobhan. It was his last night, a night he thought he would lose to the whole Treats debacle. These surprise bonus hours were a gift that he couldn't squander. Siobhan had been on his mind the minute they left the countryside.

Walsh had made himself busy doing all the things a coach would do for his fighter for post-fight recovery. He'd already fetched several buckets of ice from room service, both for the champagne and for icing Pat's bruises. Somehow, he had wrangled a small case of Gatorade.

Treats, being Treats, beelined it for the cocaine and had already headed downstairs to have a cigarette and a drink at the hotel bar at one of the tables set outside on the sidewalk. Pat didn't bother to protest; Treats was on his own. If he needed rescuing again, it'd be the universe's job. No doubt he was relishing the fresh air. God knows what kind of box or shitty horse stall they'd kept him locked up in for the last twenty-four hours.

As for Treats's side of the story of his abduction, Pat took a rain check. He'd find out on the plane. Any moment spent listening to Treats's bullshit tonight was a moment he wouldn't be able to spend with Siobhan.

Pat dressed in some of the last clean clothes he had left: a button-up shirt and a pair of jeans. It wasn't fancy, but it didn't matter. They probably weren't leaving the hotel room. With Siobhan and the champagne, he had everything he needed.

When Walsh came back from his successful quest to find some over-the-counter painkillers, he excused himself right away, seemingly satisfied with Pat's return to normalcy. He ducked out of the room to join Treats at the bar.

A rapid little knock on the door interrupted Pat's last check of himself in the mirror. His face was a touch swollen, he had a black eye, and he looked like he hadn't slept in days. *Oh well*, he thought. *It is what it is.*

He swung open the door to reveal Siobhan leaning up against the doorjamb on one arm. She was wearing a slinky black dress with spaghetti straps and a plunging neckline. She must have left her leather jacket at the coat check.

"Isn't it past your bedtime?" Siobhan asked. Her tone was playful, smoldering.

Pat smiled. She was the best thing he'd seen all week. Again.

"Get in here," Pat said, wrapping his arm around her waist and planting a kiss. She wrapped her arms around him and kissed him right back.

———

HOURS LATER, THEY LAY TOGETHER NAKED AND BREATHLESS, cratered on top of the bedsheets. Pat had no idea what time it was and didn't fucking care. Although he'd had some champagne, it was Siobhan that was his true intoxication. He lay there, staring into her eyes, extracting every last bit of pleasure from this moment before he inevitably had to say goodbye.

They both got up to get some air. Siobhan wrapped herself in a sheet and walked over to the balcony to peer over the railing. Pat threw on his boxers and brought over two more glasses of champagne.

They peered down and could see Treats and Walsh, still drinking outside on the sidewalk. They had littered their table with glasses and bottles. It was a small miracle that Treats stuck close to the hotel, thought Pat. Maybe, for once, he had decided to stop pressing his luck, at least until he got to Boston.

Siobhan waved her arms to get Treats and Walsh's attention. "You Yanks right knackered yet?" she called down.

Treats and Walsh looked up and waved back. They called back a response in the form of an exuberant drunken cheer. If they used words, they were unintelligible.

Siobhan laughed. She put her hand on Pat's on the railing and met his gaze. "Do you think we'll ever see each other again?" she asked.

God yes, Pat thought. But it's not what he said. His tongue was tied, and no words came out at first. Was this what they called love at first sight? This attraction was so powerful, yet comfortable. It was like he'd known her for years.

"I certainly hope so," Pat responded, drawing her closer. "I would really enjoy coming back and having a normal trip. If that's possible."

Siobhan threw her head back and laughed. "Of course it's possible!" she said, gripping his arms as she giggled. "If you don't look for trouble every step of the way, you might actually enjoy yourself!"

Pat chuckled. She was one hundred percent correct.

"You three look like you've been to hell and back. And now it's time for you to go already," Siobhan said.

She leaned into his chest, and Pat held her.

"Let's not think about that, Siobhan. Let's just enjoy the rest of the night. But hey, it's nice to know Boston to Dublin is a simple trip across the pond."

He kissed her again, and as usual, time stopped. They set down their champagne glasses as Siobhan led Pat back to bed.

Chapter 30

CHINATOWN

REDEEM THE TIME, FOR THE DAYS ARE EVIL.

Nate read the Bible verse that Reverend Gibbs had loosely quoted at least a thousand times since Jamal's funeral. He couldn't help it; it played over and over again like a refrain, seemingly encapsulating the present times perfectly. How could something written so long ago still be so true today? Nate knew he'd never be as religious as his aunt Carol or Reverend Gibbs, but he could still see the poetry and truth in the phrase. It had become a part of him.

He hung up the phone; he'd been talking to his mother, who he seemed to miss more and more by the day. Momentarily, he thought about driving south and escaping his dangerous dilemma between good and evil.

Today, he wanted to make it officially more permanent. He had decided to have *Redeem the time* tattooed into his arm underneath a cross. He was determined to set out and get the tattoo in the Combat Zone, at the same Asian restaurant where Pat had received his, shortly before getting pinched graduation night. At the time, he'd dared Nate to get a tattoo as well, but Nate had chickened out.

He laughed at the memory, remembering he was worried about what his mother would think or that he'd get a disease from the needle in the hidden back room. He no longer was that kid scared of what other people would think about him anymore.

Nate stood on Washington Street, at the top of the stairs to the lower entrance of the restaurant, which was identical to how it was back then. Slugs stood by his side; he had invited himself to tag along. No one could devour Asian food like Slugs, so he'd jumped at the opportunity.

Later, at the table, Slugs selected a ten-course meal off the menu. Nate laughed internally, knowing there'd be no leftovers. As the waiter came to take the order, Nate slipped him a drawing of the tattoo he wanted. The waiter nodded and prepared the back room and tattoo artist to receive the next customer.

After Slugs had stuffed himself with his pupu platter, the waiter beckoned for Nate to follow him into the hidden back room to get his ink. Slugs excused himself to stand outside, where he would light up a butt.

The makeshift tattoo parlor was behind the kitchen and, just as Nate remembered it, full of shelves and stocked with dry goods, both familiar and strange. The tattoo artist sat ready and gestured for Nate to sit down on a simple folding chair. He thought it might have been the same dude who did Pat's tattoo five years ago, but he felt it might be an insult to assume the racial profile so quickly.

Nate watched intently as the artist expertly injected the ink with a sure hand. The pain felt right and matched the tattoo's message. It was a reminder that evil was all around him and that he was committed to making the biggest impact in any way possible. A soldier of God.

Soon afterward, the tattoo artist bandaged up the completed tattoo. Nate had scarcely finished paying the artist when Slugs's massive frame burst into the tiny room.

"We gotta go, right now," he barked.

Nate knew that tone meant act first, ask questions later, so Nate hurried out the door, close behind Slugs.

They emerged onto Washington Street, heading up to Downtown Crossing. They rushed to Slugs's parked Ford Explorer. Slugs stopped Nate from getting into the passenger seat and instead handed him the keys.

"You're driving," he commanded.

Nate nodded and got into the driver's side.

"So . . ." Nate said, starting the car.

"It was Vamp Hill," Slugs explained, pointing to where they should drive. "Mothafuckas strut by me, about three of them, and made the fuckin' pistol sign with their hands. Like they own this fuckin' city. Tryin' to front and pull off some intimidation shit."

Slugs had Nate drive a few loops around Washington and Tremont Streets, then toward the South End and Roxbury, all the while looking for the Vamp Hill members. As they drove down Washington and crossed East Berkeley, Slugs noticed the three threats hanging right in front of Peters Park.

"Okay, slow down," he said.

Nate slowed down and saw three young Black men carrying some sneaker bags from High Voltage and sporting Kings gear, strolling down the sidewalk, purposely taking up space and wanting to be seen. They were by themselves. Everyone else had likely clocked who they were and was keeping their distance.

Slugs pulled out his pistol and squeezed off all his rounds, loosely aiming toward them, bullet casings flying out into the street. The Vamp Hill guys dove to the ground, and a few bystanders screamed. Slugs kept spraying the corner until all the bullets were gone.

Nate's instincts went on autopilot. His adrenaline was jacked up from the surprise attack from his cousin. He'd never seen a drive-by before. He wasn't sure if any of the rounds had connected with the targets or not.

"Okay, floor it!" Slugs shouted.

The Explorer peeled out as Nate punched the accelerator. They darted down Washington, and Nate hung a left on Waltham, ironically right in front of Cathedral High. The sight of his old school put an instant lump in his throat. He took a few winding side streets to stay off the main roads and away from BPD attention before parking in a hidden alley.

"Slugs!" he said. "What the fuck, man?"

"We had to send a message Nate. Don't worry, I didn't clip anyone," Slugs said, staring straight ahead in a calm voice. "We ain't goin' nowhere. The Norfolk Kings are here to stay."

Chapter 31

BOSTON HARBOR

AS THEY PICKED UP THEIR LUGGAGE OFF THE TRACK IN LOGAN airport, Pat was still groggy. He'd slept through the entire six-hour journey from Ireland to Boston and still felt wiped out. He was scraping the bottom of the barrel to find his last bits of energy—attempting through sheer will to make it back home to his neighborhood. As he'd expected, Pat's whole body hurt, and he had another layer of a hangover on top of that.

Even though Pat was the one who had suffered the most abuse, Treats looked the worst for wear—sweaty, pale, and shaky, the first tremors of withdrawal setting in. He smelled atrocious, as one could only expect from sweating out the toxic remains of two weeks' worth of drug abuse. He was barely able to swing his bag over his shoulder, wincing in pain and straining. Walsh was faring slightly better, but even he was depleted. Together, they didn't look so much like friends returning from vacation as they did like refugees from some ill-begotten war they had barely survived. The bustling crowd of the airport gave them a wide berth wherever they passed, not wanting to mess with men who were clearly on their last nerve.

Patrick approached the glass doors leading to the cab stand outside. Knowing that he was so close to getting home gave him a slight bounce to his step, a tiny surge of energy he needed to stay upright before he collapsed.

From behind, he heard Treats call out, "Hey, Patrick, what you say we close out this journey with a sunset cruise around the harbor?"

Pat froze in his steps. He was so close to getting home. Was he going to let Treats talk him into another misadventure? He had cruised with

Treats countless times in high school. It was Treats's father's boat docked in the harbor, but the old man had taught him how to navigate. Now, the watercraft virtually belonged to Treats.

Pat nodded, resigned to live out this final caper. It was just about late April. The boats and bars around the harbor were just getting lively. Maybe it was too early for trouble. And they would make it in time to catch the sunset. Besides, a low-key cruise around the harbor wasn't going to kill him. It sounded like a poetic end to two weeks of a lifetime.

"Say, meet me down at the South Boston Yacht Club to top it all off. We may sleep for five days once we go down!"

Treats turned toward Walsh and took mercy on him. "I know you're all done, Walsh. It's time to hibernate for the BPD Academy, right? I may never see you again, bro."

"You won't see me for at least six months," Walsh answered back, already sounding mentally checked out.

"All right," relented Pat. "I'll take a cab with Walsh and drop my bags at home to say hello to my mother, but I'll see you around six."

As Pat and Walsh stepped into a cab, Pat couldn't help but wonder if maybe this time Treats needed something more than just keeping the journey alive for one more night.

THE SUN WAS RECEDING DIRECTLY OVER THE BOSTON SKY-line in front of them. Pat had seen the sight many times before but never as breathtaking as this. The full spectrum of colors reflected brilliantly in the harbor's waters. High above in the skyscape, a 747 took off from the airport on the right, headed east right over their heads. The Boston World Trade Center was to their left.

Pat leaned back in the cockpit seat of the twenty-six-foot Wellcraft Excel. He was perched at the top of the boat, an open-air area with a small canopy covering it. The water gently lapped up against the hull. Treats was at the helm, taking in the view and rolling a joint. For the moment, Treats had turned off the motor. Pat held a cold bottle of beer loosely in his hand. He felt something he hadn't felt in days—serenity.

"I think this could be a decent Wednesday night," Treats said nonchalantly, breaking the silence. "After the sun goes down, we could buzz down to Tia's or the tavern on the water in Charlestown."

"Treats, you know I love the Charlestown girls," Pat acknowledged, "but we need to shut it down, man. Just chill out and detox for a while, you know?"

It wasn't what Treats wanted to hear. His bemused smile turned into more of a pained expression, like an emotion just starting to crack the surface.

"Hey, man," Pat said, studying Treats's face. "What's goin' on? Is this your way of still avoiding the inevitable?"

Treats looked away, straight into the sun starting to disappear behind the Boston skyline. His shoulders moved as he sighed and leaned farther back. He dug a lighter out of his pocket and lit up his joint.

"You're gonna be a great father, man," Pat offered. Once that kid was born, Pat knew that Treats would do an about-face and love and protect that kid with everything he had.

"Fuck you. I know that," laughed Treats, exhaling the sweet cloud of smoke. "But it wasn't supposed to happen now. I wanted to control when."

"Hey, sometimes in life, there are things that we just can't control," Pat replied. "But we have to make the best of the situation."

"I know. I know," admitted Treats. "No one knows that better than you, Patrick."

It was moments like this that Pat appreciated the perspective four years in prison had given him. Treats had everything. He just didn't know it. Pat leaned in. "We have to face our choices and live with them. This is a fuckin' blessing, man. She's a good girl. And look at your life! You seem to be all set right now."

Treats mirrored Pat and leaned in and contemplated a moment, staring at his joint. Something was starting to sink in.

"You're right, Patrick. You're right. I got a few revenue streams going and the union construction job to cover it. No one's gonna bother a weed dealer and a bookie from the corner." He took another pull from the joint and stared out into the sunset. "It looks like things will be turning around for you too. A little cash, a few options, construction with me, and you said Jimmy's got the gym and bartending job for you downtown. It all might just be okay."

He extended his bottle to clink with Pat's as the last few rays of the sun dipped below the Boston skyline. Then, Treats reached down into the cabin and pulled out two lines on a plate that he had cut earlier.

"Still have a little bit left. You ready to rip?" Treats asked. "Sun's almost down, kid!"

Pat shook his head no but dipped his pinky in and rubbed his gums, smiling afterward. Treats leaned down with his straw to rip the last two lines.

Then Treats sat upright at the helm and throttled the motor. "Let's grab one drink!" he shouted.

After buzzing over for about five minutes, they pulled in to Tia's Docks.

Pat noticed they seemed to be a bit wobbly coming into the docks. He glanced up at Treats. He couldn't be that fucked up yet, could he? But Treats had started gagging and jumped out of the captain's seat to run to the cuddy cabin below.

Pat took over the captain's seat, pulling the boat into the dock. As soon as he got into position, Pat tied off the boat. Once he'd secured the knots, he jumped back into the boat and rushed down below into the cuddy cabin.

There, Treats was gyrating on the floor with a bloody nose, like he was having some sort of a seizure.

Pat threw him down on the irregularly shaped V-berth mattress in the boat's stern and wrapped him in a blanket. Pat held him tight, bear-hugging him and trying to calm his body down. He rocked him a little. The shaking started to calm down.

"Hold on, Treats," Pat whispered. He knew he could get the dockmaster to summon medical help within minutes. Whatever happened next, the party was over. Boston had finally brought Treats down from the stratosphere, crashing hard into the earth.

Pat held on tight to Treats, tears beginning to form. He reached for the radio to call the dockmaster.

Chapter 32

BPD RUN-IN

PAT LINED UP THE TEN SHOTS IN A NEAT ROW ACROSS THE BAR and poured evenly in one stroke with the proficiency of a master. Young, college-aged hands grabbed at the shots, shouting and lifting them in the air to celebrate nothing in particular, other than the sanctuary of drinking together and the end of the school week. It was already three deep at the bar, and Pat knew he would have no problem keeping up.

When Pat took the job set up for him at a nightclub on One Boylston Place scarcely six months ago, the only challenging part was learning the drinks. But specialty cocktails made up barely five percent of sales; this raucous crowd ordered mostly whiskey and beer. For the most part, he served just college kids and singles in their twenties, depending on the time of night. Speed and personality were the names of the game.

One Boylston Place was in the middle of a popular strip of mixed clubs and far away from Pat's neighborhood. Any fast trouble his past could bring up was a safe distance away. It may have been only a few miles, but it may have well been across state lines in terms of neighborhood territories.

Gazing across the crowded club at the unfettered youth eager to drink, Pat felt a sense of pride in what he had built in such a short amount of time. *A bartender can work anywhere*, he thought. And on a night like this, Pat could make three or maybe even four hundred in tips, all above board. He was just a guy with a decent job. For the first time in years, life seemed somewhat . . . normal.

Six months ago seemed like an entirely different world. Typical of his insane luck, Treats had survived his little boat party. The diagnosis was severe dehydration and exhaustion, a malady he almost didn't walk away from. For once, Treats heeded the wake-up call and reversed course to intercept a more positive future with his girlfriend and baby boy. He was happy being a father—funny, given how hard he'd tried to avoid it.

Walsh had finished the academy with flying colors and was already out on the beat as one of Boston's finest. He was now a rookie on the gang unit of the Roxbury precinct area. Pat was sure he would do just fine. Growing up on O and Fourth, Walsh's whole family was dedicated to civic service. His father and brothers had joined the BPD, and his uncles were local politicians. It was just in his blood. If you weren't in the cadet program or a veteran, there was no way a White kid was getting hired with affirmative action in place. But with a connected family like the Walshes, shit was happening behind doors for years to get him on with handshakes the Irish way. No one really knew how it happened, but it sure was a bit of evidence that, in Boston, Curley's Tammany Club wasn't extinct yet!

For once, Pat felt he had a future and he could make life into something, despite all he had been through. Although he still had a passion for boxing, it wasn't his professional focus. For now, he was content to help Jimmy train the young kids around the gym, building them up and giving them confidence.

Fighting had been too much a way of life outside the ring. For once, "normal" life was feeling really good. And Pat wanted to hold on to it for as long as he could. Being here behind the bar, he thought, was like blending in with the rest of the world. Here, he was not an ex-con or a tough guy from Southie or a boxer. He was just a guy tending bar, serving college kids. The world that he used to belong to every day was far away. It was a nice escape.

The hours went by fast, as they did on any typical weekend night at the club. Before he knew it, it was nearly two a.m. By the time the last of the college kids was out the door, Pat and his coworkers launched into their efficient closing-time groove. Bus the glasses on the tables and bar, put away the garnishes in the fridge, cover the taps and bottles, wipe down the place, and turn in the bar receipts to the manager. Then came the best part—counting and divvying up the tips.

Cash in hand, Pat and his coworkers would usually be out the door by three. Most of the bars on the strip would shut down, and Pat would meet with other industry friends at the remaining after-hours places, like the Alley Cat. Or maybe they would head to Sweetwater Cafe or Zanzibar.

When they would walk out to the top of the alley where Boylston Street faced the Boston Common, all walks of life would present themselves, especially in the small hours of the night. This was an entrance to the infamous Boston Red Light District Combat Zone.

Combat zone adult entertainment area Washington Street, Boston, Massachusetts

The area had a special significance to Pat, even when he was younger. It was the location he'd gotten his tattoo on graduation day with Nate: *Vengeance Is Mine*. It was when he vowed to find his cousin PJ's killer.

The Combat Zone was full of strip clubs and drug dealers and pimps and hoes straight out of a movie scene. But to Patrick, it was old news. He'd gone to high school less than a mile away, and every day, these people were just turning tricks and scams. Not that much different from anyone else.

Typically, on nights Pat worked, he had to drive around the block ten times to find a meter so he could park—through the zone, pass by the duck pond, past the statehouse, and down Park Street until he found a meter. And after work, he would most likely have a beer or two or a puff of a joint with a coworker, talking about the night's events or the cash they'd made.

So far, this brisk evening was as routine as the others. Pat stood by the Commons entrance, passing a joint with his buddy Neos, another bartender at the club and a grad student at BC from New Hampshire. They'd become good friends over the past six months. Neos had an easygoing nature and liked to listen more than talk. The two of them had developed a rapport dealing with the weekend rush together, making a game of who could sling the most drinks. Pat's instincts were to trust Neos, so over the last six months, Neos was the only one he told details about his past, such as the altercation with the Asian gang, his time in prison, his cousin PJ, and a smattering of stories from Ireland. Of course, nothing about his safety deposit box mission. That shit was off limits.

As they were just about to part ways, a BPD cop car pulled slowly up. Pat glanced over and could see two Black cops inside. If they'd been two White cops, Pat would have been more at ease—not because of any fear of Black cops per se but because he didn't know them personally. He knew many White cops, and he could have a casual conversation with them, even joke around with some of them.

The cop on the passenger side rolled down his window and called out to them.

"What you two White boys doing out here so late?" the passenger-side cop asked, shining his light on Pat and Neos's faces.

Pat and Neos shrugged. Neos had already taken the joint and hidden it.

"I saw you passing something back and forth. Should I get out and see what it is?" the officer asked.

"No, Officer," said Neos. "We just got off work and were saying goodbye."

"All right, guys," said the cop. "Move it along, and don't let me see you around again tonight!"

Pat and Neos nodded and watched the BPD car pull away.

"I guess that's it for me tonight," Neos said. "I'll catch you tomorrow, Pat."

They shook hands, and Pat started on his way back to his car. As usual, it was a bit of a hike, about three or four blocks to where he was parked at a distant meter on Beacon Street just before the State House. He was nearly there when he saw the same BPD car cruising toward him. It pulled up alongside him on the sidewalk. Pat tensed up, already sensing that they were going to harass him again.

"Hey, you," said the passenger-side cop, in a tone that seemed a little more aggressive than their first encounter. "Thought I told you don't let me see you again around here."

Pat casually raised his hands about chest level to show the cops he wasn't carrying anything. "Just heading home, Officer," he responded. These cops felt like they had something to prove. He didn't want to upset them, but they were already coming at him a little combative. When they were in that kind of mood, even being nice might set them off.

"What did you say to me?" asked the cop, raising his voice. "Don't lie to me."

Pat knew the tone of that voice and what "don't lie to me" meant. The cops had already decided he was guilty of something or would make him guilty of something. In a fraction of a second, Pat saw a couple of different outcomes.

In one scenario, they would search him for Neos's joint, long since discarded and no longer on his person, and then plant something on him anyway. Then it would be his word against theirs. Because he was an ex-con, the mandatory sentencing laws would be harsh, and he'd be back in prison.

In another possible outcome, they might cuff him without too much incident, take him to the station, and claim that he was resisting arrest. Again, being an ex-con would be a disadvantage, and there would be little he could say to any judge that might make him more believable.

Both cases would leave the outcome entirely to the cops. Would he roll the dice and hope the cops gave him a break? It felt like the wrong decision to trust them. That left only one logical choice, the instinctive move that gave Pat any chance at all.

Run.

Pat bolted behind the police car, crossing the street, and vaulted over the pointed wrought-iron fence guarding the grassy and wooded park of

Boston Common. It was a good strategy. They could only chase by car on the park's paved walkways. They'd have to follow him on foot if he stuck to the vast grassy areas, and with this head start, it'd be tough to catch up with him. Plus, he was fast. All those boxing workouts kept him nimble on his feet, and his long legs gave him an advantage of a fast stride. This might provide just enough time to hide somewhere.

Pat could hear the distant shouts and curses from the cops fading behind him. It was dark, but he knew this park like the back of his hand. He was confident he could lose them. Once they lost sight of him, he could go in practically any direction from there. And they might just give up after chasing on foot for a little while.

He headed past a thicket of trees, took a turn, and beelined to a different park area. Then thoughts started to spook him.

Maybe he'd made a mistake by running, he thought. *Fuck.* He tried to shove the new doubt deep into the back of his mind. But he hadn't really done anything; maybe they'd just let him go . . .

He spotted a jungle gym with a sand base just up ahead. If he lay flat enough on the sand and perfectly still, they would have trouble seeing him from a distance. They might run their flashlights right over him and not even notice. It was worth a shot.

Pat lay down on the sand on his back and tried to make his body as horizontal as possible. He nestled up to the small wooden barrier that contained the sand, jutting his body up against it. He could hear his beating heart in his ears. He closed his eyes and tried to slow down his breathing.

Relax. You got this. They won't find you.

Pat opened his eyes again, with only a view of the sky. He couldn't see much else and didn't want to crane his neck over the frame of the sandbox and get caught in a beam of light. He could hear several patrol cars driving over the paved walkways. That meant they must have called it in, so now there were more of them.

Don't they have anything better to do? What the fuck?

He could hear a car slowing near the playground. Pat froze, making himself as flat and still as possible. He listened to the car door slam and someone stepping out of it. The cop strolled in his direction. Each cautious step was slightly louder than the last.

A flashlight beam grazed the top of Pat's face.

Fuck.

"All right. Let's see your hands and get up slowly," the cop announced. It was a different voice than the officer who had been harassing him on the street.

Pat threw up his hands and slowly stood up, not bothering to brush the dirt off his clothes; he didn't want to give them any reason to get spooked. His heart was practically beating out of his chest. The cop had his gun drawn, which did little to calm Pat's nerves.

He squinted past the light to see if it might be one of the cops he would recognize, any of the guys that Pat might see at the boxing gym or someone he'd grown up with from his neighborhood. He might still be able to talk his way out of this. But it wasn't. It was an Asian cop, someone he hadn't seen before.

Still, he had to try something.

"Officer, this is a big misunderstanding. I'm sorry about all of this. I'm sure we could call at least five officers that would vouch for me. Do you know Sergeant Daly, or McHugh, or Connolly?"

The Asian officer paused, then lowered and holstered his gun.

"Yes. I do know those guys," said the officer, shining the light on Pat's face to see if he should be someone he recognized. He studied Pat for a moment, apparently thinking.

"All right, fine," said the officer. "If you know those guys, let me take you in, and you'll be out in a few hours."

Pat knew the drill. Although not ideal, going to the station for a few hours to explain himself was better than getting set up and railroaded into a charge for some bullshit reason. Pat's instincts told him this was a good cop, someone who just wanted to do things by the book. He hoped he was right about that.

The officer cuffed Pat, and Pat complied without any struggle. A few other cruisers pulled up on the wide, paved walkways. They parked a short distance away, positioning their headlights to shine directly on him and the arresting officer. He glanced around, assessing the situation. The Asian officer was standing behind him, securing the cuffs and checking Pat's back pockets.

The original cop who'd harassed him on Beacon Street stepped out of the closest patrol car. By the look of his assertive gait and clenched fists, Pat could tell he was pissed. That stride oozed pure aggression. Pat's muscles tensed up, and his heart rate jumped. As the officer approached, Pat could tell he was picking up speed. From all his years of fighting, he could see the silhouette of the cop's clenched fist winding up for a punch.

That's a fucking haymaker, thought Pat.

Time seemed to slow down as his reflexes took over. He saw the punch coming at him but knew to wait for the right moment to dodge. He waited until the fist was a mere half inch away from his eye, then ducked out of the way with a dip of his knees.

Before he realized he'd missed Pat altogether, the Black cop's punch followed through and connected with the Asian officer's face, slamming him hard right in the eye.

The Asian cop, not prepared for such a violent surprise, went down, knocked out instantly. From his standing position, Pat looked him over to see how badly the officer was hurt. To his horror, Pat saw the officer's eye was partially hanging from his socket. That could have been him!

Before he could react much to what had just happened, the two Black cops picked Pat up from his knees and dropped him to the ground. They took out their billy clubs and beat him, clubbing him on his back, head, ribs, arms. Still cuffed, Pat couldn't do much to protect himself other than to writhe around on the ground, trying to shield his gut.

Sharp pains reverberated through his body, each blow another insult, another potential lifelong injury. If they hit his soft organs hard enough, he might be in the hospital for a month. Broken bones were one thing, but a ruptured kidney or spleen might send him into the ground for good. He tensed up, hoping his battle-hardened body would be tough enough to withstand the blows and protect his vital parts. With each assault, a torrent of grunts and shrieks erupted from his body. In his mind, it was a constant refrain of cursing threats.

Fuck you, motherfucker. Fuck you.

When the EMTs showed up to tend to the Asian officer, Pat was still getting clubbed and kicked. With new witnesses on the scene, the cops let up and hauled Pat into the back of the patrol car. He sat there, breathing hard, a cut above his eye bleeding heavily. That eye was already swelled shut. With all the adrenaline in his system, it was hard for Pat to tell how badly hurt he was. So far, he thought, he didn't think any bones had been broken.

He sat in the back, in disbelief at how fast things had gotten so bad. *That punch could have fucking killed that cop. And what if I hadn't dodged it? And what the fuck?*

He could hear the EMTs talking outside on their radios.

"We have an injured officer," one of them said. "On our way to Mass Eye and Ear. He'll likely require surgery. Be there in less than five. Incoming from the Common." They piled into the ambulance and took off, the siren shrieking and the emergency lights casting eerie shadows in the wooded park as it sped away.

Pat watched and listened further to see what else he could ascertain from the back seat. A group of cops had gathered, and there was a lot of talking between them. He couldn't quite make out everything the cops were saying but noticed them turning off their radios. The cop who had assaulted him talked to the gathered group, gesturing at the area where Pat was beaten and occasionally pointing to Pat in the back seat. The assaulting cop appeared to be covering all his tracks.

At one point, the cop raised his voice. "He was resisting, and that's final!"

If there were any protest to this declaration, Pat didn't see or hear any from the group of officers.

Pat shook his head. For once in his life in Boston, he could not believe there hadn't been one White officer in any of the three cruisers who had showed up on the scene. The Asian cop was solo, and the two Black cops had partnered in the cruiser. The third cruiser showed up last, and it was another Black cop and a Latino female cop.

What are the fuckin' chances of that . . . the fuckin' luck I have!

The officers' discussion seemed to be concluding. The cops were slowly getting back into their cruisers, and the two Black cops who had assaulted Pat returned to the front seat of their car, right in front of Pat.

After they had shut the door, Pat bit his tongue. He still saw red, and he held back a tirade of cursing by force of sheer will. He'd not said one negative word to anyone. Not yet.

"Let's bring him up to the BMC," said the passenger-side officer. "Get him stitched up."

Pat couldn't help himself. "Yeah, that's a fuckin' start," he snorted. "What the fuck were you thinkin', man?"

The passenger-side cop turned around and glared at him.

"For what fuckin' reason?" Pat doubled down. "Because I ran? Because I don't want to go back to jail?"

Pat knew they'd run his information already. Most likely, the computer would have said "manslaughter, accomplice to murder" or maybe even "intent to murder." They didn't know the only thing close to illegal he ever did was fight.

And I didn't even do the crime I did time for! I just kept my fuckin' mouth shut!

The irony was that Pat had kept quiet to protect Walsh, and Walsh was now a cop. Even if he'd had an early release, Walsh never would have been eligible for the academy as an ex-con.

The cops didn't know that. All they knew was that Pat had done time and that his parole had just ended. After all the bullshit, all the time and energy Pat had spent trying to set up a normal life, this was a web he never dreamed or imagined he would be caught in.

"You're done, punk," said the passenger-side cop with a snarl. "You're an ex-con. You see what happens to you."

"Yeah, okay," retorted Pat. "You fucked up that dude for nothing. That Asian cop is all done. His eye was fuckin' hanging out because of you! I may be an ex-con, but you wait and see who I know. I did nothing, absolutely nothing!"

"Shut the fuck up," said the cop who was driving.

Pat bristled but held his tongue as the cops pulled up to Boston Medical Center.

———

"I NEED HIM STITCHED UP FAST, AND GET HIM BACK TO ME."

Handcuffed to a gurney, Pat fumed as he overheard the poorly concealed whispers of the cops just outside the room. Shortly after, they both walked into his room and shut the curtain behind them. They whispered something to each other, both nodding.

When the doctor—a thirty-something serious-looking Asian man—arrived, the passenger-side cop took him aside and whispered something to him too. The Asian doctor, stone-faced, just nodded.

Glad he was at least getting some medical attention, Pat sat patiently as the doctor and nurse prepped the wound above his eye. Pat thought there was no question that he had a concussion from the multiple billy club strikes across his head and body. His whole body was starting to ache, and he had a dull throbbing pain that seemed to come from deep inside his skull.

Motherfuckers, thought Pat. He grabbed the arm of the doctor, trying to get someone on his side.

"Listen, man," he pleaded. "You have to admit me. Please! These guys did this to me. They almost fuckin' killed me! I have no idea what they will do to me next."

The doctor had kind eyes, and Pat thought for an instant that he might help him.

"I'm sorry, kid," said the doctor, apologizing. "They have already said, 'No way. He has to get to the station ASAP.'"

"Please, man, I obviously have a concussion and whatever else—"

"I'm sorry, kid," interrupted the doctor.

Pat sat stewing; a sick feeling of helplessness was growing in the pit of his stomach. "I can't fuckin' believe you," he retorted. "You're just as bad as them!"

Within minutes, the two cops came back through the curtain. The passenger-side cop freed the handcuffs from the gurney, then cuffed Pat's hands behind his back. Pat winced as the officer put them on far tighter than necessary. Both cops guided him forcefully through the emergency room door and back into the cruiser.

"Where to now, guys?" Pat asked from the back seat as the cruiser pulled away.

"To the fuckin' slammer, of course, punk," the passenger-side cop sneered. "I told you: you're done."

"Wow. What the fuck, man," shot back Pat. "Just let me know when I get my phone fuckin' call."

It was a short ride before they pulled into the Boston Municipal Court jail between Faneuil Hall and the TD Garden. Pat had already resigned himself to the fact that he'd probably be spending the night in jail, something he had vowed to himself would never happen again. He sat in booking, a bored-looking Black woman finishing up his finger-prints and all the other routine protocols before checking him in. He tried to make eye contact with her to establish some kind of human con-nection, but his attempts seemed to bounce off her.

"Do I get my call?" he asked directly.

She finally glanced up from her paperwork to look him straight in the eye. She sighed, then looked in the direction of the passenger-side cop, who was hovering over the desk. "In the fuckin' morning," he said. "If you're lucky."

"Oh, really?" Pat responded, his tone ripe with sarcasm. "Okay."

This exchange seemed to set off the officer even more. He pulled Pat-rick up and shoved him along down the hall into the jail block area of the building, clearly bent on aggravating Pat's already egregious injuries. When they arrived at the designated cell, the officer pushed Pat headfirst into the cell bars and cuffed him. He winced in pain but didn't cry out. The officer opened the jail cell door and pushed him in with so much force that he had to catch himself so he wouldn't fall.

The officer stepped into the cell and removed the cuffs. He pushed Pat against the wall and onto the bench that lined one wall. Then he stepped out of the cell and locked the door. Pat knew this drill and sus-pected he wasn't going to like what was coming next.

"All right now," the officer commanded. "Turn around."

Pat stood up and turned around, so his back was facing the officer.

"Now. Pull your pants to the floor."

"You fuckin' serious?" Pat responded. "For real?"

The officer gripped his baton, still in its holster. "I know you don't want me to come back in that cell," he threatened. "Do it now!"

Resigned, Pat complied, removed his pants, and bent down.

"Grab your cheeks and spread 'em," demanded the officer.

"This is fuckin' ridiculous!" Pat shouted, loud enough that the whole station could hear. "What the fuck?" But knowing that he would eventually be forced to do what they wanted, one way or the other, Pat complied.

Seemingly satisfied, the officer walked back to the booking area. Fuming, Pat pulled his pants back up. "When do I get my call, beautiful?" he yelled toward the booking cop. She forced her attention on the papers she was working on, refusing to look in his direction. "You have no idea what happened here tonight," Pat continued. "And I'm just planning out which cop I am calling to tell this story to."

The cops that Patrick could see in the station all started glancing at each other discreetly. The nerves in the air were palpable. Maybe they'd begun to realize they had harassed someone who had connections.

Oh, you nervous? Good. Fuck you. Fuck all of you, Pat thought.

"How 'bout I just call for my bail, and you just turn on your radio and call my friends—Sergeant Daly, Officer Connolly, maybe even McHugh, the spokesman for the commissioner?"

More officers stopped whatever they were doing and looked at each other. Their glances became more intense, and the more Pat spoke, the more the air seemed to get sucked out of the room. An older cop walked over to Pat's cell and leaned in with one arm resting on the bars.

"If you know what's good for you, you'll shut your fuckin' mouth now," said the older cop. Patrick took the note as a serious one. This older guy seemed scary to him. He had a black and gray goatee and dark-tinted glasses concealing his eyes enough so Pat couldn't get a read on his expression. Unlike the other cops in the station, he was also wearing leather gloves, which added to the whole intimidation factor.

This was the first time this cop had spoken to him. Patrick had a feeling this guy knew his partner had fucked up and gotten him in the middle of a very sticky situation. But even if this were true, Pat wasn't confident how much that might help him out. Just like criminals, officers had a code too. You never rat out a fellow officer.

"All right," said Pat, measuring his words carefully. "Tell me one thing. What're the charges? Tell me."

"Go to sleep," said the old cop, simply. "They're too long to read."

Pat hung his head, still in sheer disbelief of the reversal of fortune that was unraveling his whole life in just one evening. The older cop shuffled away, leaving Pat alone. He lay down on the steel bed, his face swollen. He felt the fourteen stitches with his fingers, starting from the corner of his eye, through his eyebrow, and up his forehead. Now that he was still and lying down, he could feel the aches and pains more acutely. They would get worse as the night went on.

I should still be in the fucking hospital, Pat thought.

He tried to relax and ignore the pain. With tears in his eyes, he began to doze off. As he rested halfway between sleep and wakefulness, thoughts of injustice swirled in his mind. Life had *just* gotten somewhat normal. He had started to think he had a productive second chance. He wanted to make good.

Would the Asian cop tell the truth? The real story? That was the biggest question. And would his White cop friends want to get in the middle of all this? Chances were slim. Why would cops start ratting on each other for Pat's sake? They wouldn't, and they couldn't. It was their code.

He didn't know when he would get his call for bail or who he would call. As he weighed the pros and cons of different people who could help him, he dozed off.

———

HE AWOKE DISORIENTED IN HIS NEW SURROUNDINGS. THE sharp pain and itching from his stitches reminded him of where he was and how he'd gotten there. Glancing over from the steel bed, he could see that the new shift had come in. The female booking officer remained the same. Pat rose from the bed, gripped the bars, and called out to her.

"Excuse me, miss, please. Can I get my call now?" he asked.

"Yes, you can," she replied, barely looking at him.

After sleeping on it, he'd decided his best bet would be to call Jimmy. He had connections and had the means to bail him out. He was simply the safest bet; one call to him could cover many contacts in the city. Pat just might have to work out an arrangement to work it off, whatever the amount ended up being.

A younger officer approached his cell and opened it, leading him to a chair and a nondescript desk with a phone. The officer uncuffed him and leaned up against the wall.

Pat picked up the phone and dialed.

SHORTLY AFTER THE CALL, SERGEANT DALY CAME THROUGH the station doors. Jimmy must have called Daly immediately.

Pat had a long history with Sergeant Daly and trusted him. Daly had helped run the Police Athletic League boxing club with Pat's dad back in the day. He was the cop who'd given him as much information as he could when his cousin PJ was killed. He'd also given it to him straight about what kind of charges Pat would be facing after the fatal skirmish with the Asian gang.

Sergeant Daly approached the booking officer and had a whispered conversation. Then he walked over to Pat's cell and leaned into the bars.

"Patrick. Yo, what the fuck happened here, kid? They got eleven assault and batteries with a dangerous weapon on a police officer."

Patrick's jaw hit the floor.

"How did this happen?" Daly asked.

Patrick attempted to explain his side of the story the best he could. Daly nodded, commenting little. When Pat finished, Daly said nothing. Pat could see him turning over the events in his mind, thinking of how he could possibly help him.

Patrick broke the silence. "Do you think that Asian cop will say anything?" he asked, wondering.

"No fuckin' way," responded Daly. "Not a chance."

Pat gulped in fear and rested his head against the bars, looking down and thinking. He hoped after Jimmy bailed him out, he could help him work out an angle on something. Next steps, anything. There was no way he'd go back to prison. He would die first.

Chapter 33

HOUSE VISIT

JIMMY DROVE SLOWLY ON THE WINDING ROUTE TO PAT'S place. Pat sat in the front passenger seat, thoughts swirling. He'd been trying to strategize since Jimmy had bailed him out at the station.

"Just go home and let this all play out, Pat," Jimmy said. "Don't leave your house for a while. Let Daly talk to those guys and see if anything can be done."

The way Jimmy said that sounded hopeful. If anyone could navigate those corridors of authority, it would be Daly and Jimmy. Having guys like them working on his side was one of the few things giving Pat any solace.

"Don't worry, kid," Jimmy said reassuringly. "I called Danny O'Riley. I'm on my way to relay the situation. He'll see what's gonna go down with this."

The strategy was a good one. Pat knew Danny O'Riley as the owner of O'Riley's boxing gym. He was also a judge in Quincy, someone higher up in the law who could maybe give them a direction or put a good word in. Those charges were no joke, thought Pat.

Maybe we can go even a step further, Pat thought. "Jimmy, I got an idea," he said.

"What is it?"

"Take a right over here and head down Dot Avenue."

"What's in that head of yours?" Jimmy asked, squinting at Pat. "Sergeant Daly said to just let this play out."

"I know, but I can't," protested Pat. "There's no way I can have this over my head. Take another right after the Emerald Isle."

Jimmy complied. His eyes darted back and forth in front of him. "So you keeping me in suspense on this mission?" he finally asked. "Where we going?"

They were passing through a nicer section of Dorchester, with mostly well-kept townhouses and neatly landscaped yards.

"Listen, Jimmy. That there is the commissioner's spokesperson's house right there—Joe McHugh. He's known me forever. He's the highest-level cop I know. Joe was my hockey coach a few years in grade school. He and his brother coach for Don Bosco, another Irish Catholic school right by the Combat Zone, about a mile from where me and Nate went to Cathedral."

"And how's he supposed to help?" Jimmy asked.

"He always said, 'You ever need anything, you call me,'" Pat replied. "Well, I need him, Jimmy. And he needs to see what they did to me last night. Now's the time. He needs to see my face and my honesty right now. Right here."

Jimmy rolled the car to a stop. Pat jumped out and walked up to the front door of the townhouse.

Pat rang the doorbell. He heard some shuffling behind the door, and then it opened a crack, revealing a little Irish woman in her fifties. She scanned his face, and then she had a glimmer of recognition. Her eyes stopped at his fresh scar on his forehead, and her brows furrowed a bit in concern. She frowned.

"May I speak with Mr. McHugh, ma'am?" Pat asked as politely as possible. "I know it's been awhile. It's important."

"One moment, dear," she said. "Let me go get him." She closed the door and shuffled off. Pat heard some murmuring before she returned to open the door.

"It's probably best you meet him at the basement door," she said kindly. "It's around the side in the back."

Patrick bounded down the stoop and walked down the alley along the side of the house. More toward the back was a heavy wooden basement door, the kind that looked fortified and old, probably original to the house. Pat took a deep breath and knocked.

The door immediately opened to reveal Joe McHugh, a tall and rugged man somewhere in his middle age. His hair was white and gray, but his eyes and face still retained an aura of youth. He recognized Pat and shook his hand like an old friend.

"Patrick. My God, it's been awhile," said Joe. "How you been? I heard you were getting your life back on track after that unfortunate prison sentence! What the hell happened to your face? Come on in. Please."

Joe ushered him into the basement, which he had converted into a classic bar. It looked like JJ Foley's, with a long, dark wooden bar and wooden finishings on the shelves to match. He even had a nail-up tin tile ceiling with ornate textured squares. A giant mirror hung in the center of the back wall, top-shelf liquor lined up all around it. It was essentially a private Irish cop bar in his own basement. Pat could easily see kicking it here.

Joe poured him three fingers of whiskey, neat, into an old-fashioned whiskey glass, before pouring himself the same. Pat gladly accepted.

"What happened, kid?" Joe said, sitting down at a stool at his bar. "Tell me."

Pat followed suit and sat next to him. "I'm so sorry, Joe," he began in earnest. "For showing up at your door at eleven a.m. on a Sunday morning. I just need ten minutes to tell you what happened."

"Go ahead, Pat. You'll know I'll help in any way I can."

Pat recounted the previous night's events, going into exact detail about how the fight went down and the gory aftermath of the Asian officer's eyeball hanging out, the group beatdown, and the nasty gash that the doctors patched up at the hospital. Joe reacted with empathy, nodding and frowning with concern.

Pat thought that degree of bogus behavior and the race card would play in his favor as he told the story. The blue wall of silence, he knew, was just like his own code of silence; you never rat out your friends, ever. But he wanted to know Joe's take on the situation, his version of the summary of the facts. Maybe it wasn't as black and white as Pat thought.

Joe listened for a few minutes and sat in thought. He took a sip off his whiskey glass and put it back on the bar.

"So first off, I want to tell you I'm sorry this happened," he said. "This shouldn't happen to anybody, ever. Second, I want to be clear," Joe explained. "You can never mention my name ever, and you were never here. You got that?"

Pat nodded, preparing for some kind of covert path that would keep Joe above the fray and safe in his police status quo.

"Third, I can't help you at all," Joe said, almost apologetically.

The impact hit Pat hard. *Fuck. Now what?* he thought.

"However," Joe continued, "this is how it'll play out, and you need to follow my steps exactly."

He can help me. He just can't do it directly. If the help was just advice, he would take it. Pat sipped whiskey as he listened.

"First, have your lawyer file an investigation tomorrow with IA—internal affairs—to keep that pressure building diligently at every court date. As things develop, I don't see this going to trial; no one'll want that. These cops will back off on the charges and throw you a few different deals. That is, if they're smart and know what's good for them. You may have to swallow your Irish pride."

Pat knew what that meant. He should give up on the idea of getting back at the cops with official charges and instead take whatever deal they gave him for his freedom. That'd be a tough one to accept, but the "true justice" option would probably be off the table.

"This is your only way out," Joe continued. "Take an acceptable deal and move on. Let it go. This is how it slowly goes away without you doing any more time."

Pat nodded and let the plan sink in. It wasn't the advice he wanted to hear, but it was probably the path he needed to take. It occurred to him how many crazy situations and high-level events had been discussed in this basement. He felt oddly safe here—like he was in a special place that kept conversations like his secret.

Pat lifted his glass and clinked Joe's. "Sláinte," he said.

"Sláinte," answered Joe.

Pat downed the remainder of his whiskey. "Joe, I don't know how to thank you," he said. "You've given me a lot to think about. And you can trust me. I was never here. We never spoke."

"I have no idea what you're talking about," Joe said with a smile. "Now get this behind you, and remember, you always have a second chance to start fresh and make something good out of your journey."

Pat returned the smile, shook Joe's hand, and showed himself out.

Joe waved to him outside before softly shutting the basement door and locking it.

The anger would not be easy to shake. Pat was still pissed as hell, but he did feel better about his situation. He had heard from the horse's mouth that there was a way out, a way that he wouldn't have to do more time behind bars.

Chapter 34

THE STOOP

PAT SAT ON THE FRONT STOOP OF HIS HOUSE LATER THAT afternoon, drinking a cup of coffee from a pot his ma had brewed earlier that morning. She always knew how to make it extra strong without it being mud. It was perfect by itself or with a little whiskey if the mood was right. For now, it was just the caffeine Pat wanted, something to make sense of his anger and the entire bullshit situation. A cup of coffee on his stoop outside was as close to a happy place as he could be at the moment.

The warm sunshine felt good on his face and helped to calm his mood. The dull pain and annoying itching of the stitches above his right eye were a constant reminder that he was anything but happy. At least the swelling was starting to go down.

Pat's ma stepped outside with her own cup of coffee. She sat down next to him and put her arm around his shoulder in a show of affection she usually kept more reserved.

"Oh, Paddy," she said reassuringly. "Everything will be okay. At least we know that you're not going back to jail."

He didn't respond at first, in an attempt to measure his words. It was hard to articulate what he was thinking and feeling, and he didn't want it to seem like he was taking it out on her.

"Yes, I know, Ma," he said, looking down. "I'm just so fucking angry."

She nodded, waiting for Pat to continue.

"It ain't right what they did," he said, shaking his head. "I can't believe that Asian cop won't say anything. I'd be furious if another cop did that to me and fucked up my eye real bad. He's probably blind in that eye now."

"Are you serious, Paddy?" his ma asked. "Look what you did. You never said a word about Walsh. You kept your mouth shut and you did four years for your best friend—all for something you didn't do!"

Damn straight I did, thought Pat, still listening as he sipped.

"You kids were protecting yourselves. You think it's any different in the BPD? It's ten times worse! The blue code, or the blue wall . . . They take an oath to stand together and protect each other's lives. That's final."

The irony of the situation was not lost on Pat. If he were a cop, would he rat on another cop? No fucking way.

"You made the right decision on going to see McHugh, and I know Jimmy has O'Riley helping out as well."

"I know, Ma," Pat said, acknowledging her point. "But I just can't believe that punk ass bitch is gonna get away with what he did. It could have been anybody—an innocent college kid from the 'burbs. Jesus, Ma, do you know that another lawyer came up to me after court and said he heard my story and would take my case immediately? He says I could get up to one million dollars, Ma. That could set us up forever!"

Pat's mother stood up, shaking her head. "Are you out of your fuckin' mind, Paddy?" she exclaimed. "Maybe we oughta get your goddamn head examined. Go up against the BPD? We'd never be free again. Every-one'd be against us. You blink wrong and you're in prison. We'd have to leave the city!"

His ma stared at him hard. He stared downward, listening.

"No fuckin' way," she continued. "You get out of this thing. Keep your head down, and get as far away from this incident as you can. You're lucky here. Did you tell O'Riley this? He would never go up against the BPD. He knows that's a fight you can't win, not even for a judge. It's a goddamn death trap. Get it out of your head."

She's not wrong, Pat thought. Did he really want to wage war with the BPD? Not only would he be fighting a battle he couldn't win, but he'd inadvertently bring down his friends with him. People like Treats or Jimmy would suffer and be assumed guilty just by association.

"You were doing so well," Ma added softly. "Your life's back on track, and you can make what you want of it—something good. It's an under-dog story. I have seen how happy you've been lately. Who knows? Maybe even Kiley will start coming around again."

Kiley wasn't exactly pressing in his mind at the moment. Siobhan was still embedded in his brain, but he had to admit he would always hold a torch for Kiley. And he wouldn't be able to do shit about it if he went back to prison.

Ma bent down and kissed him on the cheek. Pat finally looked up and smiled. They didn't always see eye to eye, but for once, she knew exactly what to say. She was fucking right.

Just as she shut the screen door to the front porch, a BPD cruiser pulled up to the curb right in front of the house. Given his recent expe-rience, Pat instinctively tensed up, expecting trouble. Were they already coming out to harass him?

The door opened and out stepped the rookie Walsh. Pat laughed and swore under his breath at the same time. *Fuckin' Walsh*, Pat thought. *Speak of the fucking devil.*

Walsh walked with a little more swagger than he had in his non-uniformed days. All smiles, he walked up to the front stoop and extended his hand.

Pat shook his hand and gave him a quick hug. "You sure you got the right house?" he asked in jest. "The junkies are down the block. We don't want no trouble, Officer."

Walsh laughed. "I did what you asked," he said. "I had a friend look up that cop's file. He's got a long list. Done this at least seven times—a real piece of work."

"Mothafucka," Pat cursed quietly.

"I know. It happens all the time. Mostly White cops doing it to the Black kids. Beating them down, robbing them for drugs and money. A real fuckin' shakedown."

"Yeah, that sounds about right," replied Pat.

"Is what it is." Walsh shrugged. "Asian cop won't say a word. Just take the deal and forget about it."

"Spoken like a true cop, Walshy. Already brainwashed by the acad-emy, huh?"

"C'mon, Pat. Think for a second."

"What I would like to do is fuckin' beat the shit out of him with my bare hands," Pat said with gritted teeth. "Maybe he wouldn't keep doing this bullshit for the rest of his goddamn career."

"I feel you, brother," Walsh conceded. "But please, don't get any crazy ideas. You got a lot of people pulling strings for you. They're all just trying to press the right buttons so it goes away, Patrick. Please."

"Yes, I know," admitted Pat. "But it shouldn't even have happened in the first place."

Walsh was about to respond when Pat noticed two guys turn up the corner and start walking up Sixth Street toward the Heights. He clocked immediately that there was something off about them. As they got closer, walking across the street, he could see they had that weird shuffle, where they seemed out of step with natural human motion, a little jerkier, a touch more confused and staggered. These kids were about nineteen or twenty, definitely strung out. Fuckin' street zombies. They were most likely cutting through the Heights and heading down to the Old Colony projects.

Pat shook his head. This had been happening much more often as the heroin had become rampant throughout the city and the South Boston housing projects. No matter how much better Pat was doing, this reality seemed to bother him even more. Sometimes the whole fucking city seemed to be falling apart.

Pat's mother rolled out the parlor window.

"Paddy, Walsh—watch these two. They're like clockwork, on the trail for money, then the fix. It's so sad." Ma squinted at them. "Isn't that Kevin?" she asked. "Remember him? He used to date your sister back in the ninth grade."

"That's him, Ma," Pat confirmed.

Off of an impulse, Pat whistled loudly and waved at them to come over. He wasn't sure exactly why. Maybe they would say hi; maybe he could help or pick up some information.

The junkies looked back and threw up a friendly "what's up" gesture with their hands. Then they picked up speed and walked the opposite direction. Ma turned away, unsurprised, and went back in the house.

Pat watched them walk right past South Boston High. His mind wandered, thinking about when he first got out of prison. His mother had showed him a newspaper article in the *New York Times* about how his neighborhood had been impacted by the forced busing, the mob, the police, and the church. Most of all, mysterious sources recently flooding his neighborhood streets with heroin for pennies on the bag. The result of all this was despair and had led to seventeen suicides—with even more attempted over the past six months.

Most people were convinced that the schools were the shrines at the core of the community. You take away the free agency and safety of the high school in a community like this one and there'd be major repercussions. The effects were like a shockwave that rippled out over every facet of the community—socioeconomic, neighborhood identity, the sense of hope. It had a class element to it; without a solid grounding in high school, how many people would graduate or go on to higher education or a well-paying job? People felt irreversibly stuck, and trapped people resorted to dealing or using or various crimes, beginning a vicious cycle that caused everything to deteriorate. People would fall off the edge, consumed by violence or addiction or despair.

Part of what kept Pat sane was his dedication to his daily workouts, which, when he wasn't at the boxing gym, meant his morning run. He had been routinely making his rounds of the city. Pat would leave H and Sixth, run down to the beach, continue out around Castle, Summer Street, and D Street, then back up Eighth and by Old Colony.

It was an amazing way to get reacquainted with the city. He'd see people from all walks of life: the street corner, the church, the gyms, the bars, construction sites—the whole gamut. But it had been almost a decade now since '87, when he was a freshman in high school, and nearly five years since that fateful night he'd brawled with the Asian gang and was locked up. A lot had changed since then. He'd been slowly processing the events of his life, taking them in, and trying to reacclimate. That's why the Ireland trip had been such incredible timing. But that trip couldn't hold off reality forever.

Walsh broke off the silence, trying to snap Pat out of whatever daydream he had been lost in. "Patrick," he said. "Yo."

"Sorry, man," Pat replied, shaking himself out of it. "I just remember the swagger in the kids I used to see around the neighborhood. It was electric! Remember?"

Walsh nodded.

"I remember Kevin," Pat recalled. "He has to be like twenty-one now. Back then, he was an athlete, a good kid. And now he's all junked out. What the hell happened?

"Damn," he continued. "The OxyContins come out, and everybody was sucking them up fast, chewing them, then snorting them. Bang! Suddenly they're chasing the needle for five bucks a bag."

"It feels like it happened overnight," admitted Walsh. "It started just before you got done with your bid at Suffolk."

"But seriously, who the hell's bringing that shit in here?" Pat asked. "I didn't think it could ever happen! Aren't there any guys left—like Nee or Shea—fucking cleaning it up or shutting it down?"

"Patrick, those names so much as jaywalk, they'll be in federal prison until the day they die. The FBI is squeezing everyone to flip on Whitey. They're uncovering decades of corruption every minute."

Another reason never to tell anyone what he'd done in Ireland. Not even Walsh.

"What you have is that next level of soldiers, drug dealers, cowboys, junkies, or wannabes just running around pumping all types of drugs," continued Walsh. "It's free reign . . . like the Wild West. No more mob crew to fear pulling your teeth, dig a hole, and bury you in it—or worse: hog tie you and throw you off the Tobin."

Walsh and Pat shared a laugh. It was just so surreal. Pat knew that Whitey had been guilty of all those things. Everyone in the neighborhood knew it. It was another reason never to betray your friends, whether you were a cop, a criminal, a gangster, or a working schmuck. At best, you were *persona non grata*. At worst, you didn't wake up at all.

"You know, Sean has his own crew going now, man," Walsh said, perking up Pat's ears. "They got it covered right now. I heard he has Talbot and Mullen pumping cocaine to Old Colony, and Jones and Mackey pumping down D Street and then up the Point and everywhere in between. I heard they're killing it."

Of course he fucking is, thought Pat. *Fucking Sean.*

"Hmm," Pat began. "I wouldn't put it past him to be pumping heroin too. He'd sell his friends to the devil to make a buck and be called a gangster."

Pat had only seen Sean once in the last five or six years, when he came to visit him at Suffolk County Prison his first year there. But that was long before Walsh's beef with Sean. And also long before Pat learned about Sean's involvement with PJ's death.

"It might be worse than that," admitted Walsh. "Rumor is that Sean's not only dealing oxys and heroin but that he's claiming protection by Choppa."

Pat shook his head, not knowing whether to laugh or curse. If Choppa really was protecting Sean, it would go a long way to explain how Sean was still alive and blowing up all at once. Rival cowboys would definitely think twice before killing someone connected to Choppa. By reputation, he was a stone-cold killer since 'Nam and the Boston Irish gang wars in the sixties.

"Hey, it's just a rumor," Walsh said. "It'll all come out in the wash soon, I hope. The heroin is definitely a major focus of the BPD."

"Gimme a fuckin' break with that shit," Pat shot back. "We've never left anything to the BPD to clean up around here."

Walsh put up his hands in a "hey relax" kind of gesture. "Okay, okay! Can we focus on getting the eleven fucking assault and battery charges on police officers dropped and behind us? Please stay focused on that deal getting signed at your next court date, and just fucking chill!"

Pat nodded through a clenched jaw. Walsh was just trying to help, but Pat feared the longer he stayed with the BPD, the more he would forget his roots and how this neighborhood actually worked.

"I need to get back over to the other battlefield of gangbangers in Roxbury and Dorchester," Walsh said, changing the subject.

Pat could see he'd had enough of this conversation. He nodded, and they shook hands.

Walsh nodded and then walked back to his cruiser.

Walsh was right. Saving his own ass needed to be Pat's immediate focus.

Chapter 35

MALCOLM X PARK

NATE SANK ANOTHER THREE-POINT SHOT FROM BEYOND THE line, warming up for his game starting in a few minutes. The satisfying *woosh* of the ball passing through the net punctuated the rhythm he was feeling, the flow of being in the moment, and had psyched him up for the upcoming game.

He was in the massive Malcolm X Park, in Roxbury, on Martin Luther King Boulevard near Humboldt Avenue. The park was peaceful, grassy, and wooded, with small, paved winding walkways that led through the green lawn filled with big maples and pines. But it meant something different to Boston's athletic youth, offering the full suite of recreational amenities, including a baseball field, a swimming pool, tennis courts, playgrounds, and—most importantly—outdoor basketball courts.

These particular courts were home to the Men's League, which hosted tournament-style games from ballers all over the city. It was the first game of Men's League, and Nate couldn't resist saying yes when he had been asked to play last week at the nearby package store. His old coach from down at the Joseph Lee School in Dorchester had asked him.

This team had solid players from Franklin Hill, Franklin Park, Talbot Avenue, and Norfolk Street. They were essentially a spin-off from that team, which was always stacked and won it all. The other team was mainly from Orchard Park, a notorious Roxbury Park public housing complex, where the famous singing group New Edition was raised. But that complex was also the home of one of Boston's largest and most intimidating street gangs, the Orchard Park Trailblazers, infamous for brutal gun violence.

It wasn't uncommon that, among the players, younger members somehow affiliated with rival gangs would be playing against each other on the courts, and the game could erupt into gunfire. Nate knew that tempers could flare. But as someone rose up the ladder in his respective gang, the less likely he'd be balling at all. At some point, it would be too hard to be both a baller and a banger. One would eventually exclude the other.

The scene at the park was lively and peaceful at the moment. Two BPD cruisers were parked nearby, one on each end of the street to make certain it would stay that way. BPD was everywhere lately, ever since the gang prosecutor Paul McLaughlin had recently been found shot in the head at a T station parking lot the night before he was to try Jeffrey Bly of the Theodore Street Posse for carjacking. Since then, cops were sure to stop, search, and shake down any young man in the community at every step of the way with no cause. They didn't need one; as far as they were concerned, anybody could be packing or at the very least carrying drugs. So, Nate knew the park was as safe as possible—not that people hadn't been shot or killed there.

But nights like this at Malcolm X Park were a BPD logistical nightmare. All the different neighborhoods and all the gangs mixed in with the great people from all over the Black community of this city—from children to grandparents and everybody in between.

Over the past few months, people at the courts had noticed Nate's impressive skills, even if they didn't recognize who he was. He'd been playing around these parks throughout Dorchester and Roxbury his whole life. Recently, he was known as one of the best ballers in any given game. As right he should, Nate thought. He had busted his ass to get his basketball scholarship, and his game had only gotten better since his disciplined training and lively games at school over the last four years. Still, the local ballers were excellent and played differently from what he was accustomed to. He may have been better, but he still had to work to win.

As he continued to warm up, he noticed a familiar face coming over from the next court. It took only about a second for Nate to recognize him as Rodney, an old friend from high school and the Boston Neighborhood Basketball League. These days, Rodney was a Castlegate banger, one of the higher-ups in the gang. A few other players noticed him and stole second looks. Most everyone on the courts seemed to know who he was. Nate sunk one more shot, then grabbed the ball and waited for Rodney to approach him.

Rodney had been with the Castlegate gang for at least the past seven years, since '89, when they were sophomores in high school. Nate doubted that Rodney would know the extent of his involvement and mission with the Norfolk Kings, one of Castlegate's rivals. But he assumed that Rodney remembered that Tre and Slugs were his family, so he had to approach the conversation carefully.

Having grown up around the Norfolk Kings, even if he had never been an official member, Nate had a keen sense of how conflict worked among the gangs. It wasn't what most outsiders thought it was. Most people didn't understand that the majority of the killings in the street didn't have anything to do with drugs. Not directly, anyway.

The killing was usually the result of a long history of beefs between rival gangs. A beef could be the result of any number of issues. It could be one gang member killing a rival gang member's uncle or cousin years ago. That person's gang would adopt a vendetta, which would spark a rivalry for years between the gangs and families. But it didn't always have to be vengeance for a murder. It could have been a conflict of egos over territory or gang symbols or colors. In a city like Boston, the beef could have been sparked by sports teams, like the Kings, the Trailblazers, Michigan, or the Raiders.

Some gangs had alliances with other gangs, and others had bad blood conflict for decades, but relations were always fluid, constantly changing on a dime. Any little thing could upset the balance of power and start a new beef, causing a chain reaction that would cascade, inevitably leading to further violence. The process was never going to stop until the root causes were changed.

Rodney stepped up to Nate, his posture seemingly friendly.

"How you been?" Rodney said, seeming genuinely glad to see him. "It's been a long time, nigga! You poppin' up outta nowhere, huh? That news about your sidekick Jamal musta hit you hard, bro. Heard about your cuz Tre too. Sorry to hear that. That's the game, though, right?"

Nate let that comment bounce right off him. He dribbled and sank another shot.

"You still out here hustling, I see," he said, bouncing the ball to Rodney as a friendly gesture. "So, what you know about Tre's death—anything?"

"Damn! Right to the point, old Nate," Rodney replied, bouncing the ball back. "I ain't hustling; I'm *running* shit, nigga. So that why you popped up out here? You looking for info for what's left of the Kings?"

If only you knew, thought Nate. "Nah, man," he replied, sinking another shot. "Just asking an old friend what the word on the street is. My cousin wasn't the type to hang himself, that's for sure."

"Nope, he was the shooter, the stone-cold OG," Rodney agreed. "But I know Vamp Hill's had enough of Norfolk Street these days, so that's where I would look."

A few other players walked on the court, getting ready for the game that would start in minutes. Nate maintained eye contact for a moment before breaking away. He felt the discussion could have continued. By the look on Rodney's face, he seemed like he had something more to say. Nate was left wondering. *Did Vamp Hill have something to do with Tre's death?*

Everyone in the neighborhood knew about Vamp Hill Kings, a violent group that had evolved into one of the most deadly gangs in the city.

A few years back, they'd viciously stormed a church funeral mid-service for rival gang member Robert Odum. On a bloodthirsty revenge spree, they'd opened fire on the mourners in church and killed one man by savagely stabbing him nine times in front of everyone. Even in gang circles, this was shocking—a bold and brutal move.

That was the last straw for many in the city when it came to violence and was one of the defining events that sparked the creation of the Ten Point Coalition. Gibbs and other clergymen in the Coalition were focused on the Vamp Hill gang as one of their biggest problems. Slugs had told Nate all about the beefs between Norfolk and Vamp Hill and how they'd resulted in a lot of bloodshed over the title *Kings*, which Tre and Ricky had claimed for Norfolk back in the mideighties. They always said they would die before they gave up the name to Vamp Hill. With Tre out of the picture and Ricky fresh out of prison and seemingly giving up the game, that beef would be left to the remaining Norfolk crew. But at the moment, the Norfolk Kings' principal concern was getting the flow of money going again.

Nate was well aware that crack had taken over the Black neighborhoods in Boston, like it had in most Black communities in the country. But cocaine and heroin were still big trade for gangs to make massive sums of money. It was why Slugs had been so focused on reestablishing a connection to a direct supply these past few months.

The organized gangs had the distribution down to a science. Most gangs had stash houses scattered around for their drug and gun supply. There would be a designated stash spot on each block—like an alley where they would hide guns and drugs. They had set up the whole operation to be highly mobile. They could deal directly from that stash spot. If they spotted a rival gang or had to move operations in a hurry, they would load up and be gone in seconds.

Everything was designed to elude the BPD. And every gang had its leading three or four known killers or shooters. Nate had learned all of this specifically from watching Tre run the Kings. Nate may have been an intelligent freshman across town in a White Catholic high school, but he got another education altogether each and every day as he came home from school and walked past these corners.

Players filled the court now, and both teams were ready for the tip-off. Nate looked back for Rodney, but he had already disappeared into a sizeable crowd gathering to watch the game, just behind the low concrete wall and wrought-iron fence surrounding the court.

Shaking it off, Nate focused on the task before him and got in position for the tip-off. When he was playing, all of these neighborhood concerns seemed a million miles away.

———

BY THE TIME THEY'D WON THE GAME, DUSK WAS SETTING IN, and people were getting amped for the night. Passing and parked cars pumped music from their speakers, with a heavy bass rattling the air. A few players were blasting hip-hop from boom boxes, and people had started to gather around the food and drink stands. The sweet smell of blunt smoke filled the air.

Out on the courts, a surge of postgame good feeling pumped through Nate, despite the BPD vehicle that he had just now noticed. It was unmarked, but Nate was sharp enough to pick out someone who didn't belong. Maybe just keeping an eye on the neighborhood? Who knew? He took a deep breath, looking around, taking stock of the neighborhood, almost breathing it in. He could feel the love he had for this city, this community, the memories of his life here. Despite the gang bloodshed nightmares, this was his home; these were his people.

After getting his fill of the scene, Nate headed for his car, instinctively making sure no one was following him—especially not that unmarked car. Ever since he'd gotten further involved with the Norfolk Kings and the Ten Point Coalition, he couldn't help but feel he was being watched. He knew this was probably just paranoia, but better safe than sorry was his justification.

As he was unlocking his door, he heard a car roll up slowly behind him. Around here, anything could go down, so he was ready to hit the floor. Nate silently cursed and thought it would be fucking ironic if he got shot the one time he wasn't packing. Because he was playing, he'd left the gun hidden in the car. He turned back to clock who was rolling up on him.

It was Rodney. That didn't necessarily mean he wasn't in trouble. He nodded hello. Rodney rolled down the passenger-side power window and called out.

"Hey, old friend," Rodney said.

"Yo," Nate replied.

"Let me know if you want to set up a discussion with Ricky and Slugs," Rodney said. "Maybe we can bridge the flow for you."

Nate looked at Rodney, uncertain whether to trust him.

"We can create an alliance," Rodney continued. "A win-win."

"I'll run it by Slugs," Nate said. "We can set something up."

Rodney flashed him the peace sign and drove off.

Nate got in his car and started the engine but remained parked. He knew right there he was just a chess piece in a strategic game that was about to unravel. Had his unexpected run-in with Rodney been just an organic coincidence of the hood he was born into? *Rodney didn't just happen to cross paths with me*, he thought. *Or did he?*

Then again, Rodney always had a play. First, every outcome was going to benefit him, and second, it would benefit Castlegate. The rest was usually collateral damage.

On the other hand, an ally like Rodney was better than any other option he could think of. Rodney certainly had access to a high-level distributor. Now Nate just needed to follow the trail.

He would need to talk to Slugs to set something up. As for what he was going to tell the Ten Point Coalition, Nate wasn't sure. The deeper he got in with the Norfolk Kings these last few months, the less he felt like telling the Coalition anything at all.

He began to slowly drive away. As he approached the suspicious vehicle, he spotted a tall White man with a radio in the driver's seat. As he passed, their eyes locked, and Nate passed by in slow motion that seemed to last for a lifetime.

Nate recognized the officer as a high-level BPD gang unit leader named Sergeant Daly. Nate was sure the cop had been watching his whole interaction with Rodney, and most likely, Rodney was on their radar as a high-level Castlegate player. Nate reached under his seat and turned on the police scanner Gibbs had given him to stay safe and one step ahead.

"I got my eyes on Rodney," the radio crackled. "He's up to something. I want to know everything about who he was just talking to there."

Nate's ears cringed upon hearing Daly's words. He contemplated the significance of being seen at that moment.

Chapter 36

COURT

SHAKING HIS HEAD IN DISGUST, PAT WALKED BRISKLY DOWN the steps of the Boston Municipal Courthouse, the late afternoon sun casting long shadows across the concrete. Shaking off the bizarre experience he had just witnessed inside, Pat breathed a sigh of relief when he saw his ma and Walsh waiting for him at the bottom of the steps.

"Wow, that was crazy," Pat said, walking alongside his ma and Walsh. "All eleven charges dropped—clean disappeared. But—get this—I had to sign a document I would not press any charges against the BPD. Man, that blue wall is colorblind," Pat said pointedly. "Black, White, and Asian are all of a sudden bonded by the blue, eh?"

Walsh just grunted and nodded. Pat's ma was silent, soaking it in. The relief on her face was unmistakable.

"At one point, it was almost going to come crashing down on me," Pat explained. "That fucking dirty-ass cop says to my lawyer, 'I would like an apology from your client.' I lost it! I said, 'No fucking way! I'd rather go back to jail than give an apology for something I didn't do!'"

"He was just trying to get back his edge on you, the fucking psycho," Walsh said.

Pat hugged his ma and then Walsh, laughing in relief and over the sheer surreal nature of the experience. After all the illegal bullshit he'd gotten away with over in Ireland, it was walking to his car after work that got him beaten nearly to death. Potentially, this altercation could have landed him right back in prison. McHugh had told him the exact right cards to play. He'd have to buy that son of a bitch a top-shelf bottle of whiskey.

So many people, not just McHugh, had played a role in pressing the right buttons to make this happen. Jimmy, Sergeant Daly, Judge O'Riley, and even his ma and Walsh . . . Pat was grateful for everyone who'd talked him down from the ledge. Making a deal was the best move to keep him out of prison.

But, he thought, what had happened still wasn't right. No one around him truly understood how heavily the injustice of the violence was weighing on his mind. He wasn't naive by any stretch of the imagination. He knew corrupt and bad cops existed. He just never thought he'd be on the receiving end of such a savage beatdown for no good reason.

Formerly, the cops had mostly been a positive influence in his life. He hadn't held them accountable for his four years in prison; that was the result of harsh sentencing from a judge who wanted to make an example out of him. The Police Athletic Association had set up the boxing gym at the bottom of the Muni, where Pat grew up and trained and where Jimmy had worked for years. Sergeant Daly had been a friend of his dad's. *My own best friend is a cop, for fuck's sake*, thought Pat.

But now . . . he felt sick in the pit of his stomach, a festering rage. Before he would fall asleep every night, the last image running through his mind was being clubbed on the ground in the park, still cuffed, with no chance to defend himself. It was a relief not to have to suffer more prison, but the fury inside of him was only growing. He'd even entertained thoughts of tracking that cop home and beating him within an inch of his life. Or worse. Left unsatisfied, the rage would inevitably burst out; it was only a matter of time. He would never trust the BPD again.

He shook the nagging feeling off for the moment, trying to enjoy the taste of his hard-won freedom.

"Let's go to the Beer Garden, Pat," Walsh suggested. The place was a relatively new one on Broadway. Close by and lively, it was a hopping place to celebrate. They'd have no trouble getting in; both Pat and Walsh knew the bouncers, a couple of tough, connected guys. Pat had worked out with one of them, Paul, quite a few times. He was actually a real good kickboxer. The other was Johnny, an ex-military Southie guy, a big musclehead biker these days.

"You boys go ahead," Ma said, hugging Pat. "Enjoy yourselves. You deserve it. And stay out of trouble, Patrick."

"Trouble finds me, but I'm with a cop now, Ma." Patrick laughed. "I'll do my best."

———

PAT AND WALSH HAD NO TROUBLE SECURING THE BEST TABLE inside, right next to the front window overlooking Broadway. The first few hours there had already flown by. Their burgers and fries were long since devoured, and they were already working through their drinks quite swiftly.

Walsh lifted his glass in a toast, the warm feeling of being full and slightly buzzed washing over him. "To freedom and a nightmare's end," Walsh announced.

"Hell yeah, bro," Pat said wholeheartedly. "From your mouth to God's ear!"

They clinked their glasses and took a heavy gulp. Pat ordered another round of appetizers to accompany the celebration.

By ten p.m., a line was starting to form outside. As Pat surveyed the scene, someone caught his eye. A familiar strawberry blonde stepped into line with a few of her friends. It was Kiley. Pat had only seen her once since prison, when he'd parked across the street from her house. He'd waved at her back then, and she had waved back. But that was the extent of their interaction. He weighed whether he should finally go up and talk to her. He'd been putting off this emotional moment since he was finally set free from Suffolk.

He probably hadn't handled everything in the best way. He'd stopped writing her while he was imprisoned, reasoning that he wanted her to go on with her life. What was he supposed to do, hold her back? She was only entering her junior year in high school, and he was heading to prison. While he was fighting guys out in the yard, she was going to college. How would they have crossed that kind of bridge?

Nevertheless, that decision nearly tore Pat apart. She was his first love and first unforgettable heartbreak. He had wanted to talk to her for so long. He must have played this scenario out a thousand times in his head.

He watched as Kiley entered with a group of friends and approached the bar. She looked around the room and spotted Walsh first. Kiley smiled, recognizing his distinctive face, and waved. Then she glanced over and saw Pat. When their eyes met, Pat's stomach dropped out a little. That warm rush returned, as if she had never left. She held her smile, but Pat could tell she was feeling something intense too.

Kiley excused herself from her friends and walked over to Pat and Walsh's table. Walsh and Pat met eyes.

"Hiya, Walsh," Kiley said.

"Great to see ya," said Walsh, returning the greeting. "Listen, Pat, I'm gonna go get us some whiskeys. Some of that top-shelf stuff."

Pat nodded, thankful that Walsh had taken the cue to give them some space.

With tears forming in her eyes, Kiley outstretched her arms for a hug. Pat rose to hug her. While they embraced, she gave him a quick soft kiss. It felt so right—familiar. When they finally pulled apart, Pat gestured for her to sit down with him.

"Well, I always envisioned the moment I would see you again," he said. "You look great! Wow!"

"You too," Kiley told him. "I heard you've been getting your life back on track. I wondered how you were going to fare after."

He nodded, feeling a weird mix of gratitude and awkwardness. Just sitting next to her, he could feel the undeniable connection. They let a few moments of silence pass between them, just looking at each other.

"You crushed me, you know," she confessed. "You were going to be my friend forever, even with everything that happened . . . and you just cut me off. No calls, no letters. That's tough love, Patrick."

"It's what was best for the both of us," Pat explained. "I had to go cold turkey. I would have gone insane. Don't you understand? It fueled me to believe I did it for you. I was saving you from my shitty choices."

Kiley sat up a little straighter and frowned.

"Look at your life now," Pat argued. "It's exactly where it should be!"

Kiley's smile didn't seem convincing. They put their foreheads together, not saying anything, just being close. It was only a moment, but time seemed to stop.

Walsh made his way back to the table with three shots of whiskey, a giant grin on his face. "For the reunion," he said, setting the shots down on the table.

Pat and Kiley had each grabbed a shot and were about to clink their glasses when sirens nearby overpowered the loud music in the bar. Pat could see flashing police lights in the street immediately outside, speeding down Broadway. Bright red and blue reflected throughout the bar, bouncing off the mirrors and glassware.

They sat to drink their shots, wordlessly clinking and downing them.

Five more cop cars raced down the street on Broadway, toward the Point. Two ambulances followed.

Walsh stood up, trying to get a better look. "This looks serious," he said. "A real incident. Maybe a house fire? Or a brawl at M Street Park?"

Pat knew something was off; something in the air had shifted. It felt negative and heavy. "No fire trucks," he observed. "Something else is going down."

Other customers were now standing up, a few standing out in the street, craning their necks to see what was happening. The bouncers were standing outside as well.

"I'm going to step out front and talk to the bouncers," Walsh said. "Be right back."

Pat rejoined Kiley at the table, sitting right beside her. She was silent, leaning into his shoulder. He stroked her hair, just enjoying the moment, ignoring what was going on around them.

Walsh returned, an ashen look on his face. He leaned over and whispered into Pat's ear, "We need to get up to the church right now."

Pat nodded grimly, embraced Kiley, and held her tight.

"We got to go, Kiley," he said. "It's not good. I'll explain later. Let's make sure and talk before you go back to school, okay?" He pulled away softly. "I'm sorry."

Kiley nodded and looked down. He made his way through the crowd with Walsh, taking one look back at Kiley. She stood alone, watching him leave.

As soon as they exited the bar, Pat and Walsh broke into a full sprint up Broadway.

———

THE SCENE WAS CHAOTIC IN FRONT OF THE ST. BRIGID CHURCH and Rectory on Broadway, just blocks away from the Beer Garden. Two ambulances and five BPD cruisers were parked outside, their lights flashing. Passersby had gathered outside, and police had already strung yellow tape around the boundaries of the church.

The church was a humble, modest red-brick building that served the South Boston St. Brigid parish. Outside was a simple green sign with gold text that read *St. Brigid Church, established 1906*, with a Celtic cross above the text. The blue and red flashing lights seemed to disturb the building's natural, peaceful appearance, giving the church an eerie quality.

Walsh, recognizing some of the detectives and servicemen, chatted with a few officers. Pat waited by the sidelines, gathered with the others trying to figure out what had happened. During the summers, when he wasn't at Cathedral High, Father Lydon had lived and served here. Whatever this was, it was a little too close to home.

Two paramedics emerged from the rectory, carrying Father Lydon on a gurney. Pat's stomach dropped. But Father Lydon didn't look dead; Pat could see his hands moving.

The paramedics loaded the gurney into the ambulance, cranked up the siren, and sped off, headed for Mass General. Pat looked over at Walsh, who waved Pat to come over.

"Walshy, what the fuck's happening?" Pat asked.

"Fucking punks robbed the rectory," Walsh replied, shaking his head. "Took twenty-seven hundred from tonight's bingo money. They got in through the front door. Father Lydon tried to stop them by closing it on them. They shot him."

"Holy fuck," Pat blurted in disbelief.

"They shot him in the arm," Walsh explained. "Then they overpowered him and got in. Put a gun to his head and made him and the parish bookkeeper open the safe. Then they ran off with the cash."

"Is he gonna be okay?" Pat asked.

"I don't know. They said he's lost a lot of blood."

Pat sat down on the curb. He put his head in his hands, feeling sick and lightheaded. Walsh sat next to him.

Pat couldn't believe his eyes or ears. This kind of violence associated with such petty bullshit theft . . . it just didn't happen around here. Nobody robs the church; that was out of fucking bounds. This was a historic area, a huge neighborhood of cops, politicians, firefighters, and, yes, ruthless gangsters, thought Pat.

What kind of fucking lowlife shoots a priest? It's purely a sign of these dark times, Pat thought. The tides of this city changed at lightning speed, from the Irish immigration to the Civil Rights Movement and from the Italian mob getting dissolved to OxyContin and heroin flooding the streets. Yes, the Irish triumph over disenfranchisement had been accomplished, but it looked like this empire would also fall.

Inside, Pat was boiling. He stood up, determined to do something. "Walsh, talk to a few of those cops," he announced. "See if there are any leads. I'll move around the crowd, see if I can pick anything up."

As Pat mingled and listened, he could tell the mood of the crowd was ugly. Already, people were murmuring about street justice. Some conjectured that a few of the BPD might go rogue and kill the bastards. Pat silently drifted behind two cops, listening to their banter as they talked about the scene. He stayed a good car length behind them, his back to them. He lit up a smoke as they spoke.

"They're probably running across the city somewhere to a drug den to load up on the heroin," said one older cop to his partner. "Use it all and sell it—all twenty-seven-hundred worth."

"Fuckin' junkies, multiplying like roaches out here," replied the other cop. "Do they think they know who it was?"

"They have a few suspects," the older cop replied. "One kid's Kevin Hanley."

Pat's ears pricked up, recognizing that name. It was that kid who had passed by his house, the one who had dated his younger sister in high school. He came from a decent family.

"He's been robbing places to get the next fix," explained the older cop.

His mind racing, Pat discarded the cigarette in the gutter and walked back toward Walsh. Media vans were starting to arrive. After they got ahold of the story, the whole city was sure to be pissed off.

"Find anything?" Pat asked.

"Something about junkies," Walsh said. "Probably a local street monster, but it's hard to tell who."

"I've got a fucking idea who," Pat replied.

Just then, Pat spotted Kiley walking onto the scene, wide-eyed. They made eye contact, and she looked at him as if to say, *What's happening here, and what happened with us?* She knew Father Lydon well, and she knew how close Patrick was to him.

How could he explain this to her? Now more than ever, he felt the gulf of experience between them. They may have been from the same neighborhood, but they were in entirely different worlds. He had been right the first time: Being around him would only sink her down, destroy her above-the-board lifestyle. She deserved better than that. She was entitled to better than what he was about to do.

Pat held her eyes before giving her a gentle wave and turning his back. He slowly walked away from the scene, his body and emotions going numb. He walked on autopilot back toward his house, watching the cityscape move around him in slow motion. Crossing L Street, the noises from the screeching brakes of the buses, the pedestrians, the random noises of the street—they all seemed a million miles away.

Before he knew it, he was back at his front stoop, walking into his house, where his grandmother and younger sisters were cozied up on the couch. They were watching the breaking news on the TV from the crews that had just rolled up on the church scene a few blocks away.

"Jesus Christ, I can't believe what this world is coming to. I was at that goddamn bingo game tonight. That's our money, Patrick," his nana exclaimed. "Those bastards are lucky to be alive. Goddamn jerks robbed the church! Poor Father Lydon. I can't believe it!"

Pat climbed up the stairs to his room. He knew what he had to do.

He entered his room, a man on a mission. He moved his bed, exposing a hidden access panel behind it on the wall that looked almost like an electrical box. He opened the panel, reached into a cubby space, and pulled out a nine-millimeter pistol, already loaded. Searching further, he grabbed a few extra clips for good measure and put them in his jacket. He examined the gun, then hid it in his pants pocket.

Right before he had gone to prison, Pat had hidden away the gun in this wall as an extra measure of protection for his family. If someone on the inside threatened his family while he was in prison, he would tell his mother where he had hidden it. It never came to that, and Pat had hoped he would never have to use it. But he was always prepared to.

Tonight was the night.

Drifting back down the stairs with a backpack, Pat wordlessly waved goodbye to his grandmother and sisters, who were still lost in the news report. They were so used to him coming in and out that they rarely asked where he was going anymore.

Pat walked down the street in the same direction he had seen Kevin Hanley and his buddy walk the other day, from the front stoop toward the infamous Old Colony projects. He knew a few things about Old Colony. All kinds of shady shit was going on in there. Many junkies hid out in the prams, which is what they used to call the utility basements of these old housing projects. They were filled with steam pipes and maintenance rooms. The prams were neglected spaces that the junkies took over with old couches and discarded mattresses, transforming them into hangout spots. They would hide drugs or shoot up there or sometimes just hide out and squat to stay low. They usually left the lower access door to the pram wedged open so they could quickly come in and out. If the city had bothered with padlocks, the junkies would probably just have removed them with bolt cutters within a few hours. But the city hadn't bothered.

He'd also heard about other junkies who hung out up in the penthouse. The penthouse had this concrete slab and some equipment up there, with an access door that led out to the roof. You'd have to make sure you were really quiet when you passed through the third floor to get up there, but then who knew what you would find.

Pat arrived at the access door to one of the prams, through a metal door that had been propped open, as he'd expected. He pulled the hood of his green Celtics hoody over his head and opened the access door. It was dimly lit down there, with only a few utility lights illuminating the virtual dungeon. He scoped out the hallway, a mess of leaky pipes and discarded trash. He walked softly, not wanting to spook anyone on some kind of trip. He saw what looked like a homeless kid, probably not more than nineteen, tucked underneath a steam pipe to keep warm, curled up in the fetal position. He crept by him, leaving him undisturbed.

Turning a corner, he saw a young junkie sitting on a shredded couch, fumbling around with his paraphernalia. Pat grabbed him by the shoulders. "Hey, pal!" he announced abruptly, doing his best impression of a strung-out junkie. "Listen, I really need a place to get some shit now and shoot it. You know anywhere? Fucking anywhere?"

The young junkie just stared at him, wide-eyed and blinking.

"Come on, man, please? You gotta have a spot somewhere."

A glimmer of lucidity passed over the junkie's face, as if he just realized another human being was talking to him. "I can show you a spot if you're buying," the junkie confessed. "It's in the South End, ten minutes from here, Columbus Ave and Mass Ave."

Pat knew that neighborhood. It was near Roxbury by the Northeastern area. "No, man," he replied. "I got this. Thanks."

"C'mon, man!" pleaded the junkie. "I got the in over there, man."

"Fuck off before I slap the fuck out of you," Pat shot back.

The kid backed off and shuffled away, lost in some fucked-up dream.

Pat had heard about the place he was talking about. The locals called it Hell House. The site was similar to this pram but ten times worse. Hell House was an old Brownstone on Columbus that should have been condemned years ago. It had since fallen into disrepair and had been claimed by squatters who turned it into a shooting gallery—a place for heroin junkies to shoot up and crash. It was riddled with pimps, pushers, homeless, zombies, streetwalkers, like a royal flush of miscreants and vagrants. The police said it stank of dead rats and human waste. Sometimes needles spilled out from the house on the stoop, all the way to the sidewalk.

If this junkie kid knew about the place, there had to be other Southie kids shooting up at the spot. That's where Pat was hoping to find Kevin Hanley.

Chapter 37

HELL HOUSE

IT WAS JUST AFTER MIDNIGHT WHEN PATRICK JUMPED OUT OF the cab in front of the run-down, boarded-up brownstone. He was on Columbus Avenue, on the South End-Roxbury line, an area where two different neighborhoods overlapped. The cabbie had seemed reluctant to take him to this part of town at the late hour. As soon as Pat had slammed the door, the cabbie pulled away fast, probably anxious to get back to familiar territory.

Pat glanced up at the building, an infamous location he had long since known from the *Herald* or the *Globe*, which had both reported stories from the site repeatedly over the years because of the criminal crowd it would draw. This was his first time visiting in person. Up close, it looked far worse than the pictures he'd seen in the papers.

In addition to being a cesspool of junkies and vagrants, the house had a corrupt and mysterious history. The owner, obviously not residing there, was smart enough to donate to several local politicians and their campaigns. Pat recalled a journalist from one of the papers who reported, "He owns the property, which is in transition and redevelopment, but the BPD can't seem to solve the homeless junkie problem that plagues the house."

Pat cased the building with a black backpack and a pair of leather gloves on, walking stealthily through the alley and creeping through the back. All the while, he stepped carefully, scanning for needles on the pavement or dead grass or dirt. The last fucking thing he needed, he thought, was a dirty needle through his foot, giving him a social disease.

He did spot a few needles near the trash, which had the pungent stench of garbage that hadn't been brought to the curb in a few weeks.

Creeping up at the back of the house, Pat scoped the back door, examining the lock. It wasn't even deadbolted, and it looked like the doorjamb was probably rotted from neglect or termites. Pat easily yanked open the door, which would have given way to far less force. The noise didn't seem to alarm anyone inside; no one came running, and he couldn't detect a single light blinking on.

The kitchen was at the back of the house, and a staircase descended to Pat's right. He decided to check the main floor first, stealthily walking slowly past the kitchen, scanning hallways, and peering into dimly lit rooms. A young couple sat sprawled out on a dirty blanket in a room with no furniture, prepping their paraphernalia for another injection. Needles and rubber tubes lay around them, along with several lighters. The emaciated man noticed Pat but seemed apathetic about his presence, mostly ignoring him in favor of the urgent need for their next fix. The young woman leaned on the man, staring off into space.

Pat reached into his jacket. The sudden movement spooked the male junkie, who clutched at his needle and held it in front of him in a defensive posture—as if that would protect him.

"Relax!" Pat said, removing his hand from his coat. "I'm looking for Kevin Hanley. Have you seen him?" Pat had pulled out an old picture from the Boys and Girls Club.

The junkie slowly put his needle down and squinted to examine the photo. It was a long shot; in the photo, Kevin was the picture of health.

"Yeah," the junkie said. "I know him. He's got a spot down in the basement. Take a look around." He then continued to wrap his bicep with a rubber tube.

Pat turned away, not eager to watch. He backtracked to the staircase. Looking more closely at the steps, he could see two bodies partially lying and partially leaning in the stairwell. They had the nods—totally knocked out and sleeping from so much heroin use. He carefully stepped over the junkies, leaving them undisturbed on the way down. The caution wasn't necessary. He could have dropped drums down the stairs and they would have scarcely noticed. Any errant needles lying around were of far more concern.

He waited for his eyes to adjust to the darkness. He noticed a light switch at the bottom of the stairs, but Pat kept the lights off in an abundance of caution. Even if they were nodding off, the junkies were still a potential threat because they were unpredictable, desperate, and irrational. A few of them appeared out of the dark, shuffling to move to another room. They had lost part of their human quality, looking more like sun-starved, malnourished creatures living in a cave. Which, in effect, they were.

When his eyes finally came into focus, he saw pretty much what he expected: people lying together in heaps, some on old, dirty mattresses, others with stringy blankets and ratty pillows. He heard a few whispers and moans, even some soft giggling, but mostly quiet. Any piece of old, dilapidated furniture was occupied by junkies of all colors and ages, either sleeping or prepping their next fix. The funk of body odor, mold, and human waste permeated the walls. It took everything Pat had to not dry heave.

Entering another large room, Pat scoped out three young male junkies on a threadbare couch that had several tears in it. As he approached them, Pat thought he could discern one of them was Kevin Hanley. The other two junkies prepped the next dose. Kevin was already shooting up, noticing Pat just as he pulled out the needle.

That's definitely him, thought Pat. *There's that miserable fuck.*

He swung back and punched Kevin hard in the face, cocking his fist back for another blow. As Kevin howled and put his hands up to protect his face, Pat kicked him in the stomach. Kevin fell in a heap to the floor, moaning, as the other junkies on the couch scattered, disappearing into the recessed shadows of the sprawling basement. Kevin lay down in the fetal position, whimpering.

Patrick drew his pistol, pointing it at Kevin's head. "Look who it is, the goddamn bingo bandit. Come on, look at me, tough guy," said Pat.

Kevin looked up from his position on the floor. He blinked, staring down the barrel. He put his open hands up and rose to a seated position back on the couch.

"What the fuck are you thinking?" Pat demanded. "I oughta snap your neck right now. You rob the church bingo money and shoot at our fuckin' priest, and you think you can just walk away?"

A faint look of concentration fluttered across Kevin's face before his expression went hollow and empty. The junk was hitting him.

"Oh shit. Set me up again," Kevin said, his eyes already scanning the floor for his discarded needle. "Hey, Patrick, what do you want here? What do you really want me to say? That this shit got me, it's all that matters?"

Not satisfied, Pat sat next to Kevin on the couch and stuck his pistol at Kevin's temple.

"I don't know, Patrick," Kevin blurted out, trying a different tactic. "Go home, will ya? Go punch the bag or something and leave me the fuck alone."

Pat sat, cold and unblinking, ready to shoot, his stare a laser beam boring into Kevin's skull. He was more serious than he had ever been at any moment of his life.

"Where's the fucking gun, Kevin?" he demanded.

Kevin eyed the needle on the ground, then looked back at Pat.

"Okay man, okay," Kevin said. "Hold on." Kevin leaned to his side, sticking his hand deep into the couch cushions. He slowly pulled out a black .22. "Here," he said, holding it by the barrel, offering the handle side to Pat. "I just tried to scare him."

Pat snatched Kevin's gun and stowed it in his jacket pocket. One person had already almost died because of this junkie; Pat wasn't going to leave him armed.

Thinking he was already off the hook, Kevin clutched his needle, desperate to get another hit into his arm. Just as he began to prepare to spike his bicep again, Pat pistol-whipped him with his nine millimeter. Kevin yelped and then fell into a heap, unconscious.

Pat stared at him, shaking his head. *I could easily take you out*, he thought. But something stopped him from going any further. There was little he could do to destroy Kevin that Kevin wasn't already doing himself.

With both guns in tow, Pat sidestepped over Kevin and slipped back up the stairs. In the back of his mind, he hoped he'd never see this little piece of shit again.

———

PAT'S EXIT WENT LARGELY UNNOTICED BY THE ZOMBIES IN the basement. Nonetheless, Pat was careful leaving the place, sneaking his way back to the street a different way than he'd come in. He found an inconspicuous corner niche between buildings and decided to wait there to collect his thoughts. He'd have a hard time finding a cab out here, so he'd probably have to hoof it back, at least part of the way.

Cars went back and forth down Columbus. Pat watched them pensively, like he was observing his own thoughts go by. He had come that close to killing Kevin. Would that really have done anyone any good? Would there be any less heroin on the street? No easy answers came to him.

A black SUV was slowing down and pulling toward the curb. Something about it didn't seem right, so Pat retreated to the shadows and walked toward the alley behind Hell House, his back to the street.

A quick slamming door signaled that somebody had jumped out of the SUV. By the time Pat heard somebody sprinting in his direction, that person was almost on top of him. Before he could turn around, he felt his body slam into the brick wall. Unhurt but surprised, Pat turned around to see who had come up from behind. Was it one of these fucking cops back to harass him?

Holy shit. It was Nate, pointing a gun in his face. What the hell was Nate doing near Hell House?

"I'm gonna ask you just once," said Nate, his eyes deadly serious. "What the hell are you doing?" He started to pat him down.

"Nate. Nate, what the fuck, man?" protested Pat. "Hold up. Listen to me. I'm not a junkie. Have you seen the news yet, jackass?"

"I can't believe this," Nate said. "You barely a year out. And now this?"

Still patting him down, Nate found one of the guns in Pat's jacket.

"Stop, Nate," Pat said sternly. "Nate. *Stop!*"

Nate pulled out the .22 that Pat had taken from Kevin. "Wow, man," he said. "What do we have here?"

"Nate—" started Pat.

"You've really crossed the line, now," sneered Nate. "A model man, huh?"

"Lines were made to be crossed, right, Nate?" Pat shot back. "Fuckin' hear me out, will ya?"

Nate stared at Pat, seemingly willing to listen to what he had to say next.

"I know how this looks," Pat explained. "You obviously have not fucking heard on the news how a junkie shot Father Lydon tonight."

"What?" Nate finally stopped, staring Pat in the face. "Why?"

"They robbed the safe at gunpoint for the bingo money," explained Pat. "That's *his* gun. He's inside. Now get the fuck off me!"

Nate loosened his grip, and his face softened from anger to concern.

"Father Lydon—is he okay?" Nate asked.

"He's in the hospital," Pat said. "But I think he's gonna pull through."

"I did not hear that," said Nate, shaking his head. "I'm sorry, brother. I was driving by with my cousin Slugs and recognized you standing beside a known shoot-up gallery in the Black community, run by Vamp Hill."

"Yeah, it's well known in my neighborhood too," Pat said. "Some junkie at the Old Colony projects tipped me off."

"Everyone knows about this place," said Nate. "I've heard about all the heroin and what's going in your neighborhood, and I saw you and I just . . . I thought the worst, man."

Nate handed the gun back to Pat, and Pat pocketed it. There was a long pause as they took everything in, letting things settle.

"I should have known," admitted Nate. "You're in too good of shape to be a junkie. I would have clocked that if I saw you in the light. But what the fuck happened to your face?"

Pat felt the fresh scar on his forehead, still healing. "Long story, bro," he replied. He left it at that.

A cop, sirens on, raced down the street. Although it was headed somewhere else, Pat tensed up a little, eager to get off the street.

"Yo, is that dude still alive in there?" Nate asked. "I got Slugs circling, so if we need to bounce now—"

"Yeah," said Pat dryly. "He's alive. If you call that living."

"C'mon," Nate said, gesturing back toward the street and the SUV. Pat nodded and followed.

They snuck out of the alley quietly, looking over their shoulders. For two Catholic school Boston guys—one Black, one White, both packing heat—they were standing in one place for far too long. Best to keep moving. Enough bad things had already happened tonight.

Chapter 38

PUG'S PUB

THEY WERE SILENT FOR MOST OF THE SUV RIDE. SLUGS MOSTLY remained suspiciously silent, blasting "C.R.E.A.M," by Wu Tang Clan, but he did offer to drop them off. Pat had suggested they go to a safe zone, somewhere both he and Nate could lie low for the next couple of hours and not draw any attention. Pug's Pub, Jimmy's dive bar, was the perfect choice. Pat had been there three or four times and knew it to be very low-key. Most people never even knew it existed.

Pug's was a dark, shady bar in Roxbury, an industrial neighborhood. The establishment was located on Magazine Street and was surrounded by old warehouses. It was off the beaten path, away from the main streets. Ninety-nine out of a hundred of the people who walked in would immediately turn around and walk out. From the outside, you could barely tell it was open—never mind a bar. Half the people inside were probably armed, so it wouldn't be out of place, nor a big deal, if both Nate and Pat were packing.

As Pat recalled, Jimmy had inherited the bar back when he was still dealing cocaine. Someone had bought a sizeable stash of product from Jimmy but couldn't cover the debt. Luckily, the guy did own the run-down bar and offered it to Jimmy instead of the cash. If he'd been dealing with anybody but Jimmy, that guy wouldn't have gotten off so lucky. A bar that, itself, was the result of a drug deal was the perfect locale to discuss the seedy goings-on at Hell House.

Nate and Pat sat in the far corner where they were barely illuminated by the dim lights. They ordered two glasses of whiskey, clinked, and tossed them back. Pat put his glass down and launched his first volley.

"Are we ready to talk about what the fuck you were doing back there?" he said. "And why the fuck you were driving around with Slugs at one a.m. near a known shoot-up gallery?"

"It's a long story, but as Marting Luther King Jr. said, one has a moral responsibility to disobey unjust laws." Nate smirked evasively. "I'm onto something with that place. I promise we'll get into it. But please, tell me about Father Lydon."

Patrick let it go for now. "As far as I know," he explained, "it wasn't a fatal wound, but I don't know how bad his arm will be fucked up."

"That shit is wack," Nate said, shaking his head. "Fucking robbing the church for the goddamn bingo money. Forcing him to open the church safe by gunpoint."

"The bastard is lucky I didn't fucking kill him," Pat said. "Nobody lays a finger on Lydon. That man did so much for us—for the community."

Nate sighed. "He was the best, back in the day. As long we kept the peace and broke up any beefs."

Pat smiled. He remembered their Cathedral days as if they were yesterday. Nate had owed his whole Cathedral High education to Father Lydon, who had spearheaded the program to integrate students of color from less-privileged neighborhoods for tuition so low it was practically nothing. Lydon was also front and center in attempting to break up any race-related fights before they happened. He was the one who had encouraged Nate and Pat to help calm things down the day of the Southie High riots, when Mayor Flynn was struck in the head by a bottle and helicopters were circling everywhere.

Pat recalled how Father Lydon tried to persuade him that Boston's shift from predominantly Irish to a more multicultural city wasn't necessarily bad. He'd said, "It's not changing because of the Blacks any more than it's changing because of the Hispanics or the Asian. Cities change. That's just how it goes. And change scares us the same way we scared the people who were here before we were."

Lydon had always believed in their higher selves. "Remember," he had said, "we of the Society of Jesus are men for others, and we need young men like you who are willing to live that out."

Having nearly blown the head off Kevin Hanley this very evening,

Pat wasn't sure how much of a "man for others" he was anymore or if he had ever been. But it touched him that Father Lydon had thought so much of them.

"We walked on water all through high school," Nate reminisced. "When I first got back to Boston to attend my best friend's funeral—you remember Jamal, right? Man, that truly broke my heart. Brother was on his way to the NBA . . . murdered for no good reason."

Pat nodded in understanding. Another young Black man in Boston snuffed out way before his time.

"Anyways," continued Nate, "I saw Father Lydon when I stopped in over at Harry the Greeks for some new gear. I'd gone and grabbed a slice across from Cathedral. And there he was, doing his thing with the kids. It was cool to see him . . ." Nate trailed off, a shadow going across his face. "Damn those junkies, huh, brother?"

"Yes," Pat agreed. "Goddamn those junkies. Man, it's crazy how something can take over like that. Once oxy came out, doctors were pumping those out by the thousands. Everyone was getting the taste. Then all a sudden, they were harder to get . . . and the rebirth of heroin began. Everyone wanted it. You could get a bag of P-dope for like ten bucks!"

"Listen, don't get me started," Nate said knowingly. "This crack and heroin been flooding the Black streets across the country for well over a decade. The people flooding the markets . . . they aren't always who you think they are." He pulled up his sleeve to reveal his new tattoo, a cross with *Redeem the time, for the days are evil. Ephesians 5:16* written underneath. "Got it at the same spot in Chinatown you got yours."

"Holy shit, man," Pat said. Nate's tattoo was larger, with two blood drops in the center of the cross. Pat sensed it had a very different meaning from his own *Vengeance Is Mine* tattoo. He didn't know quite what to expect from this new Nate.

"You ever read *The Big White Lie*?" Nate asked.

Pat shook his head.

"It's written by Michael Levine, a former DEA agent. I did my senior thesis on that book. He reveals a lot of stuff that only people inside the DEA would know. He talks about how the deep state of the CIA is largely responsible for our drug epidemic. They secure or coerce a supply in another country, sell it here, and then use the money totally off the books to fund whatever-the-fuck secret project they want."

Pat nodded, listening. Given the sheer amounts of corruption in the local government, he wouldn't be remotely surprised by it coming from the top. He'd heard too many whispered stories to dismiss anything Nate was saying outright.

"And our current president doesn't appear so clean and polished in all this either. Bush allegedly had Clinton use a small airplane runway in Mena, Arkansas, to receive planes full of drugs, and then the country is flooded with crack and heroin. Not from Florida or New York or California—but from fuckin' Arkansas! This damn city alone has had 620 murders in the first five years of the nineties—and that's just what they said on the news. It's a fuckin' war zone, and meanwhile, the world carries on, deaf and blind to the truth."

Patrick knew this was a topic Nate was ready to debate all night long. It certainly sounded like he had researched the fuck out of it. He understood what he was saying, and probably a lot of it was right. But he felt Nate would always come back to the same point—harping on the details of how the government systematically oppresses the Black community in every way. Nate always debated that if we took the bullshit billions we paid other countries and just made education equal and paid teachers professionally, Black life would instantly change. Still . . . was Nate wrong?

Patrick stood up quickly. "Wait one minute. I forgot something. I'll be right back."

"I'll get the next round," replied Nate.

Pat paced to the payphone on the opposite side of the bar. It was a beat-up machine, marked up with crude graffiti and scratches that were knifed in, spelling out curse words. He plunked in a quarter and dialed 911.

"911, what's your emergency," said the bored operator on the other line, her voice sounding like tinny static.

"Yes, I just saw two White kids walking into that drug den Hell House on Columbus. I think they had something to do with that priest church robbery in South Boston. I recognized one of them."

"Do you have the name, sir?"

"Yeah. Kevin Hanley. One of them was Kevin Hanley."

"And what's your name, sir?"

"Anonymous," Pat said, then abruptly hung up. *Fuck you, Kevin Hanley*, he thought, walking back to his corner table with a feeling that maybe, just maybe, a semblance of justice might be done.

"Listen, man," Pat began, returning to his seat where a fresh glass of cognac was waiting for him. "I was thinking about what you said. You don't have to convince me. My nana always said, 'Politics is a dirty business, but you can make a lot of money in it.' I didn't know what she meant, but I do now. It's a dirty business fueled by money; that equals corruption."

Nate seemed satisfied by that. Pat was in no mood to be combative about the finer details. The friendly familiarity of their exchange gripped him. Ever since Lydon's integration program had started, they'd had conversations like this. Patrick always clarified to Nate that being Irish was different from being White. He felt like he'd finally persuaded Nate to that point, seeing the parallels from the days where employers posted signs everywhere that said, *No Irish need apply*.

And Pat felt he'd learned a lot from Nate about the Black community and their history in Boston. Nate helped Pat understand that Black and White were not on an even playing field—not even remotely. Nate had to work twice as hard to get the opportunities that came to Pat naturally. "You think that everything is just supposed to work out for you," Nate had said back then. "That all you have to do is exist, and all that stuff will happen for you. Well, that's not how life works for kids like me."

"The water is getting dirtier around here, that's for sure," Nate said after a few silent moments with his cognac. "I know you've kept your eye on all the news from the beginning. Nothing's a surprise anymore—from that corrupt Detective Mulligan and his cronies making a fortune from shaking down criminals, to the DA being murdered."

"Yup, no one is safe," Pat agreed.

"But you must have been real shocked by all the recent rumors in the news about Bulger and the Feds. They're saying he's been a rat this whole time."

Patrick couldn't help but shake his leg with frustration, thinking about the recent news clip of Whitey being a rat. He just couldn't bring himself to believe it. Pat figured it was all bullshit just to get everyone who worked with him to flip on him, and then Whitey could be apprehended, rather than aided and abetted by everyone—including by Pat's mission in Ireland. Also, the thought of everything he did in Ireland going to benefit a fucking rat bastard made Pat's skin crawl. He didn't *want* it to be true.

He contemplated Nate's previous comment about Clinton, his nana's perception of politics, his experience with the Black BPD, and the church incident. The dots of corruption connected on every level and were everywhere he looked—and had for as long as he could remember. But was there a pattern he'd been missing the whole time, pointing to something way bigger than either of them?

He took a sip of cognac and looked Nate directly in the eye.

"We're just peasants set up to hate each other and fight each other for all eternity," Pat said. "Meanwhile, the government operates the same old-fashion way—under the radar, benefiting with billions, and fucking things up at every step on every level."

"Remember when I visited you in prison and asked you why you'd ruin your life and not rat?"

"Yeah, man, I remember."

"It was just the wrong question to ask. I won't go into it now, but I've been experiencing some challenging situations like that lately over the past six months—running around the streets trying to find Tre's killer . . . It's that constant grind of being frustrated and angry at the culture and the government that creates the very problems they claim to fix. I feel myself changing and starting to understand what it is like to be forced into very tough decisions . . ." Nate looked at Pat and lifted his glass. "We are fucking cattle, my friend!"

Pat raised his glass to meet Nate's, and they both clinked the rims and downed their drinks.

Something was different about Nate—he had an edge of fearlessness and rebellion like never before. The old Nate had an intense focus on keeping his nose clean and staying on the path to career and success.

Now, his whole trajectory seemed drastically shifted. And could you blame him? Pat remembered how he felt when PJ died—that angry, sick, helpless feeling. Nate had lost his best friend and cousin immediately afterward.

The waitress stopped by the table and dropped off two more cognacs. "What the fuck you two handsome fellas up in here for?" she asked with a playful smile. Her name tag said *Simone*.

Pat recognized that he and Nate were younger, better looking, and not as banged up as most regulars. They both smiled back.

"Hell, you have me thinking about it now, Simone," said Nate, flirting.

She winked as she turned around, showing off the view her tight pants offered.

"Hmm, hmm, hmmm," Simone said, strolling away. "You young, fine asses. Going to have to call a few of my girls down here so we can all have a good time!"

"Just a few ought to do it," laughed Pat.

Nate looked around and leaned in. "You know, how the fuck does this dude Jimmy own this place in fucking deep Roxbury? Go figure, huh? One crazy cat, and of course you're close with him! When I ran into you by the gym when I first got back to Boston, I saw Jimmy there and caught up with Papa Ray—"

"Hey, Nate, listen," Pat interrupted. "Jimmy's solid as can be. That's why he's been so tight with your Papa Ray for years. He's a good man, not part of the Irish mob or a fake gangster. He's just an independent man trying to live a decent life."

Nate raised an eyebrow in a clear expression of doubt. He laughed. "I know Papa Ray works the kitchen in here; he's been known to come out with his apron on and knock mothafuckas out cold that get out of hand!"

"The man's dedicated his life to boxing . . . opened a Police Athletic League gym," Pat continued, focusing back on Jimmy. "He opens his heart to kids from all over; you've been there, man. Yeah, okay, he's got his weaknesses like most and has had his challenges—did some time for dealing and a few other bad decisions—but he's helped out in so many ways . . ." Pat hesitated, wanting to tell Nate about the Ireland trip, his first job out of prison working at the gym, and the nightclub bartending gig that Jimmy had helped him land. But he didn't know how to bring all that up without revealing sworn secrets. But there was one thing about Jimmy he did want to bring up.

"Jimmy bailed me out of jail recently," he said.

"Whoa. What the fuck happened?" Nate asked.

"I might as well tell you this one right fuckin' now," Pat said. Just the thought of reliving this story made him tense up. "Remember every single word I say here is the fucking truth." He raised his right hand, pointing to the scar above his right eye. "I was the White Rodney King."

"Hold up. What? What the hell do you mean?" Nate asked.

"I was just walking to my car after work . . ." Pat began.

He retold the events of the evening, standing up and giving Nate a physical play-by-play—the harassment of the Black police officers, running and hiding in the park, the Asian officer apprehending him and offering him a fair deal. And then the savage eye injury the Asian officer endured when one of the Black officers took over the scene, and the brutal beatdown he'd suffered at the hands of the cops while his hands were cuffed behind his back. He told Nate about the hospital, the shady treatment at the jail, and the scummy ass-saving deal he had to make in court. "No cop, even when seriously fucked by another cop, would ever rat on their own—no matter what color," he said. "The blue wall is real."

Amid it all, they ordered another round of whiskeys.

Nate shook his head, looking down at his drink. "I'm letting it sink in, man. Unbelievable. But makes sense, knowing everything I know about the BPD. I could see it in your face—been wondering what's been going on. It's absolute bullshit, man, but it doesn't surprise me. We have Ralph Martin, a Black DA, Black judges, Black cops—but it doesn't matter that they're Black, doesn't put them on our side. They just become part of the system, conformed and programmed to the status quo. The way they behave, it's *modus operandi*—standard operating procedure."

Pat nodded as Nate spoke, agreeing with observations he knew were true.

"I remember how many times I got pushed against the wall and frisked just because I was Black. Even though there was a Black cop there, watching the whole thing." Nate trailed off.

As an afterthought, Nate raised his glass. "Well, just so I can have the last word," Nate continued, "if you were Black and that beatdown happened the exact same way, you'd be back in prison. Or dead!"

"Why does it always have to be a race thing?" Pat responded. "If the cops were White, it wouldn't have happened!"

"That's the old spirit, my friend," Nate replied. "The real problem is there's no Black and White when it comes to the blue!"

All they could do was laugh it off and take another sip. As the laughter faded, Pat's thoughts wandered back to the events of this evening and the unsettled questions of Nate's proximity to Hell House. "Wait, wait. Enough's enough," he said. "Tell me what the fuck's up with you. You're, like, living on the edge these days. What are you up to with Slugs, that place—and pulling a fuckin' gun on me? Your turn for some truth."

Nate took a deep breath. He was quiet for a moment.

The past was the past. But there was the elephant in the room Nate and Pat had not yet discussed: Tre's death and all the backstory behind it. There was the fact that Tre was the Norfolk Kings triggerman who had killed Patrick's fifteen-year-old cousin back in 1990 on Ashmont Street. Sure, Nate thought, this information had been clarified in the letters written back and forth from prison, but they'd never really hashed it out in person.

"You ain't gonna believe this," Nate started, taking another drink. "Slugs and I been reestablishing a connect for the Kings, and we been watching that Hell House. Not even sure how I got here or where this is going or, better yet, how this is going to end . . . but my intentions are good. I know . . . I must sound like you did when you decided not to rat on your best friend, and I know that cost you four years in prison, but—"

"Holy shit," said Pat. "And you're packing heat too. Well, that sure as fuck sounds like official gangbanging to me."

"It all happened so fast," Nate explained. "First, Jamal was murdered, then Tre was found mysteriously dead. Slugs was on a rampage . . . We've had enough of all the violence over the last few years. Even the Rev has formed his own street team to stop the violence."

Pat took in the information, his face in deep thought, trying to put it all together.

"All right . . . I'm still not understanding all this, brother. I know you, so either you're running with the Kings or you're not. And if you are— where are the good intentions coming from? 'Cause all this means is this stand-up straitlaced Black dude has lost his fuckin' mind. Lydon said you were picking out a law school, man. Now you could be dead at any moment?" He sighed, gazing out into space, letting his thoughts wander. He took another sip. "Nate, I'm lost in this society. Nothing makes sense to me. I feel like everything's broken. I thought I had a solid second chance here, but . . ."

He didn't know how to finish what he was saying.

"You do what you gotta do, Patrick," Nate said reassuringly. "I am on a fuckin' mission, and I'll fill you in when it develops. I promise."

Pat studied Nate's face. From everything he knew about people, everything he knew about Nate, he was telling the truth. But he could tell Nate was holding something back too.

But so am I, Pat thought.

If he wanted Nate to come clean, shouldn't he have shared that Choppa was involved in Tre's murder? But of course, he couldn't; he still knew absolutely nothing about it. Nobody was laying all their cards on the table. It felt like a bigger game was still going on, and he had no idea how high the stakes were.

It was now close to three in the morning, and Pat had lost track of how many drinks they'd had. Once they settled up, they walked out of the bar together into the cold autumn early morning. Nothing needed to be spoken. Even if they were both still hiding something, Pat knew they had each other's back.

Chapter 39

TAKEOVER SCHEME

THE SUN WAS JUST SETTING IN THE SKIES OVER RICKY'S house. Nate and Slugs sat quietly in the Ford Explorer, parked on the street outside, listening to Slugs's beats. Although the volume was relatively low by his standards, Slugs had the bass way up, and Nate could feel the vibrations in his chest. Slugs was grooving on one of his favorites from Material Love, mouthing the words and bobbing his head while methodically loading a clip into his nine millimeter. Finishing the clip, he tucked the gun into his waistband. Nate instinctively felt for the gun in his own pocket, which had become a grounding sense of security over the last few months.

"We're good, Slugs," he said. "I think we count on Rodney to be straight with us. They want to hurt Vamp Hill any way they can."

Slugs said nothing but turned down the stereo. He stared straight ahead in deep thought, his brow furrowed. He was clearly conflicted.

"He used to live over here for years before he moved over to Roxbury," Nate continued. "That's how Ricky knows him. He came to me. He needs us."

"Listen, cuz," Slugs said firmly. "I don't trust no one. Not even Ricky."

As if on cue, Ricky came outside, ambling to the front fence. It was the first time Nate noticed he had a slight limp on the same leg where Nate had seen the bullet scars the first time he'd met him. But instead of making him look weaker, it made him appear more intimidating.

Ricky leaned on the front fence. Farther back, on the front porch, another man was watching. Nate instinctively guessed that was Ricky's backup—most definitely armed, and someone who would start blasting if things went remotely askew.

Another car slowly pulled up. Nate recognized it immediately as Rodney's car, the same one that had pulled over next to him outside Malcolm X Park. Rodney parked some distance away.

Opening his door, Rodney stepped out as Slugs nodded to Nate. All three men slowly approached the fence. Nate noticed that Ricky was careful not to venture too far from the house; he was staying close enough not to set off his ankle bracelet. He moved away from the fence and sat down at an old, round, playground picnic table in the property's front yard and pulled a pack of playing cards from his back pocket.

Rodney, Nate, and Slugs cautiously entered the yard, standing near the picnic table. The yard was poorly kept, with mostly dead, ankle-high grass. The man on the porch surveyed the whole scene, never taking his eyes off the men.

Ricky removed the deck of cards from the box and started shuffling. Without a word, he dealt out four hands of seven cards apiece.

"Listen, little niggas, we just here for a little card game and a few laughs," said Ricky. "So Slugs, Rodney, Nate, sit the fuck down, 'cause that mothafucka on the porch will set off a shotgun the minute someone clinches the wrong way."

All three men complied, having already clocked that this was the case. It was no longer something that intimidated Nate. After the past few months, he had become accustomed to armed men at negotiations. You'd be an idiot not to have that kind of protection.

"You all asked about the connect me and Tre used in the old days," Ricky said, picking up his cards. "You niggas never dreamed about this type of quantity and quality. So, I figured we could all help each other out. Now, I'm just introducing a few people to each other. That's all."

The three men picked up their cards, listening.

"But I'm taking a network fee, niggas, that for sure," said Ricky, looking at his cards. "You all remember when we were supplying all these gangs in this city with this Miami connect. The Colombians were pumping that shit up the coast like Exxon. They had it down—and we had that on lockdown."

Ricky paused and shook his head fondly, remembering faster and wealthier days.

"But that all blew up in '91. You remember. The DEA seized the largest shipment in New England history—over four thousand pounds of cocaine and a five-hundred-million-dollar bust in a Norwood secret facility. That pipeline has had spotty spin-offs of shipments with different groups over the past few years. But shit's different now."

Although all three men were looking at their cards, they couldn't care less what was on them. Nate stole a sideways glance at Slugs and could tell his ears were perked up.

"I got word now that the Miami connect is back in full effect," revealed Ricky. "Now it's Dominicans every month—as much crack cocaine and heroin as needed. This cocaine is pure. The heroin's seventy-five percent, and that's what's in high demand these days. The Dominicans have these areas outside the city flourishing. Lynn. Fall River. Chelsea. Lawrence. Lowell. Rhode Island."

Ricky looked around the table, for the first time taking his eyes off his cards. He made eye contact with everyone, seeing how his news was hitting.

"And because I'm putting this together, you're getting the best pricing. Bulk rate. Now, since this is easy money and a way to snatch control, I'll be expecting my hefty grocery bag once a month." Ricky took a cigar from his front pocket and clipped the end, letting the proposition marinate in the silence.

Nate wasn't going to be the first to talk, so he waited for Slugs. Rodney leaned back, thinking; having just been reacquainted recently, it was hard for Nate to read his face.

"Yo, Ricky," Rodney finally interjected. "I *have* a connect. I thought you were calling me over to source the supply to these Kings, not get involved in a new connect, man. I don't need to fuck up a good thing."

Ricky lit up his cigar and laughed as if amused by an inside joke. "Rodney, you forgetting who you talking to," he said, chuckling. "'A good thing.' You got Academy, Vamp Hill, Lenox Street, Intervale, H-Block, Columbia Point, and every other gang creeping into your territory. You missing the point. You know this deal changes the game for both crews here. The price and the grade and the quantity don't get any better. He who controls the flow is the motherfuckin' king!"

This is fucking big, thought Nate. *He's not just talking about a connect but about controlling the whole flow into the city.* One look at Slugs, and Nate could see he was definitely considering it. But Slugs wouldn't just jump in until he was sure. Nate could tell Rodney was studying Ricky's face too, running all the possibilities and dangers of this potential deal through his mind. Would he consider it?

"I'm about to change your fuckin' lives here, nigga!" Ricky boasted. "This type of pipeline don't come around too often. I set it up 'cause I know you two could pump out enough weight to get the rate down, keep them interested, and guarantee a commitment of a grandfather deal due to our past history. You know there still's a bit of loyalty in this game."

"So how this going to go down, Ricky?" Slugs asked. "We doing individual deals here and going our different ways? Or one big monthly shipment and we both draw from that?"

"One step at a time," Ricky explained. "We build slow. Get it out on the streets first, and then you start supplying more and more bulk because the pipeline will be there flowing once a month, guaranteed. Those Vamp Hill bitches need to get cut off or shut down by the Feds, BPD, or the Ten Point Coalition—who the fuck ever. Then you two start distribution to some of these other allies."

Ricky leaned back, watching the scale of this potential deal unfold on the faces of the three young men.

"This the last time we meet like this," he said. "I won't be involved; I'm a changed man that don't participate in such activities. You'll deal with the supplier's men. Two Dominicans will meet you sometime next week at a location they will send to me. They'll be driving Pontiac Grand Ams. Pull the bricks right out of the hollow bumpers, and everyone disappears. Twenty bricks apiece to start."

Ricky let it sit, confident they would take the deal. "You down with this, Rodney?" he asked. "Or should I bring in another hustler to push this through?"

"Let's control the flow, yo," Rodney said.

Ricky looked around the table. Slugs nodded, silent. Nate could tell he was already doing the math in his head, calculating the risk versus the long-term wealth of such a big score. He could scarcely believe the sheer immensity of this deal, what it could mean, and how it had the potential to disrupt the whole fucking established order on the street. Vamp Hill might get cut out of the action entirely. Shit was about to get real.

Looks like the Norfolk Kings are back in business, thought Nate.

Chapter 40

FAMILY BREAKFAST

IT WAS A TYPICAL MORNING FOR PAT—EXCEPT FOR THE extended hangover that had lasted a few days from the cognac-infused reunion with Nate. He hadn't had that much to drink in one evening since the night he flipped the car in Ireland. Pat was thankful their evening, by contrast, had ended in peace and friendship and zero destruction. Meeting outside Hell House as they did, both packing . . . it could have gone in a very different direction.

He sat down at the breakfast table with Nana while she sipped on her black coffee and read the *Boston Herald*. Except for Nana rustling the paper, there was a dense silence. The tensions had remained high in the house since the shooting a few nights ago. It was an unfathomable event, and Nana had taken it particularly hard—seeing it as an unforgivable offense both to Father Lydon and to the church itself. To her, it was yet another sign of how the new generation was destroying everything.

Pat's ma entered from the kitchen, placing a bagel with cream cheese and an orange juice in front of him while picking up the almost empty glass of water that Pat had guzzled before he'd even sat down.

Nana cursed under her breath, shaking her head at something she saw in the paper. "That little bastard," she said, putting in her two cents. "Those drugs will possess you from the inside out. They possess you! Poor Father. Bless him."

Nana plunked down the paper in front of Pat, pointing to two photos on the front page. One was of Father Lydon speaking out in front of the

St. Brigid Church. The other was a picture of Hell House, looking like something straight out of a horror movie.

"Well, at least Father's okay and back at the rectory," his ma said. "So, they caught that junkie Kevin Hanley in a drug den. I guess it was over in the South End by Mass Ave and Columbus. We just saw him—remember, Pat? I could just tell he was circling the drain. Some residents call that drug den they found him in Hell House."

Pat remained silent, chewing on his bagel and listening. *If only they knew*, he thought.

"Yes," Nana said, getting riled up. "And the story gets better too! There've been over five hundred complaints filed about this place. And nothing done about it. Oh, it doesn't end there, Paddy, oh no. We know the owner of that property; he contributed to the new mayor's campaign, and that Black senator woman, her campaign too, remember?"

Patrick nodded, affirming he was listening. He was used to these conversations. There was so much daily corruption, and it always seemed to be a topic of discussion. From his experience, so much of it was just a lot of neighborhood gossip that managed to morph into a tale. Maybe some of these things had a kernel of truth, but by the time they got retold, they were probably blown way out of proportion. You could probably paper the Tobin Bridge with all the bullshit local tall tales about the Irish mob. The trouble was, these days, those tales didn't seem so tall anymore.

But this felt like something else. Some of these comments made Pat sick. Something was different about this story.

Wait, he thought. *They're not saying this guy paid money into Mayor Menino's campaign, are they? And what the hell is Nana talking about?*

"Who are you talking about?" he asked. "Who owns that place?"

Nana pointed to the page. "See here, Patrick?" she said, pointing to a paragraph deep within the article. "It's the Ginzo from East Boston that owns the scrapyard on Melnea Cass Boulevard. See here. Here, he blames the BPD because they have not been able to handle this drug and homelessness issue."

Pat slammed his hand down on the table, rattling the plates and glasses. Nana and his ma were quiet as he stared at the quoted line in the paper, new pieces of the puzzle falling into place. He could already tell that, one way or another, he was going to be on a collision course with "that Ginzo"—who just happened to be that scumbag Sean's uncle! It was just a matter of when.

Chapter 41

INTEL

EARLY IN THE EVENING THE FOLLOWING DAY, NATE ARRIVED for his check-in with the Ten Point Coalition. As usual, he took a circuitous route, making sure that no one had followed him. Still, his paranoia that he was being watched was getting worse. With a massive deal in play, complicated alliances of players, and getting closer and closer to the action, Nate couldn't help but think someone might catch him in the wrong place at the wrong time.

He stood inconspicuously in the park adjacent to the Ella Baker Community House, about a hundred yards away. He liked getting here early to check out who else was coming in and to case the surrounding area. With stakes this big, you could never be too cautious.

As he watched the back door from afar, he saw a group of young men in their late teens and early twenties exit the building. He squinted, struggling to place them at first. Then he was sure of it.

Those are Vamp Hill gang members, Nate thought. *What the fuck is going on?*

He couldn't believe it. Papa and Gibbs had told him that they were planning to negotiate with gang leadership to broker a cease-fire directly. The plan seemed insane. Nate was surprised they were following through. What leverage would the Coalition have against Vamp Hill— or any other gang for that matter? Maybe Slugs popping off a full clip near downtown crossing was just enough to rattle Vamp Hill and ramp up the pressure from the Coalition!

Nate also felt the shock of danger that he had barely avoided. He could have walked into the basement there and right into the hands of

Vamp Hill. Then it wouldn't have been long before everyone knew he was working with the Coalition.

He wasn't particularly looking forward to this meeting. Reverend Gibbs had called him earlier this afternoon and said it was time to meet the FBI contact for an update. He'd agreed to meet, but the idea of making contact with the FBI directly seemed foolhardy. He liked it better when Gibbs and Papa Ray acted as go-betweens and he could stay in the shadows, under a cloak of anonymity. As for this cease-fire, he didn't trust it one bit. Vamp Hill was pushing serious drugs around Dorchester and Roxbury. Where there were drugs, there'd be violence. He didn't see how an informal agreement would put a stop to anything. They must have known it was Slugs and Norfolk that blasted off.

Dusk was beginning to set in, and as the light changed, Nate calculated. Who knew? Maybe this could be the opportunity that could have a significant ripple effect and play out in a way that could benefit the Norfolk Kings, the community, his agreement with the FBI, the Coalition—maybe even Patrick. But everything had to play out just right.

Waiting until the Vamp Hill gang members were entirely out of sight, he made his way to the back stairs of the Community House. As he walked down the stairwell, he listened carefully for anyone else besides Papa Ray and Gibbs. All he could hear was the sound of his own footsteps.

He entered the basement to see Gibbs and Papa sitting at one of the long tables, waiting for him. Next to them was a white guy in plain clothes—someone who fit the perfect description of a guy who worked in high levels of law enforcement. He had a high and tight hairstyle and a mustache, with a certain stiffness and seriousness about him. Before Nate had even said hello, he could tell this guy meant business.

"Nate, this is Agent Cooper," announced Reverend Gibbs. "He has a few questions."

Nate shook hands with everyone, starting with Cooper. Cooper had a firm grip, like someone used to getting things he needed by sheer force of will. After exchanging sufficient pleasantries, they all sat at the table.

"Nate, your information has really been paying off," Gibbs began. "We had a positive meeting with the Vamp Hill leaders and have a cease-fire agreement—temporarily, at least."

"That's good news," Nate replied.

"Can you confirm the Norfolk Kings are not going to strike back at them?" Gibbs asked.

"I don't know exactly what the Kings are gonna do," Nate started. "But I don't think there's a plan to go after Vamp Hill unless we find out they definitely have something to do with Tre's death." *Interesting the drive-by was not brought up*, Nate thought.

Cooper and Gibbs exchanged a look with Papa Ray. Maybe he shouldn't have used the word *we*?

"Right now, the Kings are just zeroed in on getting product and making some money," explained Nate. "But Vamp Hill is controlling the market on the street."

Nate wasn't exactly sure where he was going next. Would he try to blow up the Kings' lifeline that Ricky had just orchestrated? Or should he provide impartial or disinformation on the potential deal to string them along?

"So, what's the word on how Vamp Hill is controlling the market, Nate?" Cooper asked, his hands folded on the table in front of him. "That's the key street knowledge I need. Even though they may agree to a cease-fire, they'll never give up the cash flow. Even without the violence, that drug supply's a major problem for this city."

Nate was relieved the topic had shifted back to Vamp Hill. That's where he was confident he could offer more carefully selected information. Cooper, for his part, sat poker-faced, hoping to pick up anything he could use.

"We've been watching their operation," Nate offered. "Seems like they have a few stash houses spread throughout the city. The crews just work in and out in an alliance with a few other gangs."

Cooper nodded, taking a few notes. *Good*, Nate thought, continuing to lead Cooper where he wanted him to go. "The junkies know where the product is and where to go," he explained. "Like that house on Mass Ave and Columbus. Hell House. Can't understand how this place hasn't been shut down."

Cooper frowned at the mention of Hell House, indicating this was probably not the first time they had heard about it. "Interesting," he said.

"We know about that house but didn't know Vamp Hill controlled it. We're trying to figure out why the BPD hasn't wiped it out. We understand there's some issue about ownership, so the city has its hands tied."

There was more to Hell House than these guys were revealing. But for now, Nate knew he had succeeded with some new information that was sufficient to help them break down Vamp Hill, which was in everybody's best interests. It was a strange united front, marked by players that would ordinarily be at each other's throats. Maybe that was why the Coalition was getting so much traction. They were willing to make alliances and concessions no one else dared to. They had skin in the game—both Papa and Gibbs fiercely loved their neighborhoods.

"Are you okay, Nate?" Papa Ray asked. Up until now, he'd remained silent, observing the proceedings. "You feel safe out there? And not in any danger? We can extract you safely at any time. Just say when!"

Safe. That was a funny word. It felt like the only way to stay safe was not to be involved. But that ship had long since sailed. He was in deep now, and he wasn't going to be deterred by fear about personal harm. Nate thought about Slugs, the Norfolk Kings, and the strange mix of underworld allies and government-sanctioned players he had engaged with in the last few months. He also thought about the gun he kept concealed—reassurance that he wouldn't be helpless if things got out of control. Nate knew he was effecting change and had some degree of power. He'd trade that for safety any day of the week.

"I'm fine," Nate replied, standing up. "I need to finish what I started."

Reverend Gibbs rose and put his hand on Nate's shoulder. "God bless you, son," he said. "You are in my prayers."

Agent Cooper stood up and shook Nate's hand. "We're close to finding the main source," he said. "We just need a little more time, and then we can phase you out."

It was an odd thing to think that Cooper, a supposed ally to the common people, felt less trustworthy than the ex-con and the Castlegate gang member Nate had just helped broker a deal with. It was hard to tell exactly who was more dangerous. Nate shook his head in doubt on the way out, walking softly up the staircase into the dark night.

Chapter 42

BEATDOWN

IT WAS TWO IN THE MORNING ON SATURDAY NIGHT IN Dorchester. The flashing neon lights of Club Cortees reflected on the shallow ice of the street and parked car windows of the club goers. Partiers who had been drinking all night had started to filter out into the frosty cold air, steam coming off their sweaty bodies from grooving to hip-hop for hours.

Nate watched the unfolding scene from the passenger seat of Slugs's parked Explorer about half a block away, only mildly interested in the goings-on. Something far more pressing was on his mind. The throngs of drunken revelers would provide excellent cover; no one would notice anything out of the ordinary among the shouts, loud laughter, and dozens of cars pulling away as everyone looked for the next place to keep the party going or hook up.

Right on cue, Rodney and his sidekick pulled up beside Slugs's SUV. Rodney rolled down his window. "Now's a good time to get the fuck outta here," he said. "Lead the way."

Slugs nodded, started the engine, and pulled away from the curb. They snaked their way out of the neighborhood, turning on Bowdoin Street, then up Quincy, and eventually onto Columbia. The road had light traffic, with only a few cars behind them. Nate wondered how much Daly and the gang unit had pursued his connection with Rodney. Nate had no way of knowing if any unmarked cars had already been following them for several blocks.

In fact, a couple of cars behind was an unmarked cruiser, with two

Black police officers in plain clothes taking care not to follow the caravan too closely. The officer in the passenger seat grabbed his radio.

"Sergeant Daly, this is Miller. We have two vehicles cruising north up Columbia. The second vehicle has the target in the passenger seat."

Across neighborhood lines, in one of the precincts, Sergeant Daly sat at a table, responding to Officer Miller's voice on the radio channel. Around him were a few teams fully geared up and ready to move.

"No problem," Daly responded. "Just stay back, observation only. Let's see what Rodney has up his sleeve."

The caravan rolled on. Slugs rolled through Columbia Square, turned onto Massachusetts Avenue, and then made a right into the Newmarket Square area. Nate knew this neighborhood well. It was not the kind of place anyone would want to be during the small hours of the morning and had been a dead zone of run-down industrial buildings for as long as anyone could remember. It was a no-man's land.

Nate smirked at the memory of having just met Pat at Pug's Pub, which happened to be only a few blocks away, one of the only dimly lit beacons that would lead people to be anywhere near this area this late at night. Where they were going was off the beaten path, you could say.

The Explorer made its way slowly through the street, its headlights casting eerie shadows through an industrial graveyard. They could see a maze of chain-link-fenced parking lots and scrapyards, locked loading docks, and ancient brick walls slathered with graffiti. Most all the fencing had razor wire coiled up top, giving it the air of an outdoor prison baring its teeth.

Nate squinted at the hard-to-see numbers of the buildings as they slowly rolled past, looking for the address of the building that Ricky had provided. Rodney followed close behind. Slugs, in an uncharacteristic move, had the radio off. Both of them wanted to listen for anything out of the ordinary.

"There it is, man," Nate said, pointing to a car parked in the shadows. They pulled into a fenced parking area on the side of a run-down building on the corner of Shirley and George Streets. As soon as the cars were parked beside each other, they killed the headlights. They were now out of the direct line of sight from the street and entirely hidden by the surrounding buildings.

Both Rodney and Slugs rolled down their windows. They nodded to each other in silence.

Slugs and Nate started locking and loading their pistols, tension thick in the air. Nate struggled to keep his hands steady. It was impossible to predict what would happen next. Ricky had orchestrated this whole deal. Could he be trusted? His relationship with Rodney was new at best. As for Slugs and Rodney . . . the Kings and Castlegate alliance was still in brand-new territory.

Nate's stomach turned. His palms sweated, sliding around the grip of the revolver that was once Tre's. Tre had died alone, murdered under mysterious circumstances, and Nate had never imagined that he would slide out of the straight life and into Tre's world.

Two beige Pontiac Grand Ams pulled into the fenced area and immediately turned out their lights.

Here we go, thought Nate.

Everyone stepped out slowly, including two of the Dominicans. They nodded to Slugs and Rodney to head back to their trunks. The Dominicans reached under the car, pulled out wrapped bricks from the hollow bumpers, and stuffed them into a small duffel bag.

So far, so good, thought Nate. *Everything seems to be under control.*

Slugs walked a bag stuffed with money and dropped it between the cars. Nate walked side-by-side with Rodney to the duffel bag filled with bricks. Rodney grabbed it, and they both returned to their vehicles.

The two Dominicans picked up the bag of money but, just as they opened the bag to count, an unmarked cruiser screeched into the caged area. Two plain-clothed Black cops opened their doors with their guns drawn.

"Freeze!" one of the officers shouted.

With no hesitation, Rodney fired a few shots out his window. The driver dodged for cover and leaped back into the unmarked police car. Not waiting for return fire, Rodney gunned the engine, ramming the gear shift into reverse, and smashed through the fence, peeling away onto the side street, dragging some of the chain links behind. Slugs had already started his car, but it was blocked in, so he aimed his gun toward the cops.

Shots rained down from all directions. Slugs and the Dominicans exchanged fire with the cops, giving Nate an opening to make a run for it. Just as Nate reached for the car door handle, the front windshield shattered, showering glass into his hair. Nate ducked instinctively and burst out of the car, taking off on foot.

Nate launched out nearly as fast as the bullets with a burst of adrenaline, as if he were spring-loaded. Not far in front of him was one of the Dominicans, who also must have escaped his car from the passenger seat only moments earlier. Behind them was an officer on foot, sprinting after them.

The last thing Nate heard as he fled the scene was the driver of the unmarked police vehicle shouting, "Shots fired! Shots fired!" into his radio. They were fucked now. Whatever restraint the cops may have had had gone out the window as soon as the bullets started flying.

Nate felt for his pistol while running, but it was gone. He must have dropped it in his mad escape.

A host of nearby police sirens rang through the air.

Nate quickly glanced back into the parking lot. One of the Dominicans rammed his car into the unmarked cruiser, the collision smashing the driving officer's head into the dash, knocking him out.

Slug's engine raced loudly as the Ford Explorer screeched out through the opening that Rodney had created only moments earlier. The two Grand Ams followed out right after through the fallen fence, and all three cars scattered in different directions.

Nate passed the Dominican, who was now four or five paces behind him. They both headed toward a tall chain-link fence at the back of a derelict building. If he could make it over, he had a better chance of losing the pursuing officer. But he could hear the sounds of many sirens getting closer. It sounded like at least four or five.

With the fence within just a few feet, he leaped, landing about halfway up. He clambered up the fence, scrambling to reach the top. He was fortunate; this one had no razor wire on it. Nate scaled to the top, swung one leg over, then the other, then jumped back down to the other side.

With a wince, he landed harder than he expected, feeling like he may have sprained his ankle on the concrete. He bent down to his ankle, instinctively checking if anything was broken. He looked up to see the Dominican within jumping distance on the other side of the fence.

I made it, thought Nate. A momentary sense of relief passed over him.

Four marked police cars screeched to a halt just behind the Black plainclothes officer. Several cruiser doors flew open at once as more officers jumped out. The plainclothes cop dashed toward the fence, about six officers in uniform right behind him. Nate could see the Dominican leap onto the fence, frantically trying to claw his way to the top. But the plainclothes officer was right behind him, grabbing his foot and yanking him back to the ground.

Then, the unbelievable happened.

The uniformed officers behind them seized both the plainclothes cop and the Dominican. One officer pulled his baton and the other his flashlight, and they both took turns beating both men in the skull. Nate could hear their sharp cries. The plainclothes cop couldn't get a word out before they smashed their blunt weapons into his head, knocking him out.

They're beating their own fucking guy, Nate thought. *The cops are beating a fucking cop!* He could hear sickening thuds as the two beaten men went quiet.

Run, you fucking idiot, he urged himself. He'd been watching, frozen in disbelief, with only a chain-link fence between him and all the cops. He wasn't even sure if anyone had seen him yet, besides the plainclothes officer, but he wasn't going to stick around to find out.

He turned around and sprinted down the short alley toward a street on the other side, but his passage was suddenly blocked by two more police cruisers. An officer from each car jumped out, their guns drawn. Nate threw his hands up.

"I don't have a gun!" he shouted.

It didn't matter. They tackled him from the front, forcing him face-down into the concrete. He felt a few kicks to the gut and a kick to the back of his head from heavy police boots. Then the batons came out.

He'd never been hit like this. They took turns beating him hard, and he took nasty blows to his side and head. The pain rippled through his whole body, which barely had time to register each impact before the next one came. He cried out, pleading for them to stop. After about a five-second respite, one officer viciously hit him one more time. Nate whimpered, bludgeoned and bleeding, unsure if they had broken anything or if anyone would ever see him alive again. It was hard to breathe. Everything hurt. Was this the end of the beating or just the beginning?

Police officers, both Black and White, handcuffed him and brought him to his feet, where he could see the Dominican handcuffed on the ground on the other side of the fence, apparently out cold. The Black plainclothes officer lay facedown in a puddle of his own blood. But the arresting officer pulled him up off the ground.

Nate's whole body throbbed. It was hard to think, and he could barely hold his head up. He said nothing; he only watched and listened. The searching officer stopped when he felt something unexpected. He pulled a badge out of the officer's jacket. "Hey!" he said, lifting the badge into the air, showing the cops who it was they'd beaten.

Nate could register the shock on their four faces, the ones who had participated in the beating, as if they had just gone off a cliff. Nate could only hear the moaning of the officer and police sirens and the crackling police radio in the gap of their silence.

The Black plainclothes officer balanced himself slowly, blood still pouring from his head. He stumbled forward, placing his hands on the hood of the police car to catch himself. Then he fell back to the ground, leaving bloody handprints on the car. The other officers tried to bring him to his feet, but he hung, limp and broken. More marked cruisers pulled up adjacent to George Street, their sirens blaring. It sounded like even more were coming, and perhaps an ambulance as well. Every flashing light, every wailing siren seemed to make all Nate's bruises throb with pain. The officers holding him kept him on his feet, not sure what to do with him next.

The new officers on the scene surrounded the bloody area. One of them—Daly, according to the tag on his uniform—emerged from one of the newly arrived cruisers and froze for a moment, registering the scene. Daly silently walked to the unconscious officer and bent down to look at him, studying his face and injuries. The name suddenly clicked for Nate. This was the cop Pat had talked about—one of the nice guys, at least according to Pat. Daly then stood up and looked around, scanning the small crowd of officers.

"This is Miller of the Gang Unit," the cop named Daly said. "Can anyone tell me why the fuck he's laying bloody on the ground?"

It was about ten seconds of solid silence before anyone said anything.

"He was climbing over the fence to pursue the suspect," said one of the cops.

The ambulance finally arrived, and an EMT leaped out and tended to Miller's wounds. "You fucked this up. This man is barely hanging on to his life as a result," Daly shouted, his veins bulging from his forehead, "and you've destroyed the name of the BPD!"

His shouts were met with silence.

Another ambulance and more EMTs arrived. The police officers holding Nate up finally transferred him to an ambulance. As they were loading him in, Nate saw a newly arrived officer on the scene and swore he recognized him.

Holy shit, Nate thought. *Pat's friend. Walsh.*

They locked eyes just before the doors closed on the ambulance.

Chapter 43

DOCKLAND BOMBING

PAT RELISHED THE GIGANTIC SPREAD THAT LAY BEFORE HIM. He always craved breakfast food when he was hungry, no matter what time of day. It didn't matter whether it was blueberry pancakes or drippy eggs with toast and sausage. He was at Mul's Diner on Broadway, which had never stopped being one of the most popular breakfast places in the city. It had been here for so long, Pat thought, that the odds were good the place would eventually outlive him too. Mul's ambiance was great, the kind of place you could see all walks of life. The waitresses were nice too.

Pat had a sip of his coffee as he glanced at the TV up in the corner. The only thing getting in the way of his breakfast high was the usual dismal flashes on the morning news show.

Walsh entered through the front door of the diner and spotted Pat right away. Walsh was wearing civilian clothes and a strained expression that Pat could see from a mile away. He sat down opposite Pat in the booth and nodded to the waitress for coffee.

"So what the fuck happened?" Pat asked, pointing to the news-flash headline. It read "BPD Probe into Black Undercover Cop Allegedly Assaulted by Their Own."

Walsh shook his head. "I showed up on the scene toward the end," he explained. "He was beat up bad, man. This is a fuckin' mess!"

The blonde waitress came by with a coffee for Walsh. He smiled and paused to take the cup. As soon as she was a few steps away, Walsh leaned in and spoke in a quiet voice. "It was a heroin deal going down," he started. "Then shots fired, and two cars on a chase. Then, a few suspects on a foot chase end up surrounded by a chain-link fence where this went down. The media has it all fucked up. He was not an undercover cop. He was in plain clothes in the Gang Unit under Sergeant Daly!"

Walsh paused. "Patrick, you ready for this?" he asked. "There was another Black guy. I saw him as the EMTs were taking him away. It was fuckin' Nate."

"What?" Patrick said.

"Nate was in this deal somehow and got his ass beat down too! I couldn't believe it. Other than being a fresh prick, that dude was always straight and narrow. I thought he was long gone, playing ball down at University of Virginia and shit? Looks like he finally got caught up with his gangbangin' cousins after all."

Pat's mind raced. He thought of the last time he'd seen Nate at Pug's Pub and all that Nate seemed to be holding back. "You do what you gotta do, Patrick," Nate had said. "I'm on a fuckin' mission, and I'll fill you in when it develops. I promise."

He silently sipped his coffee, processing. Pat knew Nate was up to something, but he'd let it go—the drive-by of Hell House with Slugs, the edgy "nothing to lose" attitude, a pistol, the bullshit about good intentions.

It was hard not to be slightly numb to the news. Pat's forehead had barely healed from his own beating at the hands of the police. The odds were good that Nate would meet a similar fate. And judging how unjust his own beating had been, wasn't it likely that Nate hadn't deserved his either? Nothing surprised him these days. He just knew one thing: Nate was up to something that hadn't made its way to the headlines. Yet.

"They're going to make a race thing out of it, for sure," Walsh continued. "They already started. I didn't see what went down, but when I got there, there was a handful of cops, both Black and White."

Patrick shook his head, making a few silent decisions at once. "Hey, listen," he started carefully. "I wanted to give you the heads-up. I gotta call in a favor in the next few nights."

"Okay," Walsh responded guardedly.

"I'm going to head back over to that Hell House or somewhere else near there and check something out. I may need an extra set of eyes and ears."

Walsh sighed and shook his head. "We got that covered, Patrick. It'll be handled."

"Yeah, yeah. Okay, gimme a break, will ya?" Pat said. "That guy, the guy who owns Hell House, greases the right palms. You know who it is, right? Mr. Future Detective? Fuckin' Sean's uncle, the East Boston guy. He owns the scrapyard D&D Metals. You can't tell me Sean isn't connected to this in some way, somehow, and God help him if I find out he's flooding heroin into this place!"

"Have you lost your fucking mind?" Walsh exclaimed. "Do you even hear yourself? You wanna spend your life in the can?" He slammed a dollar bill on the table and got up. His reaction was no surprise. Since the night Sean confessed he'd set up the deal that left PJ dead in the gutter, Sean had been a sore subject with Walsh. And Walsh's disfigured face was a permanent reminder of his drunken fight with Sean. Walsh was in no mood to listen to anything further. "I gotta get the fuck outta here. Now you're fuckin' scaring me," he snapped. "Don't do anything stupid, Patrick. Just don't! Stay out of it. Live your fucking life!"

Walsh turned to leave, heading toward the door, when he stopped in his tracks. A familiar face had just walked into the diner. Walsh glanced back at Pat, his expression full of worry. Patrick responded to the new face with a gigantic grin.

Maybe vengeance will be mine, Pat thought.

It was Treats, all smiles, strolling in like he owned the place, as usual. He appeared gleeful to see the two friends he hadn't seen in eight months—since the trip to Ireland and his boat incident. "What up, fellas?" he said, laughing. "Walsh, where you going so fast? Afraid to be seen with me, pal? I'm a model citizen now! Kiddo's about six months old. Life is all good!"

Walsh looked both happy and worried to see Treats at the same time. He stood silent.

"Oh, I get it. You only hang around with your cop friends now, huh?" He laughed and took off his coat. "The fuckin' shit we got on him, Patrick, hahaha!" Treats joked. "I'll catch you down at BAC for a workout later!"

The BAC was the Boston Athletic Center down in the Seaport District, a former industrial area that was now a hot spot for health and wellness. It was a high-profile spot, a place you could cross paths with a lot of Boston cops, college and professional athletes, or just local construction fitness freaks. The funny part was that Treats had never worked out a day in his life and would never walk through those doors. Patrick laughed at his old friend's brazenness, which didn't seem to be dampened by fatherhood at all. Walsh waved before walking away, discomfort written all over his face.

Pat stood up to embrace his old partner in crime. Trouble never had a friendlier face, and it was great to see him. After the hug, Treats made himself at home on the bench opposite Pat.

"You look great, man!" Patrick exclaimed honestly. "Helluva lot betta than the last time I saw you!"

Treats cackled as if his near-death experience was hilarious. "Everything is great," he gushed. "One day at a time. Lots of responsibilities with the baby, the girl, the union job, and still making money moving the pounds around. But I manage to get out once or twice a week too."

Pat smiled. To think Treats was worried about fatherhood ruining his life. It only seemed to make him more confident—if such a thing were possible.

"So, what's the plan?" Treats asked, signaling the waitress at the same time. "What you need me to do? I'm sure you didn't call me here to watch you eat like a pig."

Pat pushed aside his plates, now almost empty. "All right, listen. I'll get right down to it. I know you used to get your shit off Sean from time to time. Not sure if you have lately, but—"

"Yeah, he hits me up from time to time. Him or one of his runners. I've connected him with weed a few times, and I've definitely scored a few eight balls from him once or twice. But that dude is shady! He steps on his shit too much, and I only want the rocket fuel!"

"All right," Pat began. "Let him know you're trying to pick up an ounce of blow, and you heard his shit has been pretty good lately."

"You wanna tell me what the fuck you're up to?" Treats demanded. "Or are you gonna leave me hanging here?"

"Of course, man," Pat conceded. "I'm just trying to figure out if he's pumping heroin around here."

"Oh, I'm sure he's pumpin' those new oxys. That's for sure," Treats said.

"If they're available, there's money to be made, and if someone scores a script from a doctor, that's like gold right now. That shit ain't for me, though."

The waitress arrived with a fresh cup of coffee for Treats. He received it with a wink and took a sip. "Listen, Sean and I ain't that tight, and I'm sure he might have heard we all went to Ireland together. So . . . we'll see how he responds."

"No harm in trying, right?" Pat asked. "The mothafucka is up to something. He and his uncle Gino, the crazy scrap-metal guy. You remember him?"

Treats leaned back, nodding and smiling, remembering some of the side hustles he and Pat used to pull in the summer months while they were all still in high school.

"Remember we all went over to the scrapyard that day with the copper wire to cash it in?" Pat reminisced. "And his goddamn scales were rigged. He didn't know we already weighed it at A Street Metal before Sean's bright idea to bring it over there. But who the fuck was gonna argue with his batshit-crazy uncle Gino the Ginzo when he has two rottweilers and two shotguns, one on each side of his office desk?"

Treats shook his head, laughing.

"I remember that shady fuck," Treats replied, studying Pat's face. "But you all right here, Patrick. Right?" he asked. "You seeing clearly on this, man?"

"Clear as fuckin' day, Treats," Pat replied.

Treats shook his head. "I've seen that look a few times before, right before you've lost your temper. The last time I saw it, you were fighting the Tip Terror out in the Irish countryside."

Pat stayed silent. He was waiting for a solid answer.

"Okay, I heard enough," conceded Treats, changing gears. "I'll see what I can find out about what he's selling and where he's got it."

"I appreciate it," Pat said.

They stood up, both putting on their coats. Pat left a twenty on the table, and they walked toward the exit.

"Hey, you know I was thinking about that trip to Ireland," Treats said. "That was so fucking crazy, man! We ought to write that shit down! We're lucky we made it back alive."

Pat and Treats shared a laugh as they exited into the cold winter air. Pat wasn't sure if it was luck or fate. It was funny that Treats had brought up Ireland. Jimmy had just asked Pat earlier to visit Choppa, the man responsible for orchestrating the drop during his trip. Pat didn't know what this was all about, but if Jimmy asked him, then he'd do it.

Treats stopped to smoke a butt. While waiting for him to finish, Pat took a glance at the front page of the *Boston Globe* in the newspaper dispenser out front. A giant headline read "Blast Rocks London District." Intrigued, he plunked a quarter into the machine and took a paper.

"What's the matter?" Treats asked, blowing out a cloud of smoke. "You look sick or somethin'."

"A fuckin' truck bomb exploded in London," Pat said, still skimming the rest of the article. "It was the IRA."

Treats whistled slowly. "Damn," he said. "I guess that's it for the cease-fire? That didn't last long. Some of my family are celebrating now!"

"Only seventeen months," Pat said. "Hold on. I gotta make a call."

Treats nodded casually as Pat rushed back into the diner and headed

The London Docklands bombing (also known as the South Quay bombing or erroneously referred to as the Canary Wharf bombing) occurred on February 9, 1996, when the IRA detonated a powerful truck bomb

straight for the payphone. He dialed Jimmy, impatiently tapping the phone as it rang.

"Did you see the front page of the *Globe*?" Pat asked as soon as Jimmy'd picked up.

There was a long pause. Pat could hear Jimmy taking a deep breath. "I guess it's mission accomplished, Patrick," he finally said.

Pat fell silent as missing pieces from his Ireland trip fell into place. The drop had been a hefty donation to the IRA. It explained why it was dropped at the boxing club in that part of Dublin and the comment from Coley as he left the gym. Jimmy had known all along. It explained why Jimmy had freaked out when their partying antics abroad were threatening the mission. Pat's stomach turned at the thought of being unwittingly involved in an international incident. "Tell me everything," he demanded.

"Maybe you better talk to Choppa first," Jimmy said. "This is his world. He has more answers than I do. Did you see him yet?"

"I'm on my way," Pat said, quietly hanging up the phone.

Chapter 44

BACK TO PRISON

SUFFOLK COUNTY JAIL WAS JUST AS DEPRESSING AS PAT HAD remembered it. It was a dismal place, gray and expressionless, the epitome of government institutions of its kind. Once through security, Pat could feel the heaviness of the collective mood inside. He didn't want to be here. From this angle, he could also see why a few of his friends had never bothered to visit.

He was waiting in the visiting room for them to bring Choppa out on the other side of the bulletproof glass. The whole place was overlit. The fluorescent lights were aggressive, emitting a low hum, blasting unnatural light everywhere and giving everything a strange pallor. The place stank of bleach and stale air. He was already getting a headache.

Finally, a loud metal door swung open, and out came old man Choppa, his hands cuffed behind him. A guard followed closely behind to ensure he sat down in the metal chair. Once seated, Choppa flashed his toothy smile and visibly relaxed. By the looks of it, he was happy to see Pat. Then again, thought Pat, anybody stuck in this godforsaken place would have been happy to see any visitor. Anything to break up the monotony of the prison schedule was fucking welcome.

The guard uncuffed Choppa and exited through the heavy metal door. Pat picked up the phone's handset, and Choppa did the same on his side.

"How you doin', Prospect?" asked Choppa. It was Pat's nickname in prison. It had a double meaning. In the beginning, they called him that because he was a fresh-faced kid with everything going for him. He'd been a star athlete, had maintained pretty good grades, was destined for college. But in prison, the nickname was ironic cruelty. The other meaning was from what Choppa had done to him. By forcing him into the fighting arena, he became a fighting prospect. Someone to bet on. A sure thing in a prison yard bare-knuckle scrap.

Pat answered simply, "Happy to be out, Choppa. This place sucks."

Choppa chuckled, "Yeah, it's no picnic. But it's home. How you adjusting to the outside?"

"It's weird, man. My old neighborhood just isn't the same." He didn't feel like going into too much detail. All he could think about was Sean saturating the place with heroin. Pat was struggling with how to bring it up without outright accusing Choppa.

"Yeah, I told you it would be tough, kid," answered Choppa. "Most people end up returning. But not you, right?"

Pat shook his head. "Never, man. Never gonna happen ever." He was struggling with how he would bring up the subject. Finally, he pulled the rolled-up *Boston Globe* he'd snagged from Mul's out of his back pocket and slapped the front page up against the glass.

Choppa nodded knowingly, loaded with thoughts. Then, after a short pause, he offered, "We knew you were the right man for the job, Pat. You delivered in spades."

Pat eyed the phone connection into the wall nervously. He was afraid to be candid. The way he understood it, most of the prisoner conversations with the outside were recorded.

"Don't worry about that, Pat," Choppa said, noticing the discomfort on Pat's face. "All my recordings are still completely off record and disappear with a well-placed bribe."

"So it's true?" Pat demanded. "I had no idea what I was doing. You played me. I had no idea that money would be used for a confrontational moment between—"

"Easy, Prospect," Choppa dismissed. "You didn't push any buttons. You didn't do any scheming. You just made the drop. You're no more guilty than any banker that pushes money around. It's not on your hands what's done with it."

"But—"

"You gotta see the bigger picture, kid," Choppa explained patiently. "It was a solution created for a few of my allies. Everyone won here, including you. Like lots of other Irish Americans, and based on my core beliefs, I coordinated a donation to the IRA on Whitey's behalf. In return, they helped get him out of London. That's it; it's as simple as that."

"Simple as that!" Pat exclaimed. "I was the fuckin' mule, Choppa, completely unaware that I was involved in what the entire world, other than us Irish, will coin as a terrorist bombing blowing up high-rise buildings and killing innocent people—which could certainly end up with me being in prison for the rest of my fucking life!"

"Paddy," Choppa answered, shaking his head, "we've had too many long nights discussing the facts around The Cause and the history of the old country. The British reneged on the peace talk agreement, so this was an act of war. The Irish Republican Army sent a string of six public announcement courtesy warnings to clear those docks ninety minutes before the bomb exploded. The fools didn't take it seriously. But only two deaths and minor injuries—casualties of war, as they say."

Pat listened, mulling over the implications of what Choppa was saying.

"Again, your hands are clean here. I know you'll see this clearly once you calm down and think it through, but let's end this part of the conversation now," Choppa said sternly. "Is there anything else you want to discuss, kid?"

Patrick took a deep breath. "Yeah. How the hell did you get ahold of that kind of cash?" Pat asked, not sure if he wanted to know the answer. He was aware that Choppa was running a number of schemes from prison, but this was half a million they were talking about.

"It's Whitey's cash," Choppa replied. "He had stash boxes all over the world, for when this time would come. But Whitey couldn't just stroll into a bank, so I helped him move it out."

"You don't get a piece of it for helping?" Pat said.

Choppa shook his head. "I have other ways of taking care of myself," he said with a shrug.

Pat recalled the conversation he'd had with Walsh out on his front stoop, where he shared the rumor that Sean was dealing heroin and was claiming protection from Choppa.

"Are you workin' with Sean?" Pat demanded. "I heard this crazy rumor, and I'm hoping it isn't true. Is he payin' you for protection now?"

"Listen, of course I get kickbacks from a few wise guys and players out there. I gotta survive. I got a family. So I consult, make connections, offer protection, and sometimes set up a strategy or a power move," Choppa answered simply. "What do you think happened to Tre in here?"

Although Pat had long suspected that Choppa had been the one to take Tre out, the confirmation of this fact didn't make him feel any better. Choppa's not-so-cryptic message about "your vengeance is mine" was precisely what it sounded like.

"Tre had a few hits on him. His days were numbered in here," Choppa explained. "Multiple gang rivals were collaborating on it. We played a small part in it; that's all. And I get ten grand a month for my part in continuing to clear a path for Sean."

"If you're workin' with Sean, you need to know I'm comin' after that mothafucka," exclaimed Pat. "He's poisoning the city. So where does that leave you and me?"

Choppa put his hand up on the glass and moved his face closer to Pat's.

"Everything I do is to protect you. We spent almost five years together in here," Choppa said calmly. "What you didn't need to know, you didn't need to know. I would never stand in your way of handling your beefs. You do what you gotta do."

"So what happens to your ten grand a month after Sean's gone?" Pat asked.

"There's always plenty of cowboys needing my protection," explained Choppa. "Not taking sides, I just play the game. You never know what role you're going to play. You did a stand-up thing, and it'll never be forgotten.

"In the meantime," Choppa continued, "you're gonna need to stay distant for a while. The Feds are all over me now, trying to get me to flip, offering me a get-out-of-jail-free card. So we'll see what they have to prove to me that Whitey was a rat."

Pat nodded to himself, thinking it was right to be cautious. He knew that would probably be the end of conversations with Choppa for the foreseeable future. He could see Choppa had power in prison and had somehow gained from this internal power play. But it was clear Tre's death didn't have much to do with Pat's vengeance at all. For Choppa, it was all about the gains.

But at least he'd gotten the green light to go after Sean. Choppa wouldn't stop him or get in the way. There would always be someone else to fill Choppa's pockets.

"I'll see you around, Choppa," Pat said, putting his hand on the glass.

Choppa nodded and put his hand up to mirror Pat's on the other side.

Chapter 45

BOSTON MEDICAL CENTER

AS SOON AS PAT ENTERED THE MAIN LOBBY OF BOSTON MEDI-cal Center, he felt his muscles tense and his teeth clench. The last time he was here, the two cops that beat the shit out of him had dragged him in to get patched up, and the doctor had refused to let him stay. The memory of that evening brought back an ache in his forehead, exacerbated by the fresh offense of Nate's beating.

The fucking animals, Pat thought, *stomping heads first, asking questions later*. Even if Nate were guilty of dealing, like the papers were speculating, did that mean he should endure physical assault before he even saw trial?

Motherfuckers, thought Pat.

He went up the elevator to the eighth floor and took swift strides down the hallway, scanning for the room Nate explained he would be in on the phone. Finding the right room, Pat walked in quietly to not to wake him if he were sleeping, which he was.

Nate looked in rough shape. His face was still a little swollen from the beating, and he had substantial bruising. Another rush of adrenaline flowed through Pat, a wave of intensifying anger, and he found himself resisting the urge to punch a fresh hole in the wall.

Some of these rogue dirty cops think they own this fucking city.

Pat turned away from Nate to stare out the window. The eighth-floor view overlooked Massachusetts Avenue. To the left was Newmarket Square. He could almost see Newmarket Square Pizza and Cafe in the middle. The Suffolk County Prison was visible on the far left, and down off to the right up Melnea, he could see the D&D Metals sign. Pat took a deep breath, taking it all in. "Man, I love this city," he said, turning back to Nate.

"Yeah," answered Nate, who'd apparently awoken while Pat had his back turned. "As fucked up as it is, I can't deny that I still do too. That's why I set out on this mission."

Nate reached over to his bed table, to a small radio, probably something Slugs had brought in for him. He tuned it to WILD 1090 AM, the Black community local station. He turned up the music to a medium level, loud enough to drown out any soft talking audible from the outside. "Let's make sure this conversation stays between us," Nate said.

"Oh, so now you gonna tell me what happened and how you got caught up in this mess around a deal of bricks of crack cocaine and heroin?"

"Yeah," Nate sighed. "I'll tell you. I was trying to stop the bloodshed—trying to help guys like Papa Ray, Reverend Gibbs, and Ronald Lewis from the street teams, and the Ten Point Coalition. After Jamal and Tre and everything else, I just chose to fight the evil. I'm in the middle of a fuckin' war. It's a fuckin' war, Patrick."

Pat sat down in the guest chair beside the bed, listening to every word.

"I'd do anything to stop innocent people getting caught in crossfire or to shut down the fucking psychopaths at the top, flooding the streets with poison," Nate continued. "And to be honest, because of all that, Reverend Gibbs convinced me to be a source of information—a CI."

This new piece of information hit Pat like a sledgehammer. Suddenly, Nate's behavior was starting to make a lot more sense.

"I was supposed to discover and report information on the gang activities, the beefs, and the supply chain," Nate explained. "It was all run through Operation Eagle Eye, an FBI-controlled effort, separate and unknown from BPD."

"Shit, Nate," Pat exclaimed. "I knew it was something like that, but you certainly had me doubting it. You almost had me there for a minute. I thought you'd gone off the deep end."

Pat's wheels were turning fast. "But something still isn't adding up for me now. How'd you end up at the drug deal that turned into a BPD nightmare, and there was no sign of the FBI? You know what that tells me? The FBI had no knowledge of that deal going down, did they, Nate?"

"No, Patrick, they didn't," Nate confided. "But I wasn't in this for the small-time Black gangbanger-level drug deal. Isn't there always another crew or organization ready to distribute and take over? I was going for a much bigger impact like the Big White Lie, yo! Back in the day, I remember you quoted an Irishman in English class that said, 'The only thing necessary for the triumph of evil is for good men to do nothing.'"

"Yes, I can respect that, my friend," Pat admitted. "Regardless of all the shit you faced in life, you never had a small vision. Lately, I have been thinking along those same lines." Pat paused for a moment, a new thought occurring to him. "So the FBI got you covered and out of it?" he asked.

"Yeah," Nate says. "After talking with the FBI, I get to take this beating nowhere and disappear quietly back into the streets."

"Of fucking course," Pat interjected.

"Hey, at least I'm not in jail. But man—that poor cop! They beat his ass down to a pulp! Thought he was one of us! I hear he's still pissing out blood."

"I've been following it in the papers," Pat confirmed. "Now there's an internal affairs investigation and the racial spin on the whole thing, of course."

"The most fucked-up part about that is that there were Black *and* White cops involved, dishing out beatings on both of us," Nate recalled. "I saw it up close like it was in slow motion. And no one is coming forward. None of his coworkers—no one."

"Does that surprise you?" Pat asked, leaning back on the guest chair, putting his feet up on the window ledge. "The media playing the fiddle and stoking the race fire? And don't get me started on the party politics and career politicians."

Nate nodded in agreement. "The devil's working day and night," he said.

"See, the police didn't make the cultural problems they face; the government did," Pat fumed. "They're our neighbors, our family and friends—handpicked from our streets. That's why the Irish knew they had to get into politics or they'd be treated like dirt until the end of time. They knew, back in the thirties and forties, the system was corrupt and broken. Even back then, they knew. But they had to get in and play the game. You see, that's why my nana always said, 'Politics is a dirty business, but you can make a lot of money in it.' See, we Boston Irish made it to the White House, but when the Kennedys were sniped out, then MLK and Malcolm X, she knew without a doubt, multiple forces of money from corporations control the business called our government!"

Nate suddenly seemed more alert, as if a fire had been lit inside his belly. He sat up straight. Pat thought he looked ready to walk out of the hospital.

"So you getting out of here now or what?" Pat asked. "Because I got an idea. And I was wondering if you had an interest in drawing a new line and uniting on a cause."

Nate considered for a moment, his thoughts interrupted by a familiar song on the radio.

"Hey, just for a moment, remember when we used to listen to Grand-master Flash's 'The Message'—like a thousand times—after school in the parking lot?"

"Yeah and that line that says 'Don't push me,' except I think we're both beyond the edge already." Pat laughed. "You see that place right there?"

Nate stood up, wincing. He walked to the window where Pat was pointing.

"It says 'D&D Metals. We buy scrap.' There it is . . . That's the bigger impact right there, Nate," Pat proclaimed. "That there destroys Vamp Hill and Hell House and disrupts many others from selling crack and heroin throughout this city. That little fucking scrapyard breaks up a pro-tected campaign donor to many politicians around here. And best of all? It gets me my vengeance. And actually, yours too."

Nate stared at Pat. "What the hell you talking about?" he asked.

"There were multiple hits out on Tre, rival gangs in on it. Vamp Hill, probably, but if one gang didn't do it, another would have."

Tre was just another pawn in the whole game. But Tre probably knew what kind of game he was playing and that he could be taken off the board at any time. It was a war they were fighting, and nothing was fair.

"Seems like you've lost your head already!" Nate said. "All right, all right. So what you planning, man? Hopefully not something that'll land you back over there," said Nate, pointing to the left, toward Suffolk

County Prison. "Who is it over at D&D Metals, and how does that tattoo tie the whole web together?" Nate gestured toward Pat's forearm.

"I figured out how all the lines intersect," Pat revealed excitedly. "That right there? That scrapyard is Sean's uncle Gino's place, shady as hell, and he also owns Hell House, which Vamp Hill operates out of, and I know Sean is running a drug crew. The two of them are pumping large quantities of coke and heroin into both our neighborhoods."

"Okay," began Nate. "So, what now?"

"I can't move forward without cleaning up the past and the present. I think it's time we support the BPD boys in blue and behead the beast hiding in the shadows of that run-down area between our neighborhoods." Pat studied Nate's face, looking for signs that Nate would go all in. "You interested?" he asked. "Can I trust you, CI?"

They both laughed. It was an insane plan.

"Well, we are men for others; that's what Father Lydon always said," Nate admitted. "We're supposed to be of service to the world." Nate began to pack a small bag and put on his regular street clothes.

"There's a deal going down over there for a few ounces of coke," Pat said, moving closer to Nate and speaking softly. "My friend Treats is the buyer. He's going to get me some intel on the operation inside, and I'll be a few blocks away down at Pug's Pub."

"Go on," said Nate, buttoning up his shirt.

"I was inside the scrapyard once when I was eighteen, with Sean, trying to cash in some copper he stole from a job site. The uncle has two rottweilers running around and a shotgun on each side of his desk. This piece of shit intimidates and screws everyone that walks through the doors!"

Nate stopped to consider for a moment, with one shoe on and one yet to be tied. "That doesn't sound like an easy target, Patrick," he admitted.

"I'm just getting started," Pat responded with a smile.

A sudden knock on the door interrupted their moment. They turned around to see the big frame of Sergeant Daly leaning up against the doorway.

"Surprised you're here," Sergeant Daly said, eyeing Pat. "Hmm. You two in the middle of something? You see, Nate, I couldn't figure out who you were at first when I saw you with Rodney, but then all the pieces came together, and now this reunion here, well, it reminds me that we go *way back*!"

Pat looked at him blankly, keeping his best poker face firmly on.

"So I just wanted to visit the rogue CI guy who saw it all," Daly explained. "My gang unit officer got beat down, and I need some details."

Nate exchanged a look with Patrick. "Take a look at me," he said. "My eyes were shut as my head bounced off the concrete. I didn't see shit."

Sergeant Daly smirked and walked up closely to both of them.

"Taking a lesson from this guy, Omertà, huh?" Daly prodded. "Is this a coincidence? Just two old friends that just happened to both have major run-ins with the BPD? Something more going on here, fellas. If you ever listened to me, now's the time to keep your fuckin' noses clean. Out of sight, out of mind. Got it?"

Not saying a word, Nate and Pat just nodded.

Sergeant Daly shook his head. "The fuckin' odd couple here ain't so odd after all. You both have a target on your back. So you better let me walk you out!"

Chapter 46

SCRAPYARD

IT WAS NEARLY MIDNIGHT, AND NATE COULD SEE THAT THE regular stragglers at Pug's Pub were just beginning to shuffle in. It was a motley crew of drinkers, the kind who wouldn't be afraid to get wasted into the wee hours of the night in a sketchy part of town. The bartender kept the lights dim, and plenty of shadows enveloped the bar.

With Pat following him, Nate made his way over to the same booth he and Pat had used last time, nestled into the bar's back corner and facing the front entrance. That way, they had a great vantage point on anyone entering the bar. They were already a couple of rounds deep, but Nate knew the drinking wouldn't go on much longer. They had work to do.

A familiar figure entered the bar, and Nate perked up as soon as he entered. Jimmy's walk was distinctive, and he carried with him an aura of gravitas and experience.

"We ordered a whiskey for you," Pat said when he approached the table.

Jimmy nodded to Pat and shook hands with Nate, and then settled into the booth. "So, Nate," he began, "Patrick filled me in on his bright idea. You fuckin' lost your mind too? I can't believe you're doing this."

Despite the seriousness of the situation, Nate fought back a chuckle. He already knew what they were planning was crazy.

"Nate. Seriously? BPD batons brain damage the two of you? Sure I can't change your mind on this? This guy Gino usually strolls in here by midnight; it's not too late to abort this mission." Jimmy took a sip, studying their faces. "A plan can always go wrong," he continued. "And when it does, there's no turning back. One wrong turn can change your life forever. Nate, did Patrick ever tell you when I went on the run?"

Nate shook his head no and leaned in, curious.

"This was years ago," Jimmy began. "I set up a deal at a parking lot, and my father was there with the chief of police. The chief was my neighbor from a town on the South Shore, and he was in on it with us—two kilos. Wasn't the first time we'd made a deal with him involved. As I was on my way with the buyer, sure enough, state troopers raided the parking lot. They pinched my father and the chief. I got away and disappeared."

"Where'd you go?" Nate asked.

"I hid out down in the Dominican Republic for a while, but then when I was down there, I got busted with six ounces of coke and ended up in a Dominican prison. Fuck me. You do not want to be in a fuckin' Dominican prison. Total nightmare. I was fighting every day, and there were rats the size of cats. I couldn't sleep; I was scared as shit of them! Then I had a friend of mine come down and give a judge 10K to get me released. So, I fled to Miami under an assumed name, and six months later—boom! I got surrounded. I was working in a diner as a busboy, and they sent me up for the eight-year bid. My father and the chief did time too."

Nate sat listening in respect and wonder. He had heard that Jimmy had a colorful past, but he hadn't expected anything like this.

"My point is you two can't play both sides of the line. I'm telling you," Jimmy warned. "Do you want to end up in prison or on the run where you can't turn back? When I hear 'Dominicans,' Nate, I get flashbacks. You two ever think maybe those same damn Dominicans that just almost killed you are supplying this guy with his shit, Nate?"

Nate and Pat looked at each other, and Nate sat contemplating what Jimmy had just said. It was a bullet point that had never crossed either of their minds. Did Jimmy know something here? Regardless, Nate wasn't exactly sure how to break it to Jimmy that they would not be deterred.

Fortunately, Pat did it for him.

"It doesn't matter, Jimmy," explained Pat. "It's all going down."

Jimmy looked over to Nate, who simply nodded in agreement. "This is it, Jimmy, for me. After this, I'm heading straight to law school so I can fight this war at the highest level."

Jimmy sighed and leaned back. "Think about it, fellas," Jimmy cautioned. "'Cause he'll probably be walking through that door any minute."

Just then, the door swung open and a familiar lean figure strolled in, wearing a baseball cap. It was Treats, flashing his million-dollar grin. Jimmy took Treats's entrance as his cue to exit. He nodded goodbye, shaking his head as he walked away, passing Treats without a greeting. He made his way to the back offices of the bar and shut the door.

"What's up with him?" Treats asked, sitting beside Pat.

"It's nothing," Pat said. "What's up on your end?"

"Shit, that Sean wasn't lying," Treats said excitedly. "He has the rocket fuel for sure!" As if to emphasize the point, Treats dumped a few drops of powder on the back of his hand and snorted it up.

"It's done, Paddy," a freshly energized Treats explained, leaning in. "I got my two ounces, and I can certainly make a few bucks off this shizzzit. And the scrapyard site is empty—all clear and no sign of the dogs, either. From the sounds of it, there's a lot of product somewhere in there and more than just coke. He was bragging about his stockpile and how he could supply me if I needed oxys or heroin."

Patrick appeared fired up with motivation, Nate thought, and even though he didn't snort coke, his energy level looked as if he had been blasting through rails with Treats.

Right on schedule, the door swung open, and in came a petite Italian guy in his fifties, with black feathered hair.

"Sean's uncle," whispered Pat. "Gino."

On his arm was a Black woman in a miniskirt a little too small and tight—clearly a prostitute. Nate low-key eyed them both before putting their attention back in the little circle at the table.

"All right," Treats said. "I gotta get out of here so I'm not seen with you fucking criminals. I'll be under the overpass, but I got your back out there!" He pulled his hat down low and strolled out.

Pat laughed. "Even when he's involved in criminal plots, that guy's still a walking party."

They'd gone over the plan at least a dozen times. Jimmy's staff had volunteered information about Uncle Gino's hooker; she was his regular, Sally. He'd bring her once a month on a Thursday and hang out all night. *Must be his wife's bingo night*, Nate thought.

While Uncle Gino was preoccupied drinking with Sally, the plan was that Patrick and Nate would be down the street and entering the run-down brick building of D&D Metals, the one with no windows and that was covered in graffiti.

In his right mind, the only way Nate would have entered this building was if someone confirmed there was not an army and two rottweilers on the other side. He wasn't even sure what he would find. It might be money, drugs, or just piles of scrap metal, but he felt in his gut that it would be something big. Treats had successfully gathered the key information so far and he would be on the lookout—probably high as hell and hyperfocused from fresh cocaine bumps.

It was go time. Patrick grabbed his backpack off the floor, and they headed for the exit.

The air was cold and crisp outside, dulled only slightly by the couple of rounds they'd enjoyed inside the pub. They walked about a block to the train overpass, where Nate quickly spotted Treats in his car with the engine running, probably just to stay warm. They beelined to the car and hopped in.

About six blocks away from Pug's Pub, Treats pulled over on Hampden Street, about fifty yards from the front of the building. Nate could see the Orchard Park Projects behind the scrap metal yard. Pat reached into his bag and grabbed a walkie-talkie, then handed it to Treats. Then he retrieved a police scanner, which he also handed over.

"Listen in on this," he said. "Walsh gave it to me. He's just around the corner, parked in his cruiser, outside of Newmarket Pizza and Cafe. Probably eating a slice right now."

Nate and Pat jumped out of the car and walked toward the side of the building. Nate looked around carefully to see if anyone was within sight. Just like any other night, this industrial neighborhood was utterly deserted. Pat pulled a pair of bolt cutters from his backpack and quickly cut a hole in the chain-link fence into the scrapyard.

"I can't help but think back to the cop the BPD pulled down from the fence," Nate said as Pat worked to create the hole. "It was so . . . violent. Keeps flashing through my brain."

"I know," Pat said. "But just relax and focus. Concentrate on the task at hand."

Once the fence had a large enough opening, they stepped through it and ran across the scrapyard to the rear door of the windowless building. This one was secured with a chain and two master locks. Pat went to work on the chain and the locks with the bolt cutters. With some effort, the chain finally clinked to the concrete. The sudden sound made them both jump. Nate looked around to see if anyone had heard. No security lights. No one came running. They were alone.

"Here," Pat said, handing Nate one of the flashlights from his bag. Pat grabbed the other and then handed Nate a pistol. Ironically, it was the .22 that had been used to shoot Father Lydon, the one Patrick took at Hell House. Although he knew the story, Nate didn't hesitate to take the weapon and tuck it into his waistband. They didn't need to explain to each other how dangerous this could get.

They opened the door and entered slowly, the narrow beams of light illuminating the cavernous building, with its twenty-foot-high ceilings. Their slowly sweeping flashlights revealed a few forklifts and ten huge piles of metals. There were two weighing stations on opposite sides, and off in the distance was a large door and a walkway into the new part of the building.

"That's where the office is," Pat said, pointing toward the large door. "I know he has drugs and shotguns and a cash safe in there, but this guy definitely has that shit on lockdown. Probably best to stay the fuck away from there so we don't trigger an alarm or something."

"But there's nothing but piles of shit out here, man," Nate observed. "You think he's going to leave piles of drugs out in the open?"

"It's here, man," Pat reassured. "It's here somewhere. Just keep looking around."

They spent the next several minutes searching for any hidden place that someone might keep a sizeable stash. Passing by one of the scales in the ground, Nate reached to investigate the scale controller hanging in midair by a drop cord. He pressed a few buttons as the eight-by-eight-foot scale's steel plate adjusted up and down to try and register a weight. With that, Nate pressed another button, and the steel plate slowly lowered itself into an eight-foot pit.

"Pat!" Nate whispered.

Pat smirked at the unexpected find. He and Nate shined their flashlights down in the darkness of the pit.

"C'mon," Pat said.

They jumped down onto a plywood floor. They were in a hidden sublevel room, with painted lettering on the wall that said "Fire Pump Here."

"What are those?" Nate asked. He pointed at about ten large boxes that were made of metal and had wheels on the bottom, like miniature dumpsters.

"Those are construction buggies," Pat replied, "for hauling materials and moving shit around." Pat ripped the tarp off one of the buggies, revealing a lot of tightly packed material wrapped in butcher paper and plastic. Wordlessly, Nate joined Pat in tearing off all the tarp covers from the construction buggies. They each carried the same tightly wrapped cargo.

Using his pocketknife, Pat sliced into the plastic packing, revealing the contents. He didn't need to taste it; the look and texture of the white powder and the vinegary smell told him it was heroin. "Jackpot," he exclaimed triumphantly.

"Shiiiiit," Nate said, incredulous. "With this amount of weight, maybe he *is* tied in with those Dominicans! What next? You calling in Walsh to put the BPD cavalry on this? Or maybe I should call the fed?"

"Nah," Pat countered. "We can't let the bureaucracy fuck this up. Somehow this will still end up on the streets—killing people, ruining families' lives. Grab a couple of bricks, and leave them by the front door on our way out. When the cops and firefighters show up, Uncle Gino will have some explaining to do."

Nate nodded. He knew Pat was right.

They both went to work. Nate wheeled all the construction buggies close together. Pat produced some lighter fluid from his backpack and sprayed it all over the buggies, celebratory style, as if he were spraying champagne all over a group of raucous partiers.

"This gonna hurt," Nate said. "Millions of dollars up in flames."

Chapter 47

UP IN FLAMES

TREATS SNORTED ANOTHER BUMP FROM THE DRIVER'S SEAT. He anxiously scanned the street outside the building for any sign of Pat and Nate, ready to pick them up and peel out on a hair trigger. His leg bounced up and down, jittery. He felt like he needed to do something, but all he could do was wait. He had shut down the engine to avoid detection, so it was starting to get uncomfortably cold.

He saw a car pull around the corner and stop along the fence in front of the main building. It was an E-Class Mercedes Benz. Uncle Gino stepped out of the car and started to open the locks on the fence.

Treats ducked down, hoping that Gino didn't clock that a driver was sitting in a parked car not too far away from him. Treats slowly crept back up so he could just see over the door. There, he could see Gino open the fence. Inside the car, he could see the prostitute from earlier. Treats guessed Gino was taking her somewhere private inside the building so they could have a little rendezvous.

Fuck, thought Treats. *He's supposed to still be at the bar. What the fuck is he doing here so early? No warning from Jimmy?*

As the car pulled into the scrapyard, Treats scrambled to plot his next move. Were Nate and Pat on their way out, or would they have a deadly head-on collision with Gino?

He reached for the radio, knowing he had to warn the boys. Just as he grabbed it, he heard the back car door of his vehicle slam shut and felt the cold steel of a gun poking the back of his head. His mind raced on the cocaine. He had left the back doors open in case Nate and Pat needed to run in and make a quick getaway. He didn't consider that someone else would get the drop on him.

"Ahh-haaaa!" said the self-satisfied voice behind him. Treats didn't have to see his face; he'd recognize that asshole's voice anywhere. It was Sean. One look in the rearview mirror confirmed it.

"Think you can play me, Treats?" Sean threatened. "I got you a treat right fucking here. Now just fuckin' amuse me. What the fuck are you back over here for?"

Treats sat tight lipped, shaking.

"You know, I thought it was a bit random that a resourceful man like yourself needs a few ounces from me," Sean said. "But I get it. We all run into a glitch from time to time. We've hung out, made some money a few times in the past, so I obliged. But then some of the questions seemed a bit much. And now, here the fuck you are as I was coming back through this way. Then I recognize the car I saw you in earlier, scoping out my uncle's joint."

His mind raced, desperately looking for a play, a move, anything. So far, he had nothing. He tried to respond, stuttering and searching for words for the first time in his life.

"Sean, chill, man," he stammered. "I just delivered some coke right around the corner at Pug's Pub and just happened to pull over for a few bumps for myself, man." He began to sweat, and he could hear his heartbeat in his ears. His heart felt like it was about to explode.

Suddenly a muffled call came in on the radio.

"Yo, yo! We'll be out in less than five. Be ready," announced Pat's voice.

Treats winced, knowing he'd just gotten made.

"What the fuck, you mothafuckas?" snarled Sean. "Damn, I should have known Patrick was behind all this. Maybe I'll help him on his way out. How'd he get in? How many is he in there with?"

Treats felt a sharp poke of the gun to the back of his head after each question. His panic morphed into a blind rage. He'd never rat on the closest friends he ever had.

"Fuck you, Sean," Treats hissed.

"Treats, do you copy?" crackled Pat's voice on the radio. "What's going on?"

The gun prodded the back of his head again, and a thunderous boom pierced the night air. Treats saw a flash of red before everything went black.

Chapter 48

SOMETHING HAD GONE WRONG

JIMMY CAME OUT OF HIS OFFICE AT THE BACK OF PUG'S PUB TO check on the bar. He couldn't help but be worried about Pat—the least he could do was keep Gino drinking as long as possible to give the boys a chance to do their work.

He scanned the bar for Gino. He wasn't sitting in his regular seat at the bar. Jimmy combed the rest of the bar, checking the bathroom. Gino was gone. Jimmy knew all the regulars' drinking habits like the back of his hand. Gino almost always stayed until closing.

An uneasy feeling percolated in Jimmy's gut that something had gone wrong. Maybe this was more than the in-and-out simple search mission that Patrick had planned for. Pat had confided in Jimmy; Treats's role was supposed to just be observing and confirming the building was clear and that Sean was gone.

Jimmy grabbed his jacket from the hook on the office and ran out of Pug's Pub to his car. His instinct told him something was fucked up here, and his instincts were never wrong. He started the car and screeched off, barreling down Norfolk Avenue for six blocks. He took a right onto Hampden Street and pulled over, killing his lights and his engine. This was the spot.

Jimmy sat, patient and intense, his eyes scanning for any clue of what might be going on. There were only a few cars sporadically parked on the right side of the road. Then, he noticed someone running into the fenced gate.

Are Patrick and Nate still in there? Jimmy wondered.

Chapter 49

A WHOLE NOTHER LEVEL

ON THE INSIDE OF THE WAREHOUSE, PAT STOOD AT THE TOP of the scale, Nate at his side. They raised the platform back to the ground level of the floor of the building. As they stepped off, Pat grabbed the swinging controller and pressed the button to lower the scale back down. A thick silence filled the air as he reached into his backpack to prepare to light a match.

Suddenly, a banging and moaning noise came from the office area of the new building. Then the noise suddenly stopped.

Pat froze. He and Nate exchanged a look, surprised they were no longer alone. "Must be Uncle Gino and his prostitute, back for their fun," Pat said.

"I guess we can't check out the office for cash," Nate whispered.

Pat thought about it, reaching for his pistol.

Nate followed suit, then hesitated. "Nah, Patrick. Don't even think about it. Let's go. I'll leave these two bricks by the door."

Nate darted over to the door, about thirty feet away, and tossed the bricks near the threshold. "Let's drop the match down the hole and sneak out the door we came in," he suggested. "Mission accomplished, brother, and we gone. Nobody gets hurt! Come on. Let's go!"

A loud clanging sound of a heavy latch interrupted them, and the large sliding barn door between the two buildings flew open. Nate and Pat drew their weapons and fixed them on the door. Cocking his chin, Pat gestured to Nate to step behind a pile of trash metals on the side of the scale. They ducked down.

"Patrick, I got you cornered like a rat now," yelled a voice from the other side of the open door.

Pat grimaced. The voice belonged to none other than Sean.

"You stupid fuck," Sean proclaimed. "There's no way out. Got you surrounded."

Pat could read the panic on Nate's face. Reaching into his bag, rummaging for something, Pat pulled out a few sheets of scrap paper and wadded them up into a ball. Using his lighter he lit the ball of paper on fire.

Nate nodded, wide-eyed, in approval.

Patrick threw the makeshift torch down the hole, and the flames caught the trail of lighter fluid. He and Nate leaped away, just as a towering inferno blasted through the hole.

Sean opened fire, the sound of bullets ringing through the warehouse.

With the searing heat burning his skin, Pat could hear the bullets colliding with the piles of metal they were using as cover. It sounded like more than one gun. Nate fired a few shots back toward the door.

The fire continued to bellow, bursting through the hole in the floor.

Pat crept around the pile of metal, firing a few shots toward the door. He cautiously took a peek and saw Uncle Gino drop to the ground, grabbing his stomach. Then Pat spotted Sean, walking in his direction. Sean fired off a few more rounds. Pat stayed down, but Sean was getting closer.

I've got to do something, thought Nate.

"Freeze! FBI!" Nate shouted, summoning his deepest and most authoritative voice.

Startled, Sean glanced around, halting momentarily to clock his surroundings. During that hanging moment where he was caught off guard, Pat seized his opportunity. He rose above the cover of the junk pile and fired a shot into Sean's leg.

Sean dropped to one knee, keeping his other leg straight, as it was bleeding from the upper thigh. He groaned, dropping his gun to grab his leg.

Pat approached him, his gun pointed at his head at every step.

The fire was simmering down.

Pat stood over Sean with his gun aimed right for Sean's forehead.

"Time to redeem the lines you crossed," Pat threatened.

"For what, Patrick?" Sean asked. "All this for what? Your weak-ass righteous self, or for your pussy cousin who couldn't handle a couple of n*ggers? And now you here with this n*gger! You could have worked for me. We could've taken this city over. This is Dominican cartel drugs, you fuckin' moron!"

Patrick kneeled face-to-face with Sean. "You don't know me," he admonished. "I'd never work for you—ever. You're rotten to the core, man. You and your uncle have spent a lifetime doing no good, ruining people's lives, and I'm just doing my part to balance the scales, bitch."

Boom.

Patrick fired his weapon, burying a slug into Sean's head. Uncle Gino lay nearby, bleeding out, struggling through his last breaths.

Nate emerged from the junk pile, walking slowly, his weapon down. "Fuck, man," he said. "There's no turning back now. Let's go now, Patrick."

"You sure you don't want to hit the office now for the cash?" Pat asked.

"No," said Nate, shaking his head. "After those n*gger comments, I wanted to shoot him too. But this is some whole other level shit now. Let's go!"

Nodding in agreement, Pat emptied another bottle of lighter fluid on the floor and lit it up with a match. They then booked it to the back door, stopping at the threshold.

"Look, Nate, I go out first," Pat proposed. "Hopefully, Treats is out front, but if not, you run off into Orchard Park and get away fast. If I make it, I'm gonna need to disappear, my friend. But I had to do what I had to do."

"No doubt," Nate said, looking back.

Pat kicked open the heavy metal door leading into the back scrapyard. They were both expecting guns drawn, either by police or Dominicans or Sean's underlings, but instead, they were met only with silence. They walked out slowly, then turned and ran across the scrapyard, then through the cut chain-link fence. They raced toward Treats's car.

Patrick arrived at the car door and saw what remained of Treats, his head destroyed and his body slumped against the steering wheel. Everything in him seemed to explode all at once, his body reacting without his volition. He smashed the roof of the car with his hand, screaming and cursing.

Nate grabbed him just as his cries were interrupted by a car pulling fast out of nowhere with its lights off. The car screeched to a halt. The window rolled down, and it was Jimmy at the wheel.

"Get the fuck in here," he commanded. "Now, *let's go!*"

Wordlessly, they flung open the doors and jumped in. Jimmy raced away fast, and Pat turned to steal one last glance at the warehouse. He could see smoke billowing from the roof of the windowless building. Off in the distance, the sirens of fire trucks and police were getting louder.

Jimmy turned on Melnea Cass and lined up into traffic like any other vehicle. They slowly drove through the Massachusetts Avenue and Melnea Cass intersection, witnessing a BPD cruiser pass right in front of them.

Patrick locked his eyes on Walsh as the cruiser turned up Melnea toward the burning building.

Walsh tipped his hat as he drove by.

"What the fuck happened in there, Patrick?" Jimmy asked.

Patrick buried his face in his hands. "I killed those guys in there, and now I killed Treats," he wailed. "I dragged him into this, and I fucked up his life and his son's life."

Nate sat up quietly. "The amount of product we just took off the street is immeasurable," he said. "And the lives saved too. Those two punk-ass bitches would have lived a lifetime of evil. No harm, no foul with them gone." Nate held up his tattoo and showed it to Pat, in a gesture of solidarity. *Redeem the time, for the days are evil. Ephesians 5:16.* It's time for me to blend back into society, a Black man in law school, and go about this fight the other way, infiltrate the other side of corruption!

Jimmy put his hand on Pat's shoulder. "Calm down," he said softly. "Looks like the whole place is about to burn down. Focus. We need to focus. Don't think about Treats right now. You'll make it right. Call it a casualty of war." He pointed in the direction of Suffolk County Prison.

"We need to get you two cleaned up and out of sight now, or you'll be right back in there tomorrow, forever."

Jimmy merged onto 93 South. "We're going to O'Riley's for now," he announced. "Shower, new clothes. Nate will take a cab home from Quincy Center. And you and I are gonna take a long ride!"

———

JIMMY'S CAR SAT PARKED OUTSIDE PATRICK'S MA'S HOUSE. PAT ran down the steps with a few tears in his eyes. He had just left his ma in the parlor, and she too had been crying. He had comforted her the best he could, taking her hands in his and telling her he'd be back.

As he approached Jimmy's car, he spotted Kiley sitting on her front stoop. He steeled himself, then walked across the street.

"What now, Patrick?" Kiley said, standing up, a look of concern on her face. "Looks like you're off in a hurry!"

He paused a moment, taking his breath, soaking her in. "We'll see," he said softly, taking her into his arms. "I'll be gone for a while, but my conscience is finally free."

Then he pulled her into him tightly, embracing her as if it were the last time.

ACKNOWLEDGMENTS

I WOULD LIKE TO THANK MY FRIEND, JAMES MCPARTLAND, who has inspired and coached me in my business endeavors and the writing of these novels. His unwavering belief in me, guidance, and encouragement have helped change the direction of my businesses and my life. Without his consistent support and subtle teachings on how to manifest the potential within, my life would be very different. His message, "True success lies in the practice of gratitude and the unopened gifts one already has," was very impactful.

I would like to thank my spiritual coach, Chenoa Maxwell, who has been integral to my sanity during the most challenging times of my life. I remember the day we crossed paths I felt the recognition of a soul, a spiritual guide that was sent to me. I had just lost my mother to Alzheimer's way too soon. Next came the challenges of the chaotic world during the pandemic and the multiple deaths of several close people near and dear to me, including my amazing father to Lewy body dementia. Her gifts from the level of energy and conscious thought process she brings, to identifying the attachments of pain and trauma, then the required gentle healing process, were so instrumental. Chenoa's way to allow one to see their own perceptions of the relationships in life with others, with oneself, and with a high power was a grounding force for me. *When you move as fast as I have over the years, you must have someone like Chenoa by your side to raise your vibration level to keep you in flow to clear your path!*

Much gratitude is also owed to my friend Cornell Mills who I met in 1988 in an integration-type program. Without Cornell the character of Nate does not exist in my mind, and the relationship of these two main characters would not have been created. His no-nonsense, confident and proud Black soul forced me to question my own views every day throughout high school. The authentic communication process led to the conflict resolution and the development of our solid human relationship. The lessons and the enjoyment of this friendship are truly a divine intervention.

Thank God for answering my prayers and gifting me an amazing family. To my wife, for being my best friend and unselfishly supporting me as I built the vision of my life, I am forever grateful. In the first chapter of our marriage, I worked day and night while struggling with many battles within, but she always added value to decisions every step of the way. The gift of family she has created is the best life has to offer. Two beautiful girls and then a baby boy have inspired my purpose more than any other accomplishment could ever have. I am truly blessed to have you as my partner on this journey through life.

Thank you from the bottom of my heart.

AUTHOR'S NOTE

THIS STORY TAKES PLACE IN BOSTON DURING THE MID-1990S. The 23-year-old version of myself felt the culture and the society was so amoral at the time, he had to write the original foundation of this world in 1996.

This is not political point of view—not liberal or conservative—as I was raised in a hardworking military-structured, blue collar, union, democratic, JFK-loving family.

However, my grandmother was fully aware of the corruption in the deep state of American government and politics. She was the daughter of an Irish immigrant who became a South Boston city councilman and political crony of Mayor Curley.

After a century of the continued racial conflict—and more recently witnessing how America has suffered from party politics, the pandemic, medical freedoms and forced control, media control propaganda, social media censoring, cancel culture, and pedophilia—it has become quite clear that division and chaos are the playbook.

During this time, as I reached my highest stress level, I decided to recreate the second act of the original Neighborhood Lines tale and finish the journey of this commendable friendship.

At times, I felt exhausted by the continued tolerance of the nature of society within the characters' worlds. The realization set in that political corruption, crime, social hypocrisy, racial conflict, and police brutality are timeless as it has never been more evident that we live in an endless battle of good verse evil in this human experience.

The first book, Neighborhood Lines, was for the teenagers and attempted to capture the culture and show how the more things change the more they stay the same. This story is for adults to laugh and cry at this crazy journey in the American society in this lifetime. The height of the spiritual war is among us; may we awaken to not walk as fools but redeem the time and the lines that continue to be crossed. Don't take the soup. As Tom Robbins said, "When freedom is outlawed only outlaws will be free."

ABOUT THE AUTHOR

MICHAEL PATRICK MURPHY WAS BORN south of Boston and comes from a family with strong native ties to Boston. He spent ten years getting an education on Morrissey Boulevard—his high school and college years lived out in and around the areas of Dorchester, South Boston, and Boston. Inspired by stories his grandmother told him of the city's history, and of his great-grandfather, South Boston city councilor Michael Mahoney, Murphy originally wrote the foundation of *Neighborhood Lines/Redeem the Lines* while in college. This timely, heart-felt novel captures the unique atmosphere of the late 1980s and early 1990s in Boston, when the aftershocks of court-ordered busing to public schools lingered on, integration of the all-White housing projects had begun, and the murder rate had reached record-breaking figures.

Redeem the Lines is the sequel that continues the story of these two young men—Nate and Patrick, who arise out of opposing tough neighborhoods and face many challenges from their current precarious Boston culture in the mid-1990s. The decisions and ramifications of their past create a world of new circumstances that profoundly affect their relationship and the direction of their future. Murphy's hope in writing the novel is that it be used as a tool to open up dialogues about corruption, race, class, and the common ground that can be achieved by working together to solve conflicts. Murphy, who owns several businesses in the Boston area, lives on the South Shore with his wife and three children.

Printed in the USA
CPSIA information can be obtained
at www.ICGtesting.com
LVHW070506130923
758027LV00003B/207